Coldbath
Fields prison

**SPA
FIELDS**

**SPITALFIELDS**

Brick Lane

High Holborn

Crown and
Anchor public
house

mple
ar

Arundel
reet

St. Paul's
Cathedral

*River Thames*

Great Tower Street

Tower Hill

Newcastle Street

London
Bridge

**Tower of
London**

East India Dock
and Blackwall
railway terminus

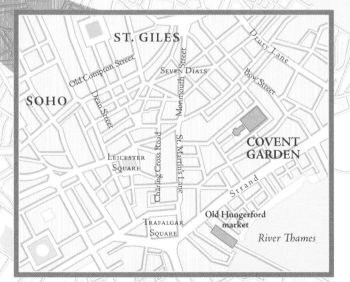

**ST. GILES**

Drury Lane

Old Compton Street

SEVEN DIALS

Monmouth Street

Bow Street

**SOHO**

Dean Street

**COVENT
GARDEN**

LEICESTER
SQUARE

Charing Cross Road

St. Martin's Lane

*Strand*

Old Hungerford
market

TRAFALGAR
SQUARE

*River Thames*

# the
## Infidel Stain

the
Infidel Stain

M. J. CARTER

G. P. PUTNAM'S SONS ✦ NEW YORK

**PUTNAM**

G. P. PUTNAM'S SONS
*Publishers Since 1838*
An imprint of Penguin Random House LLC
375 Hudson Street
New York, New York 10014

ISBN 978-0-399-17168-0

Printed in the United States of America
1   3   5   7   9   10   8   6   4   2

*Book design by Lauren Kolm*

# *historical note*

In the first half of the nineteenth century, "infidels" were political radicals with atheist and republican beliefs. They were regarded by the government as dangerous revolutionaries.

# *prologue*

The still, quiet shop was a blessed shelter from the biting cold. She had risen at four to walk the six miles to Hackney Road and back, and all the way she had held on to that half hour when she would creep in, fall gratefully into a dark corner, shut her eyes and cast aside her cares. Sometimes she thought it was the place she liked best in the world, not just for the refuge it provided, but also because of the old familiar odors—the smell of ink, of lampblack and linseed oil, the musty dry scent of paper; and the tools—the boxes of type and gravers and burins.

She did not like to come too often, for she did not want him to grow tired of her, and so she had waited and stored up this morning's visit. He never seemed to mind finding her, though, not even when at the start she had taken things—not much, but enough to land her a week in the correctional house: a bit of paper, or an empty box, or a piece of type that she would rub between her fingers. He had shown her how to get in so no one could see, and sometimes, when he was opening up, he would send her out to the coffee stall and have her buy one for herself.

The street was quite empty. The coffee seller was still on the Strand, serving the late-nighters and early-morning comers. She made her way past the darkened shopfront, into the alley around the side, behind the outside steps that led to the door of their living quarters. Under these, and out of sight of prying eyes, she cleared the bricks away from the little square door, took the small key tied to a bit of string from out of her skirts, placed it in the rusted lock and turned it.

Squatting down on her haunches, she edged through. She did not crawl as it messed her skirts and her basket and she would be selling today. There was a small cavity between the little door and the print room where they stored boxes and type and, having inched her way through the gap, she came out into the room at last.

It was very dark. She stood and brushed herself down. Dawn would not come for a while. The front was shuttered and the cracked window in the back had been blacked out—he had taken to doing this recently, claiming that it stopped the cold, but she reckoned he was working on something he wished no one to see. She knew the room well, so she was not concerned, and it was a relief to be out of the wind which whistled outside, looking for ways through the cracks. Arms outstretched, she began to walk toward the far wall, taking care not to disturb any boxes. To the right of her she could just make out the silhouette of the press. In the darkness it seemed to loom even bigger than usual.

Her boot slid from under her and for a moment she lost her balance and thought she would fall. She swore quietly as she righted herself, and clung to her basket. The floor was wet. She lifted her skirt, took another big step and grimaced. It was slippery here too. Perhaps a cat or a rat had knocked over some ink. No. He would not have been so careless to have left any lying around. Maybe one of his old workers had broken in to sleep off the night's excesses and knocked over a bottle, or spewed up, or worse. He was accustomed to working on his own, but once in a while a writer or illustrator or printer came in to help—soakers and topers, the lot of them.

"That you, Seymour?" she said. "You drunk?" But there was no answer.

"Mr. Wedderburn? Nat?"

Standing there in the dark, she began to feel uneasy. She was, she realized, holding her breath. And there was an unfamiliar smell, acrid and sharp; it made her eyes water. Some instinct told her to lay her hands upon something solid and she took a quick step back, feeling for the wall. But she lost her balance and went down, one hand reaching out to break her fall, the other grasping the basket. Her hand was wet, and the stuff was all over her skirt. She cursed again and rubbed her fingers together. Sticky, slightly thick even. Not piss then, nor booze either. She sniffed and pulled herself up quickly, keeping clear of the great piece of machinery in the middle of the room. The sense of foreboding deepened, and the thought came upon her that there was someone else there, in the dark. Fear rose in her. Quickly, quietly—though it was too late for that, she knew—she felt her way around the walls to the back window. The tool bench stood before it. She put her basket upon it and felt for an engraving tool, something sharp. Then she stretched up to pull the piece of old blanket away from the window frame, feeling herself exposed as she did so. The sky was just beginning to lighten and the room was suddenly a good deal brighter. Her fingertips and palms were stained with something black like ink. But she knew it was not ink. She did not want to turn around, but she forced herself to do so.

The sight imprinted itself upon her eye, like a flash of light.

Blood, terrible and black like ink, everywhere. As if a great, hideous bucket of it had been poured over him. Blood soaking through his trousers and pooling on the floor, where her boots had spread it into the corners. Blood painted over his face, across his arms and on his chest. Blood spewing, along with his guts, from a deep and livid cut in his stomach, as broad and wet as a mouth. And his body, bloodied and draped over the bed of the printing press, head propped against the platen, arms dangling off each side.

# Part 1

## chapter 1

The day was cold and bleak as I emerged from the Blackwall railway terminus, and the sooty brick of the city made it seem all the grayer. I had not long returned from India; after years in hot climes I was not yet re-accustomed to the English cold. I pulled my coat more tightly around me and checked my pocket watch for the tenth or twelfth time. I did not wish to be late.

It had been two days of novelties. The morning before I had taken my first ever journey upon a train, riding the Exeter mailcoach to Swindon to catch the Great Western Railway to the Paddington terminus in London. Five years before, I had left England a country traversed by horse and carriage; I had returned to find it in thrall to steam and iron.

I had stepped into the green-and-gold carriage, sat on the wooden pews of second class and watched the air fill with steam, as if we were traveling on a bed of cloud. I had felt the rush of speed and watched the curious effect of the countryside melting into a blur of green as it rushed past the window, or rather as we rushed past it. And, of course, there was the noise: the clank and wheeze of the wheels on the rail, the asthmatic puff of the engine, and those sudden unholy screeches—the wheels braking, or the air forcing its way through the whistle. We had

reached the extraordinary speed of thirty miles an hour. It was remarkable, exhilarating, unsettling—not unlike London itself.

I had been in the city less than a day. I had rooms at the Oriental
Club in Hanover Square. It was only my second visit to London; my
first had been when I was nine years old. I recalled almost nothing of it
save that we had seen my rich, scowling great-uncle at his gloomy
abode in Golden Square—a place which greatly disappointed me as I
had expected it actually to be golden—and I had seen a hurdy-gurdy
man with a dancing dog in the street.

This time, I started with a hansom cab to the Strand—where else?
It is "the first street in Europe," at least according to Mr. Disraeli. I
walked its length from Temple Bar to Charing Cross, past its arcades
and grand shops with square-paned windows, and the discreet plaques
signaling the offices of various journals and newspapers. At Charing
Cross I paused, new Trafalgar Square and the slowly rising girth of
the column to Nelson on one side of me, and on the other Old Hungerford market and its rackety steps down to the River Thames. Ahead I
could just see part of the fretted bulk of the unfinished Houses of
Parliament. On the roadway, the broughams and chaises, drays and
goods carts, rattling omnibuses and gilded chariots barely moved.

The noise was constant and deafening.

Apart from Calcutta, I had never been in such a vast multitude of
jostling people, from fine ladies and gents peering into the shop windows, to Sir Robert Peel's new police (not so new, I suppose, after ten-
odd years, but that was how everyone referred to them) walking their
"beats" in their high-collared blue tunics, to the crossing sweepers,
ragged half-starved creatures endlessly and fruitlessly sweeping away
great mounds of ordure from the roadway. I strode among them in my
paletot coat, my newish beaver hat pushed down over my ears against
the wind, a reasonably well-to-do provincial a few months behind the

fashion. I had never seen so many top hats in one place: as I looked down the Strand their bobbing throng seemed to me to resemble a moving city panorama all of its own.

The deluge of sensations was overwhelming. On the one hand, for the first time in months I felt free from the constant petty squabbles, the burdens, the boredom, the scrutiny, the disappointments of home. On the other, despite the crowds I had the strange and troubling sensation of being alone in a vast multitude of unsmiling faces; nor was I overfond of the ubiquitous, black grime—an oily, sooty extrusion that bore little relation to country dirt and seemed to coat all—and every once in a while I would taste coal dust in the air. Then there was the vast amount of ordure and dung from the horses, and everywhere glimpses of errant, ownerless children, vagabonding, street-selling, begging. I had recently finished Mr. Dickens's *Old Curiosity Shop*, and the vision of little Nell, the pauper girl, seemed ever before me. It was a relief to return to the quiet, clean haven of Mayfair and Hanover Square.

This morning I had taken my second train, from hard by the Tower of London to the East India Dock on the Blackwall Railway. There was a crowd of gawkers around the gates of the Tower, for only a few days ago a fire had destroyed the Round Tower and almost consumed the Crown jewels. A twist of smoke still wafted upward from within the battlements. The journey eastward showed a meaner London: a moving picture of shabby streets, half-finished terraces and dilapidated workshops, then a scrubland of broken fences and overgrown market gardens, and behind all these vast stretches of open dock filled with masts, populated by beetling stevedores.

I walked toward the great stone gateway of the East India Dock, which loomed like the entrance to some vast Hindoo palace. The high walls of the dock were pasted thick with bills, most of them advertising the lower sort of popular papers, the *Ironist*, *Bell's Life in London* and

*Woundy's Illustrated Weekly.* In the lee of the walls small sheds and shacks served drink and tobacco to a crowd of wretched-looking sailors. On I went, past a new church and an old timber-framed house to a rickety smoke-blackened edifice that announced itself in large faded letters as "The Hindoostanee Coffee House and Seamen's Hostel": my destination.

The door was stiff and rattled as I opened it. I found I was almost breathless. I pushed past a thick canvas curtain and entered. Perhaps twenty or thirty men sat at tables, eating. It took me a moment to see that all were Indian natives—Lascars, I guessed, from the docks. Rushing between the tables, two or three more young natives set down bowls and collected plates. The air was thick, warm and slightly fetid, a familiar marriage of perspiration and curry smells that I had not expected to encounter again. No one paid me any mind.

Most of the diners were dressed in the thin calicoes and canvases of the southern oceans, which must have provided little protection against the bitter cold outside. Some looked quite ragged, and in far from good health. There was a low buzz of talk, but most simply ate with a dedication that bespoke considerable hunger. I looked about again, more carefully. In a fireplace at the far end of the room, a large grate overflowed with glowing embers. To the left of this, in a corner, sat a lone European eating his dinner. He seemed as down-at-heel as the Lascars around him.

It was over three years since we had last met.

He was scooping up stew with pieces of roti. With a surge of concern and pleasure I pushed my way through the close-set tables toward him.

"Jeremiah!" I said as I reached him, my arms outstretched.

"Captain Avery," he said. His lips barely moved. His eyes were veiled and wary.

I felt a plunge of dismay. I dropped my arms, embarrassed.

"Sit down," he said, indicating a chair with his piece of roti, and returned to his food.

I pulled it out and wedged myself in, looking for somewhere to place my coat and hat, electing at last for my own lap. A plate was set down before me, along with a steaming bowl of curry. Reluctantly, I put a spoonful upon my plate and took a furtive look at him, remembering as I did so that insistently solitary, aloof quality that I had conveniently forgotten. He was frailer and more lined than I remembered, but his features were vividly familiar: the white scar through the eyebrow, the ragged ear, the once-broken nose, the hooded eyes. His left hand, with its two missing fingers, was beneath the table. His rusty, threadbare coat had clearly been through several owners; his waistcoat had lost all but one button, and the collar—closer to yellow than white—was pinned on, no doubt to hide a tattered shirt beneath. Next to him was a small bundle that included a battered hat.

Through the awkwardness of my reception, questions began to surface. What had become of him? How had he learned I had returned from India? How was he earning his living—was he earning his living at all?

I took a breath. "What is this place?" I said.

"Hostel for Lascar seamen," he said. He scooped another mouthful of curry onto his roti and crammed it into his mouth.

"So," I said. "Three years. More."

Blake chewed and nodded.

"How have you been?"

"Well enough. You were in Afghanistan."

I had forgotten how he intensely disliked talking about himself. I nodded.

"Decorated for bravery, promoted to captain, I heard."

"Yes." I shifted uneasily.

"Papers say the war's going well."

"Is it?" I said.

"Isn't it?"

"I do not keep up."

"You're living in Devon."

"We have taken a house near my family."

"You married Miss Larkbridge."

"Yes." I did not know how he knew these things, but I was not surprised that he did.

Silence.

Long pauses, I recalled, did not discomfit Jeremiah Blake.

"My wife is with child. . . . That is to say, it was one of the reasons we decided to return home," I blurted to fill the void.

"Must be near her confinement."

I nodded. I did not wish to speak of my marriage. He leaned back and wiped his hands on a handkerchief but so swiftly that I barely glimpsed the two stumps on his left hand, which he immediately returned to his lap. His right hand seemed red and chafed, but it was hard to be sure if this denoted he had fallen on hard times or was simply due to the ravages of the winter.

"Have you," I said, casting around for another subject, "visited Mr. Haydon's painting at the Egyptian Hall?"

"*The Death of Mountstuart?*" He shook his head.

"I went yesterday. There was an hour's queue."

"Mmm," said Blake. He took another bite of roti.

"I would say it is lively rather than accurate."

Mr. Benjamin Haydon, the history painter, was exhibiting a large canvas purporting to show the now notorious ambush and murder of the poet and adventurer Xavier Mountstuart by a gang of Hindoostanee bandits known as the Thugs. Death had transformed Mountstu-art into a saint and martyr, famous and revered across Europe. In the painting he lies in the foreground, cast upon the ground in a laundered white shirt, one arm raised in elegant defiance as a mass of blood-thirsty Thugs attack him with knives. To the left, in the background, two other Europeans fight off a battalion of savages with pistols. Jere-miah Blake and I were those two Europeans, the only living witnesses to what had actually taken place.

"Mr. Haydon wrote to me in India," I said, "asking for an account of what happened. He said he wanted 'color' and 'detail.'"

"Didn't listen to you then."

"I said that I could not help him. I didn't get the impression he would much have appreciated my version. I find I do not like to talk of it. Did he approach you?"

Blake nodded.

"I don't know much about art," I said, "but I should have said it was not a very good painting."

He met my gaze at last.

"Are you in trouble, Blake? Is that why you wrote to me? Forgive me, but I cannot but notice you seem, well, not exactly flushed with good fortune. Finding you here, among these poor wretches, I . . ." I trailed off, not sure how to proceed. "If you are in straitened circum-stances, please, Jeremiah, let me be of assistance."

He looked almost amused. "No," he said.

"No, you will not accept my help?" I said.

"No, I am perfectly well. I eat here because I like it. It reminds me of Calcutta. I talk to the sailors, keep up my dialects. And Mohammed cooks the best Bengalee food in London."

"Really?" I said. I glanced doubtfully down at the dark brown mess on the plate before me. It did not smell too bad. "I have taken rooms at

the Oriental Club. They say it has the finest curry chef in England—
you really should let me take you."

"No," said Blake.

"No?"

"I'll never set foot in that place."

"No, of course not," I said. "Foolish of me. But, Blake, I have to say,
you do not look well. And your clothes are . . ."

"I've had a bout of fever," he said testily. "That's all. It returns once
in a while. Especially in winter."

We glared at each other.

"Well, you have managed to mystify me entirely, Blake. You should
know that when I received your letter I dropped everything and came
at once. I have journeyed seventeen hours to see you. Why we are here,
save that you have a taste for the cooking, I have no idea. I suppose I
should not be surprised. But I would be grateful if you would oblige
me with some explanation."

"I wrote to you because I have an appointment with someone who
wishes to meet you too."

"Me?" I said, bemused.

"You may decide you don't want to meet him, but since you're
here . . ."

"Someone in London who wants to meet me?"

"Viscount Allington."

"Viscount Allington, the peer? The evangelical? The Factory Act
peer? The one who helps the chimney sweeps?" I said, even more
puzzled.

Blake nodded.

"Asked for me? For us?"

"He has some particular work—a case. But you are under no obligation. You can leave if you want."

"But how—"

"Theophilus Collinson knew you'd returned. Recommended you." He raised his eyebrows for a moment and the white scar through the left one lifted into his forehead.

We had both had dealings with Collinson, the former head of the East India Company's Secret Department. In India, it had been said that he had a finger in every curry. Blake did not trust the man, but when both were returning to England, Collinson had very forcefully offered his patronage. It seemed Blake had accepted it.

He brought out a small envelope and drew from it a leaf of paper of fine quality. He handed it to me. The writing was an elegant, spidery scrawl:

> *Lord Allington has a fancy to employ both you and William Avery, who, as you may recall, is now returned from India.*

Below was written my address in Devon, and at the end, in a less formal hand:

> *I think that in this case even you will not be able to question the client's principles.*

I was flattered, and at the same time felt a pang of disappointment. It was not Blake who had summoned me at all.

## chapter 2

From outside there came a great jangling of trappings and horses' hooves. Through the small, smutty panes of the establishment's front window I glimpsed a large black coach and four draw up. Four figures alighted from it.

The front door opened. Drawing aside the canvas curtain with great aplomb, a black-and-gold-liveried footman stepped in, bringing with him a blast of cold air which caused many of the diners to look up apprehensively from their bowls and hunch their shoulders. Through the door, dressed in black, processed a tall, gaunt gentleman and a youngish woman, quite handsome. They were followed by a short man in a brown cape with a small, fussy mustache who clutched a brown leather bag—clearly a secretary. The room fell silent. From a door near the back fireplace there now issued a middle-aged Indian native wearing a small white cap and an approximation of Indian dress—kurta, waistcoat and pajamas—but made in thick gray worsted woolens. He was followed by a white woman anxiously smoothing her hair and struggling to tie a clean apron, and behind her a small golden-skinned child, about six. The Indian native, whom I took to be Mohammed, the proprietor, bowed, then righted himself and spread his arms in welcome. The white woman in the apron curtseyed low.

The gentleman visitor removed his shining beaver hat—his face was pleasing in an ethereal, ascetic manner, though very pale—and nodded loftily to his hosts, leavening his regal manner with a brief, serious smile. Then, to my surprise, he knelt before the little child and very solemnly took her hand. She grinned and kissed him on the cheek. His female companion watched, her expression demure but guarded. The man in the brown cape stood behind, hat in hand, very much the practiced, impassive retainer. The gentleman straightened, and the small girl ran up to the Indian proprietor and took his hand. With the other the proprietor beckoned one of the rushing waiters and had him lift a bowl of curry up to the gentleman. He bent slightly—with a hint of trepidation—sniffed, his pale nostrils quivering, and gave a tiny nod. The proprietor lifted his daughter into his arms and ushered the visitors around the room, stopping at a few tables where the tall gentleman made short solemn inquiries of the diners, and the proprietor appeared to translate their replies. At last the visitors were conducted through the far door by the white woman, who was if anything more flustered than she had been before, and they all disappeared.

The dumb show over, the diners returned to their food.

"That's him," said Blake.

"Lord Allington? What is he doing here?" I drawled, doing my best not to sound too interested.

"He is chairman of the Committee for the Rescue of Destitute Lascars. The Navigation Acts forbid Lascar sailors from working their passage back on the ships that brought them to England. Once their ships dock they're left onshore until they can find another passage, but

English ships don't want them because they've mostly got little English. A few freeze to death on the docks each winter. This place feeds them and tries to find them passage. It's run on charitable donations. Allington gives the most. Today's his first visit."

"So you approve of him—Allington?"

"Won't know till I meet him."

I rolled my eyes. "Who is the white woman in the apron?"

"Mohammed's wife. They met in Dublin. The child is their daughter—Noor or Nora."

"And why are we here?"

Blake finished his roti. "Collinson mentioned Allington had an interest in the place and I suggested we meet here."

"Perfectly talkative when you want to be," I muttered, not quite loudly enough for him to hear, though he looked up sharply. "And what does he want with us?"

"Don't know. But I say again, you're not obliged to take part."

"Allington is an admirable man. If he were to ask for my services, I should feel inclined to say yes. Unless, of course, you would rather I did not."

Blake gave nothing away. His brow hooded his eyes; his mouth was a straight line. "It's up to you. You'd be paid."

"Money is neither here nor there," I said, though this was not quite true. "Look here, Jeremiah, I should be more than content to embark on another endeavor with you, but not if I am regarded as a useless piece of baggage. If that were the case, I should rather know now, and take myself home."

"I don't know if you'll be useful. I don't know what the job is."

"How encouraging to find you have such faith in me," I said, "given that I have traveled so far."

A young waiter now appeared at the table and murmured in Hindoostanee that we were awaited upstairs by the grand sahib. I glanced at Blake's shabby getup and wondered what a lord would make of him.

"Did you really have to come attired like this?" I said.

"Suits me to go through the streets like this. People don't remember a poor man."

"I think you will be fairly memorable to Viscount Allington. And please, Blake, mop your face. You look like a piece of wet fish."

He ignored me, pulled on the remains of a pair of gloves that looked as if they had been half eaten by exceedingly hungry cats, then retrieved the rest of his bundle. Twice he stopped at a table to greet a diner, who looked up companionably and exchanged a few sentences, mostly in dialects I did not know. The young waiter led us through a tiny dark kitchen full of huge steaming tureens and pots, and up a flight of rickety stairs. We continued through three bare but clean dormitory rooms hung with hammocks, next to each a sad roll of possessions. As we approached the door at the far end of the last, it was opened by the black-and-gold footman and there stood Mohammed and his wife, with the child now holding her mother's hand. The proprietor grinned at Blake and raised his eyebrows as they left and we entered. The Viscount and his companions were clustered round an old deal table, looking over a number of ledgers. The man in the brown cape beckoned to us grandly. "Your Lordship," he said, "Mr. Blake and Captain Avery."

The Viscount stood between the brown-caped man and the lady like the apex of a triangle; both looked expectantly up at him as at an admired saint in a religious painting. He was perhaps five years older and a little taller than me, and clean-shaven. Had he not held himself with the confidence and poise of an aristocrat, one might have described him as lanky. It was clear, close to, that his severe black clothes were immaculately cut and of the finest wool; I suddenly felt my own garb to be both frivolously bright and cheap by comparison. On the table, along with his beaver hat, were a fine silver-topped cane and a pair of silk gloves. His most distinctive features, apart from his pallor and slenderness, were his large pale blue eyes, which were ringed with long dark lashes and gave him an air of unworldliness and a slightly effeminate look—one, I suspected, that women liked. This effect was not altogether mitigated by a head of thick, lustrous dark brown hair worn slightly longer than the fashion, and dark brows.

Brown Cape, whose short, stubby figure and punctilious gestures could not have been more in contrast to his master's languid gracefulness, said, "Lord Allington thanks you for responding so speedily to his summons."

The Viscount inclined his head and took us in. The sight of Blake in his full glory caused him to blink several times and for some moments he was unable to tear his eyes away, nor to moderate his slightly appalled expression. I was convinced then that Blake had deliberately dressed in his worst in order to conjure just such a reaction, and felt a burst of irritation. The Viscount's gaze alighted upon me; his relief was tangible.

"Gentlemen, I hope you will join me in prayer," he said, bringing his long delicate fingers together, and bowed his head. I followed. Blake looked stonily ahead.

"Dear Lord, show us the way. Give us the strength to gain self-mastery, to do good, to help the weak, the lost and the fallen. To see evil and to lay waste to it. To fight wickedness and to defeat the snares of pride, vanity and indolence. Amen."

After a considerable silence His Lordship opened his eyes, looking dazed, as if he were having to drag himself down from some higher heavenly plane.

My knowledge of Anselm Bertram Vickers, Viscount Allington,

derived from *The Times* and political gossip from my father's circle in Devon. He was a member of the new Tory government, but better known as a philanthropist and for his religious piety—not qualities readily associated with the aristocracy. He was very well connected. Through his mother alone he was related to the Earl of Aberdeen and the Duke of Buccleuch. He chaired a legion of committees of charitable and religious organizations which were especially devoted to the needs of children. In Parliament he had attempted with some success to prevent young children from working in mines, mills and as chimney sweeps. He had seen through laws to improve the treatment of lunatics, and had led the thus far failed campaign to reduce working hours in factories and mines to ten hours a day. There were those who said that his work denied poor families the chance to bring home a decent income, and that he was at least partly motivated by the desire to confound the rich mill and mine owners of the Whig party. As for his personal life, he was unmarried but considered highly eligible. I had seen him described as "the prince of philanthropy, with the looks of an angel." It was also widely rumored that he was on very ill terms with his father, the famously unpleasant Earl of Pewsey, who had tried and failed to stall Allington's inheritance of a fortune from a great-aunt, and that the two could not be in the same room together. Since Allington was a Tory, my father more or less approved of him, though he was suspicious of the Viscount's churchiness and philanthropy. He delighted, however, in the fury Allington's campaigns inspired among the opposition, the Whigs, whom he regarded as the enemy.

Brown Cape began to speak, but His Lordship raised his hand.

"Gentlemen," he said, "I asked Sir Theophilus Collinson to recommend two men with a strong sense of duty, two men incorruptible and undeflectable. He named you. I must admit, this was most agreeable to me. Apart from this refuge for the poor Lascars, I am on the Indian

Board of Control and am much concerned both to improve the lot of the natives there and to combat the evils of Hindooism." At this, Blake's brows twitched into the briefest frown.

"Your association with Xavier Mountstuart was for me no small added incentive for seeking you out," His Lordship continued. "I applaud your brave efforts to save him at the hour of his death.

"Captain Avery, may I congratulate you on your various acts of bravery, most recently on the Afghan campaign. The Company's loss is England's gain. Mr. Blake, Sir Theo likes to say of you simply that you have a talent for 'finding things.' I know, however, that your exploits are something of a byword."

I will confess that it was exceedingly pleasant to find myself complimented by Lord Allington. At the same time I had the strongest feeling that Blake had taken against His Lordship and was about to say something disobliging, and that the whole enterprise would collapse before it had begun. I did not wish this to happen and so I struck out before he could.

"Your Lordship, I know we would both be glad to help in any way we may."

Blake said nothing. I judged he would hate an untidy contradiction and it felt peculiarly satisfying to have outmaneuvered him, if only for a moment.

"Perhaps you might tell us about the task you have for us," I continued.

Lord Allington turned to his female companion, who had thus far barely shifted her attention from him. "The subject is, I fear, not one suitable for ladies' ears."

"Come, Allington, there is no real reason for me to depart," she said.

"My dear," he said, warningly.

"But, Allington—"

He raised his hand and she fell silent. "Mr. Threlfall," he said to Brown Cape, "would you see my sister back to the coach?"

The lady sighed loudly and gave us a mutinous look. "The footman will escort me," she said stiffly, lifting her skirts and rustling noisily from the room, the silent footman gliding behind her.

"Gentlemen." The Viscount unmeshed his fingers and pressed them onto the table, staring into its unpolished surface. "I have a dark and ugly task to ask of you. I do not know if it may be resolved, but I think it must be attempted and I believe that the act of doing so will cast light into the dark places where it is most truly needed. The matter concerns an unsolved murder—two, indeed."

I felt a thrill of shock, and also of excitement.

"One took place three weeks ago, in the back streets below Drury Lane—a hive of degeneracy but also of great poverty and wretchedness. It was not some drunken brawl or cheap revenge played out upon the street. The victim was the poorest sort of printer, of chapbooks and the like, and he was attacked in his own shop."

"Printers, even poor ones, are hardly the most wretched in London," said Blake sullenly, for the first time. Looking up, Lord Allington became instantly once more mesmerized by his appearance.

"Your Lordship," I said, "I see you are surprised by Mr. Blake's attire. I should perhaps explain that he is accoutred thus so as to pass easily through the lowest and poorest parts of the city—just such places as you describe. In India this skill saved my life. Indeed, I would go so far as to describe him as a very 'master of disguise.'"

Lord Allington nodded and looked patently relieved. Blake glared at me but said nothing. I had judged once again that his natural antipathy to complicated explanations would make him loath to contradict me, and so—for the moment—it proved.

"Please, Your Lordship, pray continue," I prompted.

"I know nothing personally of the victim, but we have been able to obtain copies of a police report as well as several descriptions of the body from those who found it. Mr. Threlfall has the papers. As I said, the man was a printer and his name was—"

"Wedderburn, My Lord," Mr. Threlfall supplied smoothly.

"Yes," said Viscount Allington. "His premises were in Holywell Street, a poor and dishonest neighborhood, as you will know. The circumstances of the murder were strange and bloody, there were no witnesses, but the manner in which his body was discovered has impressed itself most dreadfully upon everyone who saw it."

Mr. Threlfall retrieved from his leather bag a portfolio and handed it to his master. His Lordship studied it for a few moments, shut his eyes as if in distaste, then handed it back to Threlfall, opening his blue eyes wide. He spoke in a low, urgent voice.

"The matter was almost immediately abandoned by the police for lack of evidence. But the body was found in an exceptional and horrible state. It was very particularly draped—spread-eagled, indeed—across the printing press, as if the assailant had taken very particular pains to place it there. Its face and neck had been cut, carved even, so that it was hardly recognizable. It was covered in blood—in monstrous quantities, and on the hands this had been mixed with ink. The stomach had been . . . well, the only way to describe it is sliced open, like some butchered creature. Moreover, this abomination was committed as the man's family slept quietly upstairs."

He paused for a moment, and exhaled as if to rid himself of the horrible picture the words had conjured.

"Good heavens!" I said.

"As far as the new police's hurried researches could tell, he had no debts, nor any particular enemies."

"I've heard nothing of this," Blake said musingly. "You'd expect to see something in the press, a broadside or two at the very least, or a ballad. Especially if the man was a printer."

"There were a number of brief mentions of the murder in the press the day after it occurred, but since then, nothing."

"You mentioned a second murder—Your Lordship," Blake said, and the tiny pause between the words insinuated an unmistakable sliver of disrespect which Lord Allington affected not to notice, though he straightened his back even more and it seemed to me his manner became even loftier.

"Not long after I learned of this crime," he said, "news of another death was brought to my attention. Another printer, by the name of . . ."

"Blundell, sir," said Threlfall.

"Thank you, Threlfall, six weeks ago. The matter was complicated because there was subsequently a fire at his premises, but I have it on good authority he was murdered in similar, if not identical, circumstances, and the fire came after. He lived in the area of Monmouth Street by Seven Dials. The police have concluded that he died accidentally in the fire."

"Surely even without the newspapers, such tales would have spread by word of mouth, Your Lordship? Comparisons made?" I said.

"It would seem that both crimes have been all but forgotten already. I have been informed that in the immediate streets about, the stories have gained local notoriety. There has been a renewed interest in foolish superstitions, talk of Spring-Heeled Jack and such. But there is also a reluctance to speak about the crimes themselves."

"May I ask how you came to hear of the murders?" said Blake.

"They were brought to my attention by a member of one of our societies who runs what is commonly called a 'ragged school' in the vicinity. He was dismayed that so little attention had been devoted to these crimes."

"And the police have given up on the murders?"

"They say with no murder implement, no apparent motive and no further evidence, there is no basis upon which to continue an investigation."

"But you do not believe this," said Blake.

"I do not."

There was a silence.

"I imagine, Your Lordship," said Blake, the gentleness of his tone surprising me, "that sometimes the work you do must lead you into conflict with established and respected authorities you never thought that in your position you would have to question. That must be difficult for you."

Lord Allington, who had been staring deep into the table again as if seeking some great truth in its surface, looked up at Blake almost gratefully, his eyes wide again.

"I must ask you for your discretion given what I am about to say. Please understand I have the highest respect for the London police. But it is a not uncommon story: difficult cases in the poorest, grimmest parts of the capital, where the inhabitants are, let us say, less than welcoming to the police, are neglected. It is also the case that the senior figures in the Metropolitan Police are preoccupied with the Chartist threat almost to the exclusion of all else. The police commissioner, Sir Richard Mayne, is quite obsessed by it. He may not be entirely incorrect to be so." He lowered his voice. "There are suggestions the fire at the Tower might not have been the accident we have been led to believe it was but a deliberate act of arson."

My first reaction to this extraordinary news was to look to Blake; his expression was quite inscrutable.

"It is also the case that since the Bow Street Runners were disbanded in '39, there has been no detecting unit within the Metropolitan Police, and so such cases have not been dealt with as well as they might. Nor have the police or the parish chosen to offer a reward for information.

"To be blunt, gentlemen, from what I can gather, since the murders have not caught the public's attention, and took place in some of the most degenerate regions of London, the police have chosen to neglect them. I regard this as both a terrible mistake and an injustice."

The statement seemed to require another question. Blake remained silent, so I obliged, though I was not sure what precisely I was supposed to ask.

"Sir?"

Lord Allington lowered his shoulders as if settling himself to deliver a speech. Or a sermon.

"As you may know, I am no stranger to the poorest parts of London. I have become aware of what the city—and its new modes of work—does to the poorest and most desperate: how it robs them of dignity, of the community and customs of the village. How it crowds them into places where ignorance, profligacy and drunkenness reign, where cleanliness is impossible, disease is rife, and misery, depression and discontent abound."

As he spoke, his voice grew rich and fervent, and he seemed transported by his own words.

"Moral degradation surrounds them, religion eludes them and salvation is denied them. The children of these places come of age without decency, without comfort, without hope, without God. The city is the sump of degradation of human traffic. The old bonds have been broken, godlessness is rife. There is terrible want: such poverty and ignorance and hardship that make it near impossible for those who suffer them to do more than struggle to exist, and which encourage many to fall into sin, degradation and corruption. Only by improving the conditions of life and work of the poorest can we encourage them to look higher, to consider their immortal souls, to love God and find the way to salvation." His blue eyes brimmed, and his voice took on an incantatory quality. Next to him Threlfall gave a small emphatic nod from time to time.

"Another effect of the great changes that have taken place in manufacturing in the last forty years has been to transform us into a country inhabited by two nations, between whom there is less and less intercourse and no sympathy. Two nations who are ordered by different manners and governed by different laws: I mean the rich and the poor. We might as well be inhabitants of different planets. There are those among the poorest who have come to believe—not altogether without reason—that their rulers, or at least their masters, do not care as much for their welfare as they should. I wish to show this is not true."

The words had clearly been spoken before, though this did not detract from their power.

"It has been a hard year. The poor are hungry. They find little relief, and so they are driven to extremes. They talk of universal suffrage, democracy, republicanism as answers to their problems. They look to Chartism and the Chartists. I see the Chartists as the great and looming danger of the age. I believe that if we do not take care we will be in danger of surrendering the working classes to them and their dangerous ideas. We would be ruled by the mob. There are those, like the police commissioner, who believe such threats can be quelled with police truncheons. I believe we must win hearts and minds by showing the laboring classes that we can and do govern in their interests and care about their welfare."

"I do not share your opinion, Lord Allington," said Blake abruptly. "I do not think the Chartists want revolution: I think they simply want the vote. I agree with them: it should be the right of every man. Can you find no common ground with them, given your desire to bring your 'two nations' together, and their desire for better pay and conditions?"

"Mr. Blake," Lord Allington said in a kindly voice, deliberately ignoring his impertinent tone, "as I understand it you are a man of singular intellect who has triumphed over very modest circumstances. I can quite see why you should believe this to be true. But you must agree that the multitude is not ready for the vote. They are not sufficiently educated for the responsibility. They may one day be, but not yet."

Blake bristled; His Lordship was oblivious. "As for the Chartists, I did at one stage believe it might be possible to find what you call 'common ground' with them, but I was disappointed. And they are dangerous: they have the power to rally a whole class, and for all their peaceful claims, their true aims are revolution, the death of property rights, anarchy. I know that in the eyes of some, the governing class—I mean the aristocracy—may sometimes seem to enjoy its privileges and do little enough in return for them. But we are the best hope for the stability and greatness of this country, though I admit we must do more to demonstrate our concern for every soul."

"So," Blake said, "you believe that by sending us to investigate these murders and even solving them, you will restore the downtrodden multitudes of Drury Lane's faith in their betters and draw them away from Chartism?"

"As Shakespeare says, Mr. Blake," said Lord Allington, smiling reprovingly, "one good deed shines in a naughty world. Every good act makes a difference. Many good acts can make a great difference. 'Let us not be weary in well doing: for in due season we shall reap, if we faint not.' Galatians six, verse nine."

"I see," Blake said, as if he did not. There was a silence.

"I do have another reason," His Lordship said at last, in a tone more personal, more anxious, than the confident tone of his sermon, "for engaging in this case, one more prompted by sentiment perhaps than reason. I am haunted—how could one not be?—by the thought that there is in this city some monster, or monsters, conceiving of these murders and then carrying them out, killing with impunity because it has silently been decreed that these victims are not worthy of concern. Two murders the same. I think it entirely possible that there may be more to come. Perhaps even others before. The police have chosen not to act. I have the resources to do something, therefore I have a duty to act."

Blake paused. "It will not be easy," he said at last. "The locals will likely be wary of us, and the sites of the murders are likely to give us nothing after all this time."

Lord Allington looked pleased. His eyes drifted heavenward. "I do not believe that you will be deterred by such trifles, Mr. Blake. If we—if you—catch this man, the inhabitants of these streets can rest a little easier and feel a little safer. And they will have trust in their rulers."

Blake muttered something I could not hear.

His Lordship, half hearing, said, "Mr. Blake, may I ask you something?"

"Sir?"

"I recollect now that Sir Theo intimated that you might perhaps be an atheist. Is this true?"

"Mr. Blake," I broke in nervously.

"I can answer the question, Captain Avery," said Blake. "I'm not a believer. I lost my faith a long time ago. If you'd rather find a godly in-quirer, so be it. I won't lie about it."

"I see," His Lordship said. "You are at least honest. Faith is not a prerequisite for the task. I asked for honest and undeflectable, not de-vout. Besides, I believe that God works through everyone—even you, Mr. Blake."

"And I that the institution of religion exists only to keep mankind in order."

"I beg your pardon?" said Lord Allington, bemused.

"I believe Mr. Blake is quoting Montaigne," I said, recalling his pre-dilection for such things.

"Voltaire," said Blake. "I was quoting Voltaire."

"The French infidel?" said His Lordship.

"Not a word I've heard in a while," Blake observed. "But no, I should have said he was a skeptic, not a non-believer, Your Lordship."

Lord Allington stared at him for a moment, genuinely perplexed, and then, almost to himself, "Well, Sir Theo did say you had your enthusiasms." He coughed. "Captain Avery, may I ask, are you ob-servant?"

"I am a churchgoer, Your Lordship, though I cannot swear that I am saved," I said, grinning. His Lordship did not return it. "But I must be honest too. I am not familiar with this kind of investigation—even if Mr. Blake is. And I do not know London at all."

"But I must have you both," said His Lordship, "Blake and Avery—it is what I discussed with Sir Theo." I saw the thought of dealing with Blake alone alarmed him. If nothing else I might be a polite bridge be-tween them both.

"Will you do it, gentlemen?" Allington said.

We turned to Blake. I had no idea what he would say. He caught my eye and raised his brows just a little. I stared back at him hopefully.

"I—we will look into it," he said, "and determine what use we can be."

"I thank you. I will pray for a fruitful outcome. Mr. Threlfall has all the papers. He will make terms and discuss remuneration." He picked up his gloves and turned away; the matter of money was clearly distasteful to him. "And now I must depart. I wish I could linger and ask you about India, but I fear I have other pressing engagements. I should like you to call on me in the next few days at my Charles Street residence in Mayfair to report on your findings. I hope to have more time then. Good day, sirs. And thank you. Ah yes, if the families of the dead men are in want, I should like to do something for them. Let us know."

*With his master gone,* Mr. Threlfall the diffident servant swiftly became Mr. Threlfall the pompous steward.

"Do you have cards?" he said haughtily, his chest swelling like a farmyard cockerel. I informed him of where I was staying and was greeted with a small nod of approval which I found mildly insulting. Blake produced from his ragged pockets a small purse from which he extracted a bent card. Mr. Threlfall took hold of it with the tips of his fingers as if it might be contagious.

He handed the leather portfolio to me. "Here are the documents, including the papers provided by the new police. There are also letters of introduction from Lord Allington with his seal. I suggest you do not come tomorrow. His Lordship has a very full day and is dining with the Earl of Aberdeen."

"Is the name of the man who brought the murders to Lord Allington's attention in there?" said Blake.

Mr. Threlfall nodded, his mouth a moue of distaste. I suppressed a smile. I knew Blake cared nothing for his disapproval.

"As for your . . . wages?"

"I assume Collinson has already named a figure," said Blake.

"He has."

Blake sighed. "We'll take it, but we shall need in addition some money for expenses. For bribes and payments and so on."

Threlfall looked alarmed. "Is information to be obtained by payment?" he said.

I suspected Blake was amusing himself. "The lower classes have so little to sell, we shall have to pay for information."

"Well, I suppose you may sign for it and account for it later," said Threlfall dubiously.

Blake wandered off toward the door.

Threlfall caught hold of my arm. He muttered, but not so quietly that Blake could not hear, "Captain Avery, can you please ensure that Mr. Blake is more appropriately dressed next time he meets His Lordship?"

"I'll do my best, Mr. Threlfall," Blake called over his shoulder, almost cheerily. "I sense, sir, that this has been a trying day for you. You would rather have been dispensing charity elsewhere."

"I am devoted to His Lordship and his sister," Threlfall said. "Personally I believe charity is better expended upon our own deserving poor, rather than those who have irresponsibly washed up on our shores. And Hindoos at that. As the Bible says, 'if any provide not for his own, and specially for those of his own house, he hath denied the faith, and is worse than an infidel.'"

"Didn't stop you dipping one of your fat fingers into one of those big pans of Hindoo curry though, did it, Mr. Threlfall?"

"I do not know what you mean."

"It's all over your sleeve, Mr. Threlfall. It's in your fingernails and on your coat," said Blake drily. "Tasty, wouldn't you say?"

Mr. Threlfall tried to look at his sleeve while pretending not to—it was indeed soaked in something thick and stew-like—reddened, picked up his case and stomped from the room. We heard his boots clattering crossly down the stairs.

"Fire and fury!" I said, laughing despite myself. "He deserved it, but was it a good idea to so provoke him?"

"Shouldn't think so," said Blake, looking moodily after him. "You don't have to do this, Avery," he added.

"Allington asked for me. Why should I not stay? I've a mind for it—it beats drilling the South Devon militia, believe me. And you need me. Look at you: you are in no state to work on your own."

"You said yourself you've no experience in such things," he retorted. "What can you do round the back of Drury Lane or Monmouth Street in your fine frock coat but get yourself sharped or buy a cheap whore?"

"Oh, Jeremiah, you have become coarse in your old age."

"I was always coarse, you just didn't understand because I was speaking Hindoostanee. Besides, this thing, it's impossible. The bodies will have been buried long since, there will be next to nothing to find."

"You did not refuse it."

"I've nothing better to do."

*I, too,* I thought.

We passed down the stairs in silence. At last Blake turned to me and said, *"Master of disguise?"*

"Why not?" I said, and I laughed.

I felt my melancholy start to lift for the first time in months.

# chapter 3

On the train back to Tower Hill, Blake took the leather portfolio from my lap and began to flick through the papers, as I stared, fascinated, out of the window.

"Is there much to read?" I said at last.

"Police report of death of Nathaniel Wedderburn, printer, aged forty-two. Lived above his shop with his wife and five children. Thirty-six Holywell Street, Holborn. Description of body. No sign of forced entry. No sign of a struggle in the room. No murder weapon. No one saw anything. Body found by a young girl, Matty Horner. No relation to the deceased. A coroner's report. A statement from a Thomas Dearlove of the London City Mission and the Society for the Suppression of Mendicity, describing how he saw the body shortly after it was found."

"The 'ragged school' teacher?"

"Should think so."

"And the other dead man?"

"Even less on him. Matthew Blundell, printer, Monmouth Street, Seven Dials. A police report from six weeks back, saying the body was discovered in the premises after a fire. No witnesses. Another letter from Dearlove dated two weeks ago, addressed to His Lordship, saying that he had heard word of another murdered printer in Monmouth Street. He says that the body was discovered by neighbors, and had been stabbed and left on his press just as Wedderburn was, but that the place caught fire not long after the body was discovered. Someone brought a candle into the shop and the room combusted. Several burned, but no one seriously."

"How shall we proceed?" I asked.

"We will do our best to build a picture of Wedderburn and his associates. See if he knew Blundell. Find this Dearlove. Follow what threads we can." He sighed and ran his hand through his hair. He looked suddenly weary. "This kind of murder, it's rare. But when some-one goes so far as to arrange bodies in such an elaborate way, rational thought, logical connections, usual motives"—he shook his head—"more often than not, they do not apply. Whoever has done this has a kind of sickness of the soul. But one that is not necessarily in plain view."

"You have seen something like it before?"

He nodded and clamped his mouth shut. I saw he would say no more on the matter. "Still," he relented, "we'll go to Holywell Street. Ask the questions. See what we can find out."

At Tower Hill I looked up from retrieving my ticket for the inspec-tor to find Blake on the other side of the shed, gazing at the black steam engine attached to the huge metal cable which stretched all the way to the wagons we had traveled upon, snaking around them and up the track itself.

"You take an interest in steam engines, Blake?" I said, surprised.

"Never seen one of these—the engine's stationary and the cable draws the wagons along the track."

"It seems to me as if the whole world has changed since I left England."

"Not yet, but it will. The railways'll be everywhere. Devon too." On Great Tower Street we spied an omnibus caught in the traffic like a fly in honey. I had always longed to travel in one. With an air of worldly resignation Blake gestured me on, and I hauled myself in by the leather strap. There was at once an overwhelming and uncitified smell of wet horse and old straw, and I had to pack myself in, my knees knocking over-intimately against those of passengers opposite us, my feet deep in the straw. The omnibus itself was equally trapped in a sea of coaches, donkey carts, carriages, horses, squeaking brakes and rattling wheels, all striking out in different directions. As we snailed west, I fell to daydreaming, marveling that the last time I had seen the man next to me, we had stood in the warmth of an Indian spring on the banks of the Hooghly River, watching the clippers sailing past. The passengers' faces—cross, musing, fatigued, dazed—changed and rearranged themselves, and our trousers grew increasingly muddied as ladies dragged their wet skirts over them, fighting their way on and off. In Devon I would have worn gaiters to weather the mud; in the city it was not done, but the place was quite as muddy. By the time we reached our destination, we might have walked the distance in half the time. And when we were discharged from the "bus," we were, I saw, on the far side of the old Temple Bar.

"I was here yesterday," I said.

"Holywell Street is off the Strand," Blake said. "There you'll find the similarity ends." He strode through the archway, heading north, his pace exposing a very slight limp. There was a gust of chill air. I shivered.

"Cold still catch you out?" he said.

I nodded, gasped and pulled my coat about me.

"Me too," he said.

Holywell Street was a bedraggled mishmash of battered old and ugly new, with a distinctly disreputable, even sinister air. Blake fitted in perfectly. Dreary flat-fronted tenements alternated with timbered houses so bent, mended and patched it was a wonder they stood at all. As it was, the whole street gave the impression that at an antique moment before the flood some great geological pressure had squeezed it, forcing it all upright; some premises had emerged barely wide enough to fit a front door; others had walls warped and curved like crooked old men. The oldest buildings leaned forward so far over the street that it seemed a miracle they had not yet toppled into it.

It was busy. Street sellers offered coffee, hot potatoes, sandwiches and the like. A young girl sold winter cress. A couple of patterers hawked ballads and stories and love letters allegedly sent by famous aristocrats to lowly seamstresses. A few painted creatures stood about in bright, cheap dresses, with plaid shawls that only half hid their low necklines. Farther away a couple of small boys were dancing to a barrel organ. A no-less-ramshackle company observed the wares: clerks taking coffee, idlers in caps and cord breeches leaning against walls encrusted with advertising bills, and pimply boys staring at the whores and the shop windows.

Above all, the street was lined with small run-down bookshops, print shops and sellers of secondhand clothes. Several had elaborate shop signs over their doors: above one was a huge grinning plaster mask and the words "Masquerade and Fancy Attire"; above another was a huge smiling half-moon. There was also a tavern; a couple of those "marine stores" that sold a jumble of worn-out odds and ends; a barber's; and a small brown shop, the tiny panes in its window darkened, that went by the legend "Letters Wrote." Outside the shabby book and print shops were trestles on which were displayed their mostly disappointing, well-thumbed stock: old journals, torn sheet music, chapbooks and soiled penny bloods with lurid names: *Varney the Vampire* and *The Gallery of Terror*. The clothes dealers made a better show: their threadbare wares were displayed all down the street, hung on poles in front of their shops, a rainbow of dingy hues, with rows of shoes, implausibly blacked, below, set out like exotic piano keys.

We stopped at a shop whose window was strung with old beaver hats, bright neckties, and trousers and jackets with black-patched knees and elbows. Most looked as if a little soap and water would have improved them immeasurably. An old clothes seller sat immobile before it, lost in his pipe fumes.

"I suppose this is where you acquire your wardrobe?" I said to Blake.

"I wouldn't buy here, it's three times the price of Rosemary Lane."

"*Rosemary Lane?*" the old man sputtered, coming to life. He had a long, thin yellow face, a straggling pointy beard, and a black skullcap, denoting his Jewish faith, with a frizz of gray fuzz beneath it. He appeared to have concluded that the best way to exhibit his wares was to wear as many of them as possible at once: he had at least five layers on—greatcoat over frock coat over several waistcoats, and his gnarled fingers emerged from two pairs of ragged fingerless gloves. "Rosemary Lane!" he said again. "I'll have you know my clothes are a sight finer than them shreds. And my prices are very good, cheap, cheap, cheap. But quality too. See these?" He stood up and pointed at a row of baggy-kneed trousers. "Bargains all. And what about a surcoat?" He grabbed Blake's coat and rubbed it between his fingers, then pointed at something only very slightly less ragged.

"You could do with something warmer. Twenty-two shillings." I grinned delightedly: he sounded like the cockney Sam Weller from *The Pickwick Papers*—or the pickpocket Fagin from *Oliver Twist*.

"Twenty-two shillings?" said Blake drily. "If I gave you half you'd be rolling me."

"Carn take it, sir, cost me a great deal more than that. See the sleeves, lovely work."

Blake shook his head.

"That's a nice bit of levver too," the old man went on, glancing at the leather portfolio. "But what about the young gentleman?" He gestured at me, then ran his hand caressingly along a row of brightly colored squares. "You can never have too many handkerchiefs—here, a billy every one."

I looked confused.

Blake said, "He claims they're silk. Care to help me with something else, old man? Tell me where Nat Wedderburn's shop is?"

At once the old man's face closed like a door. "Carn help you with that," he said, and turned away abruptly.

The murdered man's shop was almost opposite. It looked as if it had been closed not for three weeks but for many years. The window had been blacked out and already a few bills had been pasted over it. The sign, "Nathaniel Wedderburn, books and engravings," with a pretty decoration of thorns and leaves in white, was very worn. It seemed to me that as they went past passersby sped up and took care not to look at it, as if the grisly happenings that had come about within might cast a taint.

Blake knocked on the door.

"Even if they are there, would we not be intruding upon their grief?" I said.

"You've a better notion?" He knocked again.

"Let us at least have Lord Allington's letter to hand," I said, looking about nervously. On the other side of the road, the old clothes dealer eyed us balefully. From the portfolio I pulled out the envelope sealed with His Lordship's arms and slipped it into my coat pocket.

The two boys with the barrel organ had followed us down the street and watched us from the gutter. Blake beckoned me close, and from a pocket in his rags brought out two thin iron tools—a piece of wire filament with a curved end; and a thicker, flat-headed implement—and quickly inserted them into his palms, tucking the ends up his cuffs.

"Blake?" I said doubtfully.

Shielding the keyhole and handle with his body, he pushed the thicker tool into the lock and gave it a hard downward yank, then slipped the wire filament in above it and twisted.

"Blake!"

He turned the handle and the door opened smoothly. I swallowed my censure, wondered where he had learned such skills, then followed after him, closing the door behind me.

It would have been hard to imagine a room more grimly empty. There was not a book or scrap of paper anywhere, just a layer of fine dust over a short wooden counter, behind which were bare shelves. The air was acrid with the smell of chloride of lime. Behind the counter was a door through which we passed into the much larger room at the back. The chloride smell was even stronger here. Gray light came through a side window, before which was a long black-stained workbench. The higher parts of the brick walls were blackened with smoke. There was a door in the back wall, presumably leading into a yard, and an empty fireplace. Opposite the window and workbench was a rickety stair, under which there was a small cupboard door.

The room was dominated by a great black iron printing press. It comprised an upright rectangular frame, attached to which was a giant vise holding a heavy square metal plate which hovered threateningly over a flat table below. It was all too easy to imagine Wedderburn lying across it. The floor around the press had evidently been scrubbed hard but it was still stained with black. The only other furniture was a deal table, a round-backed chair, a few metal plates and some wooden boxes.

Blake paced slowly about the room. He tried the back door, which was locked, and the small cupboard, which was not. He walked around the press, never touching it, stepping back from time to time to look at it from another angle.

"Should we not ask someone's permission before we do this?" I said.

He seemed to be in some kind of reverie and barely heard me.

"Blake?"

"Let's see if the family's upstairs," he said.

There was a door at the top of the stairs and I made to climb them.

"No," he said. "We'll go up the outside steps. Don't want to frighten them." Ostentatiously he "locked up" the shop behind him, and we walked around the side where there were steps up to another door. At the top, Blake knocked. Silence, then a creak. He knocked again. Eventually a cry: "Ma!" The sound of footsteps.

A listless voice. A woman's. "Who is it?"

"Mrs. Wedderburn? My name is Jem Blake. May we talk to you? We have come to try and help you."

"Leave us alone. Who'd help us?"

Blake looked at me, cleared his throat and spoke in a warm, reassuring tone that was his voice and yet was not.

"Someone who wants justice for your husband and to see that your children are fed. We have no wish to frighten you. We want only to speak to you. If you are alarmed we will stand away from the door, and you may question us outside."

"I don't know." We heard her sigh behind the door. Farther away a child again cried, "Ma!"

"All right," she said. "Wait." There was a good deal of shuffling about, then the sound of a heavy bolt being drawn. The door opened.

Mrs. Wedderburn wore no cap and her hair, long, chaotic and red, spilled around her shoulders. Her face was white, her eyes red-rimmed, and she stared at us dully. She wore a coarse brown frock with a cotton kerchief around her neck and a creased apron tied around a small waist. Even in the wreck of her grief, one could see that she had been—still was—a very striking woman; grief gave her a strange, otherworldly quality, as if she were sleepwalking. Two small children clung to her skirts, and behind her was another girl, about ten, and a boy a little older.

"I am Jem Blake, Mrs. Wedderburn." We had taken a few steps down the stairs. Blake stood with his hands out, palms upward. "And this is my companion, Captain William Avery." He drew out a card and offered it to her. She looked at it without seeing it and then let her arm drop uselessly to her side. Behind her, the children watched us, warily.

"You'd better come in," she said. She drifted back into the room, the previous small show of defiance having used up all her resources.

The older boy and girl closed the door, bolted it and dragged several heavy boxes against it. The girl gave me a bleak look and hunched her shoulders.

"In case they come back," she whispered.

The room, not ill-sized, had bare brick walls and wooden boards, and was well lit by two windows. There were rudimentary stairs to an attic floor above, and a door open to a small kitchen and scullery at the back. Inside the main room were a worn table, three upright chairs, two stuffed mattresses and an old cylinder desk against a wall. The door to the shop below, on the other side of the room, was barricaded by five or six wooden boxes, with two baskets on top in which ropes were coiled. There was a fire in the grate, a little coal in a bucket, and on the table the remains of a meal—bread, cheese, some wrinkled apples and small beer. The family did not seem in immediate want and yet the place felt stripped of comfort, as if something had been irretrievably lost.

Blake stood locked in his own thoughts and took off his gloves. The children at once noticed his missing fingers and stared at them with something between fear and fascination.

"Mrs. Wedderburn," I said, for the moment seemed to require something, "will you sit down?" I led her to a chair. The children clustered themselves around her, the little ones still holding on to her skirts. The oldest girl began to arrange her mother's flaming hair.

"Let me assure you," I said, "we have not come to take anything from you, or to force anything upon you. We want only to help you."

Mrs. Wedderburn seemed not to hear.

The oldest girl bit her lip in frustration. "Ma! Ma! Listen to him," she said. "He says they've come to help. Talk to them, Ma!"

The woman made a visible effort to gather herself and looked up at me.

"Things been hard the last weeks. Carn sleep or hardly think straight. I'm sorry."

"Mrs. Wedderburn, I have a letter of introduction. It is from Lord Allington. The philanthropist. Perhaps you have heard of him?"

She nodded vaguely.

"He heard about your husband's death from a young man who runs the ragged school near here. Mr. Dearlove? He is dismayed at the lack of progress. He believes more must be done to discover whoever is responsible for your husband's death."

The older girl pulled at her mother's skirt. "Ma!"

"Carn bring him back," Mrs. Wedderburn murmured.

"Do you not want to know who could have done such a thing, and have them brought to justice, Mrs. Wedderburn?" I said. "To stop them from doing such a terrible thing again?"

"Who are you to do this?" she said, suddenly more awake and wary.

Blake stirred from his reverie. He came over and crouched down, holding on to the arm of her chair to balance himself, and gave her a steady look. "Mrs. Wedderburn," he said.

She met his eyes. "My name is Connie," she said.

"Connie. I am an inquiry agent. I find things. I'm good at it. Captain Avery is helping me. He is"—he hesitated—"a good man."

"Carn bring him back," she said again, stubbornly.

"Connie," he said, and he took her hand and looked into her eyes, "I know well how hard it is to lose someone. I do. But I must ask you some questions about your husband's death."

She gazed at him; the wariness receded and the grief returned. "There's not much to tell."

"Perhaps the children should not be here?" I said. She nodded, and though the older girl protested, they took themselves up the rickety stairs.

"Connie," Blake said, never losing her gaze, "how long have you been here?"

"Six years."

"Did he employ many men?"

"Not for a long time. Daniel, he'd been helping, but he went his own way." Her eyes were suddenly brilliant with the sheen of unshed tears.

"Daniel?"

"My son. He's not here."

"Did Nat have particular clients?"

She shook her head, stubborn again. "I wouldn't know. I didn't see that side of it."

"I've a hard question, Connie. Can you tell me what you remember about when Nat died?"

"That's the thing," she said, agitation breaking through her torpor. "I didn't see him. He went down to work that night. He has to work overnight when the orders come. I didn't think anything of it when he didn't come up. We went to bed. I heard nothing. I thought I'd see him in the morning. Now I never will. They said I couldn't see him after they found him. I should remember him as he'd been. My poor Nat. He gave up so much for me." Two great silent tears rolled down her cheeks.

"Who is 'they'?"

"The ones what found him. Matty was first, then Abraham over the street. That man who teaches the school. The others in the street."

"What time did he usually close up at night?"

"About ten o'clock. I'd bring him a bit of supper earlier. Left him to it. Didn't like me to come down when he was working."

"Anything unusual happen in the days before his death?"

She shook her head. "I carn remember anything different. Nothing."

"Do you have any thought, however unlikely, of who might have done this?"

She broke from his glance and looked at the floor.

"No. Carn think of no one."

"No one to whom he owed money? No one who might have been

angry—an old apprentice, a client, a rival? An enemy. Anyone who wished him ill?"

"I said," she said stonily, "I carn think of no one."

"I don't want to upset you, Connie. But what kind of help would I be if I didn't ask that question?" Her expression did not soften.

"I'll need to speak to other people who knew him," said Blake. "To those who found him. I'll need names. Will you help me?"

At that moment the side door to the outside steps burst open. In the doorway stood a tall, thick-set young man, barely, I should have said, eighteen years old. It was at once apparent that he was in a high state of excitement. Seeing us did nothing to calm him. He stepped menacingly into the room, his fists balled.

"Who are they?" he said brusquely to Connie Wedderburn, and to us, "What are you doing here?"

My fists were itching and I had crossed the room to meet him before I even had time to think. "Who are you to visit such violence and ill temper to those who have suffered so much?" I said furiously.

"Daniel!" Connie Wedderburn cried, standing up.

"William, he is Connie's son," said Blake mildly, placing a hand on my shoulder. If he had not done so we might have come to blows. The young man, I saw, had the look of his mother but was twice her size. The other children now appeared quietly at the top of the stairs.

"These men say they want to find the man who hurt your father, Daniel," said Connie, her voice thick with pleading. "They mean no harm."

I collected myself and stood down, a harder task than it should have been. "My apologies, Master Wedderburn. I did not know you."

He ignored me and instead addressed his mother. "I've nothing to say to you. I'm here to pick up some clothes and nothing more."

"Daniel!" she said again.

"What's she been saying?" he said, turning at last to Blake and me. "You ask her about Eldred Woundy. That's who you should see."

He stamped up the stairs, returned with a bundle tucked under his arm and made for the door. The smallest boy began to snivel. The young man turned round. He came back, bent down, picked up the child and kissed him gently, not looking at his mother.

"Hush now, Charlie, I'll be back. There's things I have to do." He rocked his brother back and forth. The child quietened, but the mother broke into heaving sobs. Daniel kissed the smallest girl, embraced the two older children and stroked their heads, picked up his bundle and walked out. Once he had left, the older girl came over to her mother, who gazed after her son, and put her arms around her.

"Connie," said Blake.

"He is right," she said. "You should go and see Eldred Woundy. He won't like it, but it is true. There've been enough secrets."

"I'll do that," he said. "But I must ask you a few more questions."

She gazed at him mulishly, her face still tear-stained, and gave a stiff little shrug.

"Who found your husband's body?"

"Matty Horner. Poor girl. She came in to get a bit of shelter from the cold."

"Where will I find her?"

"In the street. She's always there."

"What happened after she found the body?"

"She called the others then the blue bastards came. They took him away. Asked us questions and never came back. Not that anyone wants to see them in the street. But now it's as if the place Nat had in the world has disappeared, as if he'd never lived at all."

"Blue bastards?" I said.

"Coppers, bluebottles, peelers, new police, they've plenty of names," said Blake. He came up close to her, too close perhaps, so he almost touched her cheek, and whispered something. She looked at the children.

"No," she said, "we won't leave. Where would we go?"

"His Lordship has offered to help your family. I believe he could find you somewhere else," I said. The two older children stared at me hopefully.

"No. I won't leave here," she said, suddenly flinty. The boy's expression returned to its former dullness; the girl looked resigned.

Blake nodded. "I shall need to see his work."

"There's nothing left," said Connie Wedderburn. He stared at her and after a moment she bowed her head awkwardly. "I'll see what I can find." She pulled herself up, wrapped herself carelessly in a shawl and went outside. The oldest girl got up and pushed the door shut behind her mother. The mute older brother shadowed her.

"In case they come back," she said quietly, again.

*They are very afraid*, I thought. "They will not," I said firmly. "Is that not true, Mr. Blake? They will not return."

"What?" He looked at the children as if seeing them for the first time, and I prayed he would feel disposed to offer some reassurance.

"No," he said. "They will not come back. You should not fear that."

His words seemed to console them. "Mister? Captain?" the girl said, turning to me. "You said the Lord wanted to know if we needed anything."

"The Lord?" I said, confused.

"That Lord what does charity. You work for him," she said impatiently. "Can he give us some money. Today? Till Ma's better and we know what to do."

I looked at the food on the table. She followed my glance.

"Someone brought that. Dunno if there'll be more."

"What do you need?" I said.

"Two shillings? Half a crown?" she said hopefully.

Blake said nothing. I counted out five shillings. She took the money from my palm, coin by coin, looking meaningfully at her silent brother, then undid a small handkerchief from around her neck and wrapped them up in it.

"You tell that Lord thanks," she said, pocketing it quickly as her mother returned.

Connie Wedderburn held out a bulky package wrapped in crumpled paper.

"I'll pay you for them," said Blake. She shook her head.

He passed me the package and brought out from one of his pockets a notebook and a metal implement that proved to be some form of pen which appeared not to need ink. "Give me the names of people who knew your husband," he said, removing the lid and beginning to write.

"Carn think of anyone," she said.

He prompted her gently. "People in the street? People who worked for Nat? People he bought from or sold to?"

She came out with a few names, haltingly, denying they were of significance even as she did so.

"Ever hear of a man called Blundell?" he said at last. She shook her head.

"Thank you, Connie. We are truly sorry to come on such sad business. We'll return to tell you of anything we find. If you need food or rent or fuel, you have my card. Lord Allington has said he wishes to help if he can."

As we opened the door to depart, she passed her hand across her eyes. "Something I meant to ask. What was it? Yes. You related to old Billy Blake?"

"No," he said.

## chapter 4

———◦}◦◦{◦———

Evening was coming on and the east wind cut against every exposed inch. The two young organ-grinders had set up outside the shop and were dancing again. One, barely nine or ten, solicited me with a cup in which a solitary coin jangled; he had a leering, knowing look. The other turned the handle to make the gasping organ play. Across the road, the old clothes seller glared at us. Above his door was a sign, "Abraham Kravitz, clothing merchant." I supposed he must be the Abraham of whom Connie Wedderburn had spoken.

"What now?" I said.

Blake restored his pocketbook to its pocket. "Find the girl Matty. Talk to Eldred Woundy," he said. "He started out printing penny bloods but set up a newspaper a few months back called *Woundy's Illustrated Weekly*. Big success. Got himself famous—big man, fancy dresser. See, there's a bill for it." He pointed at the wall behind me. It was thickly pasted with advertisements for theaters and pleasure gardens and the admirableness of certain journals, among them *Woundy's Weekly*: "The Latest News and the Best." He unwrapped a plug of tobacco, installed it in one cheek and began to chew.

There came suddenly from behind me a yelp, and Blake lunged. Or rather it was the other way around; it was so fast I could not tell. When I looked round, Blake had the cup-wielding barrel-organ boy by the arm.

"What the devil—"

From the boy's sleeve Blake plucked my silk handkerchief.

The child's face puckered in fury and he began to scream abuse—though not in any language I understood—as he tried vainly to twist from Blake's grip. The other boy picked up a handful of filth and stones from the street and pelted us with it, then took up the barrel organ in his arms and ran off as fast as he could.

Blake jerked the boy round, waved my handkerchief at him, ceased chewing and spoke to him calmly and imperturbably in his own tongue. In reply, the boy produced a stream of impassioned, incomprehensible words, the meaning of which was only too clear: the accusation was outrageous, he was utterly innocent. The diatribe continued for several minutes until he ran out of breath. Blake asked him another question. This time the answer was briefer and accompanied by a smirk.

"You've acquired another language since we last met," I said.

"Italian. All the organ-grinder boys are Italian."

"What does he say?"

"When I pointed out he was caught red-handed, he said you deserved to be stolen from as you take so little care to protect your possessions." Blake looked me up and down. "He's not wrong."

I bit back my reply.

Blake questioned him again. The boy looked at him craftily and shook his head. Blake gripped him harder and gave a chilly smile. Gesticulating expansively at Wedderburn's shop, the boy answered, increasingly volubly, and after a while started to grin. Then Blake let him go. The child scrambled off down the street, turning back once to make an obscene gesture and shout something offensive. I turned to Blake indignantly. He pushed my handkerchief into my pocket.

"He told me what I wanted. If he's taken by the police he'll be put in jail or transported."

"He is a thief."

"He's ten years old, has no other livelihood and there'll be some kidsman waiting to take his coins from him at the end of the day."

I shook my head, exasperated. "Kidsman?"

"A man who sets him and a bunch of other children thieving. They take the risks, he gets the fruits."

I sighed. "And did he tell you something useful?"

"He said Holywell Street is a good pitch because you never see coppers. They move street sellers on: it's the new dispensation. They'll arrest boys for rolling hoops in the street, let alone playing a barrel organ. Even so, the shopkeepers down here don't like him and his brother—they say they drive custom away."

"I can see why," I said.

"But Wedderburn let them stand outside the shop sometimes when others moved them on. The boy said everyone knows about the murder but no one talks about it now. He and his brother were here the day the body was found. Nothing like it had ever happened before. A big crowd gathered outside to try and get a look, but they took the body out in a box with a blanket over the top. He was told it was carved up like a piece of pork and there was blood everywhere. All the shops closed the next day: shopkeepers too scared to open. He said there are some 'bad men' in the street, but Wedderburn wasn't one of them and some of his clients were grand men, gentlemen in fine clothes."

"Is there any talk about who might have done it?"

In answer, Blake leaned forward and spat a stream of tobacco into the road. I winced.

"The boy said nobody knows and no one saw anything." He sighed. "The popular choices include various demonic apparitions, including Spring-Heeled Jack, and the Duke of Cumberland."

"What?"

"You know," he said, suddenly looking extraordinarily tired, "the Queen's uncle Ernest—he's the King of Hanover now. Profligate, gambler, said to have slit his valet's throat, fathered a child by his sister and murdered his mistress's husband, and has a face to frighten children with."

"Perhaps we should return tomorrow, Blake," I said anxiously. "You look all in."

He waved me aside. "The street will be lively till ten. We must find the girl, Matty Horner. She'll be selling cress or chickweed in a basket, the boy said. Everyone knows her. Old black bonnet, gray plaid shawl. You got any inside pockets? Take your valuables out of your coat and put them in your waistcoat at least."

Red-faced, I passed Connie's package to Blake, who slipped it inside his coat, then I stuffed my loose possessions into my waistcoat pockets until they bulged, and buttoned my coat from top to bottom. My attention was caught by the shop next door to Wedderburn's: "Dugdale's, printer's and bookseller's"; it too had an arrangement of white leaves and thorns around the name. It was one of those on Blake's list and it appeared to be thriving—as much as anything on that grimy thoroughfare could. A number of youths were clustered around a table outside the shop window on which there were various well-used pamphlets: *The Pirate's Bride*, *The Mad Monk*, and several more titles with suspiciously recognizable names: *Oliver Twiss*, *The Adventures of Nick-*

*erlarse Nickelbee*. It was not these that the boys were straining to see, however, but the window behind. Here, among more battered copies, were displayed handbills in which certain teasing phrases stood out in especially large letters: BACHELORS' CHOICE, CONFESSIONS OF A BLUSHING NEWLYWED, RACY SECRETS and PRIVATE COMPANION. When you got close enough to see, you realized that the wording around these, in much smaller letters, was utterly innocuous.

"Let me see what I can discover," I called to Blake, pushing my way in.

The shop was not unlike Wedderburn's but a good deal larger, with a long counter and shelves arranged with prints, worn volumes, pamphlets and chapbooks. Behind the counter was a short, square man with a rubicund face and a jaunty manner.

"Welcome, sir! It is always good to see a real gentleman in the shop. What might I help you with? Anything in particular you seek? I have a fine collection"—he gestured at his dog-eared stock—"and plenty more out back." He winked.

"I would indeed be grateful for some help. I have just seen Mrs. Wedderburn next door. I should like to ask you a few questions about her husband's death."

The man's congenial manner vanished. "We will have none of that in here. I sell books and pamphlets, that is all." He looked over my shoulder as the door opened and one of the eager youths came in. "If you wish to buy something, all well and good. If not, get out of my shop. I'm saying nothing."

"I have been formally engaged to look into Mr. Wedderburn's demise," I said.

"Be off with you! I have nothing to say about that matter. We do not talk about it here. Get out!"

Blake was standing outside.

"It did not go well?"

"No."

"Did you offer to buy something?"

"No."

"Good idea to smooth the feathers first. Some'll be happy to talk, others won't, not in front of the customers—bad for business. Next time you put some money down and ask to speak somewhere quiet. Likely he's frightened being right next door to the murder."

"Or knows more and is hiding it."

"That too. Next time, wait for me." He was taken by a fit of coughing and bent over, wheezing, shooing my attempts to help him.

"Find me Matty Horner," he said. "I'll catch my breath."

*It took a while* to come upon the girl. My inquiries were met with suspicious looks, but eventually the judicious application of a sixpence caused her to be revealed to me. She was of middling height, but looked smaller because she was so slight. She wore a black bonnet—so old and faded it was almost purple—pulled as far forward as it would go to shield her ears from the wind, and a large stringy plaid shawl that swamped her. She carried a basket.

"Sell you some cress, sir, or a nice juicy apple?" She seemed very young, though her voice was husky from shouting her wares. Her dress was not far off a rag and the bottom was edged with an uneven ink-black stain. Her face was pale, dirty and pinched with fatigue. But she had a bright, agreeable manner and a ready smile, which distinguished her from most on the street. I looked at the things in her basket. It seemed dishonorable to purchase a sorry bunch of cress merely to retain her attention, but I retrieved a small coin and pointed out an apple less wizened than the rest.

"Miss Matty Horner?" I said as she handed it to me.

The smile disappeared. "Who wants to know?"

I removed my hat. "My name is Captain William Avery, I have been asked to look into the death of Nat Wedderburn. I think you knew him."

She took a step back. Her eyes darted from side to side as if she were looking for some means of escape. I took hold of her basket. It felt like the act of a cad.

"Let go of me," she said loudly. Heads turned.

"Miss Horner," I said, flustered and speaking hurriedly, "please hear me out. I have just seen Connie Wedderburn. I know that you found Mr. Wedderburn's body. I cannot imagine how dreadful that must have been for you. My friend Mr. Jeremiah Blake and I are determined to find the man who did this appalling thing. But we need your help. I am loath to ask you, but we need to speak to you about what you saw. We would, of course, be willing to pay for your time."

The girl considered. I hoped my courteous words would have some effect. And I still held her basket.

"You are *determined*, are you, Captain?" she said sarcastically. "Owe you money, did he?" Her expression became sly, but oddly this merely emphasized how frail and small she was. I released the basket.

"No, Miss Horner. It is not that at all. We have been asked to look into the matter because the new police have done so little. I was a soldier in India, as was my friend Mr. Blake. He is an inquiry agent—"

"India?" she said, her curiosity for a moment outpacing her mistrustfulness. "Never met anyone from India. Where's your friend then?"

I pointed Blake out. He was leaning against a wall, his hand on his chest, watching us. She looked back and forth at us. Not for the first time I was reminded of what a strange couple we must make—me in my country gentleman's smart clothes, he looking as if he had recently been discharged from a paupers' hospital.

"Look, I'll talk to you," she said in a low voice, "but you'll have to pay."

I nodded disapprovingly.

She laughed wearily. "Nah. I'm not pricey. I want a cup and two thin from the coffee stand. And maybe a shilling. That'll do to start. I'll meet you at Abraham's. He'll let me sit in the back."

*So, you again,*" said the old clothes dealer, scowling from beneath his shaggy eyebrows. "Not here, I think, to buy a few garments. But poking into the Wedderburn business."

"Keep it down, Abe, and let him in," said Matty Horner.

"You sure, Matty girl? You all right?" He spoke to her fondly, in a tone quite different from his addresses to us.

"Nothing a cup and two thin won't sort. They come to ask me about when I found him. They say they're going to find who done it to him."

"What you doing nosing round here? You're no blue bastards."

"I am Captain Avery and this is Mr. Blake," I said patiently. "We have been asked to look into the matter by Viscount Allington. He does a great deal of work in places like this to help the needy, and is most concerned at the lack of progress made by the new police."

Abraham Kravitz was unimpressed. "What you want with her, then?"

"We need to ask Miss Horner about what she saw."

"She shouldn't have to speak of it again. No one else does."

"Abe," said Matty, her exasperation transforming the word into two syllables, Ay-abe, "come on. Let them sit in and I can have my coffee. They're buying. It carn hurt and if they can do something about it . . ."

"There are things it doesn't do to remember," he said.

"But they are already in here," she said, tapping her head. "And not thinking about them doan help. I've tried."

"You just be careful." With a great show of reluctance, the old man stood aside to let us in. "All right, Matty girl, take them into the back and rest your legs. I hope they're paying you good."

We followed the girl into the rear of the shop past mounds of old clothes, piled high and giving off a musty scent. In the back, wedged between two such piles, were a small table and some odd chairs. I gave Matty her cup of hot coffee and the bread and butter, and pulled out a chair for her. With exaggerated ceremony she sat down upon it, placing her basket carefully on the floor, setting her prizes upon the table and removing her bonnet. Then she set to eating with great bites, chewing each mouthful thoroughly as if to wring from it as much nourishment and satisfaction as possible. I had also purchased a ham sandwich. It turned out to be a slab of gray flannel set between two slices of something not far off cardboard. The enthusiasm with which she then tucked into this made me wish I had bought her something better.

"You know who I am, Matty?" Blake said.

"The captain here says you was—you were," she corrected herself, "a soldier in India."

"I was that," said Blake. "Now I'm a private inquiry agent. I'm not a copper, but I sometimes work on matters that the police don't have time for. I have a piece of paper says I can look into such things. The captain, he's helping me. If I ask you some questions, will you think carefully before you answer and tell me all that you remember?"

She nodded. "Can I see it?"

"What?"

"Your piece o' paper says you can ask questions."

"Can you read?"

"Yes." With an expression most skeptical, Blake retrieved from yet another of his pockets a small black wallet and took out an official-looking paper.

"Fingers clean?" he said.

In answer she wiped them on her dress. He gave it to her, watching her intently. She perused the paper like some old judge, then handed it back to him with such a dainty flourish that I covered my mouth to hide my amusement.

"All in order?" he said. She nodded. He sat down opposite her, took out his pocketbook and the special pen he had used before. She glanced at the stumps of his missing fingers.

"What's that?"

"Called a fountain pen. It has a steel nib and a little reservoir inside which stores ink."

"Not seen one of them before. Looks pricey. Can I see it?"

"Maybe. How old are you, Matty?"

She looked him square in the eye. "Twelve, sir."

He stared back. "Coster girl, are you?"

"Wasn't born to it, no. But I sell a bit of this and that. Run a few errands."

"Who takes care of you?"

"Take care of mesself, and my brother, Pen. My ma died when we was little. My pa was a printer. We were up near St. Paul's. I learned my letters then. I write a good hand. Pa died three years back. He got sick, then he couldn't work, then he got into debt. When he died, there

wasn't nothing—anything—left. Me and Pen do all right now though,"
she said. "We've kept out of the pan. We've our own place."

"That must be hard."

"S'all right." She spoke matter-of-factly.

"How do you know the Wedderburns?"

"When Pa died we was on the street. Ended up down here. Nat and
Connie was kind to us when no one else was. Abraham too. Nat didn't
mind if I came in the back of the shop and took a sit-down out of the
cold. Sometimes there was still a bit of fire in the grate—late at night
or if I started very early, walking out to Hackney Road to get water-
cress or something. They sell the green stuff cheaper up there than
Farringdon market. If I walk further I make a bit more. That was what
I was doing the day—" She stopped. "He showed me how to get in
round the side. Gave me a key. When things were easier, sometimes I'd
watch the littl'uns and then they'd give me a bit of supper."

"Things been hard?"

"Aren't they for everyone? Food's scarce, work's scarce, that's what
they say," she said.

"Was Mr. Wedderburn ever robbed?"

"Not as I recall. Not beyond the usual. He was in the shop all the
time, or upstairs."

"Did he have anyone work for him?"

"No one regular. An illustrator or maybe a writer. But no one of
late except Daniel—his son. He used to work in the shop."

"But not anymore."

She looked down at the hem of her skirt with its odd black stain.

"Daniel doan speak to me much no more. Got politics and I doan
know what. Argued with Nat about it. Nat said no point getting caught
up in all that."

"We met him earlier. He seems a very angry fellow," I said.

"Yeah, he's always angry now." She caught herself. "But I doan mean—"

Blake interrupted her. "How did Nat get on with the other printers and booksellers in Holywell Street?"

"All right. Not specially friendly. They're always looking over their shoulders at each other. There's a few I doan like, but far as I know Nat never had a beef with any of them. Some said he gave hisself airs, thought he was better than them. But he didn't care much what anyone said. The clothes dealers are more companionable. Maybe it's because, you know, they're all Jews. Nat got on all right with Abe. Abe's all right. But, mister, you mustn't think Daniel—he'd never do anything . . ."

Blake nodded. "I believe you. What about the printers? Did they argue?"

"I never seen any fighting or nothing. They just like to sound off about each other. Think of ways of doing each other down. But Nat never did anything like that."

"What sort of thing?"

She looked over at me. "Here, Captain whatever your name is, I'm doing a lot of work here, I want a plum duff and a hot elderberry wine."

"Tell you what," said Blake. "We'll give you the money for it when we've finished. You can go and get it then. I promise."

She pursed her lips. I put some coins on the table and pushed them toward her. "Take it now, Miss Horner. And my name is Captain Avery."

She picked up the coins and squirreled them away in the folds of her shawl. "My thanks, *Captain Avery.*"

"So how did they do each other down?" said Blake.

"Oh, I doan know, always looking to get ahead of each other. Copying each other's stuff and undercutting prices. Bad-mouthing each other. Dugdale's prime on that."

"Ever met Mr. Woundy?"

"Dunno anyone by that name."

"He'd be a big man, fat. Flash dresser. Ever see anyone like that?"

"Well, a fat man did come sometimes. Didn't catch his name."

"What do you remember about him?"

She thought for a moment. "Lots of chins. Reminded me of . . . what's it called, a great frog or toad, with a big throat and small brown eyes. Flabby red cheeks. Green suit, silk waistcoat. Not a sight you forget. Another time a big brown greatcoat with a dark fur collar. Very particular about his hair. Sideburns round his face till they turned into a little beard. I remember because he and Nat were chalk and cheese. He was big and loud and looked like money. Nat was thin and quiet and a bit worn. Might have been him?"

"How many times did you see him?"

"Three, maybe four times."

"Was he a client?"

"Dunno."

"Did Nat have regular customers, anyone you'd recognize?"

"I was working when his customers came. But sometimes one or two would pull up in carriages—quite the swells. Couldn't say I knew a face, and none of their names."

"All right, Matty, I want something else of you," Blake said. "I want you to go to the shop with us, take us through what you saw. You are the only one who can tell me. I will make it worth your while. More than you'd earn in a day."

"Blake," I said, "do you really—" His fierce look silenced me.

"I doan have a key," she said. "I did, but I doan have it today."

"I can fix that," he said curtly.

"Well then," she said, just as curt, "all right. Today is three weeks to the day it happened. I know because I mark off the days, keep a record. My dad taught me. Like he taught me to read. And I've a very good memory. I'll do it for two shillings. I'll meet you round the side, under the Wedderburns' steps, in a few minutes. I'll go first. You come after."

"Don't want to be seen with us?" said Blake.

"Got my reputation to think of," she said archly. "Doan want people seeing me go in."

She stood up and I saw her feet were bare. Blake did not seem to have noticed. She picked up her bonnet, shawl and basket, shouting thanks to Kravitz, and struck out through the milling idlers. A few minutes later we joined her under the Wedderburns' steps.

She pointed to a small door in the wall. "This is how I used to get in, round the side so no one could see. I'd walked to Hackney for winter lettuce."

Blake bent down on his heels and took out his tools.

She smirked. "House-breaker, eh, Mr. Blake?" she said. "Very respectable."

The light was not good, but the door sprung open after a few minutes and she edged in with us following behind. We crawled through a dusty cavity and then out into the back room itself. As she stood up, she braced herself.

"Tell me everything you remember," said Blake, taking out his pocketbook and pen, "however small."

"It was before six, not quite light. The room was really dark, but I was used to that so I didn't think nothing of it. I'd find my way over there"—she pointed to the far corner—"and lie down for a bit. It's quiet and there's no drafts."

She described coming in and finding the floor wet. She described stumbling, walking to the window, pulling away the shades, then turning to find Wedderburn lying across the press, his feet leaning upon the ground, his arms spread out. At each stage, Blake stopped her, probing every detail, how many steps she had taken, where she had stood, what she could see. He watched her every movement. She replied to his inquiries with a dispassion that I could not decide was plucky or alarming.

"Tell me more about the body," said Blake.

She took a breath. "There were these long thin cuts over his chest, but his stomach . . ." She gulped, at last losing her composure. "I've not ever seen anything like it. It was gouged open and gutted. Like a pig. Like a fish. And the insides spilled out." She put her hand over her mouth.

"I think we have heard enough, Blake?" I said. But Blake was not satisfied.

"Was the room disordered?"

She took a moment. "Nat's tools were laid neat on the workbench. Chair and desk in the usual place. But the pamphlets on the folding bench were spattered with blood. There could have been a struggle by the press. But it wasn't just blood, it was ink too. There was black ink on his face and more on his chest and fingertips. I mean, not just the usual printer's stain, but like his fingers had been pressed in it. There was a pool of blood at his feet, and his trousers were soaked with it."

"Your skirt," I said.

She looked down at the uneven black stain around the hem. "I washed it but I couldn't get it out. Carn afford to throw out all my clothes."

"The wounds on his chest, what made them?" said Blake impatiently.

The girl considered. "It's been nagging at me. Gravers and burins—

printer's tools—would do that. But I doan recall any were dirty. And acid—they use it for burning the metal away in engraving."

"Anything else? Any small detail. The press, the floor, his body?"

"The way he was lying. I said it later to Abraham, it was like he'd been laid there, special. It was like Jesus, come down from the cross. My pa took us to church. And it's funny that, cos Nat Wedderburn, he was about as far from a churchgoing man as you could imagine."

"What did you do after you found it?" Blake said.

"It?" she said, puzzled.

"The body."

She ran her hand across her face. "I wanted to spew." She paused. "Then I thought Connie and the children shouldn't see it. I ran to Abe's. I knew he'd be up. He knocked on a few doors. Moises next to him. Dugdale and Wenham over here. They called the copper from the Strand. He looked a bit green. The fellow who teaches the school, Thomas, he was walking past and came in. People were starting to gather outside, so we had to lock the door. Thomas, Abe and I went up to tell Connie. She fell on the floor. She couldn't speak. I stayed with her. When I came down there was a coffin brought and an undertaker took the body out. Another copper made me tell what I'd seen. Then I helped to clean up. We moved all we could upstairs."

"Good of you," Blake said.

"I wouldn't have done anything else," she said sharply, "they been kind to me."

"Was there a coroner's court?"

"Yeah, it was at the back of the Spotted Dog tavern."

"And?"

"And the coroner, he and the jurors go and look at Nat's body. And when they come out, most of them were looking sick. Then he calls the witnesses. Abe and me and the others. Asked me what I saw. So I told him. Then Thomas, he stood up and said that Nat had it coming to him, cos of what kind of a man he was and what he did. He said he consorted with criminals and it was the Lord's judgment."

"Thomas the schoolteacher?"

"Yeah. He's always up and down here and the courts with his Bible, trying to turn us from sin. I say, I would if I could afford it. He's from one of them missions on the Strand. Them societies for this and that."

"Exeter Hall?"

"That's it. Where all them evangelicals come from. Nat used to call them the Society for Telling Off the Poor. I never thought Thomas meant any harm: Pen goes to the ragged school when I can get him to. But I could have landed him one that day."

"Was there a doctor to look at the body?"

She shook her head. "After Thomas said Nat was a bad 'un, all the other printers went quiet. Coroner asked if anyone had any notion of who might have wished him ill. No one spoke up. He said, was it possible that Nat had done hisself in, or could he have had an accident on the press? I couldn't believe he could even say that. The jurors were sent to another room to decide what happened. They took a long while and when they came back they said they couldn't agree. Six said it was 'unlawful killing.' Five said it was 'accidental death.' Made no sense to me. They buried Nat in St. George's Gardens the next day. Connie said Nat would rather have been buried at a crossroads with a stake through his heart than put in a churchyard. But there wasn't nothing she could do. And I never heard nothing more about looking for who done it till today."

"Does the back door lead onto an alley?"

"Yeah. The fat man would come in that way."

"Show me how the press works," he said.

"Think I doan know?"

He shrugged. She described to him the frame, the metal type, the bed, the power of the thick, screw-like vise to press the paper down on the type and ink.

Then at last she said, "I've had enough now. Doan want to be in here anymore."

Blake shrugged and we crawled out into the darkening afternoon.

"What did people on the street say after?"

"To start with, booksellers like Dugdale and Wenham, they was all looking over their shoulders. All kept their shops closed. Thought they might be next. But they couldn't stay closed forever. Nothing happened, and people stopped talking about it, like it was bad luck."

"What about gossip?"

"Some said Nat must have owed money. Some said it was that evil duke what killed his servant and that girl. What's his name?"

"Cumberland," said Blake briskly. "It can't be him. He's King of Hanover in Germany now."

"They say his footmen used to come and get girls from round here." Then she said in a low voice, "Some of the girls up the road. They say maybe it was an apparition or, you know, Spring-Heeled Jack."

"Spring-Heeled Jack?" I said.

"Everyone knows who he is," she said, frowning.

"I was in India for five years."

"A story to frighten children," said Blake scornfully. "A creature in a black cloak who leaps ten feet at a time and wanders the streets, attacking women."

"And he has great claws and red eyes and breathes fire," protested Matty.

"Believe me," said Blake firmly, "it wasn't him. But it seems strange to me that no one seems to know about it beyond the street. You'd have thought that a patterer at least would have made up a ballad or a song."

She grimaced. "Carn really explain it. Maybe because the blue bastards never came back—but that's no surprise, they never come down here."

"Surely they must by law. It's part of their beat," I said.

She gave me an old look. "They should, but they doan. And all that with the coroner's verdict. And Nat keeping hisself a bit apart. And people down here not liking anyone poking their noses into their business. Dugdale—he likes to throw about his weight—told everyone to keep quiet. It'd be bad for business."

"We are done for today," said Blake abruptly.

"I'd like my money now," she said stoutly.

He counted out two shillings and dropped the coins into her hand.

"Heard of a printer called Blundell?" he said.

She shook her head.

"And how old are you, Matty?"

"Sixt— twelve, sir, like I said."

"Sixteen, more like," Blake said. "You're never twelve. Who runs you?"

"No one," she said, aggrieved. "Mesself. Abe's kind to me. Wedderburns helped us. Doan need no one else."

Blake looked at her. It was a hard look. I could not help liking the way she had stood up to him, and in turn regretting his brusqueness to her.

I stepped across him. "Miss Horner, may I escort you to the corner of the street?"

"Why, Captain," she said, half laughing, "I should be delighted."

I offered her my arm, leading her away, and noted how light she felt.

"You've no shoes, Miss Horner," I observed.

She pulled the hem of her skirts over her feet and for the first time looked abashed. "I had some, but the blood—I couldn't keep them. S'all right, I'm used to it. I'm saving for a new pair."

"It is very cold to be without them, to say nothing of the dirt. Perhaps you should use your shillings for new shoes."

"Perhaps I will, Captain," she said, wrapping her shawl about her as well as she could. "But first, I shall get some hot supper. See you, Captain."

I watched her hurry up the street, hunched over her basket to avoid the rain. Blake came up behind me just as Kravitz appeared at his shop door, rubbing his dry, frizzed beard between his fingers.

"I want to talk to you, Mr. Kravitz," Blake said.

The old man regarded us grumpishly. "Carn work you two out. The toff in his shiny clobber and you in yer rag fair getup. You make sure he doesn't get any ideas about Matty. She's a good girl."

"If you care so much about her," I said, "why do you not give her some shoes and a new skirt? She should not be out in bare feet."

"See any ladies' things here?" he said gruffly.

"There are plenty up the street and I am sure you know the merchants. Here. Three shillings. You will know her size better than I. Pick her out a pair. No need to tell her it was me. But I shall be back to see she has them."

Abraham Kravitz looked at the coins for a minute, then picked them up.

Blake drew some more coins from his pocket.

"Ten shillings. I'll take that coat and whatever you can tell me about Nat Wedderburn. Connie said we should talk to you."

"Ach! Keep yer money! Ask yer questions!" the old man said.

"Tell me about the day when Matty found Wedderburn."

"She ran over here. She was very pale, she could hardly speak. She should never have seen it." He gave his account, which in every particular echoed hers.

"Did you know Nat well?"

"Not well. For about five, six year, since he came here. He seemed all right to me."

"Know where he came from?"

The old man shook his head. "No one tells much about themselves round here. The street don't pry."

"Did he have any enemies?"

He sniffed. "I'd say not. He was not one to make trouble. Coppers done very little, it's true, they only come down here to take someone away, but they's no obvious answer to who killed him."

"Did you ever see Nat with a man called Eldred Woundy?"

He shook his head.

"Is there someone with a good memory round here, one who remembers the street from way back, who would know all the printers, where they came from?"

Kravitz laughed. "Carn think of no one now. Like I said, few round here want to talk about the past."

"But there was someone?"

He shrugged. "There was Dick Carlile. He knew them all, and they reckoned him. Well respected. Free-press man and all that. In and out of prison for years he was. His sons live nearby, but he moved away long since and he don't speak to them anymore. Word is, he's dying. Dying man's easy to respect."

"And how do you know so much about it?"

His mouth curved up, but not quite in a smile. "Been here a long while mesself. Me own brother was a printer. We don't speak. Turned goy, changed his name, eats his bacon."

"Turned goy?" I said.

"Converted, became a Christian," said Blake.

Kravitz spat. "He was in a hurry. Turned his back on his family, made his money." He picked up a stray handkerchief and pinned it carefully back on its line. "If you're going to see that Eldred Woundy, you'll need a better coat."

"*You were very hard* on the girl," I said.

"She didn't tell us everything."

"For heaven's sake, she talked and talked. Her memory was excellent. And did you not see she had no shoes? How do you know she is holding back?"

"I simply know."

I snorted. "And yet you were more than gentlemanly to the handsome widow, who must know more than she claims."

Blake stumbled slightly. His face was pouring with perspiration and his shoulders shook.

"Blake," I said anxiously, my exasperation forgotten. "You are ill. We must get you home." He tried to shake me off, but was immediately seized by a bout of coughing. I made him lean upon me and we hobbled down to the Strand where I hailed a hansom cab, pushed him into it and climbed in after.

"I do not even know where you live."

"Soho, north of here."

"Well, I am none the wiser."

The streets were all one to me, this one leading to another and another, until we came to a thoroughfare called Old Compton Street.

"I shall get out here," said Blake.

"But we will take you to your door."

"No."

I sighed and stopped the cab but placed my hand upon the door. "So you will not let me help you. Do you have a powder for your fever?"

He gave me his inscrutable look.

"Jeremiah," I said, "it is a long time since we saw each other. But what took place in India, what you showed me there, changed me. I have persisted in thinking of you not only as someone to whom I owed a great debt but also as someone whom I esteemed and admired, despite our differences—and despite those mulishly stubborn traits which I find my memory had conveniently erased. I fancied that you did not think entirely ill of me. Tell me, did I delude myself?"

He was silent for a moment. "You owe me nothing, William," he said. I took this for the dismissal I had been half expecting. But then he said heavily, "This city is a cruel place, William. Vigorous, full of novelties and innovations, but implacable and pitiless too. It has hardened me." There was another silence. "I am sorry. I cannot promise to be better humored, but I will try." He clambered slowly out of the cab.

"How shall we meet tomorrow?" I said. "What if you take a turn for the worse?"

"You will get my message." He handed me the package that Connie Wedderburn had given him.

"I recall you are a keen reader. You can look through that."

*I felt as if my eyes* and ears had seen and heard in one day what would pass for a busy month in the country. What to make of it all, and of Jeremiah Blake's reappearance in my life, I was too all in to consider. At the Oriental I made my toilet and descended in anticipation of a quiet dinner. I did not know many other members—most were a good deal older than I, having returned to England after successful careers in the East. I had, however, acquired a modicum of fame, and the night before a number of clubmen, learning I was among them, had made a fuss of me. A red-faced and mildly inebriated Tory Member of Parliament—a former East India Company civilian—had insisted upon standing me dinner, while others had pressed me to recount my various Indian adventures and plied me with invitations.

"Avery! Over here!" The Tory Member was upon me before I could escape.

"Captain Avery! You must come and join us. I will not be refused." He dragged me into the smoking room where I was surrounded by a group of gentlemen, none of whom I knew. Too tired to put up much of a struggle, I allowed myself to be hustled into the dining room. It was a good dinner, and reassuring after the day's strangeness. I drank a great deal of claret and let the talk wash over me: disquisitions on the quality of game to be expected over the winter; the extent to which the Queen disliked the new Prime Minister; the fire at the Tower of London; the arrival of the second royal baby; and the arrival of the King of Hanover in London for the arrival of his niece's heir. I was reminded of my nights in the officers' mess. The Tory MP suggested that I might consider standing for Parliament in the landowning interest. Eventually I pleaded exhaustion and retired to my rooms.

"A shame, young man," he said. "There's a deal more port to be drunk."


*I had drunk enough* to ensure that sleep would come at least for a while. But in my room, I recalled in a guilty rush that I had made the decision to remain in London with no consideration of my domestic obligations, to my wife Helen and the child-to-come. I pushed the thought away. Helen had been far from sorry to see me go. Some time apart might perhaps improve matters between us, as my sister Louisa had suggested. There was certainly no business in Devon that urgently required my attention.

I wrote to Helen, explaining that I would have to remain in London for perhaps a week, implying, with not complete honesty, that I would have ample opportunity to ingratiate myself with a number of men of influence, among them Sir Theophilus Collinson. To my sister Louisa I wrote at greater length, explaining what had taken place and how much I wanted to stay in London, and asking her to summon me should she judge that I was needed. There was no need to mention that I had not been as candid about my situation to my wife.

It was only after I had undressed that my eye caught the bulky bundle that Blake had given me. I unwound the paper and string and understood at last the nature of Nat Wedderburn's business.

On the top was a smutty song about the Queen and her consort, called "What 'e gets up to round 'Er Majesty." It did, I admit, raise a small smile from me. This was followed by a number of engravings purporting to depict "the aristocracy and church at play." The first showed disrobed nuns and bishops—identified only by their headgear—engaged in various obscene acts and was entitled "The Arse Bishop and His Friends." The next item was a slim pamphlet called *School-mistress of Love, or Birchen Sports*, and appeared to be a prolonged advertisement for the various "modes of punishment" offered by a "Miss Tess Thrashington," a marvelously well-endowed "Governess of Love," at her premises in Charlotte Street. The first page showed her administering "discipline" to a gentleman clad only in a vest. Subsequent pages illustrated her "whipping machine," which resembled nothing so much as a pair of stocks attached to a long board with holes in it: in the picture, a naked man placed his head and hands through three of the holes and these were then further tethered with thick bonds. An unclothed buxom young woman with flowing locks was administering a beating to his posterior with an outlandishly long switch, while another unclothed young woman sitting on the other side of the board manipulated his member. The last page featured illustrations of young, unclothed women beating unclothed mustachioed men with a variety of bludgeons, birch switches and whips until the blood ran down their backs.

Then there were two books with text and illustrations: *The History of Lord Byron's Voluptuous Amours* and *The New Epicurean, or The Delights of Sex*. The author of the latter volume went by the name of the Reverend Erasmus Cumming, and, having described in some detail various obscene escapades, he declared his "credo of the cynic and realist," announcing that virtue and honor in women were mere appearance, principle in men a mask, morals simply a cloak for the rich to do as they liked and law was the robbery of the poor. The pursuit of hedonism and the pleasures of the flesh were the only honesty. The engravings were of surprisingly good quality, and the writing, though coarse, was larded with Latin quotations and limp attempts at *bons mots*. In my soused state I found the whole thing strangely lowering. Finally there were two more pamphlets with more of the same, entitled *Lady Bumtickler's Revels* and *The Lustful Turk*.

Thus I discovered what Blake had understood well before me: why Nat Wedderburn was not a good man. Troubled, fatigued and depressed by my own compulsive curiosity and that the stuff failed to stimulate anything in me but a general sense of melancholy, I fell asleep.

*In my dream* I am standing upon a narrow ledge in bright, bright sunlight. It is so bright that I must screw my eyes up to see. My uniform is drenched in perspiration. Around me are craggy peaks and burned rock forms. I know at once that I am in Afghanistan.

I have an intimation that something bad is about to happen. Beside me, one of my men, Mohammed Abdoo, looks to me questioningly. The next moment he is crashing off the ledge beside me. As he falls into the deep, deep void below, he looks back at me with horror and disbelief. Then another of my men, Faisal Khan, is tumbling off the ledge; then with dreadful swiftness another, and another. I reach out to catch a hand, to warn them, to call out their names, but they go, one after the other, and I cannot stop them. I know there is something I must do if I am to have any chance of saving them. It comes to me that I must turn to see who or what is pushing them to their deaths, though I fear that if I do so I will fall. But if I do not turn, I will eventually fall too. Fighting the sickening dread, I look behind me, but as I do so I feel a pair of hands thrust me off the ledge. Then I see myself falling into the void, my face a picture of horror and disbelief.

## chapter 5

I woke anxious and cloudy-headed. It was late morning and I was shamed by my tardiness. More of a worry, however, was that there was no message from Blake. I imagined him sickening and in need of a doctor. Then the summons came after luncheon: we would meet in the dining room of the Crown and Anchor at four o'clock.

I imagined the Crown and Anchor would be some old tavern with a fire and cozy nooks. I could not have been more wrong. It was a vast, four-story building in the classical style, the length of five town houses on the south side of the Strand, barely a hundred yards from the end of Holywell Street. Inside, it was a little chipped and battered at the edges, but still most impressive. The large stone atrium was lit by a glass lantern in the roof and framed by a grand ironwork staircase. The dining room would happily have accommodated five hundred, and was decorated with painted panels and elaborately carved festoons, with two huge inglenook marble fireplaces at each end in which roaring fires burned. It was so large that the usual tavern smells of tobacco and beer were mere traces in the air. There were few diners and Blake was easy to find, sitting at a small table by the wall. On the table was a large bull's-eye lamp; by his side, a large cloth bag. His color was better though he was still pale, but he was dressed in a worse state than he had been the day before: today he did not even have a collar but wore a handkerchief tied around his neck.

"Good afternoon," I said, hiding my exasperation at his getup, but not my anxious scrutiny of his health.

"Stop your clucking," he said peevishly. "The fever broke in the night, I am quite well." A waiter brought a pot of coffee and a bowl of kitcheree from which the scent of familiar spices wafted.

"What is this place?" I said.

"They called it the Temple of Freedom. It was the heart of radical politics in London. They celebrated the storming of the Bastille here in 1795. And the return of Tom Paine's bones from America in 1819. Chartists held their first London meeting here." He half smiled. "But it's not what it was. Do not fear, I'm sure there are none lurking under the table."

"I suppose you are familiar with the Chartists," I said.

"I have met a few."

"Well, in my opinion they are dangerous. They encourage the disruption of relations between master and men, and landowner and tenant. They foment dissatisfaction among ordinary people. They preach the confiscation of property and the destruction of the propertied class. They are the rule of the mob."

"Ah, the mob," said Blake. "Do you know what your hero Byron said about the mob? 'It is the mob that labor in your fields, and serve in your houses—that man your navy, and recruit your army—that have enabled you to defy all the world, and can also defy you when neglect and calamity have driven them to despair. You may call the people a mob; but do not forget, that a mob too often speaks the sentiments of the people.'

"In my opinion," he said quietly, "the Chartists have good reason to be angry, but what they want is the vote for all, not merely the rich and privileged. They believe, foolishly perhaps, that if they could vote, Parliament would for once address their needs and act in their interests."

"Parliament acts in the interests of the whole country."

"Does it."

"Are you saying it does not?"

Blake closed his eyes in irritation.

"Tell me what you think then," I said. "Explain it to me. I ask you honestly. I wish to know."

"Parliament functions to allow the privileged to maintain their privileges," he said. "It has consistently fought Lord Allington's attempts to shorten working hours for the laboring class. It forestalls his attempts to regulate children's work in mines and factories and votes down his plans to introduce universal education for children. It fights tooth and nail to maintain the Corn Laws which keep bread prices high, so landowners like your father are secure in their wealth. Meanwhile the harvests fail and the poor go hungry. In whose interests are these things done?"

"But the children of the poor need to work to help feed their families. Everyone knows that."

Blake gave me his look. I looked away. We lifted our cups and sipped our coffee.

"Was it really necessary to come dressed as a tramp again? Admit it, there are times when you do it merely to provoke consternation."

Blake scratched his ear. I assumed that, as so often, there would be no answer, but then he said, "Now and then I tire of dancing for Collinson's clients. Now and then I tire of making a good impression."

"Have there been many clients?"

"It's how I earn my keep." From out of a pocket he brought a small silver case and drew out a card.

"Jeremiah Blake, Private Inquiry Agent." Underneath was written, "Messages may be left at Jenkins's, 62 Dean Street, Westminster."

"And Sir Theo?"

"To do the work I need a license from the coppers. Sir Theo has connections."

"If you dislike it, why do you do it?"

"I'm good for nothing else," he said.

"But surely this case is different—a death among the poor, help for the neglected and the needy. What is there to complain of?"

Blake pursed his lips slightly.

"What?" I said.

"Nothing."

"Something. You do not like Lord Allington's religion, granted. But let us agree he is unlikely to enjoy much success in converting the Hindoos, and you cannot deny he does real good. Your Lascars were fed and sheltered."

He nodded.

"So what is it?"

He thought for a moment. "He has the God-given arrogance of his class."

"As I recall, arrogance is a quality in which you are not exactly deficient, Mr. Blake."

"Someone's been sharpening your wit, Captain Avery."

"I found a whetstone and did it for myself, Mr. Blake," I said tartly. He almost smiled.

"I assume that you knew all along that Nat Wedderburn was a seller of obscene books, but you did not see fit to tell me," I said.

"It is what Holywell Street is known for, but I could not be sure until we saw his wares. Now you have confirmed it. You said you wanted to play your part. What are they like?"

"You expect me to describe them?" I said.

He shrugged. I thrust the packet into his lap. He unwrapped the paper and leafed quickly through the contents.

"This is high quality of its type. The paper, the engravings, the claims to learning, the particular tastes. This comes at a price. No wonder Matty Horner said Wedderburn's customers were swells. There's money in this. He should have made a good living."

"It begs a question, don't you think?" I said.

"It does?"

"Do you really believe Lord Allington will wish to continue with this matter when he discovers what kind of man Wedderburn was?"

"He should have an idea already. Holywell Street's wares are hardly a secret."

"But, Blake—"

"If you wish to walk away from this, you can."

"Damn it, Blake, will you stop saying that!" I collected myself.

"What of the other murder?"

"Matthew Blundell, printer, six weeks ago, in Seven Dials."

I remembered Seven Dials from *Sketches by Boz*. "Is that not a particularly grim place?"

"All the want, degradation and sins of London crammed into a few dismal crowded courts. That's what *The Times* says. I went by there this morning. The fire did a good job of bringing down the whole building. There's little left but some blackened walls. The neighbors say his wife and children escaped but left a few days later. They had nothing and it would have been the pan otherwise."

"The pan?"

"The workhouse. He had had his shop six years or so—same as Wedderburn. No one knew where he was from, but he was thought to be an educated man or even a preacher fallen on hard times. They knew him as a drunk and clown. In his cups he would make great blaspheming and lewd speeches which kept the street amused. A couple of prosecutions for theft and fraud. Seems he was in the same business as Wedderburn—lewd books sold illicitly."

"Had the neighbors heard of Wedderburn?"

Blake shook his head. "But several described seeing the body, and their description is almost identical to Wedderburn's with one difference. Blundell's hair had been covered in red paint. Then someone brought in a candle to get a better look and the room just seemed to catch fire."

"Good God! Spontaneous combustion?"

"I suppose it is a possibility."

"And nothing from the police?"

"As I say, they did not arrive until after the fire and concluded the man died in it."

I found such talk dispiriting. "What must we do next then?"

"I plan to see the schoolmaster Dearlove, and then to go to the rookery behind Drury Lane. If the men were murdered over a feud or money owed, it would be the crims who'd likely know. But if you're to come with me dressed like that, you'll be a walking magnet for every gonoph and rampsman."

I took another sip of coffee and did my best to look as if I did not mind.

"Here," he said, and he hauled out of his cloth bag a long, worn velveteen coat and an old cloth cap such as the kind laborers wore. "Put this on. You'll have to take off your collar and necktie and put this on instead." He handed me a well-used, brightly colored silk handkerchief.

"I shall look like a laborer!"

I will not describe the look he gave me. Hurriedly I took off my coat and put his on; it had a damp, musty odor like Abraham Kravitz's shop. A number of other diners gave us wondering looks.

"Put your money and anything else you value in the deepest inner pocket and do up the coat nice and tight." He permitted himself a sneaking smile. "You did say that I was a master of disguise." He picked up his bull's-eye lamp and we walked into the still crowded and darkening Strand.

"How can you stand the noise?" I said, as we picked our way through the carts and carriages.

"You get used to it," he said. "And there are the side streets to take refuge in."

"Was it always like this—before, when you were a child?"

"I cannot remember."

"It makes me long for the countryside."

*Thomas Dearlove's school lay* at the end of a grim alley that led off Newcastle Street, a drafty thoroughfare that passed west of Holywell Street. Ashes and filth were heaped up by the sides of the flat-faced, ugly tenements; not an unbroken pane of glass was there anywhere. Halfway up the lane a cluster of pinched, insolent-looking boys leaned over some game, passing about a pipe. They watched us approach with an unwavering surly gaze.

"Got a penny for us, have ya?" one said, and two more came swaggering toward us.

I would have dismissed them, but Blake said, his accent smoothly thickening into those of the London street, "I've got a penny. But I want to know wotcha think of the schoolteacher up there."

"The holy groaner?" said one, and the others laughed.

"Goes on about the Lord and that. Looks like he's never had a woman, know what I mean?" said another, his profane words at odds with his diminutive stature—he looked barely twelve.

"He's all right," said a third. "There's a fire, and we get bread and butter and tea."

Blake leaned over the game and tossed three small coins into the air. The boys went skittering after them.

The school's premises were a former stables. Boards had been laid to cover the hard earth. There were low stools and long deal tables with the legs cut down so they were low enough for the stools. On the walls, spotted with damp, were large printed cards showing the alphabet and a number of admonitory and encouraging texts: "Thou Shalt Not Steal," "Try, Try Again" and "God Goes with Thee." It was a poor, grim place indeed. At the back a fireplace had been contrived. Over it was hung a tripod and next to it stood a large kettle. It was to this that a slight, black-clad man—the teacher, I supposed—was now attending.

As we walked in he stood up, nervously rubbing his hands against the sides of his trousers, looking from one of us to the other, no doubt dismayed by our getup. His most obvious quality was his extreme thinness. His bony wrists protruded several inches from his coat, and his trousers were almost worn through at the knee. A thick knitted comforter was wound several times around his neck, his skin had a waxy pallor, and he seemed to be in want of at least one good meal. His gauntness, it seemed to me, was not dissimilar to the austere intensity of Lord Allington, but His Lordship's angularity had been flattered by wealth and comfort. Dearlove looked, in other words, most unloved, and indeed the picture of a hard-pushed schoolmaster.

"May I help you?" His words steamed in the cold air.

"Mr. Dearlove," said Blake, bringing out His Lordship's letter, "we are the men who have been asked to look into the two murders by Lord Allington."

Dearlove took the letter—his fingers were almost blue—and looked over it.

"Oh, yes. I am afraid you have not chosen the best moment. The children will be arriving for evening lessons soon. They expect something hot when it is this cold." He gestured at the kettle, then took out a handkerchief and blew his nose.

"Please, continue your tasks," Blake said. "We will not take up too much of your time."

"Perhaps I might help you?" I said.

He brightened. "If you could bring in some logs from by the door, and help me fill the kettle?"

I busied myself with the logs.

Blake said, "Mr. Dearlove, I am told you are the one who informed Lord Allington of the fact that the police had dropped the matter of Wedderburn's death, and made the connection to the earlier murder of Blundell."

"I did."

"Why do you think no one seems to know about these murders?"

"I . . . I cannot say for sure." He coughed, a shallow, rattling sound, and dabbed at his mouth with the handkerchief.

"Have you spoken to the new police?"

"Of course. I was taken aback when I found that so little had been done—indeed, nothing at all—to pursue Mr. Wedderburn's murderer. And then to hear some days later that a similar crime had taken place barely half a mile away—I felt I must take the matter up. I first spoke about the murders to a constable on the Strand, then to another who walks Monmouth Street by Seven Dials. As a rule I enjoy good relations with the new police—the constables know me. When I pressed them, both more or less admitted that nothing more would be done. And so I went to Bow Street station and was given short shrift. They said I should not bother them." He lowered his voice. "There was no doubt in my mind that they did not want to know about the connection between the two deaths. I was shocked. I know there is no love lost between the new police and the people around here—but I considered the police honest and did not think that they would go so far as to leave a monster upon the streets."

"A monster?"

"If you had seen Nat Wedderburn's body, what had been done to it, you could not but believe that it was the work of some godless monster."

"Do you have any thoughts on their inaction?"

He shook his head. "The Bible says, 'Deliver the poor and needy: rid them out of the hand of the wicked' and 'Whoso stoppeth his ears at the cry of the poor, he also shall cry himself, but shall not be heard.'"

"Do the poor cry?"

"Have you not heard? And if it were not enough, in the streets they are saying it was some supernatural sprite, Spring-Heeled Jack or somesuch, come to take souls to hell. All the foolish superstition against which we fight is resurrected by this dreadful crime."

"The people in Holywell Street are very reluctant to speak of the murder at all."

"I believe they are frightened."

"Of whom?"

"Oh, I mean of the murder. They would rather not think of it. What do you mean?"

"I meant, someone has told them not to speak of it."

"I had not thought of that. It is, I suppose, a possibility."

"Who would have the power to frighten a street into silence?"

Dearlove looked perplexed. "I do not know. The printers in Holywell Street work for themselves and jostle with each other for crumbs."

I filled the kettle and helped him haul it onto the hook over the fire.

"I suppose Dugdale is something of a bully and likes to give himself airs. There are, of course, the criminal gangs who inhabit the courts behind Drury Lane, but I believe they remain in the courts. I know little of them in any case—my task is to bring God and learning. But I would be most surprised if Mr. Wedderburn had any dealings with them."

"What about Eldred Woundy?" said Blake.

"Who?" Dearlove shook his head. "The newspaper proprietor? Why should he take an interest?" He knelt down to start the fire.

Blake changed the subject. "Did you not say at the coroner's court that Mr. Wedderburn deserved his fate?"

"I said his death was the Lord's judgment."

"Because of what he did, or what he believed?"

Dearlove twisted round awkwardly to look at Blake. "He was a godless man. He called himself an infidel. His publications corrupted the mind. He laughed in the face of the Lord." He lowered his voice again. "That does not mean I would wish such a death upon him. And I was happy to teach his children. He understood the importance of reading and writing and they would send the little ones to me from time to time."

"How did you hear of Blundell's death?"

"From a woman in the rookeries off Seven Dials. She told me that a man had been murdered, and that when the body was found a candle was brought into the shop and all caught fire. I work for the London City Mission. We strive to bring the gospel into the darkest courts. Apart from us there are not many who venture into those places and speak to the unfortunates who live there. Lord Allington is a patron of the mission and his office at Exeter Hall helps the school here with food and other necessities. After my brush with Bow Street I be-thought myself of him and brought the matter to his attention."

"What do the people in the courts and rookeries make of you, Mr. Dearlove?"

"They know me now. The children come to the school. At first most simply see it as somewhere they may get some food and shelter, but they are learning too. At Seven Dials it has taken longer."

"There are some streets both here and there that I would think twice about venturing into," said Blake.

"I have had my fair share of tribulations. But it does not deter me."

"What kind of tribulations, if I might ask?" I said curiously.

"Oh, I have been spat at, thrown downstairs, had ordure emptied over my head. But, as I say, it does not stop me. It is nothing compared to the sacrifices of our Lord."

"And in Holywell Street? They know you there?"

"They do. I walk through on my way to Exeter Hall and I persevere among the street sellers."

"Do you know Matty Horner?" I said.

"Her brother Pen comes sometimes to the school, but he is a wild and wayward child. She found Wedderburn's body. It must have been a dreadful shock for her."

"Does she come to you for instruction?" I said.

"No, like many older children round here, she denies herself that her brother might reap the benefits of education."

*Drury Lane*, famous for its theater, had a shabby and disreputable air. We had barely set foot upon it when, with no warning, Blake slipped between two tall buildings into a dark lane barely wider than our shoulders and exceedingly muddy.

"Stay close and mind your feet," he called back at me, "if you want to keep those boots shiny."

"Where do we go?" I asked.

"To see a man who knows the lie of the land," he said. "Trap shut now, William, and follow briskly."

After a distance of perhaps fifty yards we turned left into a wider, more crowded thoroughfare, from which three further lanes led off. Blake took the rightmost. It was dirty, odiferous, piled with debris and thick with life, though I should say the poorest, meanest, dirtiest and bleakest I had seen in England—far worse than Holywell Street. The despairing, the cunning, the dangerously vigorous: all pressed in upon each other. We strode on through a maze of mean lanes, divided in the middle by an open trench down which pure effluent flowed. Had I not been with Blake I should have immediately been lost. As it was, I felt as if I had entered another city, and I was glad now of the rough clothes; in my own attire I should have feared for myself. Lines of ragged gray laundry fluttered enervatingly above the lanes. Below, livestock snuffled. Old women wrapped in dirty shawls, their faces masks of ill use, sat against damp walls in the mud. Hard-faced urchins minded swaddled infants and played at knucklebones. Pinched-looking men in greasy corduroys lolled aimlessly. Down the middle of the lane a knot of bulky, ill-meaning youths in tight trousers, loudly patterned calico waistcoats and over-oiled curls and whiskers barged into whomsoever they liked, the threat of violence in every noisy laugh. The buildings were crammed in like nothing I had ever seen. Doors swung off hinges, broken windows were packed with straw and old clothes. On one side a small beaten-down premises advertised itself as a skinner's:

"Good money paid for dogs and cats."

"Don't look so avidly," Blake muttered, seizing me by the cuff and dragging me forward.

We stopped at last before a ramshackle public house, "The Cocko' the Hoop" by name, before which more degraded humanity was carousing.

The interior could not have been more different from the Crown and Anchor. It was a crush of bleary-eyed men, women, children and dogs in various stages of inebriation, excitement and collapse. The smell of soured beer, wet sawdust, dried herring and bodies was overpowering. The noise was deafening. Standing at the threshold, Blake surveyed it for a moment, then pulled me out of the way as a man in the last stage of angry intoxication prepared to hurl himself upon me, though I felt quite equal to the challenge. Grabbing my fists, Blake pushed me toward the edge of a long table crowded with drinkers, where we took two empty stools.

"Pull your cap down, keep your own counsel," he muttered. A large florid woman slapped a jug of beer down before us, together with two none-too-clean pewter mugs. Blake said a few words and she jutted her chin in the direction of another table.

A tall, thin man in a white shirt with a gaudy silk handkerchief about his neck, a beaver hat and moleskin trousers, skin taut over gaunt cheeks, a mustache long and narrow as a shoelace, his expression as guarded as Blake's: there was no mistaking him for anything other than a villain. As he talked quietly to his neighbor, his eyes—small and shrewd—fixed upon Blake. He finished his business, picked up his stool and brought it down next to Blake. The other drinkers at the table at once and sheepishly shuffled as far as they could away from us.

"Jem," the thin man said by way of greeting, his face quite expressionless.

"Joe," said Blake steadily. They might have been competing for whose face revealed the least. "Thought you might be up in the Holy Land tonight."

"Down here, as you see. Who's your friend?" He looked me over.

"My friend."

"Doan know him. Doan like him."

"He has no interest in you. Nor I. Want the lay on a matter. And you owe me."

"Mebbe."

"It's none of your pies, Joe. A murder in Holywell Street and another in Seven Dials. Two printers. Wedderburn and Blundell. What d'you know about it?"

"Not a thing."

"Both selling bawdy books, perhaps a bit of black and fencing on the side. Maybe whoremongering. Any bad blood in the courts? Someone out to get them? A commission even?"

The villain Joe thought for a moment. Then shook his head. "Means nothing to me."

"Wedderburn was the printer found dead on his press. Heard about that, didn't you?"

Joe nodded. "Heard of it but I didn't know him or the other. Far as I know, they got nothing down here and there was nothing out on them. If there was, I reckon I'd have heard."

"You'll ask?"

"I'll ask. But I'd say their deaths ain't nothing to do with our'n."

"Wedderburn has a son. Angry-looking cove."

"Doan know him."

"What of Eldred Woundy?"

"What of him?"

"You know him, then?"

Joe looked up at the ceiling. "Respectable gent these days, they say."

"And before?"

He grimaced. "Had a few lodging houses down here. Said to own a tailshop up near Tottenham Court Road. A few years since it was said he was in the business of paying for dirt. Slippery cove. Never pin anything on him."

He rose, carrying his stool with him, and returned to his previous spot, for no one had commandeered it, though the place was heaving. He sat down, tapped the table and two men instantly attended him. He muttered something and they both moved off.

"Don't watch him," said Blake. "He doesn't like it."

"Who is he?"

"A man with influence. The less you know of him, the better." He filled my mug. "How does it compare with Calcutta?"

I recalled the chaotic, midden-filled streets of the native parts of that city. There was little to choose between these streets and those. Not that I would admit as much to Blake.

"What is the Holy Land, and what is 'black' and a 'tailshop'?" I said. "And how in heaven's name are fencing and the courts involved?"

"Lord. And I ask myself why I brought you. The Holy Land is the great rookery around St. Giles by Oxford Street. Much bigger than this. Black is blackmail. A tailshop is a whorehouse, a fence is someone who receives and deals in stolen goods, and a court is the name for these slum lanes."

"You think Wedderburn was engaged in such things? And that Woundy owns a whorehouse?"

"It's possible. Such things can fit with their line of work. Pimping and smut shops often go together. Gentleman Joe would know, as he would if Wedderburn and Blundell had enemies here, or if someone was paid to knock them off. If their deaths were rookery killings, it might explain why the coppers ignored them."

"But he says he has never heard of Wedderburn and Blundell."

"That's right."

"Is he to be trusted?"

"Unless he has a good reason to lie."

We sat quiet while the maelstrom went on about us. Gentleman Joe's attentions apparently encouraged others to leave us alone. Once or twice I saw Blake look up to meet the eye of someone I guessed he knew, but not a word was exchanged. Meanwhile at the villain's table there was a deal of to-ing and fro-ing. At length Gentleman Joe returned to us, leaning intimately across Blake.

"However they met their ends, it weren't none of our doing. I'd swear to it."

Blake nodded. "Know anything about Lord Allington?"

"The churchy toff who wants to save the poor? Not much. Owns a netherskens round here."

Blake looked surprised.

"Nah. It's a 'model' lodging house. Even the bedbugs get a bath and go to church Sunday. Strict hours and the clergy exhorting you as you eat your dinner. Not for everyone."

"You hear anything . . ." Blake gave Gentleman Joe a look square in the eye.

"You'll know," the other said, dropping his gaze. "Now, you're giving my men the jitters."

"We'll be off."

"Tell your friend next time he comes to the Drury Lane courts, he'd better change his fine boots if he wants to keep them."

Back we went through the maze of darkling alleys, Blake walking swiftly. Having had my fill of following several steps behind, I strode to catch him up, almost walking into an open cesspool; wordlessly he thrust his arm out to bar me just in time. It was only then that I saw the glint of the dark greasy water. Ruefully, I took my place behind him. In Drury Lane the theater had brought out food sellers, their wares lit by smoky red lamps, and brightly dressed courtesans idling under the gaslights. Blake turned left and, apparently lost in thought, trudged toward the corner where the cabs stood.

"Take a hackney cab," he said. "You'll never find your way back from here on foot. I'll see you tomorrow. We'll visit Woundy then. His premises are just south of Temple Bar."

"For goodness' sake, Jeremiah, you are barely over your fever. Come with me, I will drop you off on the way."

"I've things to do," was all he would say. He raised his hand and limped off north up Drury Lane.


*That night* I dreamed again.

My men are dropping off the ledge to their deaths and there is nothing I can do to prevent it. This time, however, I can hear someone laughing behind me: a long, scornful, hearty laugh. Then I too feel the thrusting hands, and fall.

# chapter 6

The offices of *Woundy's Illustrated Weekly Newspaper,* "Proprietor Mr. E. Woundy"—the letters picked out in smart gold edged with black and embellished at each end by a design of pretty leaves in white—took up the ground floor of a soot-blackened warehouse with a large yard by the Thames at the end of Arundel Street just south of Temple Bar. On the far side of the yard there was a smaller door over which were painted in black the words "Woundy's Penny Miscellany" and "Woundy's Penny Atlas," with the same design of white leaves. In the yard a pair of dray horses stood patiently while rushing boys unloaded boxes from their carts and ran with them into the building. There was so much coming and going, it was easy to wander in unchallenged.

Inside, the impression was of constant, fervid activity accompanied by the relentless clacking and grinding of machinery.

On one side there was a beehive of small rooms with low partitions from which issued a stream of shirtsleeved clerks. On the other was a flight of stairs and beneath them a pair of large double doors from which the noisy clack emanated. Through the doors came men in plain cotton shirts, coarse waistcoats and aprons spattered with ink, carrying metal plates and frames full of metal letters. In the midst of all this activity, two large heavyset men in matching rough homespun blue jackets stood at the entrance, each leaning on a long walking stick which might also have been a cudgel. Both had faces that had evidently taken a good share of blows, and one had the great splayed red nose of a hardened drinker.

"See the nobblers?" Blake muttered.

"Those two bruisers by the door?"

He nodded.

"Why should a newspaper require the services of such men?"

"Can I help you, gentlemen?" A slight young man detached himself from the fray.

"We are here to see Mr. Woundy," said Blake.

"Yes, he is expecting you. Will you come upstairs?"

Blake nodded.

At the top of the stairs it was quieter and the large room was dominated by two great workbenches perhaps thirty feet long; dozens of men were working at them. At the first, men pored over sheaves of paper and checked over ledgers. At the other, men loaded boxes with what appeared to be little pieces of lead. Small boys darted between them, carrying paper, boxes and metal trays.

"He won't be long," said the young man. "Perhaps in the meantime I might furnish you with two copies of *Woundy's Weekly* itself?" He smiled happily, pressing them into our hands.

Mine was eight pages long, like *The Times*, but there the resemblance ended. Along the top of the front page was a panorama of London, with St. Paul's, and the river filled with small boats. In the sky ran the legend "Woundy's Illustrated Weekly Newspaper." The front page was devoted to a surprisingly radical article exhorting the Chartists to fight "those rich factory owners, namely the Anti-Corn-Law Leaguers," who campaigned for free trade and low wages, and who would "give our labor to the foreigner," and telling them to guard against being "gulled" by the Whigs, who in government had been "inflexible tyrants and the oppressors of their families, the destroyers of their homes, engineers of the Poor Law and the workhouse, the plague of the poor."

The rest of the paper was filled with alarming headlines: murders, rick-burnings, accidental shootings. In among these were reports on the happenings in the law courts, police stations and racecourses, some poetry, a review of Mrs. Forbes Bush's two-volume *Memoirs of the Queens of France*, and a page of "goings-on about town," which consisted largely of innuendo about the activities of the aristocracy. There was an article purporting to describe the life of the emperor of China, with whom, of course, we were at war, and a small column labeled "Foreign Intelligence" in which it was reported that British troops had taken the mouth of the Pearl River and had moved on Canton. There was no mention of the war in Afghanistan. The last page bristled with more blood-curdling headlines. In "Cannibalism in Liverpool," a certain Mr. Griswald "averred that he had indeed acquired a taste for human flesh that could not be satiated." In "Stepson Murdered by His Father in Kensal Green," the victim, little Jim, was said to have cried out, "Oh! Mother! Oh! Mother!" as his father beat him to death. It all seemed unutterably vulgar.

A man in a worn black suit appeared at my elbow. "Mr. Woundy will be with you very soon. Perhaps you would care for a tour of the premises?"

"We would indeed," said Blake, quite unconcerned at being mistaken for someone else.

"Well, as you know, the paper has been a remarkable success. Mr. Woundy's idea: a Sunday paper for the working man. This is the editorial office. See, here at the bench, our editors work to make the copy fill the page. Of course, it is quieter today than it sometimes is, as we have put this week's paper to bed. You can hear it printing now downstairs." He smiled fondly. "Mr. Kean over there is one of our best penny-a-liners: he has a wonderful turn of phrase when it comes to a parricide or a house burning. And over there we are fitting in advertisements. We have found there's a deal of interest in advertising due to the numbers of copies we are selling." His voice grew husky with pride. "Here"—he pointed at the second bench—"our typesetters make up the pages." He stopped a boy carrying a box full of metal letters.

"Type," he said with a grin. "May I show you the presses?"

Blake nodded, and we were led down the stairs.

"Who are these gentlemen?" said Blake innocently, pointing at the bruisers.

"They are Mr. Woundy's men," said our guide brightly. "Through here," he said, beckoning us toward the double doors, "and here"—he pushed through the doors and the sound was suddenly deafening—"are the presses. Two genuine Koenig and Bauer double-cylinder steam-powered printing presses," he bellowed proudly. "Just like the ones at *The Times*. Six thousand sheets an hour! And we have laid orders for two more."

The steam presses were like nothing I had ever seen or heard before. They were distinctly odd-looking, resembling nothing so much as giant winged insects with two large eyes, settled upon a long table. The eyes were two long cylinders which spun round, bringing with them at great speed leaves of blank paper that slid across one wing, disappeared, and then emerged a moment later covered in printed words, spilling from the other end with whirling proliferation. Each machine was fed with paper at one end by two boys, while at the other another two boys carried away piles of printed pages to a bench where more boys folded them. The black iron printing press in Wedderburn's shop was to these a phosphorous match to a bonfire. They were remarkable, but within a few minutes the noise had become almost unbearable to me. Blake, however, was entranced. I retreated to the relative quiet of the other side of the doors.

Even without Matty Horner's description one would have picked out Eldred Woundy in a crowd. He was above six foot in height and immensely broad, and his large, emphatic gestures were the kind that drew attention. He was impatiently divesting himself of a heavy greatcoat with a large fur collar, and, as he did so, he was addressing a group of young boys whom I concluded must be hawkers for his newspaper. His deep voice was such that even across the room one could hear snatches of words. Underneath his coat he wore a snug-fitting green frock coat and trousers, a green-and-black satin waistcoat that strained around his considerable girth, and a fob watch attached to this waistcoat by a large and shiny gold chain. Having concluded his lecture, he tossed the boys a coin each and they departed remarkably cheerful, given how sharply he had harangued them. As they left, a new column of supplicants swarmed about him. Once or twice he glanced in my direction and it was with some relief that I saw Blake emerge from the printing room, just as Woundy surged purposefully toward me.

"Gentlemen!" he cried, stretching out the great hams of his arms. I cleared my voice. "I am Captain William Avery and this is my colleague, Mr. Jeremiah Blake."

"Blake, eh?" said Woundy, looking him over appraisingly. "Welcome! I am, as you have no doubt guessed, Eldred Woundy, proprietor, creator and editor of *Woundy's Illustrated Weekly Newspaper* and a host of other titles, including *Woundy's Penny Miscellany* and *Woundy's Penny Atlas*. Honest radical, and man of the people." The voice was Welsh but overlaid, I now recognized, with London vowels. He smiled broadly. "I am delighted you have come. May I offer you one of these?" From his pocket he produced two coins, half crowns.

"See what it says?" he said, handing one to each of us. Stamped on the tails side of the coin, over the usual coat of arms, were three words, "Woundy's Illustrated Weekly."

"Is this legal tender?" said Blake.

"It is until they say it is not, and in the meantime it is a pleasing— and most inventive, do you not think?—little advertisement for our publication," said Woundy. "I am paying my staff with them. They will be all over London in a week. I understand you have had at least a brief tour of our premises. Let me explain a little more about our heroic un- dertaking." He brought his hands together and rubbed them in a ges- ture of anticipation. "I can assure you that *Woundy's Illustrated Weekly Newspaper* is a genuine innovation in the history of journalism! As you know, we launched only a few months ago and already our circulation outstrips that of every other publication in the country! We have cre- ated a Sunday newspaper that the working man can enjoy, and from which he may also learn, and which he chooses to purchase again and again. We are selling upward of ninety thousand copies each week!

"We have employed the most skilled writers and the most talented illustrators. We utilize the finest and most up-to-date steam presses! We are in talks to purchase our own paper mill! We are expanding everywhere and for this reason we are looking for a select few investors to join us on this journey to the heights of creative endeavor and even greater profits!"

His manner reminded me of a street patterer—or a preacher. I re- called Allington's lecture of two days before. About his elbows another pack of underlings had begun to gather, waiting for his attention, like so many small fry about a much larger fish.

He stared at Blake. "You remind me of someone. Old Billy Blake, the printer and engraver. Any relation? Lived across the way, by Fountains Court. A bit touched, crazed even. Had a way with words."

"No," said Blake, garrulous as ever.

Woundy shrugged. "Thought you had the look of him."

"Mr. Woundy," I said awkwardly, "I fear there may have been some confusion about our visit. Your newspaper and printing works are quite magnificent, but we are here on another matter entirely."

The generous bow of Woundy's broad smile snapped into a straight line. The small fry scattered, as if in anticipation of some explosion.

"Confusion? Who are you then?"

"Mr. Woundy," said Blake softly, "we are here to talk to you about Nat Wedderburn."

"Nat who?" said Woundy.

"You know him. He was murdered three weeks ago. Not far from here in Holywell Street. Horrible murder. Your paper had an article about it."

"Never heard of him. Gentlemen, if you are not the investors I was expecting, you are wasting my time. Time and money are things I do not waste. How this confusion came about I do not know, but the culprit shall know about it."

Blake placed his hand on Woundy's fleshy arm. "We had a long talk with Connie. We should like to ask you some questions."

Woundy looked at Blake's hand on his sleeve and brushed it off. His voice was low and threatening. "We run five murders every week. I do not know the names of all those victims. Once again I say I do not know your Nat Wedderburn—or whatever he is called."

Blake spoke as I had never heard him before—hard, low and equally threatening.

"I think you do, and I think it will be a small matter to prove it, Mr. Woundy."

Now Woundy grabbed Blake's arm and drew him toward him.

"Take care," he said calmly but with a certain menacing air. "I say again I do not know this man. I have never met this man. I am a respectable gentleman. I will not have my reputation trampled and I forbid you to suggest that I have any connection to this man. If you do so, make no mistake, I will bring the weight of my considerable influence upon you. I will call my lawyers upon you, Mr. Blake. I will see you in court. Or worse."

Blake pulled away. He was smiling. "That's a deal of heat to expend on someone you've never heard of, Mr. Woundy. What of Matthew Blundell? Spontaneously combusted, they say. I suppose you did not know him either?"

"Throw them out!" shouted Eldred Woundy. The two burly men at the door lumbered toward us.

"We are leaving, we are leaving," I said.

"Why the muscle, Mr. Woundy? Something to be worried about?" Blake said.

"Out!" Woundy roared.

"We need no help, we are leaving," I called out. The room fell silent; only the clack of the presses behind their doors could be heard.

The bruiser with the red nose came up behind us, intending, I supposed, to be seen to eject us. Before he could lay a hand upon me— before, indeed, clear thought had formed—I turned and knocked his arm away. In response he tried to bring his cudgel down upon me. I let the cold, almost pleasurable, rage overtake me. I grasped the stick and wrested it from him with more force than he expected—I saw his surprise as I cracked it upon his head and shoulder and he stumbled and fell. I also saw the looks of horror on the faces of Woundy's watching staff. I dropped the stick and we walked into the yard. The bruiser's twin came after us, however, taking hold of my shoulder with the intention of pulling me round to deal me a blow on the jaw. I hit him fast in the stomach with such force that he doubled up, then I kicked his legs out from under him. He went down. I did not give him a backward glance.

"William. Enough," said Blake. I retrieved my hat, which I had lost in the melee, caught Blake's elbow and dragged him swiftly into the street.

At the top of Arundel Street by the Strand we stopped. My hand was shaking.

"I am glad to be away from that infernal din," I said, brushing off my hat, pretending to a nonchalance I did not feel. "How can anyone work with it?"

Blake pulled on his gloves. Tactfully, he did not refer to my loss of composure, nor to my difficulty in regaining it, but his eyes did not leave me.

"Noise is the coming thing," he said at last. "There'll be plenty more of it."

Once I had put my fists away, however, the remorse came on. "I am concerned that Woundy might blame Connie Wedderburn for our visit," I said. "That she might come to harm because of us."

"There is a deal of bluster about Eldred Woundy," Blake said dismissively. "I reckon he must have known that someone would come calling about Wedderburn eventually. If he's that keen to keep the association quiet, I reckon he'll keep clear of Connie. And if he were to come, it would prove that he knew them."

"What if he sends his bruisers?"

"Look, we can try to find who murdered these men, or we can station ourselves outside Connie Wedderburn's home. We cannot do both."

"I should like to warn her," I said. "And should we not try to divine the son Daniel's whereabouts?"

"We'll return to Holywell Street," he said. "You may go and tell her. And ask her about Wedderburn's clients too. Anything she can remember."

*The oldest daughter* opened the door a crack and peered out suspiciously.

"Is your mother at home?"

She let me in. There was a small fire in the grate and food on the table, but I was again taken aback by the bareness and sadness of the scene. Connie Wedderburn was standing, once more as if dreaming or stunned, her hair defying its pins and tumbling round her shoulders. She had been in the midst of a halfhearted attempt to tidy the room and was holding two plates. She barely noticed my arrival.

"Where are your brothers and sisters?" I asked the girl.

"Took them to Mr. Dearlove's," she whispered. "He and Pa argued, but he's good at letters and writing and there's food."

"It seems to me that you are a very brave girl and do a great deal here, helping your mother."

She nodded solemnly. "Can I have another shilling?" Slightly rue-fully, I counted the coins into her small palm.

"Look, Ma, it's the captain from the other day come to see us," she said when she had tied them away in her handkerchief. "Here he is. He wants to talk to you again."

"How are you today, Mrs. Wedderburn?" Very gently, I took the plates from her hands and led her to a chair, pulling one up for myself. I remembered Blake had held her hand, so I did the same now, giving her my best smile. It felt somewhat dishonest.

"We saw Eldred Woundy this morning," I said. "I am afraid he was not much pleased to see us. He denied knowing your husband alto-gether and told us he would take us to court if we pressed it."

"He's always been so taken up with appearances, Eldred."

"We mentioned your name, Mrs. Wedderburn. I am concerned that our doing so may have placed you and your children in an awkward position. He may be angry. I wished to warn you."

She looked at me directly for the first time and gave me a sad smile. Her skin was creamy white against her red hair, and her lips were swollen from biting. Even in her dulled state there was something about her that stirred the blood.

"Eldred? Harm me? You don't understand. He never would. Never in a million years."

"Then I am relieved," I said. "And I have another question."

"Yes?"

"We would like to talk to your son Daniel. Can you tell us where we can find him?"

She started and drew her hand away. "What do you want with him?"

"To ask him what he remembers about his father's death."

"Carn you just let him be?" she said hoarsely. Then her face broke. "I don't know where he is. He won't tell us. You saw him. I don't know what to do."

"Perhaps we could speak to him? Try to persuade him to see reason," I said.

"Could you?" She took my hand again.

"We would need to know where he is."

She gave me a watchful look. Then she said, "You see Matty?"

"Yes, we did. She was most helpful."

"She's a good girl. I'd have done more for her if I could."

"I must also ask," I said, reddening slightly, "if you might remember any regular customers of your husband's who, er, purchased his publications. I know it is a delicate matter, but it may be important."

"They did not exactly leave their cards at the door," she said. "Nat always kept that side of the business to himself. I wouldn't know where to begin."

"Can you tell me about your husband and Mr. Woundy? How they knew one another?"

"No more today, Captain, please," she said firmly. She closed her eyes. The little girl ran and wrapped her arms around her mother, looking at me reproachfully.

I made one last attempt. "What is it that so worries you about Daniel, Connie?"

She looked at me and there were tears on her cheeks.

"Carn say," was all she would offer.


*Holywell Street* was no more alluring in the gray late-morning light than it had been in the dusk, though I fancied the passersby were giving us a wider berth. Blake was leaning against the shop in an ill humor.

"Shall we speak to the shopkeepers then?"

He sighed and turned to the large bookshop next door—Dugdale's—where I had fared so poorly two days before. The red-faced man behind the counter remembered me at once. His expression curdled like milk with vinegar. One or two other customers were browsing furtively. Blake put a shilling on the counter and waited them out.

"Mr. Dugdale—" he said.

"I know what you want," the man said unpleasantly, interrupting him. "*I* want you gone."

"Well, you may not know that Wedderburn wasn't the first victim and I don't think he'll be the last," Blake said to him. "And that ought to worry you. Unless you have good reason to feel safe—and that ought to worry you more. I'm no blue bastard, but I have a powerful patron who wants the truth. And if I decide it, Wedderburn's murder will be in every paper by tomorrow morning, with all the attendant fuss someone in your line would go far to avoid. My only interest is the murder. This is my card. When you're ready to talk you can send a boy. I think we have things to say. Good day, Mr. Dugdale."

Dugdale scowled.

"Do you think he will speak?" I said when we were outside.

"Maybe, if he thinks it worth his while." Through the shop window I saw Dugdale take up the card and read it.

"Should we go to the next shop?"

"No. They're all like that. Something or someone's made them jittery. Call it a day. I need to think."

I was, I saw to my disappointment, being dismissed, but I could not deny that Blake looked as if he was in need of rest. We continued toward Drury Lane, and I became sure that I was not imagining that the clothes dealers and shopkeepers turned from us and avoided our eyes. At the corner with Drury Lane a few bored, worn-looking whores in low-cut garish dresses had gathered, their shawls draped to expose their shoulders. I thought how cold they must be.

"You're the one looking for the printer's killer?" one called out to Blake. "The one with two fingers missing? Let's see your hand, go on."

Blake walked over to them, took his hand out of his pocket and showed the two stumps. They gathered round, giggling and shrieking equally with disgust and curiosity.

"You're out early, girls," he said. He seemed quite at ease. I hung back, awkward.

"There's only a little trade in the afternoon, but we gets to talk and laugh a bit among ourselves, and the blue bastards don't move us on here. Nights we're up at the theaters."

"You wanna beat some lard and honey together and rub it on the stumps, it'll stop them chafing," said one girl.

"I got something what'll stop it chafing," jeered another, hitching her skirts suggestively. "If there's any beating to be done, it won't be a bit of lard and honey."

The rest of the girls shrieked.

"My ma used to make it," the other girl said haughtily. "And she added an egg yolk an' a drop of rose water an' all."

"Anything to tell us?" Blake said. "About the printer?"

"He said we wasn't to say nothing—" one girl said.

"Oh, give over! What's the harm?" the first girl retorted, grinning at Blake. "You know what they're saying? It was Spring-Heeled Jack what done him. Took his soul to hell."

Blake sighed impatiently. "No such animal, ladies."

"It's a mystery then. Because no one saw nothing."

"What did people say of him?"

"Better than some, no worse than others. Didn't know him well. Never took liberties. Reckon she kept him on a short leash."

"She?"

"The wife. Thinks a lot of herself, doan she? They say his stuff is pricey. Maybe they murdered him for his money."

The others nodded.

"Doan think them other printers much liked him. But they're a rum lot," said another, soberly. "They doan like nobody."

"Son's nice-looking, I'd give him one for free." The others laughed again.

"What about him?"

"He's not here much these days. Argued with his pa, they say. A Chartist."

"Well, we must move on, ladies, but we'll be around and if you think of anything . . ." said Blake.

"Likewise—you and your friend," said the first girl. "We're always ready and waiting." There was another shriek of laughter.


*As we were about to turn* into Drury Lane there came a cry behind us.

"Mr. Blake! Captain!" Matty Horner, basket flying, was running to catch us up. There were points of pink color in her cheeks, her eyes were bright and she had shoes: a pair of worn black-laced leather boots. Not the most delicate of footwear for a young woman, but practical enough and not monstrously ugly.

"Mr. Blake, I want to ask you something."

"Yes?" Blake said impassively. Once again I was annoyed by his brusqueness.

"I want to say," she said, gasping for breath, "that I know about you, Mr. Blake. I knew I'd seen you, here and in Soho. I remembered your hand. You find things, and people. That's what they say. Look, I could help you. I'm on the street all the time. I could watch for you. Who comes and who goes. I'm good at remembering things. You know that. I could be useful. See, I write a good hand too." From a pocket she produced a crumpled bit of paper which on closer examination I saw she had carefully folded. "It's my own hand, I swear it."

"What do you want in return?" said Blake, looking unconvinced.

"I've something to ask you. Later. You could try me for a while, and you'd see, I'd be worth it."

He frowned. "Then tell me why no one will speak of the murder today and we are watched with such suspicion."

Her eyes widened. "I d-dunno," she stuttered, taken aback. "I suppose they doan like outsiders."

He turned away from her and she stood, trying to wrestle her features into nonchalance, her disappointment palpable.

"I think we may have a use for you, Miss Horner," I said firmly. "Mr. Blake will think on it, and I shall look at your writing." I took the bit of paper from her. "I see you have shoes."

"Oh, Abraham found them for me. Gave them to me this morning," she said, looking past me at Blake. I brought out a coin from my pocket and tried to press it upon her.

"No," she said, giving me a hard smile. "You're all right. Plenty of ways of earning a penny." She turned on her heel and walked back down the road, where I could see Abraham Kravitz staring fiercely at us.

"Why be so harsh?"

"I said, I do not trust her."

"Everything she said has been confirmed. Come, Blake, we could ask her to watch the Wedderburns' house in case Woundy comes," I persisted.

"I'll think on it," he said sharply.

"Or we could ask her to look out for Daniel," I said.

"No need to. He's over there."

Hands in pockets, hunched and purposeful, Daniel Wedderburn was weaving his way through the hawkers and idlers. Matty had seen him too and watched him intently.

"Daniel," Blake said when the boy—hardly a boy, indeed: he was almost as tall as I and far broader—was level with us. He did not recognize Blake. "We were at your mother's two days ago. We want to ask you about your father. We want to find his murderer."

The boy set his jaw and walked briskly away from us, but Blake remained doggedly by his side.

"I will follow you until you answer," said Blake. "It will be easier to talk now."

The boy tried to push him out of the way but Blake stayed with him, and I trailed behind. At length he gave up, glowering with rage.

"Coppers ain't interested. Why should you be? Who are you anyway?" He seemed to seethe with anger, as if he might catch fire at any moment.

"I'm an inquiry agent, Daniel, and the captain is my colleague," Blake said calmly. "We've been asked to look into your father's death because there was another like it some weeks ago, at Seven Dials."

"Another murder, like my pa's?" The boy looked confused.

"A printer called Blundell. Ever heard of him?"

He shook his head. "Seen Woundy, did you?"

"We did," said Blake. "He insisted he didn't know your father. Tried to set his bruisers on us."

The boy gave an angry laugh. "That don't surprise me. He always came at night, skulking at the back of the shop. Didn't wish to be seen."

"Why's that?"

He shrugged. "Pa'd not tell me. Don't doubt it was to do with the filth he sold."

"Do you have any idea why your father might have been murdered?"

"Because he sank himself into the mire," he said, as if it were obvious. "He brought it upon himself."

"Did you work with him?"

"Not unless I had to." He seemed to swell further with rage.

It was then that I had a strange vision. Despite the disparity in our stations, I realized that he reminded me of myself a few years before— full of angry thoughts so large and inexpressible I feared they might choke me.

"Look," he said. "I'll tell you about my pa. He disgusted me. He betrayed his family and everyone about him. He was a godless, lewd man.

But what is worse is that he had an education. He should have known better, but he dragged himself into the gutter and brought us with him. I can never forgive him for that."

"Maybe it was the only way he could make a living to keep you all."

The boy shook his head.

"Should have been a good living," said Blake.

"You ask Woundy about that. He had my pa on a short rein. Pa bowed to Woundy, never stood up to him. I tell you, all that about Woundy being the respectable gentleman? You take away his fancy suits, and he is the worst of all."

"So Woundy is in the same business as your pa?"

The boy looked deflated. "Don't know. But there was something between them. When he came round they would talk about money. Pa wouldn't tell me."

"What do you recall of the night your father died, Daniel?"

"I wasn't there. We'd argued weeks since. We hardly spoke."

"But you saw the body?"

The boy looked ashen.

"Where do you work now, Daniel?" Blake said. "Where do you live? Work's short for lots of trades but not for printers."

"It's not as easy as you'd think." He was relieved to change the subject.

"No?"

Angry red suffused his cheeks again. "It's all changing in printing. Holywell Street is the end of something. Printers don't set up on their own anymore, masters in their own shop. It's all big works and steam presses, a few masters reveling in wealth and luxury served by men who once worked for themselves. Woundy's printers are nothing more than wage slaves. He takes plenty on, but he's forced down wages and he demands longer hours. And if you won't do them, there's plenty who'll take your place. It's the same all over. Tailors, stonemasons, furniture makers. The weavers over in Spitalfields, they're starving."

"You sound like a Chartist," I said.

"I am a Chartist, signed and sealed!" He almost shouted it, and a number of passersby looked round. "Live it and breathe it. From where I stand, the rich have but one goal. To keep their wealth and their privileges, to grind down the poor and to keep them poor. We must fight back. But I wouldn't expect you to understand. And now I'm going. I've a meeting to attend."

"A Chartist meeting?"

"In a manner of speaking," said the boy cryptically. "It'll be a Chartists' meeting by the end."

"Where is it?"

"Crown and Anchor, on the Strand."

"Your father didn't approve of your beliefs," said Blake.

"He told me to stay away from politics. He said it would bring only trouble—as he lay down for Woundy to wipe his boots upon. As he scraped and bowed for his flash customers. He said, 'You cannot turn the world upside down—authority will have its way and slap you down.' He yielded. I will not."

"Woundy's paper is pro-Chartist," Blake said.

"A sop to his readers."

"What about your mother?" I said.

"What about her?"

"Does she not at least deserve some support and comfort?"

"Not from me," he said sullenly.

"I have just watched her weep over you," I said. "She misses you sorely."

I thought he might soften, but he did not.

"Someone else is putting food on the table and coal in the grate. I am not needed."

"Who?" said Blake.

"Eldred Woundy!" he said triumphantly. "And what do you think she provides in return?"

"How can you say such a thing of your own mother!" I said, shocked.

He gave me a sullen look. "See, she's drawn you in too. She catches everyone."

"We are concerned that Woundy might hurt your mother," I said, and Daniel started. "We told Woundy that we had spoken to her. He was not pleased. Would you consider staying with your family for a while? If not for your mother, then for your sisters' and brothers' sake?"

He frowned. "I can't go back home. I have other obligations. But I'll look in on them tonight, after the meeting, if I can."

He stepped past me, hunched his shoulders once more and set off at speed in the direction of the Strand.

"I should like to be at that meeting," said Blake.

"A Chartist meeting, Jeremiah? Truly?"

"I am a dangerous radical, remember?"

"Then we should ask Matty to keep watch over the shop."

He looked skeptical but he said, "All right. We'll give her a penny or two," and dug into his pockets.

"I have it," I said curtly.

# chapter 7

Is there a meeting here this evening?" Blake inquired of the porter as we stepped into the Crown and Anchor.

"Anti-Corn-Law League, up the stairs, Mr. Blake," came the reply. "The ballroom. See the gentlemen going up? Follow them."

"But—" I said. Blake shushed me with a look.

"Why are we attending an Anti-Corn-Law meeting?" I demanded in a whisper as we took the stairs.

"We'll find out soon enough," said he.

The room was large and fairly well filled, though there were plenty of empty seats and the audience were mostly attired in smart black coats and hats. There were even a few women. Well-turned-out young men briskly handed out pamphlets. At the front, four men of aldermanly bearing sat on a raised stage. Above them was a banner which read, "He that witholdeth corn, the people shall curse him."

Again I would have questioned our presence here, and again Blake shushed me, gesturing that we stand at the back.

"Let us watch."

One of the gentlemen on the platform stood and called the meeting to order, introducing himself as a Mr. Elliot. It seemed to me he was not altogether at ease as his eyes constantly darted toward the doors behind us and he kept mopping his brow. Gradually, however, as he continued to talk he became less guarded, even describing the Corn Laws as "a mechanism for maintaining the incomes of landlords so they may employ a superfluity of grooms and gardeners," a bit of leaden wit delivered with a considerable wiggling of eyebrows in case the audience should fail to spot it as a joke. The audience obligingly sniggered—no doubt with relief, since it would be the last piece of levity they would be hearing in some time. "The laws are deliberately maintained with this object in mind," the gentleman went on more seriously, "therefore it is just, it is only reasonable, for all human beings to struggle against them."

It occurred to me that my father would probably disown me if he knew where I was.

At that moment there was the sound of many people coming up the stairs and shouts coming from outside the doors. Two of the brisk young men ran to the doors to try to keep them shut, but they were too late: they sprang open and in surged a mighty column of men carrying their own banners, upon which were written, "Liberty, Freedom, Let the People Serve," and underneath, "The National Charter Association."

The speaker, Mr. Elliot, raised his arms in a gesture of exasperation. His companions on the stage stood in consternation. The interlopers, meanwhile, pushed to the front. It was immediately apparent that they far outnumbered the Anti-Corn-Law Leaguers: there must have been at least a hundred of them, perhaps two. Blake pointed out Daniel Wedderburn, who was making his way to the stage, clutching his cap in expectation.

Members of the League began to berate the Chartists and in some places where the two groups met, blows were exchanged. For a moment the event threatened to become most unpleasant. From the stage the speaker began to appeal for order. I might have stepped in myself had not Blake laid a hand on my shoulder.

"We are here to observe," he said.

"You foresaw this," I muttered.

Five of the invaders now stepped upon the stage and one, a small man in clerical black, raised his hands for silence. Gradually the room quietened.

"This is too much, Mr. Watkins!" said Mr. Elliot furiously to the small clerical man. "This is a private meeting! I demand that you leave!"

The Chartists launched into unmannerly jeers.

"Mr. Elliot," said Mr. Watkins, the clerical Chartist, "you have called the meeting to order, and now we are part of it. We seek only to pass an important motion and then we will be on our way." He had a lively face, bushy dark hair and a northern accent, though I could not have identified it any more precisely than that.

"This is merely another example of the foolish insolence of you Chartists, who encourage and stir the unnatural hatred of the have-nothings for the have-somethings!" cried Mr. Elliot. The latter part of his speech was drowned out by the boos of the Chartist army. In among them, however, I could still hear a few cheers from the Anti-Corn-Law Leaguers.

"No, my friend," said the Chartist Watkins. "It is you who have stoked this feeling, by betraying us in '32 with the so-called 'Great' Reform Act, which brought the vote to the manufacturers and the masters but left us, the workers, without. Now you campaign upon a matter which is a distraction from the true needs of the poor, but you pursue it because it will allow you to lower wages." The Chartists cheered. "Your league claims to welcome all, but your membership subscription of fifty pounds a year shows to whom it truly belongs." At the front, Daniel Wedderburn applauded and waved his cap.

"And now, Mr. Elliot," said Watkins, "I will ask you and your friends to return to your seats. No ill will befall you, but we have some business to transact, and we will have our way."

Mr. Elliot rolled his eyes, advised his supporters to wait for the invasion to pass, and sat down, glowering. It was plain that this was not the first time such a thing had taken place.

"We shall now propose our own motion," said Watkins, "and I have a feeling that this meeting of the Anti-Corn-Law League will pass it with a great majority! I have with me some well-known members of the National Charter Association."

He introduced the men who had stepped onto the stage with him. First there was Mr. George Harney, "the well-known journalist and speaker," a slight fellow with a lively face who waved his revolutionary red cap at the audience. Then the unsmiling Dr. McDouall, "surgeon and devotee to our cause," with long sideburns and a dark frock coat. There was Mr. Charlie Neesom, "bookseller, journalist, temperance man, who has paid for his devotion to the cause many times over," a gaunt, bespectacled man with a quiet, commanding air. Finally, there was "Major Bennywhisky, our Polish brother, who, having labored for Polish independence, has committed himself to our own struggle for freedom." Major Bennywhisky wore a blue military jacket with gold epaulets, and a pair of remarkably elaborate side whiskers. He stood to attention and saluted. The gesture seemed to me rather overdone. The rowdy cheers and applause that greeted him, however, lasted for several minutes.

"Friends," Watkins said at last, "we are not here merely for frivolous reasons. We find ourselves at the end of three years of terrible hardship for working people, particularly for our friends in the North. In Nottingham, Sheffield, Glasgow and Manchester, we have seen destitution and misery on a scale that we never dreamed. I have seen parents sit through the night for weeks at a time so their only bed might afford their families some rest. I have seen babies born on wet flags without a rag to cover them, or a bit of food for their mothers. I have seen men fast for days uncheered by the hope of better fortune, sinking under the pressure of want into premature graves. Children left without parents, starving on the streets."

By the time he had finished speaking, the room was utterly silent. Unbidden, the image of Matty, struggling to feed her brother and herself, came to me.

"I see a community of careworn looks, of desolate homes," Watkins continued. "A community in need, denied help by the masters and manufacturers who campaign for the repeal of the Corn Laws, but who obstruct attempts to limit working hours, to combat dangerous work conditions and to raise wages."

On the dais, the Anti-Corn-Law men sat, stony-faced. Though I could not condone the rudeness of the Chartists, I could not restrain a smile at the former's discomfort.

"Mr. Charlie Neesom will now address you," said Watkins. Neesom, the gaunt man in spectacles, stood and came to the front.

"London! The depredations that have already wrought devastation upon your brothers in the North have come to you," he said. He had the blunt, matter-of-fact accent of the North and this, I saw, gave his dramatic words more force than a more colorful delivery would have. "The death of crafts and trades, among them the silk weavers of Spitalfields, who starve before our eyes while the princes of commerce build their gaudy, tinseled palaces. Our country is the richest in the world, the envy of the world, and yet the vast fruits of its success are denied us, we who carry this country upon our shoulders. The inequality of riches in England is a byword among foreigners. In no country in the world is there so striking a contrast, so defined a partition, so easy and dreadful a comparison between rich and poor as there is here."

There were loud calls of "Hear, hear!"

"How can we combat this assault upon our livelihoods and our families? Are we to bleed like our northern brothers before succor comes? We ask for a fair day's pay for a fair day's work. But when will it come? Again and again, Parliament ignores our plight. The old government, the Whigs, the most infamous government that ever ruled, passed laws that lowered our wages and raised the price of food, consigned us to the workhouse, divided families, allowed the needy to die of want and in shame. Now they try to woo us. The Tories are no better: they give seventy thousand pounds to the refurbishment of the Queen's stables, they send thousands more to compensate the rich owners of former black slaves in the Caribbean, but they ignore the starving poor.

"A couple of rich men do try and buy us off with promises of cheaper food or a few less hours' work. But their fellow parliamentarians will not acknowledge our desperate need. We must have a new beginning. It is only through fair representation in government that our needs and our just demands can be met. I ask you to vote for the motion: a motion in support of our Charter and for universal suffrage, the vote for every man."

At this, the Polish major, Bennywhisky, leaped up, stood on his chair in a highly excited manner and cried, in an accent only just intelligible to his audience, "Brothers in bondage! We must protect ourselves from the ferocious monster Capital, who is at all times eager to appease his greedy appetite upon the very miseries of the sons of industry, and would—given any opportunity—make tools and slaves of us all! We must respond in kind. With fire and fury! Let us light the fire of liberty in London so that it shall never die!"

Many in the audience, Daniel Wedderburn included, shouted, "Aye!" The major sat down, evidently very pleased with himself, to noisy applause and whistles—amid which one could still hear a few boos.

"Thank you, Brother Beniofsky," said Neesom, pronouncing the man's name with a knowing air, though I wondered how much he had actually welcomed his Polish colleague's intervention. "The National Charter Association demands the just representation of the people of Great Britain and Ireland in the Commons House of Parliament, through the six points of the Charter. What are these six points? Firstly, the vote for every man above twenty-one—true democracy."

There was a grumble in the audience and a woman shouted, "And what of women?"

Several male voices rose to hush her, but the speaker raised his hand. "That we will come to by and by. Secondly, we demand the abolition of a property qualification to stand as an MP, and thirdly, we want payment for MPs so that we may be represented by men like ourselves: poor but honest men who will speak for us. Fourthly, we must have annual parliaments. Fifthly, electoral boroughs must be of equal size, and sixthly, there must be secret ballots to protect the voter in the exercise of his vote."

"All those in favor of the motion," said little Mr. Watkins, "that the Anti-Corn-Law League should adopt the six articles of the Charter?"

There were a few boos and hisses, but the motion was easily carried.

"Mr. Elliot, let it be entered in your minutes that a motion in favor of the Charter was passed at this meeting of the Anti-Corn-Law League."

The man who had not spoken, McDouall, took the ledger from one of Mr. Elliot's colleagues and proceeded to write in it, offering it to Mr. Elliot to countersign. The latter shook his head. "This only weakens your case. It changes nothing!" he shouted.

"It shows that numbers, not privilege, will out in the end," said Neesom.

"May we now be permitted to go?" said Mr. Elliot sarcastically. Neesom nodded. Then a voice from the audience called out,

"May I ask one question?" It was Daniel Wedderburn.

Neesom smiled and said, "One of our younger members—Brother Wedderburn. Ask away."

"We tell ourselves that the rulers of our country must be in ignorance of our state." Wedderburn's voice was hoarse with nerves, and he stuttered a little. "Yet when, two years ago, thousands brought a petition to Parliament, imploring our governors to hear testimony of our situation, it was dismissed and their demands scorned. I believe in the Charter but it is hard not to feel that our legislators, our magistrates and our employers have abandoned us. I ask you, Mr. Neesom, where are you on the matter of physical force?"

Neesom smiled, took off his spectacles and said, "A good question, Brother Wedderburn. I say, 'Peacefully if we can, forcibly if we must!'"

There were at once both cries of approval and boos and hisses. Mr. Elliot raised his hands in the air and looked at his pocket watch.

"Let me explain, my brothers!" said Neesom, stretching out his arms in a plea for quiet. "We must show Parliament that we mean what we say. That for us the Charter is a matter of life and death, and that we cannot be deflected by the opposition of an assembly in which none of us has a say. They must understand that we are in earnest. Let us not forget, moreover, that the government has created its own militia force, those skull-cracking ruffians, those kitchen spies, those bludgeoners, those blue devils, the so-called new police!" This last raised a cheer. "They must know that if they turn their forces on us, the mills and fields of England will burn. Too long have we remained in bondage, too long have we turned a smiling face to oppression!"

At this the Polish major stood, nodded emphatically to denote his support of Neesom's words, and roared, "Yes! Yes!"

Over the heads of the crowd I saw Daniel Wedderburn nodding vigorously too. But not all were in agreement: the clerical type, Watkins, shook his head.

"I do not support physical force," he said, "and I am as true a supporter of the Charter as any man. I say, such agitation can only be harmful and injurious to the movement. Parliament tries to discredit us by branding us anarchists and plunderers. It says that universal suffrage means universal pillage. It claims that threats of force prove we are undeserving of the vote and if we accomplish it, it will be the first step to disorder, revolution and the redistribution of property. Violent words do not threaten the enemies of our movement, but they undermine its friends. We do not want muskets and pikes but education and schooling."

The Chartists seemed split: most cheered, some booed.

Daniel Wedderburn turned for a moment. Our eyes met, then his slid away.

The Chartists began to push out of the room. A few angry words and insults were exchanged with the Leaguers, but their retreat was more or less peaceful. Blake and I watched them depart but Daniel Wedderburn had vanished, and so we too passed through the doors, leaving the Anti-Corn-Law Leaguers to their own devices.

"I know you, do I not?" It was the bespectacled man from the stage, Neesom, and he placed a hand on Blake's arm. "Charlie Neesom at your service. And this is George Watkins, Charter organizer, cabinetmaker by trade—though there's precious little of that work about just now—and Methodist lay preacher. We have seen you at the Mechanics Institute and the Philosophical Society and such like." Neesom pushed his spectacles up his nose. He looked thoroughly mild-mannered; it would have been hard to imagine anyone less like a revolutionary fire-brand.

"We saw you at the talk on Thomas Paine," said Watkins eagerly.

"And when you translated for Mr. Matseeni," said Neesom.

"Jem Blake," Blake said, taking Neesom's hand. "This is my companion, William Avery. I saw Mr. Watkins recite *Paradise Lost* in its entirety. Quite a feat."

Watkins nodded modestly, and then, "We are surprised to find you among the Leaguers."

"But is this not a Chartist meeting now?" Blake said innocently.

"You heard we were coming?" said Neesom.

"I heard it might be a possibility."

"Blake and Avery, Blake and Avery," said Watkins. "Why is that familiar?"

"The men who were with Mountstuart when he died," said Neesom, taking off his spectacles and starting to polish them with the edge of his shirt.

"Good Lord, of course! You knew Mountstuart?" said Watkins, his face lighting up with excitement. "I was—am—a great admirer of the man. Well, it is even more of a pleasure to meet you! I should certainly like to take the opportunity to ask you about him."

Blake nodded absently.

"Thank you," I said hurriedly, "but it is still a slightly painful subject for us."

"Of course," said Watkins, looking mortified.

"No matter," said Blake, "I'd be happy to talk of him sometime. But perhaps Mr. Neesom might answer a question for me. Is there a natural link between printers and booksellers and Chartism?"

"The fight for the vote has often gone hand in hand with the fight for free speech," said Neesom pleasantly. "There's many printers and booksellers who fought the stamp in the twenties and thirties, were committed to suffrage too and went to prison for it."

"The stamp?" I said.

"The duty on newspapers to keep them too dear for the working man, a tax on knowledge," said Neesom. "You are no doubt too young to remember."

"I've another question, for Mr. Watkins," said Blake. "You do not share Mr. Neesom's opinion on physical force, and yet you share the same stage."

"I hold that we must win the battle through moral argument. But if anyone has a right to argue for force, it is Charlie. He has been arrested many times for his beliefs. And next year we will gather signatures for another petition, and it will be so great that there will be no denying that it represents the will of the people and Parliament will not be able to refuse us."

Neesom said, "May I ask, Mr. Blake and Mr. Avery, where you both stand on the Charter?"

Blake gave a small smile and said nothing.

"For myself," I said, "I think such disruptive tactics weaken your case. I have no great love of the Anti-Corn-Law Leaguers, but I cannot understand the point of your performance today. Some might say you demonstrate your unworthiness to vote by such rowdiness. And your Polish major, Bennywhisky or whatever his name is, seems more a pantomime creature than anything else."

"I am sorry you think that," said Neesom quietly. "You must understand that though they are many fewer in number to us, the Leaguers have almost infinite resources and much more influence in Parliament. We have to find striking ways of showing that they do not speak for us, and that we will remain an irritant until our demands are met. As for Major Beniofsky, he has done a good deal for our cause."

"You can hardly be surprised that someone of my background would be no supporter of your cause," I said. "Though I do agree that something has gone terribly wrong in the dealings between masters and men. I do not know what is to be done, but to me your movement threatens chaos and anarchy."

"I must assure you that you are wrong," said Watkins. "I am glad to have the opportunity to say this to a man such as yourself. Whatever *The Times* may say, Chartists are not revolutionary hotheads. We believe in debate and the rule of law. I would say those of us who talk of force do so more to try and frighten Parliament into acting than because they wish to rise."

"Would you agree, Mr. Neesom?" said Blake.

"What of the work of Lord Allington?" I interrupted. "I do not believe he wants to 'buy off' the laboring man. He is entirely sincere in his desire to improve lives. This is the backbone of good Toryism. For hundreds of years the right-thinking country gentry have kept their tenants' needs at heart."

"I'm sure Lord Allington is an admirable gentleman, Captain Avery," said Watkins, "but he is one man, and his own party challenges him at every turn. What we the workers want—nay, deserve—as subjects of the Queen and creators of wealth, is the right to have a say in the regulation of our own lives, not to be reliant on the passing kindness of masters or landowners. And not to be dismissed as a tiresome group whose circumstances can never be bettered."

"You have not said where you stand, Mr. Blake," said Neesom.

"Oh, Mr. Blake is a veritable radical," I said.

Blake shook his head. "I see the justice of the Charter. But I fear it will take more than signatures to bring the change you seek."

"We are prepared for that," said Watkins. "We are out to change hearts and minds. To persuade the country that the laboring classes are respectable and responsible, not rootless and threatening. All these things take perseverance and time."

"I wish you well of it, but I'm no joiner. Not anymore."

"But, Mr. Blake, politics is life," Neesom said. "Association makes one man part of a great combination which can enable wonderful changes. Strength resides in community, combination and trust. If you will not join, then what good are you?"

The shadow of a smile flitted across Blake's face. "It is a good question."


*A cold rain blew* into our faces when we emerged from the Crown and Anchor. I thought of Matty Horner in the street with her basket, struggling for a few coins. The poor are always with us, my father liked to say.

"Did you find that illuminating? Are you any closer to a solution?" I said.

Blake scratched his ragged ear. "Why, are you?"

I laughed. "I am perplexed. All I can say is that Woundy was lying, Connie Wedderburn is hiding something, Dugdale is unpleasant, the poor are starving, the Chartists are disruptive and Daniel Wedderburn is alarmingly angry. But I thought that you might have certain theories by now."

"This work is not like a steady climb up a flight of stairs. It's more like gathering crumbs, and hoping that at some moment you may find yourself with part of a loaf."

"So it was a day of crumbs then."

"In a manner of speaking."

"I lost sight of the Wedderburn boy," I said. "I am sorry."

He shrugged, rubbing his ear again. "Never mind. We'll find him. Thought I'd go to the Cyder Cellars. Frequented by journalists and hacks. Might pick up something about our dead men." He gave me an uncharacteristic sideways look. "Come if you wish. It's not far from here. Unless you are dining with your Oriental gents."

I was pleased by the invitation, though I was careful not to show how much. Also I had one errand to fulfill. The Chartists' descriptions of want had so moved me, I was filled with a desire to help Matty Horner in some small way.

"I should release the girl, Matty, first," I said. "Inquire if she has seen anything."

He looked at me, having entirely divined my intentions, and as so often chose not to comment on them, for which I was grateful. Then he tore a page from his notebook. "I'll draw you a map. Take care. Do not lose yourself."

*She stood opposite* the Wedderburn house, a small wet figure clutching an empty basket, taking what shelter she could under Abraham Kravitz's awning. The rain had eased, but many of the shopkeepers had already closed and the street was quiet save for a couple of drunken vagabonds, too far gone to stand up.

She gathered herself when she saw me. "Anything to report, Miss Horner?"

"Yes, Captain. Daniel came in about ten minutes ago. Out of breath he was. Hasn't left yet. And that copper from the Strand. Never comes up here normally. He walked up and down about an hour ago. No one else."

"Thank you, Miss Horner. Here is something for your trouble, and I should like, if you will let me, to buy you a hot meal. What will you have?"

"A 'tater if you please," she said. I purchased one from a man with a small, brightly polished tin brazier at the top of the street by Drury Lane. The potato was cut in half and slathered in butter and salt. I wrapped it in my clean handkerchief. We stood under a gaslight, and she warmed her hands upon it before eating it. I removed myself while she ate, returning with a large orange which I had bought from a costermonger on the corner of Drury Lane. Seeing it, she shook her head.

"Oh, Captain, you're a babe-in-arms."

"I am sorry," I said, disappointed. "Have I done wrong?"

"The orange. It's no good." She took my hand and pressed it into the skin. "See? Like a sponge. It's been boiled. Coster trick. They do it to the old ones—makes them swell up—but if we opened it, all the juice'd be gone. Where'd you get it from?"

I hesitated, feeling foolish.

"It was from him up on Drury Lane, wasn't it?" She marched off.

"Oi! You!" she said, her hands upon her hips, her head jerking angrily. She looked unpredictable, almost threatening. I very nearly felt sorry for the orange seller. "I know you. Give him his money back or you'll tell me the reason why."

The man looked most taken aback. He at first pretended ignorance but soon caved in beneath the onslaught of her threats.

"I'll tell the whole street you're boiling. I'll queer your pitch even if I lose me own. You doan cheat my friends!"

"Calm down, Matty, don't shout about it, he can have his money back."

I bought her a cup of coffee, a jam puff and a halfpennyworth of "hard-bake" treacle, which she put in her pocket.

"Can I ask you something, Captain?" she said.

"Anything."

"How is it that Mr. Blake is, well, in charge? You're the gentleman, ain't you, and Mr. Blake is, well, he's not. It's hardly usual."

"I suppose it is not. But Mr. Blake, though he may seem brusque and even rude, saved my life in India, and when others lied, he saw through their lies and told the truth."

"Will you tell me about it?"

"Well, it is a long story and not really mine to tell."

"Tell me about India then. What it's like?"

And so I told her about India. As she listened, her face opened and I saw how the ugly bonnet and shapeless clothes and a certain boyish jauntiness of manner disguised her delicate features, the fine curve of her neck, a burgeoning womanliness. She caught my look and I saw she disliked it—somehow her expression shifted, and she retreated to the wary, boyish girl again—so I glanced away and all was easy.

"He did look at my writing, didn't he, Mr. Blake?" she said at last. "He does know I can write?"

I realized I had forgotten her crumpled bit of paper. "I am sure he did, Miss Horner," I said guiltily. "You work very hard. I hope your brother does his share?"

The amiability that had struck up between us suddenly faltered.

"Yes, sir," she said, "when he can. Thank you, sir. I should go home now."

# chapter 8

I am ashamed to say that even with his scrawled map it took me well over half an hour to find the Cyder Cellars, a walk that should have taken not much more than five minutes. I circled Covent Garden market, taking wrong turn after wrong turn, my sense of unease and helplessness growing by the minute. When it came to finding my way around the city, I was quite incapable. At last, with a sense of inexpressible relief, I stumbled upon the place. It was very heaven to descend its greasy steps and find myself assailed by a miasma of cigar smoke, the reek of beer and roars of inebriation.

Gaslights hung from the high ceiling, there was sawdust upon the floor and the walls were paneled with old cider casks cut in half. Parties of raucous drinkers and diners were ranged on long tables. At the far end was a stage—if one could dignify with such a name little more than a raised platform framed by a pair of skimpy curtains. Upon it, a skinny man in theatrical makeup, white-faced with two red smudges on his cheeks, was singing, but such was the general uproar I could not hear the words. Blake was in a corner, observing the scene with his usual dispassion, nursing a mug of beer. I fought my way across the floor. Two other men were seated with Blake. They shared a bottle of claret and were helping themselves to a plate of oysters and brown bread. Both men's hands were stained with ink.

"Ah, you must be Mr. Blake's friend," said the older of the two. He was a short man with a curved back and a pointed face, unruly gray hair, shaggy eyebrows and a considerable stomach. "I am Douglas Jerrold and this is Henry. He has not stopped talking since we sat down. He is a writer of humorous and satirical ephemera, and the editor of *Punch*." He eyed me expectantly.

The younger man closed his mouth and raised his hand in greeting. He was plump with a plain good-natured face and a general air of chaos—his hair stuck out at odd angles, and his shirt had worked itself out of his trousers. "Henry Mayhew at your service. Douglas, the poor man will most certainly not have heard of *Punch*."

"I will be sure to read it now," I said, and introduced myself. And then, because I could not resist it, "Might I ask if you are acquainted with Mr. Dickens? I am a most tremendous admirer of his."

"I have that honor," Mr. Jerrold said wearily; behind him, Mayhew pulled a comic grimace. Evidently I had said the wrong thing.

"He is a fine writer and a good friend. I cannot, I fear, procure for you an autograph. Mr. Dickens has declared he cannot sign any more."

"Oh no, please forgive me, I would not dream—"

"Mr. Jerrold is himself a famous playwright and wordsmith," said Mayhew quickly. "You may recall his play, *Black-Eyed Susan*? It ran for three hundred nights at Drury Lane, which I believe is a record."

"Henry is too kind," said Jerrold drily, "and prone to flatter me. He wishes to marry my daughter."

Mayhew blushed.

"Avery is West Country–born and has been in India these last five years," said Blake. "You'll have to excuse his ignorance."

"It is, of course, excused," said Mr. Jerrold. "You know, this is the first time Mr. Blake has ever introduced us to an associate. We had no idea what to expect. But then Mr. Blake always tickles our curiosity but never quite satisfies it. He is a very elusive gentleman."

"I have often thought so," I said. Blake said nothing.

"In the meantime he has been kind enough to stand us a bottle of claret and these oysters," said Henry Mayhew, "and has promised to give us a tour of the most wretched parts of London. Here, let me pour you a glass."

"May I ask how you met?" said Jerrold.

"We were sent on a commission together in India some years ago," I said, "and now Viscount Allington has retained us both to work on a particular case."

"Viscount Allington, eh? Is this the matter on which you wish to consult us, Blake? I am not sure I wish to come to the aid of the aristocracy," said Jerrold.

"You should know, Captain Avery," said Mayhew, "that Douglas has a very particular list of bêtes noires: lawyers, bankers, aristocrats and Tories. The rest of the world he looks upon with an indulgent eye."

"Then I am afraid we must differ," I said stiffly. "I am a Tory born and bred, and I can think of many admirable aristocrats, Viscount Allington being one of them."

"An admirable creature I am sure, in his lofty evangelical way. But one cannot justify the creaking privileges of a whole class on the back of one well-meaning toff," said Mr. Jerrold. "Your Duke of Wellington—a man who in my opinion should have been pensioned off after Waterloo—denies the existence of poverty and hunger among the poor in London. And why? Because he has counted five and twenty turkeys at his own poulterer's."

Mr. Mayhew laughed, drained his glass and refilled it. There was something both mournful and engaging about him.

"Lord Allington has asked us to look into a couple of murders which the new police have given up on," Blake said. "Two printers, murdered in their shops."

"Printers? I've heard nothing of this. What is Allington's interest in it?"

"He tried to persuade the police to pursue the cases. They seem determined to bury them. He has retained Captain Avery and me to discover what we can. I intend to find out the truth behind this, and when I do, I can bring you the story. But now, I need intelligence."

"Well, well," Jerrold said, looking at Blake keenly. "What are the names of the two dead men?"

"Nathaniel Wedderburn and Matthew Blundell."

"I do not know them."

"Maybe because the first had premises in Holywell Street, the second in Seven Dials."

"Ah well, they are several rungs down the ladder, even from us. There are thousands of disreputable publishers at that end of the trade constantly setting up and sinking back into the mire. Nevertheless, I should have expected to hear something of this. And Henry spends a good deal of time in the Shakespeare's Head tavern in Wych Street."

"My fellow editor Mark Lemon lives above it," Mayhew said hastily. "I did hear tell of a grisly murder nearby. But I do not recall a name, and there were no broadsheets about it and nothing in the newspapers. We have been so taken up with the paper, I must confess I had forgot it."

Blake shook his head. "That is not my question. My question is, what do you know about Eldred Woundy?"

"Now that is a most interesting question." Jerrold leaned back into his chair. "Mr. Woundy is leading a revolution in publishing. His paper outsells everything. He has realized that with cheaper paper, faster steam presses and the reduction of stamp duty, there is now the potential to reach a readership greater than anything we have ever seen before. I will also say that though I know almost everyone in the world of journalism, I know very little about Woundy. He has risen, as they say, without trace, though interesting rumors cling to him. Did you not work for him for a while, Henry?"

Mayhew, in the midst of eating an oyster, swallowed quickly and tried to suppress a belch.

"I had that dubious honor," he said, his gray pouchy eyes dwelling on Blake, "some years ago. There are times when one must take what comes along, and I was short . . ."

"You are always short," said Jerrold.

Mayhew nodded vigorously. "Woundy published—still publishes— penny bloods. I wrote the words to accompany the illustrations. He was a great shouter and blusterer: 'More blood!' he would say. 'Bigger eyes!' Not an easy man to work for, fractious, far from generous—but entertaining: large in all things, full of energy and swagger, and he knew his audience. From our pens streamed a veritable flood of tales of murders, baby swaps, cannibalism and vampires."

"That how he made his money?" said Blake.

"He certainly had a nose for what sold, but there's scarcely a fortune to be made in such things. He had a reputation as a lively but small-scale publisher. I should be amazed if he had made enough to launch *Woundy's Weekly*, but he was very close with his money, and he was not the most scrupulous of men, though that is hardly a rare thing in our trade. There was talk that he had other, let us say, less salubrious interests, though we never knew quite what. Odd fellows would arrive; he would retire with them into his office and lock the door. We liked to think he was hatching nefarious plots. How he has come into his current fortune and respectability is something of a mystery. Of course, he may simply have a wealthy backer . . . who must be delighted with the return on his investment."

"Is he married? Has he a family?"

"Never saw any sign of it. He liked to play the dandy, liked a good meal and good wine."

"We went to visit Mr. Woundy this very morning," I said. "He mistook us for would-be investors."

"Did he?" said Jerrold, raising one luxuriant eyebrow.

"You said that there were certain rumors about Woundy," Blake interjected.

"There was a story some years ago that he had an interest in the *English Spy*."

Mayhew paused. "Come to think of it, I heard that too."

"What is the *English Spy*?" I said.

"A cheap scandal sheet of very low morals," said Jerrold, his nose wrinkling, "purporting to cover the world of fashion and swells. Reviews of courtesans, gambling dens and such. A breed of publication whose time, thankfully, has largely passed—it must have closed two years ago. But again, one would hardly expect it to have made the kind of money needed to buy two steam presses."

"Did Woundy know the two printers who died?" Mayhew said.

Blake smiled. "I believe he did but I have no proof."

"It is not impossible to imagine that Woundy might have had connections in that line. *English Spy* did, after all, make a point of writing up the best-known brothels and courtesans."

A small dumpling of a man was pushing his way through the crowd toward us. His red face and a slight list in his walk—he righted himself with the use of a silver-topped cane—proclaimed him to be an admiral of the red. That is to say, he clearly liked a drink.

"This is a coincidence indeed," said Mr. Jerrold, staring at the tubby little man. "Here is someone who might well know more about Eldred Woundy, though he may not be minded to help you. Renton O'Toole, vulgarian, rogue and charlatan. If anyone knows whether Woundy was engaged with the flash press, it would be him."

The little man made straight for our table.

"Jerrold, Mayhew," he said, combatively picking up one of our glasses and taking a mouthful of wine. "Not bad," he declared. He pointed at Blake. "I know you. The inscrutable Mr. Blake. Pacer of the streets. Possessor of secrets, and two missing fingers. Some say they were bitten off by a tiger. What say you, Mr. Blake?" There was no mistaking his Irishness.

"You behave yourself, someday I might tell you."

"Promises, promises," said the little man, swiveling round and pointing to me. "You, I do not know."

"Mr. Blake and Captain Avery," said Mr. Jerrold, disapprovingly, "may I introduce Renton O'Toole, former proprietor of the *Ironist*. Have you nowhere else to be?"

"Douglas Jerrold, you know I have the hide of a rhinoceros. I am unsnubbable. Avery, eh?" He put his finger to his nose and then mimed great surprise. "Surely not Blake and Avery, the brave companions of the great Xavier Mountstuart in his final struggle against the murderous Thugs of India? Am I right? I know I am."

He gave a little curtsey, in the midst of which he almost lost his balance.

"Good heavens!" said Mayhew. "All this time you were *that* Blake. I cannot believe we did not realize—and you never said a word! Why, we saw Benjamin Haydon's painting just last week!"

Jerrold looked at Blake with one bristling eyebrow raised. Blake gave a tiny shrug.

"Well, Mr. Blake, you surprise us yet again!"

"And you, Captain Avery," said Mayhew warmly, "you are the one who shot the tiger and saved the maharaja! What a story!" Then he said more quietly into my ear, "*Were* Mr. Blake's fingers bitten off by a tiger?"

I shook my head.

"I must say," said O'Toole, drawing up a chair, "that you look nothing like your portraits."

"Since Mr. Haydon has not met either of us, that is hardly surprising," I said.

Jerrold nodded sagely. "Engaging man, Haydon. Dreadful painter."

"I am most wounded, Captain Avery," said O'Toole, "that you have not heard of *me*. I am very well known in London: writer, actor, man of fashion, satirist, seeker-out of truth—"

"Blackmailer," said Jerrold.

O'Toole raised his—our—glass. "I pride myself on knowing everyone's business, and I will not deny that I made tidy sums from encouraging the rich, powerful and not so well behaved to recompense me in return for keeping certain unfortunate escapades out of print. But of course that is all over now."

"It is said that Renton extracted five thousand pounds out of half a dozen courtiers over some court scandal a few years ago," said Mayhew, beaming. Douglas Jerrold looked disgusted.

O'Toole waved his arms about extravagantly. "I'll not deny it. I am no hypocrite. I am a man of many talents, among them a gift for a telling phrase."

"He means he never stints on heaping abuse on those he takes against," said Jerrold. "Renton has been horsewhipped at least twenty times by those he has attacked in print."

"Is it twenty times?" said O'Toole. "I cannot recall." He lifted his cane and essayed a rather lopsided attempt at a saber thrust.

I struggled to restrain a smile.

"What Renton is chiefly famous for is inflicting scabrous reviews," said Jerrold severely. "The *Ironist* was a nasty item—I am glad its day is done. The readers want something different. Humor that is not coarse, immoral or malicious."

"Like that bleeding-heart excuse for a humorous rag you persevere with," O'Toole snorted contemptuously. "What is its name? *Pinch? Hunch?*"

"It is called *Punch*, as you well know," said Mayhew, thumping the table. "It is a good deal more amusing than your sorry publication. Comicality and satire do not need to be ribald and dirty."

"Well said, sir!" said Jerrold.

O'Toole assumed a tragic look. "Ah, the times are against me. And yet I scrape a living. How many does your pathetic publication sell?"

Mayhew hung his head.

"I heard *Pinch* is losing money hand over fist each week, and that you went to your publishers to ask them to buy you out, but they refused because your debts are so high. How much longer can you last, Mr. Mayhew? Hmm? But enough of this. It is Mr. Blake I came to see. A little bird tells me that you paid a somewhat curtailed visit earlier today to the premises of Mr. Eldred Woundy."

"Why," said Jerrold, "we were just speaking of him."

Blake sat up, his eyes hooded in shadow.

"If you are looking for intelligence about Woundy, I am your man. I could tell you many, many things that he would prefer to remain un-known."

"You dislike him," said Blake.

O'Toole put his forefinger on his chin as if pretending to think. "I do. I should go so far as to say I loathe him. And I am willing to talk. But I'll need a good bottle of claret, a plate of beef and oyster stew, and something more on account. But we can discuss that later."

Jerrold sniffed. "I should not bother if I were you, Mr. Blake. At best, Renton's intelligence is worth a couple of oysters."

"Please yourself," said O'Toole.

"I'll stand you dinner," said Blake quietly.

O'Toole called for wine and stew, made a great fuss of settling him-self and tucking into his dinner, then looked up with the expectation of our avid attention. He had it.

"Mr. Blake," he said. "You have a certain reputation. I may be in need of your skills one of these days. If I help you now, I expect to be able to call upon you in future. I believe Dean Street in Soho is where you reside?"

"You're well informed," said Blake.

"I make it my business to be."

"So. Woundy."

O'Toole leaned forward, his voice suddenly urgent. "Such a low-life swindler as ever existed. Capable of anything. You think I am without principles, Jerrold, but Woundy . . . And now he seeks respectability and influence with his cheap little weekly. Well, I know a few things about his past that would put paid to that."

"Why should you reveal them now?" said Blake.

"Who before was interested? Two months ago, Woundy was a no-body whose ostensible business was penny bloods. Now he is currency and I know how he made his money. He was secretly the proprietor of the *English Spy*. Old Spendhall was merely the editor. You think I was bad—Woundy made an art of blackmail, he was engaged in money-lending, forgery and he kept a brothel. The journal was merely another medium for amassing money. He turned up a story, then demanded payment for keeping it out of print."

"The *English Spy* was the *Ironist*'s chief rival," said Mayhew.

"The *English Spy* my rival? Please. My publication was a thing of wit and elegance. The *English Spy* was a coarse and shabby copy."

"You were had up for corrupting public morals," protested Jerrold.

"Oh, indeed," said O'Toole, "the Society for the Suppression of Vice had me in its sights. But I exposed the hypocrisies and crimes of the rich and titled, and surely, Douglas, you cannot argue with that?"

"How did he turn up enough stories to make a fortune out of it?" said Blake.

"He had a finger in many pies. But first, let me tell you what he did to me. He stole my ideas and tried to put me out of business." O'Toole's voice throbbed with emotion. "Some six years ago, when old King William was still alive, I was setting up the *Ironist* and he approached me about becoming joint proprietor. However, he wanted his role to be secret. He had a good deal of capital, to which I shall return. We worked together for some months and were on the point of publication when he suddenly withdrew his funds without explanation. My plans were in ruins, but I managed to scrape together enough to launch. The next thing I knew, the *English Spy* had started up. Its editor, Spendhall, tried to lure my people away, then began to chase my stories, and the sources I had cultivated. I had a very damaging story about old Ernest of Cumberland. You would not have believed it. And he was about to pay me for it too, but just to spite me the *English Spy* printed parts of the stories, incomplete and without the evidence, so no one benefited, and the old devil simply shrugged them off.

"Then I began to receive threatening letters demanding that I close down my publication. I am used to such menaces. I made myself scarce for several weeks. One night two nobblers arrived at our offices. They broke my chief compositor's foot. I know it was Woundy who sent them. Nevertheless, I persisted."

"How do you know it was him?" said Blake.

O'Toole looked around the table intently. He clearly believed himself the hero of his story. I wondered what had become of the compositor.

"I know. Next thing, the bluebottles were set on me over accusations of extortion. I was almost put out of business."

"But, Renton, you *were* extorting."

"Yes, but who knew? Only I, and those who had cause to pay me. And Woundy, who had learned everything from me. I soon found out he was behind the *English Spy*, and the rest too, though he did all he could to put me off the scent. Even in those days he wished to appear blameless."

"Opening a rival paper is not a crime," said Jerrold exasperatedly. "What is your proof that he tried to have you closed down?"

"I have no actual paper proof," said O'Toole angrily. "But there was the lawsuit between the *Ironist* and the *English Spy*, which again almost put me out of business. As I was saying, I could not help wondering how it was that Woundy had come into so much capital, and so I began to sniff about. And what did I find? Mr. Woundy was not merely adept at extortion, he was also a substantial publisher of obscene and lewd material, and he had a brothel in Charlotte Street that catered to interesting tastes." Here Renton permitted himself a knowing smile.

"A former bookshop that he turned into a knocking shop. I have it on good authority that he was not above a bit of forgery and fraud too. They all fed usefully upon each other. Certain men of rank partook of certain services in which Mr. Woundy had a confidential interest, then found themselves blackmailed for it. And with his various interests he amassed a small fortune."

Jerrold threw his hands up. "But, Renton, you are hardly one to talk." I thought at once of Wedderburn's illustrations for "Miss Tess Thrashington's" premises on Charlotte Street.

"What I produced was not illegal," O'Toole persisted. "Woundy's stuff was—is—filth of the first water. Extremely profitable, high priced, sold to the gentry and aristocracy—with a specialism in 'birchen sports.' He goes to great lengths to hide his involvement. He stakes the cash and has others make it and sell it for him. They take the heat if the law or the Society for the Suppression of Vice comes calling. He always has two or three booksellers working for him."

"And you know this because . . ." said Blake.

"I have been watching the man for years, waiting for my moment."

"Why not publish all this yourself, Mr. O'Toole?"

"I know how people think of me. But you, Mr. Blake, you have the ear of important men. You could take him down."

"And why should I do that? For the sake of a few dirty pictures and a few toffs blackmailed for bad behavior?"

"No," said O'Toole sulkily. "Because three weeks ago that poor excuse for a man, Nat Wedderburn, was murdered at his own press. Ah! You did not think I knew about that, Mr. Blake? But I do. Wedderburn was one of Woundy's creatures, dependent on his charity, selling his filth and running some moderately successful blackmailing himself. Matthew Blundell was another. A drunken, ribald oaf who

died in very similar circumstances a few weeks before and then immediately caught light and burned. Did he not?"

"You are certain Blundell worked for Woundy?" said Blake.

"Caught your attention now, have I, Mr. Blake? There's a good deal
of money in their end of the trade, but neither of them lived as well as
they should've. Woundy was creaming off the profits. I went so far as
to pose as a client for Blundell's publications. You know how they furnished their customers with the real filth? Hid it in a basket under
piles of dirty laundry—most appropriate—and lowered it by ropes
into the backyard."

I recalled the great baskets with ropes in Connie Wedderburn's
lodgings.

"Why do you believe these men met their ends, O'Toole?"

"Why, Woundy's ambitions are boundless and he is ruthless. Now
that his paper is doing so well his pet printers are no longer useful to
him, and he doesn't want them to be traced to him. He will have decided that he can no longer afford to be connected to such men, and he
will not wish to continue paying them. He is a man of blunt reasoning.
He cannot be certain of their silence, so he will ensure it. And he has
the means to do it: you have seen his punishers. Once it was done, he
ensured that no one would speak of it."

"You think he threatened the whole of Holywell Street and silenced
the coppers?"

"I think his bruisers could easily let it be known that the matter
must be kept quiet. And as for the bluebottles, a little grease across
palms will do wonders."

"What about the editor of the *English Spy*? Is he still with us?"

"Died a few years back."

"Of what?"

"Who can say?"

"Oh really, Renton!" said Jerrold crossly. "Spendhall died of old age and drink, there was no mystery about that!"

"A very elaborate way of dispensing with one's employees' services, wouldn't you say, Mr. O'Toole?" said Blake.

"But so appropriate for the publisher of 'penny bloods,' wouldn't you say, Mr. Blake? Blood and ceremony. Woundy knows all about that. He hoped no one would take an interest in such lowlifes—and the police obliged. But just in case the murders should attract further attention, do they not appear to be the work of someone crazed with disgust for these purveyors of obscenity? Certainly not someone with whom the murdered men enjoyed a fruitful financial connection."

"You seem to know a great deal about it all, Renton," Mayhew broke in, his words a little slurred.

O'Toole ground his teeth. "Because I have good reason to take an interest in Woundy and his ways. I'll not let him get away with this."

"Do you recognize Woundy from Mr. O'Toole's account, Mr. Mayhew?" Blake said.

Mayhew chewed his lip. "He was a man of loud and angry passions. I must confess it does not sound quite as outlandish as it should."

"Do you have proof of any of this, O'Toole?" said Blake. "Or is it all just hearsay?"

"Not paper proof," O'Toole grumbled. "But there might be something. Woundy was a methodical creature. Liked to keep things written down in big black ledgers. Chances are there's a record somewhere."

"Blake," I muttered. "If Woundy is indeed capable of such things, should we not be concerned for Connie Wedderburn? Blundell's family disappeared. What if that was Woundy's doing? I will not feel easy now unless I see that they are safe."

Blake rubbed his ear. "I am not sure what to make of your story,

O'Toole," he said. "But since we mentioned Wedderburn's widow to Woundy, we cannot take the chance that he might do her harm. Mr. Mayhew, Mr. Jerrold, we must leave you. But before we go, O'Toole, what can you tell me about Lord Allington?"

"Why should you take an interest in him?" said O'Toole beadily.

"There are marks of his charity everywhere round Drury Lane. I am curious."

"Pure as driven snow, so far as I know," said O'Toole, yawning, and I fancied not entirely convinced by Blake's nonchalance. "His parents were a pair though. Father, the Earl of Pewsey, was a cruel old turk, ran through the family money, had some very interesting pastimes. I had a few guineas from him in my time."

Jerrold rolled his eyes.

"The story is," O'Toole went on, warming up, "that such was the coldness of the parents, the Viscount and his sister were brought up by a servant, a very devout, pious woman. Provided the only kindness they had in their whole childhood. That explains the religious mania. The sister too. It's said the Earl, short of money, did his best to deprive Allington of a trust he was due when he was twenty-one, and then of a legacy from an aunt. Then tried to marry the sister off to some old crony of his, twice her age. She refused. He cut her off and she took refuge with Allington. Such was the father's reputation that brother and sister occupy the peaks of irreproachable respectability, devoting themselves to their poor little chimney sweeps and whatnot, while the Earl and his lady stew in the country, contemplating their debts, relics of a freer and more permissive age. Much like myself." He smirked.

I stood, ready to withdraw. Mayhew got up tipsily and took our hands. "I hope we will meet again, Captain Avery. I shall wait with bated breath to hear the outcome of this evening. And, Mr. Blake— our tour, you promised."

Jerrold stood too, revealing a very curved, almost hunched, back.

"Yes indeed, gentlemen, we look forward to hearing the end of the story."

O'Toole, meanwhile, retrieved something slightly bent and frayed from his very tight waistband. "My card," he said. He proffered it to Blake, his arms describing a great arc like some tragic actor making a grand gesture. It read:

RENTON O'TOOLE, SCRIBE, ACTOR, SWELL
*"If I chance to talk a little wild, forgive me."*
—*HENRY VIII*, ACT I, SC. 4.

Underneath there was an address in Old Street. I caught Blake's eye and was forced to choke back my amusement.

"Do not forget, Mr. Blake," said O'Toole, quite oblivious to our mirth, "you owe me, and I shall not be slow in calling upon you when the need arises."

*A reed of light* shone from between the shutters of the Wedderburns' rooms. I ran up the stairs to the side door, Blake trailing behind me, and knocked. No reply. I battered upon it and called out. There came the sound of footsteps.

"Who is it?" asked Connie Wedderburn from the other side of the door.

"Mrs. Wedderburn, it is Captain Avery. We were concerned about you."

"Captain Avery, you cannot pursue us at such hours. You must leave us alone."

"Connie," Blake called through the door, "we've heard some worrying intelligence and we wanted to be sure you were safe."

There was a pause, a whisper, a scraping of locks and bolts, and the door opened slightly. Connie Wedderburn stood in her nightdress, her hair a penumbra of dull fire; on either side stood the oldest daughter and the silent son. She gazed at us for a moment, pushed the children back inside, took up a blanket and, wrapping it around herself, stepped out to us, closing the door behind her.

"Is Daniel here?" I said. "We saw him. He said he would come."

"He came, then he left."

"We hoped he would stay."

She shivered. "I think he meant to, but we argued. He is so angry with me he can hardly bear to be near me."

"What did you argue about?" said Blake.

She pulled the blanket tighter about her. "About his father. About Eldred. Things he doesn't understand but won't take on trust."

"What time did he leave?" Blake said.

"I don't know. It was dark. Not long ago."

"Mrs. Wedderburn," I said, "we are worried that Eldred Woundy may intend some harm to you in his desire to keep his association with your husband a secret."

"You are concerned about Eldred?" she said. "I thought . . ." She trailed off.

"We cannot address the matter properly until tomorrow, but we wanted to keep watch tonight."

"Believe me, Captain Avery," she said, "Eldred would never harm us."

"Nevertheless I would not feel right if we were to leave you and something happened," I said. "We would be like sentries, guarding the gate. We do not wish to alarm you on our account—we will simply be outside."

"But it is perishing cold," said Connie Wedderburn.

"I insist," I said.

Blake produced a pitiful dry cough. I ignored him.

"I tell you, it isn't needful," she said. But I would not be deflected and so she found us two old moth-eaten blankets and, shaking her head, gave us the key to the shop, then returned inside.

I took the first watch outside the side door. Blake said not a word, but went to sit in the shop lest someone try to enter by the back door.

It was too chill to sleep. I remembered how I had yearned for the cold in the headache-inducing heat of May and June in India. Gloomy thoughts of home pressed upon me. I pushed them away and other, more immediate, questions surged in their place: Woundy's intentions; O'Toole's and Jerrold's stories; Daniel Wedderburn and his anger.

Blake relieved me at around two, still wordless and gray with fatigue. I moved into the shop where the wind did not cut, and I dozed at last and for once did not dream. I heard a clock strike. It was still dark. Blake stood over me, holding a lighted candle. He was pale, haggard and feverish.

"You look ghastly," I said.

"And I slept so well," he said.

"Was I wrong?"

"No. Come, we'll visit Woundy."

"What time is it?"

"Just after five. We will get into the works before anyone else, see if we can find his papers. And then we'll plan to beard him when he arrives."

"What about the Wedderburns?"

"The coffee seller is outside."

I picked myself up, feeling the creases in my clothes and body. I had become soft. We bought coffee, which was gritty and bitter. The light beginning to illuminate the city was of a sinister hue—an odd bruised yellow as if presaging worse weather—and the biting easterly blow found its way to our necks and ears.

*Woundy's yard* was empty but for a carter in a calico smock, gaiters and a large hat unloading wooden crates from a cart pulled by four dray horses. The contrast with the clamor of the day before could not have been more marked.

"Baren't no one here," he said to us, "I'm early."

Blake took out his lock-picking tools and padded about the yard, pushing at the doors like some hopeful burglar. The one to *Woundy's Penny Atlas* was firmly locked. The one to *Woundy's Illustrated Weekly*, however, was not, and from within one could just hear the infernal rattle and hiss of the printing presses.

"They run the presses through the night?" I wondered.

"The noise will cover our entry in any event," Blake said, walking in.

Despite the chatter of the presses in the background, the newspaper's premises seemed eerily empty, as if all the people who had bustled here the day before had suddenly been spirited away. It was chill, and my breath colored the air.

"What now? Do we hide ourselves in his office?" I said.

"You think we should leap out and surprise him when he arrives?"

"I am new to this inquiry business. How should I know?"

He did not reply. Instead he walked off toward the room with the steam presses.

"Yes," I muttered, "why do we not instead simply indulge your appetite for loud machinery?"

Blake pushed open the double doors. He stopped suddenly. I was just behind him.

One press was working as if in a manic rage, plates and rollers rattling and slamming back and forth. But there was no paper upon it; the plates crashed together and drew apart, and crashed together and drew apart. No one fed the paper in, no one took it away, no one watched over the endless hiss and shuttle.

On the other press, its weight hindering the machine's relentless will to motion, was draped the horribly slashed and bloodied body of Eldred Woundy, a pool of dark blood gathering, drop by drop, at its feet.

# Part 2

## chapter 9

The picture of Eldred Woundy's vast, mottled, blubbery frame is one I will not easily forget. It lay there, propped awkwardly on the press, the suety hips and belly bursting from the top of the blood-soaked trousers, the arms dangling out over the rollers, the naked upper body; ink spattered over the face, the arms, the hands; one hideous slice through its stomach where the guts, leaking blood, spilled out, and slashes all around it. The thought came to me: *This is what Wedderburn looked like. And Blundell.* I thought of Matty—the horror that she had seen. Men do barbarous deeds in battle, and I had seen my share of them, but finding a body in such a place, so arranged, as if each wound had been made by deliberate design—I had never seen anything like this.

Blake prowled around the body, standing as close as he could without disturbing the blood accumulating at the corpse's feet, his face inches from its livid wounds. He stared at its eyes, he inhaled the air around its lips, he gazed at its fingers, traced over its face and chest, and then he touched the head, pressed upon the neck and pinched the back of the upper arm.

I gasped and expressed my dismay. "You must not!" I said.

"Don't you see, William?" he said, as earnestly as I had ever heard

him, drawing out his notebook and his steel pen. "It is Matty's description of Nat's murder made flesh. I can learn from this. I can draw conclusions about what killed him and when he was placed on the press."

"But surely he was killed by the cut through the stomach."

"By no means. That could have been done after. There were blows
to the head, see?"

"I hope for his sake it was so. But does it even matter? Our duty is
to inform the police, and Woundy's workers will arrive soon."

"All of it matters. Look, I'm sure the fingertips have been deliberately coated in ink, just as Matty described Nat's. The face is red and
congested. The body is not yet stiff, but he is fat and it is cold, so that
will have slowed down rigor mortis, and the blood has started to collect in the back and the backs of the arms. See, the skin here is purple
and when I press it, it blanches white." He shook his head. "How long
has he been here?"

"Blake! We must report this! We must tell the new police."

Blake dragged his attention from the body. "Yes. But we must also
look in his office first. See if O'Toole's ledger is there."

"Blake?"

"When will we have another chance?"

Woundy's office, among the honeycomb of small rooms next to the
presses, was not locked. It was clear that someone had already entered
it, already rifled, thoroughly and carefully, through the piles of paper
and the little gray ledgers with their neat columns of numbers, and almost certainly left with what they wanted.

"We must report this, Blake. We cannot delay any longer," I said
at last.

"There should be a copper in the Strand," he said. "I'll go back to
the body. Like as not this'll go badly for us."

"I know."

Within the hour there were five constables from Bow Street police station in the yard, holding back an anxious crowd of Woundy's employees. Inside, Woundy's most senior men had been herded up the stairs to the main office, where an inspector and a sergeant of the new police questioned each in turn. We were sitting on our own at the far end of the room. They had left us for last.

"So you found the body." This, unsmilingly, from the taller of the two, Inspector Forrester, a heavy man with salt-and-pepper hair and a carefully trained mustache which had been teased onto his cheeks. His companion, Sergeant Loin, was pale and slight with a tight mouth and sharp black eyes.

Blake nodded.

"Yesterday Mr. Woundy ordered you from the premises and your friend administered a violent beating to one of his employees and laid another out on the cobbles," said Sergeant Loin, in an equally unfriendly manner. "Today those men are both missing. You may wish to explain yourselves."

Blake said, "If they are missing, we know nothing of that. They were Woundy's nobblers, tried to knock us about. We came to ask Mr. Woundy about another matter. He mistook us for investors. When we explained the mistake and asked our questions, he lost his temper and ordered us out. I believe he had a reputation for being quick-tempered, but we would not know for sure as we had not met him before."

"The men back there say you posed as investors."

"We were mistaken for investors and delayed in correcting the mistake as we were keen to see Mr. Woundy promptly. As for the fight, Woundy's bruisers came at us with cudgels. Captain Avery was defending himself—and me, my health is not good."

"My sergeant says you're a private inquiry agent, Mr. Blake. But you were never one of us, were you?"

"I was never a copper or a Bow Street Runner, no," Blake said calmly. "But I have my license. Signed by Sir Richard Mayne."

"He has a fancy patron," said Loin dismissively, "Sir Theophilus Collinson. Loans him out to his toff friends like some doxy."

"That's enough, Loin," said Forrester. "Who is your friend?"

"I am Captain William Avery, an old associate of Mr. Blake's from India, engaged like him to look into the murder of two printers some weeks ago in Holywell Street and Seven Dials. It was about this that we came to see Mr. Woundy."

Loin looked incredulous. "I know of the Holywell Street murder. Nothing much to it. Case closed. I had no idea Mr. Blake and his friend had taken it upon themselves to stick their noses in."

"Explain your business with Woundy," said Inspector Forrester. Blake explained.

"And what brought you back here so early?" said the inspector skeptically. "Something of a coincidence, you arriving at that moment."

"We were concerned he might intend some harm to the dead man's widow. What with the violence of his bruisers and their quickness to attack us, and some further intelligence we received last night, we decided to get here early to see him and let him know that if any harm came to her we would make sure the authorities would hold him responsible."

"The authorities being us?" said the inspector.

"Yes."

"You look somewhat bedraggled for a professional visit."

"We stayed up all night keeping watch over the widow," I said, my temper fraying. "We had not had time to change. She will confirm this."

"The carter was already here when we arrived this morning," said Blake. "He will testify to that."

"He also said you took your time coming out again. Could've killed him in that time," said Loin.

"I took a moment to examine the body," said Blake patiently. "I did not think I should get the chance again. Captain Avery then went to summon help, while I made sure the body was not disturbed. Your constable will confirm that when he arrived with Avery I showed him that the body was starting to become stiff and its color was livid. He must have been dead for two hours at the very least before we got here, as any good medical man could confirm. And if we had killed him, do you not think there would be some traces of blood still upon us?"

"Fancy you know something about reckoning a man's time of death?" Forrester said.

"It's an inexact science, but yes," said Blake.

"Anything else?"

"Well, it's clear that Woundy was murdered by whoever did for Wedderburn and for Matthew Blundell, a printer murdered in his shop some six weeks ago. Don't you agree, Sergeant Loin?"

It was evident that Sergeant Loin knew no such thing. "Blundell died in a fire," he said.

"He was murdered first and laid on his press, then the place was burned. Witnesses say Wedderburn was also laid out, like Woundy, on his printing press, with his arms outstretched, chest and feet bare, and a hole in his stomach with the guts coming out. What else can one make of it?"

"It seems, Mr. Blake, that you know more about this than we do," said Forrester coldly. "Anything to add, Loin?"

Loin shook his head. "I—I did not see the bodies," he stuttered, looking most awkward.

"I suspect Sergeant Loin was not party to the murder reports," said Blake briskly. "If he reads them he will find the similarities unmistakable. You might also ask who has engaged us and why he has done so."

"I shall ask what questions I choose," snapped Forrester. Then, after a pause, "Well, who is your employer?"

"Lord Allington."

Forrester coughed incredulously. "Lord Allington, the evangelical peer? Can you confirm this?"

"I can." Blake pulled from his coat the Viscount's letter of introduction, which the inspector snatched from him.

"And his reason for employing you?"

"He believes the new police have given up on the cases. He believes there is a dangerous madman loose on the streets and no one is seeking to stop him."

Forrester looked as if he would happily have arrested Blake there and then, and Loin as if he wished he were somewhere else.

"Do you have a suspect?" said Forrester, smoothing down his mustache with his thumb and forefinger.

"I did."

"Well, who is he?"

"Eldred Woundy."

"Anything else you would like to apprise us of?"

"Yes. I do not think the stabbing killed him. He took a couple of blows to the head—to stun him, I imagine. Then I think he was suffocated. See, he is gray around the mouth. And the eyes: the pupils have spread and covered the irises. That takes place when the body is denied oxygen. I have not been able to get close to the body, but I would imagine there is bruising at the back of the neck. I reckon he was choked from behind first, then laid, perhaps as he was expiring, on the press. But there's a strange smell about the body and I don't know what it is. I am sure, though, that the stomach was cut after he was dead, when he was on the press. The ink on the hands and fingers, and the arrangement, were made then too. I think you'll find no cuts on his back. Also, I think given Lord Allington's letter and my patron's influence, you'll find it hard to detain us much longer."

They did not like us, that was clear, and if we had been less well connected I have no doubt we would have been arraigned on some charge. As it was they kept us as long as they could, they repeating their questions, we repeating our answers. At length it became clear there was nothing more to be said for the time being, and so—with an ill-tempered stipulation that we remain for the time being in London and at our present lodgings—they released us.

*Lord Allington lived* in a handsome town house on Charles Street in Mayfair, not far from my rooms at the Oriental Club. Freshly attired, we were ushered by a splendidly if soberly liveried doorman into a marble entrance hall in which gray *trompe l'œil* sculptures were painted into gray *trompe l'œil* niches. Inside, there was great activity. A deputation of ladies in black emerged through one door; several black-clad young men mounted the stairs, their arms full of piles of papers, while a footman descended with a small tray. Such was the dominance of gray and black, I felt quite ostentatious in what I had considered to be a discreetly elegant blue silk necktie and patterned waistcoat. The doorman consulted a footman, who vanished then returned with Mr. Threlfall. He loftily indicated that we should leave our coats and then ushered us into a small drawing room.

The room was sparsely, though richly, furnished. There was a marble bust, a small desk on which there was a pile of religious tracts—the uppermost being *The Road to Hell: Listen to Your Conscience*—a hard-looking settle and two spindly high-backed chairs, all pushed to the room's edges. Over the fireplace was a framed Bible text embroidered in black thread: "Go to the Ant, thou sluggard; consider her ways and be wise." It was, I concluded, the most uncomfortable expensively furnished room I had ever entered.

"Lady Agnes Bertram Vickers," said Threlfall.

Standing before the settle was a woman in a black silk dress with a high lace collar and a small waist. I recognized her: she was Lord Allington's sister; I had seen her at the Lascar hostel where she had been so disappointed at her dismissal. The first impression was of someone demure and unassuming. Her thick soft brown hair was parted in the middle and twisted loosely over her ears into a wide knot. Her eyes were a dark brown but fringed with the same thick lashes as her brother's.

"Gentlemen," she said, but her glance rested chiefly upon Blake. "I am Lord Allington's sister. I oversee his household and contribute what little I can as a female to his charitable causes. You must understand that he is very busy today and very likely will not have time to see you. He has to see representatives from the Society for the Relief of the Spitalfields Weavers, then delegates from the Short Hours movement who have come all the way from Manchester. Later, he will be dining with the Home Secretary and the Duke of Buccleuch." The imperious manner in which this was said at once dispatched any impression of diffidence or shyness.

"We have news which may affect the direction of future investigation, madam," said Blake. "We need to speak to him."

"You may speak to me. And you will address me as 'Lady Agnes' or 'My Lady.'"

"I beg your pardon, Lady Agnes," I said, "but I am not sure the details are fit for a lady's ears. Your brother did ask that you leave the room the other day when the matter was discussed."

The comment did not please her but she assented to it with ill grace, giving a small cross nod to indicate that we might sit. So we perched on the two spindly chairs and waited, and she sat still and very upright and stared at Blake's hand with its missing fingers.

"What a contrast your appearance presents from two days ago, Mr. Blake," she said.

He smiled. "My work obliges me to adopt a variety of different guises, Lady Agnes."

"But which is the real Mr. Blake, and does he know it?" There was something almost coquettish about her tone. "Tell me about yourself."

"I am a private inquiry agent. I find things, people. Avery is a former East India Company officer. We worked together in India."

There was a long, awkward silence.

"If I might, Lady Agnes," I said, "Mr. Blake has many admirable qualities, but describing himself is not his greatest strength. Sir Theophilus Collinson, however, would give you a most thorough recommendation."

She tapped her knuckles impatiently. "Might I ask in more general terms how your researches are progressing?"

"We have not yet found what we are looking for," said Blake, "if that is what you mean."

"Do you believe you will be successful?"

"Hard to say. We have made some progress."

"I will be honest, Mr. Blake," she said. "I strongly believe that my brother's pursuit of this matter is misplaced and potentially dangerous. Nor am I convinced that you are the right man to conduct this inquiry. Our work is to bring salvation to the poor and charity to the needy. That is what we do best. I fear my brother strays into territory that might bring upon him unwelcome attention, even criticism and censure. My brother is a shining star—a beacon of salvation. Nothing must be allowed to diminish his brightness. What do you say to that?" She gazed at him with a curious mixture of severity and appetite. Fatigue sent my mind into odd byways and I found myself wondering what woman other than the daughter of an earl would have so brazenly and directly stared at and addressed a man she did not know. The only other answer that presented itself was a whore. I knew I must be very tired indeed.

"My answer is that there is a murderer at large and he should be stopped."

"Surely that is the task of the new police? Besides, from what I can gather, his victims were infidels, men who had already by their own actions damned themselves."

I was taken aback by the casual ruthlessness of her words.

"We disagree, Lady Agnes," he said. "And I too will be honest. As I told your brother, I do not share your religious convictions. I do not believe anyone is damned, though life can produce its own kinds of hell."

"Indeed?" she said, closing her mouth as if someone had dropped something unpleasant into it. She rose. Threlfall opened the door for her, shooting us a disdainful look, and she swept out, he following after.

"Could you not have been just a little more tactful?" I said in a low tone, knowing all too well the answer.

"I'm not employed for my tact. And she has none."

"She is an aristocrat, and your employer's sister."

Still we waited. Despite the discomfort of the chair, I began to doze. I was roused by a sudden cacophony of children's voices proceeding from beyond the drawing room door. It took me a moment to recognize that they were giving a not-altogether-tuneful rendition of the hymn "Lo, He Comes Down."

I went into the hall. His Lordship towered over a troop of small, well-scrubbed children in gray smocks. A cluster of footmen and maids, soberly dressed secretaries, as well as Mr. Threlfall and Lady Agnes, stood on the stairs, listening. When the children had finished, His Lordship applauded, as did the rest of the audience. He knelt down to thank them and they crowded about him. It was a magical scene and everyone seemed delighted. Lord Allington rose and the children were ushered outside by their white-capped matrons.

"Captain Avery," said His Lordship, glancing apprehensively over my shoulder at Blake. Seeing him slightly more appropriately togged, his expression turned to one of relief. "I am so glad you are here. You heard our orphans? I am patron of a home for abandoned children in Norwood."

His Lordship wore a pristine white shirt beneath his waistcoat and a cream silk ascot around his neck. He looked the acme of somber elegance.

"I shall speak to the gentlemen alone, but Threlfall will take notes. Come, Threlfall," he said, and a footman strode over to escort him into the room. Lady Agnes looked at us both searchingly. Threlfall seemed hardly more pleased to be staying, his hand creeping up to his mustache, which he toyed with distractedly until His Lordship shot him a pained smile.

"Well, gentlemen," said His Lordship, his blue eyes cast heavenward, "I would be grateful if you would tell me what you have discovered."

Blake sketched out our various encounters, disclosed the matter of Nat Wedderburn and Blundell's occupations, but painted a poignant picture of Wedderburn's family. He recounted the meeting with Woundy but gave a somewhat abridged description of my fisticuffs,

then went on to what O'Toole had told us of Woundy's history. He
omitted Daniel Wedderburn's violent outbursts, our visit to the Chartist meeting and his belief that Matty Horner had been less than honest, and ended with our discovery of Woundy's body and interview
with the new police, making light of their all-too-palpable dislike of us.

His Lordship's angelic brow puckered anxiously. He began to pace.

"It is most unfortunate that you were the first to discover Mr.
Woundy's corpse. There is something I should tell you. Some months
ago I met this Mr. Eldred Woundy. He introduced himself as a self-
made man of some substance who had voiced a desire to make a sizable
donation to several charities, and perhaps to serve on several charitable boards. We do not want to attract the wrong kind of attention.
This is most awkward. I suppose I shall have to disclose this to the
new police."

I could almost hear Blake grinding his teeth. "Can you tell us anything about your meeting with Mr. Woundy?" he said.

"He came to the Lords to meet with me. I take a number of such
meetings from time to time, to encourage donations and enlistment to
our causes. I spoke to him for perhaps ten or fifteen minutes. He
seemed a forceful, if somewhat coarse, man. He said he had done well
for himself and wished to do something for the London poor to allevi-
ate their needs and salve their souls."

"If I may speak for my colleague," I said, "I believe Mr. Blake thinks
that the fact that we were the first to find Eldred Woundy's body has
given us an advantage. We know much more about the murders now
and their perpetrator."

Lord Allington continued to pace. "There is something terrible in
the thought of advantage accruing from the discovery of a poor murdered soul," he said, "though I take your meaning. You are certain then
that all three men were killed by the same person or persons?"

Blake nodded.

"Captain Avery, you agree with him?"

"As I have said before, I am no expert, but I feel certain that this is the case."

"If I may, Your Lordship," Blake said, so quietly that I suspected he was twitching with irritation, "the question is, do you wish us to proceed? As your sister has informed us, in the eyes of your church these men had by their own actions already damned themselves."

Allington's pale blue eyes grew round. "Mr. Blake, I may abhor what these men did, but their untimely ends deserve as much investigation as a good man's. I engaged you to carry this thing through to its conclusion. Besides, you may have the advantage over the police, for you are further along than they."

Then, a strange thing happened. He suddenly looked utterly dejected, as if something had knocked the air out of him, and he seemed to almost forget we were there.

"We could turn what we know over to the police," I said. Viscount Allington stared at the floor and did not reply. Mr. Threlfall looked alarmed. "Your Lordship?" I ventured.

"What? Oh yes, I trust you will do that anyway." There was an awkward silence.

"Sir?" I said. His Lordship was startled and distracted.

"What? Yes, quite well, thank you." He sat down on the settle and clasped his hands together so tightly the veins stood out. Threlfall bit his lip and looked desperately at the door but did nothing. Allington wrested his attention back to us, but it was an effort to do so.

"Gentlemen, you must persevere. I hope the police will now act, but whatever happens we must pursue this. Such evil cannot be left at large." He took a deep breath. "Are you of a mind on how you might continue?"

"Yes."

"And?"

"The murderer might have been blackmailed by these men, or had an association with them and did not wish it to emerge." Blake's brusqueness made me wince. "The ways in which the bodies were laid out, however, suggest to me that their deaths might have been intended both as some kind of punishment and also as a warning."

"For what?"

"I do not know yet," said Blake.

"Mr. Blake, forgive me, I do not wish to interfere in your inquiries, but is it possible that the Chartists might be in some way responsible?"

Blake scratched his ear.

"Do you have any reason for thinking that, Your Lordship?" I said.

"Nothing I can say with any certainty."

"Something," said Blake.

"No, no," he said, "I should not have spoken. I must confess that I feel almost defeated in the face of such darkness. I have seen many instances of cruelty, ignorance and want, and I rejoice in meeting these head-on and fighting them. We are making progress. We should pass the new factory bill in the next parliament and I shall be proud to put my name to it. I believe it will both help the poor and discourage the Chartists from their foolish ideas. But there are certain kinds of darkness, of god-lessness, that leave me close to despair. When my thoughts should be with the victims and their families I find myself thinking of the perpe-trator. One who murders has moved so far from God, must be so lost, in so dark and terrible a place. It is a thought I can hardly bear."

Threlfall had long since stopped writing and hovered uneasily be-hind His Lordship, frantically smoothing his mustache.

"Captain Avery," His Lordship said, "would you join me in prayer? Threlfall?" He knelt down.

I could hardly say no, though my old wound made the act of kneeling somewhat painful. Threlfall went down on his knees too. I reflected that he must have to do this several times a day and felt almost sorry for him. Blake remained seated and looked pointedly out the window.

His Lordship clasped his hands together and shut his eyes tightly.

"Lord, show us a way out of the darkness. Give us light in the darkest places. Deliver us from our sins and our fears." He stopped. I waited. I was wretchedly grateful when he at last said, "Amen."

"You know," Lord Allington said softly, "from time to time I attend public hangings. They are horrible affairs. I hate them, everything about them, but I feel an obligation to attend. The crowds crow with pleasure. I look at those about to die and I think how terrible it must be to be so lost from God. I think of Christ at the end bearing the derision of the crowd—I know it is almost a sin to think of the two in the same breath, but I find myself praying that somewhere in themselves the condemned can find a way to ask the Father for some tiny drop of forgiveness. I long for it, I look for it. Their remorse. God's mercy. But I fear their souls are irredeemably damned. Then I find myself having to examine my own conscience, asking myself, do I go for impure reasons? Is my conscience in some way falsely salved by the apparent contrast of my piety with their evil?"

He seemed to drift off into some reverie of his own. Then, "What do you say, Mr. Blake, who believes in nothing?" His voice was bitter.

"I cannot answer for you, Your Lordship," Blake said.

"What can you know of the scrutiny and agony of the soul?" said Lord Allington.

There was another silence. Mr. Threlfall looked around anxiously for some way out, but inspiration evaded him.

"I think it best if we depart, Mr. Threlfall," I said. "If we are needed

His Lordship can send a message to the Oriental, or to Mr. Blake's premises. You have his card."

In the hallway Lady Agnes waylaid Blake. Without preamble she took hold of his hand and pressed a paper into his palm. "Even the most determined impenitent may be saved," she said, staring into his eyes. He took it, looking back at her, and shook his head.

*The blowy chill* of Charles Street was a relief. Blake briefly inspected the religious tract Lady Agnes had given him—for that was what it was— and dropped it into the gutter. I, meanwhile, tried to exorcize that last troubling image of Lord Allington.

"Was Woundy truly your main suspect? I thought you doubted O'Toole. And what of Daniel Wedderburn? Should you not have mentioned his animus against his father to the police?"

"I cannot give names to the coppers until I am sure," said Blake.

"But what if it were Daniel and he were to kill again?" I persisted.

"It is still just a supposition—we have no proof."

I plunged my hands into my pockets. At the bottom of one I found a twist of paper. It was the scrap that Matty Horner had given me the day before. I unfolded it. The black script was cramped but perfectly legible: "The LORD bless thee, and keep thee; the LORD make his face shine upon thee, and be gracious unto thee; the LORD lift up his countenance upon thee, and give thee peace."

I handed it to Blake. He glanced at it, then pulled something from his own pockets.

"What's this?" he said, and handed me a bunch of leafless twigs.

"Where are they from?"

"They were laid about the press and round Woundy's body. Do you know the tree?"

I had not noticed them at all. I rolled the twigs about in my hands. The bark was a creamy gray and knobbly to the touch. It was too early for buds, so I peeled back the bark and scratched into the soft pith underneath.

"I should say it was elder."

He thought for a moment. "Are there not stories about elder? Country stories?"

"When I was a child I was told the fairies made flutes from it, and it is good luck to have one by the doorway, it wards off the devil."

"Anything else? A Bible story perhaps?"

"Not that I can recall." I held out the twigs to him and he slipped them back into his pocket. We walked on in silence to Berkeley Square, I dreading Blake's verdict on Allington and at the same time impatient for it. It was not forthcoming. "On the matter of elder," I said at last, "it occurs to me that my nurse used to say Judas hanged himself on an elder tree. Why did you not mention the twigs—and the other details—to His Lordship?"

"I told you, I am not ready to say everything that's in my head. I need to have more than suspicions. Clients often lose heart if the facts become too complicated or unpleasant. Given Lord Allington's mood, I would rather keep things simple."

I had to admit this was not unwise counsel.

"Where are we going now?"

"To find Woundy's tailshop, 26 Charlotte Street."

"Miss Tess Thrashington? Do you think that wise?"

Blake spat into the gutter, somehow managing to imbue his expectoration with disdain. "And I thought India had all but stamped the prudishness out of you."

"What will His Lordship say?"

"Does His Lordship have any notions of who might have murdered

Eldred Woundy? And can you suggest another place likely to yield the kind of secrets that might get a man killed?"

"No," I answered sheepishly. "Are we certain it truly belonged to Woundy?"

"His publications advertised it. And if he did have an interest in it, better we get there before they've had time to scarper or come up with a story."

He set off, his limping gait reminding me of my own uneven deportment. We hobbled together past the elegant curve of Regent Street's fine shops, then along the congested cacophony of Oxford Street—my head ringing, my senses once again overwhelmed. At the end of that busy thoroughfare, the road divided into a dozen dark and smelly alleys yielding glimpses of a grimmer, more dangerous London, the famous St. Giles Rookery. We turned left, skirting around it, threading our way up through a web of quieter lanes until we arrived at Charlotte Street, a comfortable-enough enclave of plain-fronted brick houses dating from the last century, with a coffeehouse on a corner. Number 26 did not draw attention to itself. A set of railings ran close to the yellow-brown brick, a pair of steps setting it back from the road. The windows were heavily curtained and hung with thick lace, the front door was painted black and there was a discreet brass plaque with the legend "26" upon it. Blake gave a double rap on the lion-faced knocker. When there was no response he rapped again more loudly. A large, well-turned-out doorman stuck his head round the door.

"Be off with you," he said combatively.

"We need to come in." Blake was insistent.

"By appointment and introduction only."

"We've information for Madam. She needs to hear it. It concerns her partner. We've been sent. It's urgent and if you don't let us in she's sure to be angry. All kinds of consequences."

The doorman hesitated.

"Your funeral," said Blake.

"I'll ask her. Round the back. Five knocks."

The back of 26 Charlotte Street was not nearly as salubrious as the front. We rapped our five raps and the footman put his head round the door with a gruff, "Who sent you?"

Blake told him Eldred Woundy. He denied having heard the name. Blake told him he should ask Madam. The door was shut, then after a few minutes he appeared again and told us to follow. The servants' quarters were as dingy as one might have expected, but when we crossed into a long hall the furnishings became luxurious and fashionable: polished floors, thick rugs, shining brass door handles, damask wallpapers. From beyond one door came a series of alarming cries. From another two pretty young women emerged in almost translucent peignoirs. They gave us a bored look and took to the stairs. Blake was all set to follow them when a woman in a midnight-blue silk dress appeared in the hall.

"Not there. In here," she said shortly, pointing a finger at us and then redirecting it sharply toward a door on our left. "For all I know you're some cheap journalist looking for a tall tale. If that's it, then it'll be the worse for you." And she disappeared.

We followed her in. It was a charming room. There was a lively fire in the grate, pretty sprigged wallpaper, a yellow settle upon which she sat, two small tables covered in fine lace cloths, two wooden chairs and a daybed upholstered in velvet. She picked up a box from one of the tables and took from it a cigar which she proceeded to light with a phosphorous match. I had never seen a woman smoke.

"I know you," she said, pointing at Blake as she took a long draw. At first sight she might have seemed a prime example of respectable matronhood. Her dress was of the best embroidered silk, and around the neck was pinned a piece of very fine lace. Its artful arrangement, however, only drew attention to the large expanse of generous bosom displayed beneath. Her face was heavily powdered and rouged, and her lips were painted.

"You might," said Blake. "I've been around."

"I mean, one of my gentlemen had need of you."

"It's possible, Miss . . ."

"You can call me the Governess." She exhaled and smiled, the red curve of her lips looking almost devilish. "Now, what do you fancy, a light birching?" She called out and a statuesque girl with shining black skin and a short fuzz of black hair, dressed only in a petticoat, came in. "Ebony Kate can do something in the flogging line for your pretty young friend." Her eyes flickered over me and I prayed to God I was not blushing. "If you have the money, I can have you whipped, fusti-gated, scourged, needle-pricked, half hanged, furze-brushed, stinging-nettled, currycombed, phlebotomized and tortured to your heart's delight. Or perhaps you'd like to see the thrashing machine?"

"Oh no, madam, we are not here for that," I protested.

"Really? Never tried it, I'll bet. It's remarkable what deep desires are dredged up if you are willing to dig deep enough. But if you'd rather"—she yawned—"we can provide something more in the milk-and-water line."

Blake shook his head. He said he had news to trade for the answer to a question, and warned she would not like the news, though she would be glad to know it. At once her amusement was extinguished. She dismissed the girl and became stony.

"Don't bargain with me, mister," she said.

"You should know that Eldred Woundy—" he began.

"Never heard of him," she said.

". . . is dead. Captain Avery here and I found his body early this morning. On his press. He had been murdered. It will be everywhere by tomorrow."

She sat quite still and struggled to show nothing, but she took a great breath and with her fingers she squeezed her cigar in half. The two pieces fell onto the carpet where the lit end smoldered until I stamped upon it.

"Why would you come to me with this?" she said, her jaw clenched.

Blake said that we were looking into the murders of two of Woundy's printing associates and that Renton O'Toole had been telling anyone who would listen of Woundy's association with the place.

"Renton O'Toole!" she said scornfully. "That bastard. Do not say that you listened to him! I tell you, I own this place. Eldred Woundy had nothing to do with it."

Blake answered that the coppers would be coming sooner or later, whether it was true or not.

"And what do you expect in return for tipping me the wink? A backhander? A free tumble? They'll never shut me down. My clients are too important. You'd be amazed who comes here."

"You think they'll stick by you if you're tied to a gruesome murder that's reported in every paper in the land? Who might have had it in for Woundy?"

"Anyone who had dealings with him." She managed a hard laugh.

"Anyone he blackmailed for coming here?"

She shook her head. "Don't try me. We never did that."

"Whoever did for him has killed two other men in the same way, printers who worked for him in the bawdy-and-blackmail line. Nat Wedderburn and Matthew Blundell, they were called. They printed advertisements for this place."

"Didn't know them."

"Butchered on their presses. Killer has a taste for it, I'd say. Just like your clients."

"Look. Most of my clients wouldn't hurt a fly. They come here for punishment."

"And the others? Come on! The coppers will give it to you all right—they'll be scouring your customers. Your business will be dead in a week, and if whoever did it does come through here, you may be next."

She moved the ends of her painted lips upward. I would not have gone so far as to call it a smile.

"Don't try and frighten me," she said. "I'm not giving up my customers' names. Won't do it. Anyway, we never put the moves on them. We live on returning custom, we'd be out of business in a moment. I know Eldred got up to some things in his other lines, but we didn't play that one here. I swear it."

"Then you're going to have to come up with something else for me."

"I don't know about the rest, he kept it all apart. You're trying my patience."

He gazed at her.

"Did they hurt him?" she said.

Blake nodded.

"Any idea who did it?" She rubbed at her eye.

He shook his head. "His bruisers have gone missing. You heard from either of them?"

She shook her head. "Didn't know much about them. Common run of nobblers, no better or worse than the rest."

"They been with him long?"

"Not long. He'd had a nobbler from time to time in the past—his line of business, sometimes it was useful to look well protected. But having two all the time was new. Didn't make nothing of it though, just said the paper brought more attention and you couldn't be too careful. Never gave the impression of being fearful, but then he wasn't the kind to show it, and these last months he was so taken up with the paper."

"Did he bring his bruisers here?"

"Sometimes, not always."

"And he slept here?"

"He had a room here. But often he slept at the paper."

"Can we see it?"

"You'll find nothing."

"Nevertheless."

She took us up the stairs and along a corridor, lavishly decorated with more fine wallpaper and a new carpet. One door was open and as we passed I glimpsed a collection of what I could only describe as instruments of torture, mounted on the walls like trophies: whips, flays, rapiers, something resembling thumbscrews, various cuffs and tethers, and two metal helmets that looked designed to pinch the head or impede the breathing.

"Ah, my sweet innocent, you are shocked," said the Governess. She opened a door farther along. An empty room. By which I mean a room quite empty of all character: richly decorated in velvet swags, a large feather bed with a silk bedspread, elegant tables, but nothing that volunteered that it belonged to anyone. One suit in the wardrobe with nothing in the pockets. No books, no papers. Nothing.

"Do you imagine he would have left anything here that might have been found by one of my clients or even one of my girls?" she said scornfully. "He would never have been so careless. Anyway, he was hardly here after the paper took off. This was small fry."

"Didn't have a taste for your skills?"

"He tried it once or twice but his heart wasn't in it. What got him going was making his way. That was his first love. But I'll shed a tear for him. We were fond of each other. He was fair with me. Good to me even." She dabbed at her eye. "Now," she said, recovering herself, "you'd better go or I'll have my bruisers on to you. And we don't want that."

Blake paused a moment as if deciding how far he might press her.

"My card, madam. You send to me if you hear anything. You know I'm discreet."

She glanced at it, her sangfroid quite returned. "Mr. Blake—yes, I recall now. I hope you find them, and I hope they hang. If I think of something I'll send to you. If I'm still here."

# chapter 10

"Good day to you, Mr. Kravitz," Blake said to the old clothes seller.

"Is it though?" said the old man. He was puffing on his thin pipe and dressed in so many layers that one wondered if he would be able to prize himself out of his chair.

"Seen Matty Horner today?"

"She was out early. She went home."

"Tell me where her lodgings are. We need to speak to her."

"Do you." Abraham Kravitz gave a long suck on his pipe and blew out a thin twist of smoke that snaked into the air. "Don't trust you, Mr. Blake, or your friend. Something tells me your meddling ain't going to do her no good, nor the Wedderburns neither."

"You care so much for her," I said, "yet you let her go barefoot through the streets."

He had the grace to look abashed then.

"I need to speak to her today, old man," said Blake, his voice cold. "If I don't, believe me, it will go hard for her and you'll be the cause."

"Why don't you ask the Christian boy?" Kravitz said sarcastically, waving over our shoulders.

The schoolmaster Dearlove was walking past, hands and wrists folded under his arms against the cold, head bowed, his bulky comforter wrapped clumsily around his neck and shoulders. Blake had already stopped him.

"It relates to the murders," he was saying.

"Why, yes," said Dearlove, startled. "I know where it is. Hard to find though. I suppose I could lead you there. But I must be quick, I have preparations to make, a deputation including Lord Allington and his sister are coming to inspect the school in a few hours."

At the Drury Lane end of Holywell Street Dearlove stopped, with a sense of dutiful laboriousness rather than ease, to ask an old flower seller how she did; on the corner of Wych Street, he called to a group of running boys that he had not seen them at school in a while. Then, without warning, a stout man barged into Blake, who in turn stumbled into me. The man's face was a mask of rage. He grabbed Blake's arm, bared his teeth and hissed into his face, "Stay out of the street. You're not wanted here. You hang around, we'll finish you. Understand?"

Unperturbed, Blake extricated himself from the man's grasp, and drew me after.

"You're a familiar face round here, Mr. Dearlove," he said.

"I have been here awhile now," the other said, quite oblivious to the scene that had just been enacted, "they know I am sincere."

"What are we to make of that?" I muttered.

"Someone who thinks it's bad for business. Someone with a hand in the murders, perhaps," Blake replied.

"You seem remarkably unconcerned."

"I'd say we'll find out soon enough."


*Off Drury Lane* we passed into another labyrinth of grim passages and alleyways as poor and broken down as anything I had seen before. I knew that I should never be able to navigate them on my own. At last Dearlove pointed us into a bleak dead end of flat-fronted tenements calling itself Vinegar Yard.

"It is the tenth house along. In the cellar," he said. "I must be on my way." He marched away, a spindly figure, his thin jacket flying up in the wind and his hands still clasped under his arms against the cold.

A gutter ran down the middle of the alley and overflowed with puddles of filthy water, the cold allaying the filthy smells. To one side of the front doors were stands of steps down to cellars crudely gouged out of the ground. We descended. It was as dank as anything one could imagine, the door at the bottom little more than a few slabs of rotten timber. On this Blake knocked.

"Who is it?"

"Matty, it's Mr. Blake and Captain Avery. Will you let us in?"

"Could it not wait? I'll be in Holywell Street soon. I have been watching, honest."

"It cannot wait."

"I'm . . . I'm not decent."

"Then we will wait. Get yourself ready."

At last there was a shifting of a bolt and a pulling and a pushing, and the door opened.

Matty Horner stood there, her hair falling about her shoulders, wearing her old gray dress, a blanket about her. She looked startled and not altogether pleased to see us.

"May we come in?"

She nodded diffidently.

Behind the door the cellar was divided in two by a flimsy partition. Matty led us into a small dark space, longer than it was wide, reeking of fetid damp. Yellowing plaster peeled from the ceiling and walls; most had long since come away, exposing the old dank brick. The floor was uneven stone flags, though she had contrived a scrap of blanket to cover a little of it. At the back, the bottom half of a window, two of its broken panes stuffed with rags, let in a little light. To the side a recess had been dug out of the wall to make a fireplace, next to which there were a few pieces of coal. Two old produce boxes, such as I had seen at Covent Garden, were upturned. One had a candle upon it and a solitary pansy in a small jar filled with water, the one pretty thing in the room, and a well-thumbed copy of a periodical, *Master Humphrey's Clock*.

"Abe gives them to me sometimes," she said, seeing my gaze rest upon it. "It's got *The Old Curiosity Shop* in it. It's the story about Little Nell, the pauper girl."

On the floor was the seat of a chair without its back that had been dragged in from the street, and a little farther away a moth-eaten mattress and a box filled with straw. In a corner a tin pail and an old china jug. Some hooks had been screwed into the brick and upon these were hung a few pieces of clothing, including Matty's old bonnet. A makeshift shelf had been set up on a wall for storing food.

I did not know what to say.

"It is not much, I know, but at least we're not in a lodging house or the spike—the workhouse," she said, "and that's something. I do not have much to report, Mr. Blake," she went on hurriedly. "I heard that Daniel left and you stood guard—"

"Where is Pen?" said Blake.

"He's out," she said. She rubbed her nose and looked away. "I was meaning to talk to you about him."

Blake shook his head. "There's been another murder, Matty."

She slipped onto one of the old boxes, aghast. "Not in the street? I was there this morning. I didn't see anything."

"Not in the street. The fat man, Eldred Woundy. We found him this morning, spread out over his press, just like you described Nat, just like Jesus. I need to ask you again about Nat."

"Blake," I said, "not this again."

"I need you to describe it once more so I can compare them, so I can be quite sure—"

"That they was killed by the same person," she said.

"Yes."

She took a deep breath as if to steady herself.

"Blake," I said, "can this not wait?"

"It's dark in here," he said, ignoring me. "Let's light the candle." He brought out a phosphorous match and lit the poor candle stub. It seemed surprisingly inconsiderate of him to use it up by daylight.

He led her through her description, once again watching her intently, scrutinizing every expression, every fidget, every shift of the voice, but he was gentler than he had been the first time. She rehearsed it all again, her voice low, her eyes downcast, and I marveled at the vividness of her memory, and wished she might have exercised it in more benign circumstances.

"Eldred Woundy was just as you described him," said Blake. "Your memory is very, very good. So I need to ask you, Matty, can you think of any other small detail you might have forgotten to tell us before?"

Matty shook her head. "I told you everything I remember, truly."

"You see," said Blake, "the other victims each had something different, something extra when they were killed. The first man—his name was Blundell, Matty—he was killed in just the same way, but he had red paint thrown over his hair. Woundy, he had these twigs scattered all about him." Blake drew the twigs out of his pocket and began to twirl them between his fingers.

"Captain Avery says they come from the elder tree. Does that make you think of anything, remind you of anything? Is there anything you can think of now?"

She scratched her nose and shook her head. But she could not pull her gaze from his.

"I got to thinking about these murders, Matty, these terrible deaths. And I started to think about betrayal."

Her eyes never moved from his.

"You're smartish, Matty, you've had some education. You write a good hand. I'm sure you read well too. Do you remember who the greatest betrayer is in the Bible?"

She did not answer.

"It is Judas, isn't it? There are lots of stories about Judas. Not the ones in the Bible, but other stories. I knew an old woman who used to tell me those kinds of stories, as if Jesus had lived in her village and Judas had been a neighbor that had gone to the bad. She told me that when Judas hanged himself, his stomach burst open so his soul could escape his body and descend to hell. It could not come out through his mouth because his mouth had kissed Jesus and so it was too pure."

Matty's hands pressed hard on her knees.

"The first victim, Blundell, had red paint splashed all over his hair. I saw a book of Bible stories once with pictures and Judas had red hair. Do you remember that, William? The old stories say he had red hair."

"I think I remember something about it."

"Eldred Woundy had piles of twigs cast about him. William says they're elder. In the stories elder's the tree Judas hanged himself on. Is there anything else that might have been left around Nat?"

She shook her head.

He sighed. "Tell me, Matty, do you recall your Bible? What else did Judas do? What did he betray Jesus for? Do you remember?"

Matty hung her head and whispered, "Thirty pieces of silver." There was a silence.

Slowly Matty dragged herself up and took herself over to the wall by the shelf. She prized out one brick, then a second, then a third. She slipped her hand into the space behind and drew out first a small box and then a dirty knotted bundle. Not meeting our eyes, she placed both upon the upturned crate. In the box was a pretty hairbrush and comb, several metal tools that looked like pens, a small ragged doll and a few pieces of metal type, an "x" and an "m": a pitifully poor collection of her prized possessions. Then she untied the bundle. Within there was a pile of silver coins.

"Thirty half crowns," she said, tonelessly.

"Matty!" I said. "What have you done? You could be transported for less. Much less."

"I know it," she said, her voice dull, her head bowed. "I needed it. I'm sure it wasn't Nat's. No one asked after it." Her voice became thicker with every word, whether with anger or tears I could not say. "I haven't spent none—any—of it."

For a long moment no one spoke. Blake said, "Where is Pen, Matty?"

"I told you. He's out."

"He hasn't been here for a while. There's barely enough food for one. One dress on the hook. One mattress slept on. It's plain you're on your own."

"I was going to tell you, I was. I just thought you wouldn't listen."

"Tell me now," said Blake.

"Pen was caught by the blue bastards the day before Nat died. They charged him with larceny. He's going to be transported. He's twelve."

"What'd he do?"

"He took a penny tart from a shop, Taylor's in Wych Street, and a finny—five pounds—too, though he swears he didn't. Look, I know what thieving means. It's near as bad as murder to the law. But the thing is, no matter how hard I worked, crossing-sweeping, walking to Hackney for winter cress, running errands, I couldn't bring in enough to feed him and me—he was always hungry. That was how he started."

"It is not his first time then," I said, the disapproval seeping into my voice.

"No."

"Go on, Matty," said Blake, as kindly as he had ever spoken to her. Now the words began to tumble out.

"My pa died and left us nothing. We were on the street. No one to help us, nowhere to go. I was thirteen, Pen was nine. Parish overseer came to take us to the spike. We ran away, we knew it would be the end of us. We'd be separated and we'd never get out. We slept in a doorway. We was arrested that first night for vagrancy. Just for sleeping in the street for lack of anywhere else. Three days in Tothill prison. Pen didn't mind: there was food and shelter at least. When we came out, well, it's a different world on the street. No God, no book learning, but hunger and recklessness. I didn't want to be part of it, but I am. I thieved and he did too. It was that or the spike. We stayed in lodging houses, sometimes thirty bodies to a room, sometimes on the hard floor, payment in advance. You don't want to know the things I was made to do, the things I did, what I saw. I don't like to think of it now. And not for riches, just to put a little bit of food in our mouths, and a shelter over our heads, because no one would help us."

I looked away, dismayed.

"What?" she said with great bitterness. "You are shocked, Captain Avery."

I shook my head.

"But I kept us out of the spike, and I got us out of the lodging houses. I saved a tiny bit of stock money and bought cress and fruit. Every day I must decide if it's worth walking the six miles to Hackney and back where I can buy them cheaper than Farringdon market. I'll make more, but the walk'll take it out of me. I got us this place. I know it's nothing to you, but to me it's a step up.

"The whores up Holywell Street, some of them's been kind to Pen and me. Bought us food when we was hungry. They say I'd be better off joining them, making a living on my back. But I'd rather thieve. Not every girl of my class thinks nothing of selling herself." She looked at me with a face both furious and pleading. I could not meet her eyes.

"So you stopped thieving," Blake said.

"Till now," she said. "Yeah, I stopped and it was for a reason that's no reason. I keep holding on to this idea that sometime I'm going to get my chance, and I must be ready for it. So I tried to keep us both straight. But Pen, he came by some bad habits on the way. I sent him to the ragged school, but it was only a few hours a day and the rest he ran wild. I don't know why I keep trying. I know in my heart that chance ain't coming, not really. Not now."

I thought she might cry. But she did not. She sat with her hands clenched in her lap.

"I have tried to get better work. Pa showed me compositing, but the men, they won't try me out. I'm clever. They know I'm honest—well, honest enough. But it doan—it doesn't—do me any good. No one will give me that chance because I'm a girl, and work's hard enough for men to come by. For the good jobs women come by, I'm not presentable. I got nothing decent to wear and I carn hardly keep clean. Not in here."

Blake listened, his eyes in shadow.

"This isn't what I thought would become of me, what I imagined for mesself. When Pa was alive and we were clean and there was enough to eat, I had such plans. He said there wasn't nothing—anything—I couldn't do. I thought I'd be a printer like him, or maybe even a teacher, or if I couldn't I'd work in a shop. He taught hisself Latin, my pa. But sickness and debt did for him and then us."

She pulled her hair back from her face and rubbed her eyes. "Must seem strange to you, a poor coster girl wanting such things."

"No," said Blake.

"It was all for nothing anyway, cos Pen is to be transported. Every day I see printers on Holywell Street selling their dirty books, salting away their money, what'd go to prison if they was taken, but the coppers doan care to look. How can that be fair?"

"It isn't fair," said Blake quietly.

"So I've thieved again, and taken far more than Pen ever did. And from a dead man. Mr. Blake, you do what you must do." It was as if all hope had been stripped from her. A part of me wanted to give her words of comfort, and yet I could not.

"Tell me how the coins looked when you found them," said Blake.

She glanced at him, hopeful.

"They were in three piles to the left of Nat's body, on the bed of the press. The blood was everywhere but it didn't touch them. I was sure they weren't Nat's. I never saw money like that round his. I thought I could use it to get Pen out of jail. Or maybe after, we could go to a small town, find somewhere cheap to stay and I could get mesself presentable and find decent employment. When he was taken, I couldn't find anyone to help. Even Abraham'd lost patience with him. I went to see the coppers but they laughed at me. So I hid the coins in the backyard and came and got them later. No one asked after them."

"How did you plan to use the money to get Pen out?"

"There was a man that Nat and Connie used to know. A Member of Parliament who used to be a lawyer. Nat said he helped the poor. I thought I could ask him for help, and I could offer him the money. But it was hard to ask Connie about him when she was in such a state. So the days passed and I did nothing. Then you came. I knew you wouldn't think well of me stealing, but I thought if I showed you I could help you, I could be useful, with looking out and such, you might help us. Everyone says you're a clever man, Mr. Blake. And you know people. You're working for that lord."

"Tell me more about Nat and Connie's friend."

"They knew him from years back, he's respectable now. I was going to buy fine paper, write a good letter. Go to his house."

"And where is Pen?" I asked.

"Coldbath Fields. There's been cholera at Millbank prison, so they got some of them in Coldbath. It's close-ish at least. And cos he's going away, they're letting me see him once a week. I am going day after tomorrow."

"How long until he's shipped?"

"They won't say for certain. A week. Two. He swears he didn't do it. Not this time. Says the grocer swore an oath against him to get him transported on purpose."

"Do you think that's true?"

She shrugged wearily. "He swears it's true. But I dunno what to believe when it comes to Pen. So, you going to take me in?"

"No. You can keep the money," Blake said, Matty's hands flying to her mouth, "for the moment. But I advise you not to tell anyone else about it and not to spend it. It's known that you found Nat's body. Whoever killed him may have heard."

I had not thought of this and, it was evident, neither had Matty.

"Too late to worry now," said Blake. "But take care. Watch out for yourself." He took two shillings from his pocket and put them on the table.

"This will buy you dinner, a new candle and something to take Pen when you see him. I never make promises if I can't be sure of keeping them, so I will tell you, I don't know if I can do anything for Pen. But there are some people we might ask to help. What I want from you is the name of the Honorable Member."

Matty let out a great ragged breath. Her eyes threatened to tear up. "He's called John Heffernan. I know he lives in Chelsea, by the river, Cheyne something. They talked about him a few weeks before Nat died. I'd had a long day and Nat had let me in the shop. They knew him from when he had lived near them, Islington way. He's Irish, from a good family, with land. Nat said he still worked for the poor, despite being in Parliament, but Connie got angry and said he'd left his old friends behind. I remember it because it was the night he and Daniel almost came to blows."

"To blows?"

She gulped, as though she had made a mistake. "I didn't mean—"

"Matty, I need you to tell me what they argued about. I can't work this out if you don't help me."

"Politics," she said. "It was always politics."

"The Chartists?"

"Daniel was all fired up about the Chartists," she said at last. "He said with the vote poor men would become masters of their own fate, not like now, when the workers starve and the masters grow fat. Said he was going to take the pledge—not to drink, I mean, and to give up tobacco. He said what Nat did—the books—was shameful and dirty and a sin before God. The vote was worth fighting for and he wanted to be worthy of it. Such talk made Nat furious. He said Daniel should leave the Chartists well alone.

"There was nothing to be gained by it. He said the meetings were full of informers and Daniel would end up in prison and no one would hire him. Daniel said he wouldn't work for Nat no more. That he was a coward and a man of no principles. Connie begged them both to stop, told them off, but Daniel walked out and didn't come back for three days."

Blake stood. "We'll leave now, Matty. But we will be back."

"Will you come with me to see Pen? I'm going the day after tomorrow at two o'clock."

"I can't," he said.

She looked startled and disappointed.

"But," he said, "I will do what I can."

"I will come." I spoke before I had thought. I did not know why I had offered.

"Thank you, Captain," she murmured awkwardly.

Blake took her hand in farewell. I could not. But I found myself looking at her wrists and thinking how fragile and thin they were.

"I will see you the day after tomorrow, Miss Horner," I said.


"*I'm hungry,*" he said. "You coming?"

I followed him up St. Martin's Lane, over Charing Cross Road and across the pigeon-filled seediness of Leicester Square, where a small man with thick, curling brown hair in a greatcoat swept past us, going south at a tremendous pace. He gave the impression of great purpose, and marched so quickly his coattails appeared to be chasing after him.

A few moments later Blake muttered, "That was your Mr. Dickens."

"That was *Charles Dickens?*" I turned on my heel, but he had long since disappeared amid the pigeons and the shooting galleries. "Why did you not say before?"

"See him all over town, always at a rattling pace. Not a man who wants to be stopped."

We arrived in a place called Old Compton Street. Here between the emporiums selling books, quack medicines and old curiosities, there were a number of shops with foreign signs. One called itself a "Boucherie Charcuterie"; the one next to it was a "Librairie/Imprimerie," and next to that was a "Tabac." Blake halted at an odd little place, with a sign bearing the legend "Dubourg," and beneath it, "table d'hôte." I hesitated.

"A French dining room?" I said doubtfully.

"The hero of Doora unnerved by a French restaurant. William, the food is good and I am hungry." And he went in. Scraping as much of the London mud off my trousers as I could, I followed.

It was crammed with small tables, was stuffy and warm and smelled of garlic and butter. A man rose from a table and swooped down on Blake, taking him by the shoulders and kissing him on both cheeks. Blake submitted to this with a kind of dumb acceptance. Then the man cried, so the whole place could hear, "*Comment ça va? Eh bien, ça fait bien longtemps! Je vous attends toujours au Reform Cloob!*"

I had had a little French instruction as a boy, but almost none of it had stuck. It was the man's getup, however, that really arrested my attention. He wore a loose jacket of purple velvet with cuffs of lavender silk, loose trousers with a purple stripe down the seams, and a soft velvet hat perched on the side of his head. He had a prominent nose, a small, sculpted, almost feminine mouth, and his long dark hair grew down from his sideburns to form a neat beard under his chin.

His usual reserve quite intact, Blake replied in French, and I smiled and waited. This, I saw, would always be my fate with Blake, to be the one standing politely by while he prattled on in some unintelligible tongue. The man now enveloped my hands in both of his, shaking them vigorously. His hands and wrists, I saw, were covered in little scars.

"*Enchanté!*" he said. His smile spread across his whole face and he peered into my eyes as if to emphasize that he truly was enchanted.

"It is very good to meet an old friend of Monsieur Bleck. He like to be mysterious, *non?*"

I nodded, carried by his enthusiasm.

"Avery, this is Alexis Soyer," said Blake, somewhat overwhelmed by Soyer's high spirits, I thought. "He is the chef at the Reform Club."

Soyer grinned and gave a little bow. "*Eh bien*, Bleck, I do not see you for months! Why do you not visit me at the Reform Cloob?"

"I have been working. How is Emma?" said Blake.

"She is, *comment dit-on?* Blooming! She is marvelous! Her paintings amaze and delight! The world beats its way to her door! But, Bleck, the kitchens at the Reform Cloob! You must see them. They will fascinate you—truly. *Il n'y a rien au monde comme elles!* They are unique! We have a grand invention—a gas stove with five small gas fires. Each lights immediately and may be regularized to any heat—and no dust and no smell! And steam power *partout*! It drives the rotisserie, heats the bains-marie, keeps the food warm! We have hot water and ice whenever we need! And the size! The scale! I guarantee you, Bleck, will find it of unsurpassable interest!"

Blake tried to disengage himself but Soyer was insistent.

"You must! And bring *votre ami*. I will send"—he made a gesture with his fingers to show someone walking—"my sous chef to summon you. It will please you. And I will cook for you."

Mr. Soyer took his leave, assuring us that the "dobe" was good. The

French proprietor, a man in shirtsleeves and an apron who greeted Blake with only marginally less eagerness, led us to a small table by the fire, already laid with cutlery and two glasses. In swift succession, there appeared a bottle of red wine and a loaf of pale bread shaped like a long baton. At other tables, men in soft French caps and, to my surprise, even ladies sat over plates of cold meats and stews, murmuring to each other. There seemed to be not an English voice among them. A plate of something heavily dressed in a thick dark sauce and smelling strongly of garlic, which proved to be the "dobe," was placed on our table. Blake launched into it without hesitation.

French cuisine might be the height of fashion in London, but in Devon we were used to plainer fare. Warily, I took a little off a spoon, for I was very hungry. It had a rich, robust, almost rank flavor, and despite the strength of the garlic, it was extremely satisfying. The bread had a marvelous thin crust on the outside and was impossibly light and fluffy and white within. For several minutes we did nothing but eat.

When I glanced up, Blake was giving me one of his bland hard looks. I fidgeted under it.

The Frenchman brought to our table a plate of winter cress and a slice of something yellow, melting and exceedingly pungent.

"Ugh, what is that?" I said, though I knew.

"It's cheese," Blake said.

"It reeks! Dear God, you cannot mean to eat it?"

In answer he cut himself a sticky wedge, spread it upon a corner of bread and put it into his mouth. "It's no different from Stilton."

I pushed the plate with its stinking contents as far from me as possible. Blake's lips twitched.

"I suppose this is a hostel for displaced Frenchmen?"

"There are French round here and Germans and Italians. They

meet their compatriots at such places and eat the dishes that remind them of home."

"You live near here," I said, accusingly.

Again he fixed me with that look. "What is it you really want to say?"

"Nothing. But may I congratulate you on the manner in which you put the crumbs together with Matty: Judas, the money. How you persuaded her to confess. I am in awe."

I knew that was not what he meant. "For God's sake, Blake," I said at last, "she is a thief. And in such circumstances, and you knew and said nothing."

"And you wanted to believe that she is"—he cast about for a moment—"an innocent, untouched by her surroundings. Now you see the reality of her life, and you dismiss her."

"You cannot talk. One minute you have barely a kind word for her, now you lecture me?"

"No one could live that life in those streets and be untouched by it."

"By God! I think you like her better as a thief."

"I think I know her better." He wiped his hands on his handkerchief.

"Oh, it is the old story: William sees only what he wishes to see or what others tell him to see. But the great clear-sighted Jeremiah Blake sees everything clearly."

"No, but I could see you forming some fancy idea of helping her, of raising her hopes. Now you can hardly bear to speak to her. She is not a plaything. When you return to Devon, her life goes on here."

I flinched and he saw it. "I have said I will go to the prison with her," I said stiffly.

"If the magistrates are determined to send the boy down, there may be nothing we can do. And it may be that transportation to Australia is better than a life in London in the shadow of the workhouse. He'd be better fed and free by the time he was eighteen, with a chance to make a new life."

"How can you think that? Can you not see how it would be for her to be parted from him? I suppose not, since you keep yourself so resolutely apart from everyone else!"

I regretted the words as I spoke them. "I am sorry, Jeremiah," I said humbly.

"You forget, transportation transformed my life." *And mine too in a way*, I thought.

We paid, and as we made to leave, the proprietor, Monsieur Dubourg, brought Blake a generous bowl of the beef stew covered in a clean white cloth, with a pewter spoon.

"*Pour madame*," he said. Even I, with my sorry schoolboy French, understood this to mean, "For the lady," or indeed, "For the wife."

Blake shook his head, "*Pas aujourd'hui*," he said.

"*J'insiste*," said Monsieur Dubourg, and thrust the bowl into his hands, smiling benevolently. Blake awkwardly drew out a few coins, but the proprietor waved them away.

"*C'est mon plaisir*," he said magnanimously.

"Where now?" I said innocently.

"We'll go and find the MP, Heffernan," he said.

"With that bowl of stew?"

Blake puffed crossly, sighed, hunched his shoulders as if the world were against him, and turned right. It was a cobbled lane named Dean Street, not especially prosperous, but busy with life. Two respectable-seeming women with baskets of purchases exchanged news; they nodded at Blake. There was a French shop selling bread and cakes, a barber's advertising itself as "Figaro-coiffeur," and a place apparently under German management selling cigars, snuff and tobacco. Though the houses had seen better days, some had elegant details and fine windows. Down the middle of the street came a large, ugly-looking man with an only slightly less large and ugly dog on a string; all who passed them gave him a wide berth.

"This is where you live," I said. Blake said nothing.

Halfway up on the left he stopped. A small shop. It was hard to tell precisely what it sold: there were bits of ribbon and small handkerchiefs in the window, along with tins of tea. Before Blake could open the door, a woman in a black bonnet appeared.

"Oh, Mr. Blake!" There was no mistaking the pleasure in her voice. She looked to be in early middle age, her clothes much mended but very neat, lines of worry about her eyes, a warm smile.

"Monsieur Dubourg insisted," Blake said, presenting her with the bowl.

"Oh, Mr. Blake, that is too kind!" She looked inquiringly at me.

"And this is your friend?"

"May I present Captain William Avery, lately back from India. Avery, may I introduce Miss Jenkins."

"A pleasure, ma'am," I said.

She blushed. "Mr. Blake's famous colleague from India! How marvelous! How do you find London, Captain Avery?"

"Most stimulating, ma'am, if rather colder than India."

"Well said, Captain! Oh, Mr. Blake, how I shall enjoy this. You must let me repay you for your kindness."

"The kindness is all Monsieur Dubourg's. Besides, I think I must owe you . . ."

"Oh no! I have taken no messages today. You owe me nothing. Now do tell me, what is the dish's name?"

"It is called a daube—beef, red wine, carrots and bacon," Blake said.

"Captain Avery, you should know your friend—though so very

busy—has been the soul of kindness ever since I acquired my shop."
She hesitated as if she had said too much, and looked anxious. Blake
smiled awkwardly.

"Miss Jenkins takes messages for me, and her maid-of-all-work does
for me."

"Mr. Blake"—and she gestured at her bowl—"has introduced me to
some of the interesting customs of our foreign neighbors. As a lady, of
course, I cannot venture into their 'restaurants' and 'cafés,' but occasionally he brings me a choice dish so that I may enjoy it in respectable
circumstances, and I must confess to having acquired quite a taste for
French cuisine!"

"You must eat it while it is hot, Miss Jenkins," Blake said. "And we,
I fear, must be on our way."

"Another of your mysterious inquiries, Mr. Blake?"

"Another of my mysterious inquiries."


*I never discovered precisely* how the officer at Westminster Hall knew
Blake, but clearly he did, and when Blake arrived at the gates claiming
to have an appointment with the Honorable John Heffernan to discuss
a "thorny" matter, a boy was at once dispatched into the building's depths.
He soon returned, however, with the information that the Honorable
Gentleman had not been seen in the Commons for some weeks. Blake
sighed irritably. The officer nodded us inside and the boy led us to a
clerk in a black gown who also regarded Blake with wary recognition.
Blake explained he had papers for John Heffernan MP but the gentleman was absent and he did not have the precise address; it was either
Cheyne Walk or Row in Chelsea. Nervously, the clerk initiated an investigation which yielded the address: 23 Cheyne Walk.

"How is it that the clerks of the House of Commons quail before Jeremiah Blake?" I said afterward.

Blake shrugged. "Collinson's clients. I've spared the blushes of a few men in there."

We were preparing to take a hansom cab—I had suggested we arrive at the gentleman's home without our feet and trousers drenched in city mud, and was also beginning to feel the effects of the night's sleeplessness and the day's length—when we were hailed by a lively shout. Henry Mayhew was laboring across the muddy sward next to the great sooty church of Westminster Abbey, intermittently waving. He was, as he had been the night before, a little chaotic in appearance: his hair stood up in tufts, his coat was misbuttoned, and he was struggling to keep in order a bundle of papers which threatened to spill out of his arms. He seemed very pleased to see us, if a little abashed.

"Mr. Blake! Captain Avery! I fear I was somewhat in my cups last night. Have you heard about Eldred Woundy?"

"Blake and I found the body," I volunteered. "After O'Toole's words, we decided to beard him at his offices early this morning."

"Fire and fury!" said Mayhew, looking back and forth between us. "But I suppose you make rather a habit of finding yourselves in dramatic situations. I wish I did. How extraordinary! I don't suppose you would care to describe the circumstances in which you found him? It will certainly be a big story. I can promise that I won't cheapen it— well, not as much as some others would."

"I can't tell you now," said Blake. "But if you are willing to wait, I fancy there will be something to tell later."

Mayhew smiled and shrugged. "Ah well, murders were never really my métier. But I am serious about writing something on the London poor, Mr. Blake. I was hoping I might visit Tothill House of Correction behind the abbey there, but it seems I shall have to make representations to the Governor first, which may take weeks. Douglas, of course, thinks I am foolish, but then he does most of the time."

"It so happens that we have another story which may interest you, Mr. Mayhew," I said, and gave a brief account of Matty and Pen Horner, explaining that I would be visiting the boy at Coldbath Fields. I asked if he would accompany me.

"I should be most gratified," Mayhew said. "I cannot promise that I will definitely be able to publish something, but I should very much like to come."

We said farewell, and Mayhew was knee-deep in mud again when he turned back to us.

"Bless me, I had forgotten! Renton O'Toole has vanished! At lunchtime today there was a notice delivered at the Cyder Cellars. O'Toole paid for it to be read aloud. It announced that as a result of certain circumstances he has elected to leave town for his own safety. No one knows where he has gone. We assume it is because of Woundy's murder. At the Cyder Cellars they have opened a book on whether he is in fear of his life or is in fact the murderer himself!"

## chapter 11

Cheyne Walk was a picturesque row of houses that looked onto the Thames in the quiet suburb of Chelsea. In the gathering dusk, a low mist from the water spread the contours of the gaslights and threw a gentle illumination over the bare plane trees and the crooked wooden fence which marked the river's edge. The sounds—grinding cartwheels, boatmen's shouts and occasional foghorns, dampened by the water—were a pleasant respite from the constant clamor of the city downriver. Down the road, however, was the unmistakable figure of one of the new police in his hat and high-necked tunic.

Number 23 was a tall, handsome red-brick town house with elaborate iron gates and a fine plum tree which held on tenaciously to its last, half-crisped leaves. A maid answered the front door. At first she intimated that we should do better to return via the servants' entrance. My affront at the suggestion, however, changed her mind and she reluctantly agreed to take our names to her master, while we waited on the doorstep.

"He is not in," she said briskly on her return.

"Then we shall wait," said Blake, pushing his foot in the door and sliding into the hall despite her efforts to close the door upon us. "We have no pressing engagement."

"You will be waiting a long time then," she said crossly. She stood there for some minutes, then took herself upstairs.

"He's here," Blake murmured.

Some fifteen minutes later she descended, followed by a gentleman who clearly took his toilet very seriously. He was dressed immaculately in a modish, tight-waisted, cutaway dark blue frock coat, cream trousers, a cornflower-blue silk patterned waistcoat with a fine gold watch chain, blue silk ascot and muslin shirt with fashionably long cuffs. One hand mopped his temples with a handkerchief; the other gripped the stair rail as he descended slowly. His face seemed familiar but I could not tell why.

"You are lucky to find me home," he said. He was perhaps a little too advanced in years to play the dandy quite so enthusiastically, but he was still handsome, and he spoke with an Irish lilt. "I should be at the House, but I have not been well. I've been abed for several days. Do I know either of you gentlemen? You are, perhaps, electors? Might I ask you to return another day?" He smiled easily but held his shoulders very tight.

"No, Mr. Heffernan."

"Then what—"

"I am sorry to disturb you here. We had hoped to find you at the House," said Blake smoothly. "We come on a matter of some urgency from the office of Lord Allington. I have a letter of introduction." He pulled the Viscount's letter halfway out of his pocket.

"Lord Allington?" said Heffernan, his shoulders still hunched. "We have not always seen eye-to-eye politically, but of course I admire his efforts on behalf of the poor. I would be happy to help if I can. I am convalescing, however. Perhaps another time? Does it concern the factory hours bill? Or a philanthropic matter?"

"It is complicated. Perhaps we might sit down, Mr. Heffernan."

"Well, I—"

"Is there a good reason why you cannot? We shall not take much of your time," said Blake, somehow both innocently and rudely at the same time.

"Well, er, indeed." Heffernan wanted to refuse us, but felt he could not. "We will go into the green study, Martha. Will you attend to the lights? And some tea if you please."

The room was well proportioned and filled with furniture: two sofas, an elegant desk, a collection of small tables, carved walnut chairs and shiny *objets*. A large window looked out onto the river, and the walls were covered in dark green silk which glowed under the gaslights. It was the room of a man who saw himself well measured in his fine possessions. Heffernan sat down at the desk.

"Mr. Heffernan, would you permit me to ask you where you would place yourself politically?" said Blake.

"I am on the radical end, sir, but would probably now call myself a liberal."

"You have worked, I think, on prison reform and a number of radical bills for poor relief?"

"I voted against the Poor Law in '34," said Heffernan. He sat back into his chair and smiled as affably as he could manage. "As any right-thinking man should have, in my opinion. My fellow MPs disagreed with me, however. We may be from different parties, but as I said, I could be persuaded to back Lord Allington's factory bill, with a few amendments, though it will certainly not make me popular within my own party." He smiled, as if the thought amused him.

"As it happens, we are here on another matter, sir, but one I hope you will help us with, as it touches on your interest in justice."

Heffernan nodded uneasily. Blake held out Lord Allington's letter of introduction.

"His Lordship has charged us with the investigation of three murders that recently took place between Seven Dials and the Strand. We believe you may be able to cast some light on at least one of them."

Heffernan started like a hare. He took the letter and as he did so he noted, with surprise and revulsion, the stumps of Blake's fingers.

"Who are you?" he said, his voice unsteady.

"I am a private inquiry agent. Captain Avery is working with me. You may perhaps recall our names, Blake and Avery? We were the companions of Xavier Mountstuart when he died in India. It is how I lost my fingers. You may recall that Mr. Haydon's painting of the event is currently on show in Piccadilly."

I was amazed that Blake volunteered this, but it had the necessary effect. Heffernan's anxiety immediately gave way to curiosity.

"Truly, that was you? How remarkable! Xavier Mountstuart, indeed! But my dear sirs, I cannot imagine what I could have to do with these murders. We are a very, very long way from Seven Dials."

"We are indeed. And from Islington too."

Heffernan pressed his handkerchief to his forehead. "I do not take your meaning."

"Mr. Heffernan," Blake said, affecting great weariness, "Nathaniel Wedderburn was murdered at his shop in Holywell Street by the Strand approximately three weeks ago. Please do not do me the discourtesy of pretending you have never heard of him or his wife, Connie. I have it on very good evidence that you knew them well twenty years ago."

Heffernan went a peculiar color and seemed to choke.

"I—I . . . what are you suggesting?"

"As I said, Nat Wedderburn was murdered. We are looking for reasons why he should have met such a violent end. And we have been led to his past." Blake sat quite still, a stark counter to Heffernan, who seemed unable to stop fidgeting.

"I do not believe I can help you. It is a long time since I encountered the . . . the Wedderburns."

"Is it? They were discussing you only a few weeks before Nat died. I wonder what can have prompted their recollections?"

"No encounter between us, I assure you," Heffernan said, pressing his palms together tightly.

"You can think of nothing else?"

He shook his head.

"It seems that Nat Wedderburn was engaged, along with his fellow victims, in blackmail. They threatened respectable men with the exposure of shaming secrets unless they paid up. I wondered whether perhaps Nat Wedderburn was blackmailing you."

There was a short silence. The man's cheeks flushed red; he laughed shakily.

"I assure you, Mr. Blake, that he never blackmailed me, not now or ever. I will not deny that I know—or rather knew—the Wedderburns. I have not seen them for years, and I am sorry to hear that Nathaniel has come to such a dreadful end. I had heard he had taken up an unfortunate profession, but I thought it was the printing of immoral books. I assume he must have fallen on bad times. He seemed a decent man when I knew him, and his wife, Connie, an admirable woman. Are she and the children provided for? What is the oldest son's name? Daniel? I should be sorry to think they were in distress."

"Perhaps you might explain how you came to know them?" Blake said.

"Twenty years ago, as a young man, I was a firebrand radical, a naive boy, dreaming of utopias. My father had estates in Ireland, but I came to London to fight for 'freedom and equality.'" He laughed at his younger self. "I was supposed to be training as a lawyer, but I was determined to live 'among the people,' and so I took a house in Guildford Street near Spa Fields, south of Islington. The Wedderburns were the most appealing of my neighbors. Connie was a beautiful girl. Nat was a man of modest means and background but intelligent and surprisingly well read for his class. Not much came of my fine intentions save a few bruising exchanges with the new police—no, it was before their time, it was the Bow Street Runners we crossed swords with. Well, I saw the error of my ways in the end. I did not lose my devotion to reform, but I realized that the way to change was through the workings of Parliament. I attained my majority, matured, finished my legal training and moved to more respectable lodgings. After I left Guildford Street the Wedderburns passed out of my life. I do not recall seeing them again, though I have thought of them over the years. I am not the man I was twenty years ago. I have not been him nor thought of him in a long time."

The words spilled from Heffernan, as I was sure they would not have had not Blake first distracted him with the mention of blackmail.

"It has been very hard to find anyone who knew him in his youth. Would you oblige me by telling me what you remember of Nat then, and how, for instance, he made his living?"

"Well, it is a long time ago. He was not from London. His father, as I recall, had been a provincial . . . a shopkeeper perhaps or cabinetmaker? I am not certain. The family was not doing well. Nathaniel had hopes of becoming a lawyer—I think that may be how we first met. I lent him law books and such. He failed: he had not the funds to finish his studies and get himself articled and could find no one to

take him on. The legal profession does require funds. But my memory
is that his true aspiration was to be a 'member of the republic of letters.' He read widely." He smiled in recollection. "He met the poet
Shelley."

"Indeed?"

"Oh yes," Heffernan said distractedly. "We read a good deal of
poetry," and he began to recite in a rich voice:

> "Who fought for freedom more than life? Who gave up all,
>     to die in strife?
> The young, the brave, no more a slave, Immortal Shell! That
>     died so well,
> He fell, and sleeps in honor's grave."

"That is Shelley?" said Blake doubtfully.

"The life of the man of letters provided, as it often does, thin pick-
ings," said Heffernan, "and so Nathaniel took on other work: writing
for the unstamped press, working as a printer's assistant, even as a
mason. Connie too had some education. At one time she ran a little
school, teaching children their letters."

"Was Nathaniel an infidel?"

"That is not a word I have heard for some years." Heffernan laughed,
but it was not a comfortable laugh. "He did not set much store by religion—but then the times were less devout, and many of the London laboring classes felt the same."

"Can you put a precise date to your acquaintance?"

"Oh." He paused to think. "I suppose it must have been between
1821 and '23, sometime around then."

Blake nodded. "I am not certain of the children's ages. Would Connie have by then been a mother?"

"Do you know, I cannot quite recall."

"As I said, Mr. Heffernan, we are looking into several murders—three to be precise. I wondered if you were acquainted with the other two men: a printer called Matthew Blundell and the newspaper proprietor Eldred Woundy, who was found dead in his premises this morning."

Heffernan was very still and looked Blake in the eye.

"They mean nothing to me. Though of course I have heard of Mr. Woundy. Found dead this morning? Good heavens. From the way you speak, I assume you think the deaths are connected."

Blake's eyes bored into Heffernan's. The man tried to meet them but eventually he looked away, as most did under that unnervingly direct gaze. He coughed a dry little cough and pressed his chest.

"Is there anything else, gentlemen? I am on a strict regime, I need my rest."

"Mr. Heffernan, with your permission I should like to ask a great thing of you. I should like to describe these murders to you."

Heffernan looked horrified—as I should have done.

"I know this is a great deal to ask, but as a man devoted to the betterment of the poor, I believe you would not balk at doing something that may bring justice to a dark corner where it might otherwise never reach. The truth is, the murders have confounded the police and leave us with many questions. We feel there may be clues, hidden meanings, in the way the men were killed. With your memory of the past you might be able to throw light on some tiny yet significant detail."

I should certainly have said no; but Heffernan nodded his assent.

"They were all killed in a very similar manner, Mr. Heffernan. They were strangled, stripped of their shirts, cut about the face and body, and knifed in the stomach. There was a great deal of blood. Blundell's hair had been painted red, money was left at Wedderburn's body, and

Woundy was sprinkled with elder twigs. The pads of their fingers had been dipped in ink and all three were found lying draped across their presses. It seems certain they were murdered by the same man."

Heffernan swallowed and raised his hand as if he had heard enough.

"How appalling. I cannot believe that Nat Wedderburn could have done anything to deserve such a terrible fate. But I cannot say that any of those details seem to me of any special significance. They simply sound like the actions of a violent madman."

"I am sorry to have pressed the details upon you," said Blake. "We are grateful for your time. We shall not take up more of it. Here's my card in case something comes to you. Or you may write to the office of Lord Allington."

Heffernan did not get up. "If something comes to me . . ." he trailed off.

*What did you make of that?* Blake said as we stood beneath the gaslight's aureole. He brought forth a small flask and took a swig before offering it to me. The police constable we had seen earlier strode past and nodded to us, then continued on his way, his hands clasped behind his back.

"I should say he was extremely nervous and was hiding something."

"I'd say everything he said was a lie, including 'and' and 'but.'"

"That's a little excessive."

"Well, maybe. But he's seen the Wedderburns more recently than he claims. He asked after Connie and the children, and knew Daniel's name, then said he hadn't seen them in twenty years. Then he said he could not remember if Connie had already had a child when he lived near them."

"A simple mistake, perhaps? He might have heard news of them."

Blake shook his head emphatically. "I'd say he already knew about Nat's death and feared we knew more about his association with Nat than we did. O'Toole says Wedderburn, Woundy and Blundell knew each other. Now I am certain that Heffernan knew them all too. I fancy Wedderburn was more engaged in politics than he had admitted to his son. Heffernan all but called himself a revolutionary. Wedderburn was a forthright non-believer. The Chartists claim that God is on their side, but twenty years ago radicals prided themselves on being infidels. And Shelley, whom Heffernan said Wedderburn admired, was a true revolutionary, for all they try now to make him out to be some daydreaming romantic. Did you ever read Shelley?

"Men of England, wherefore plow
For the lords who lay ye low?
Wherefore weave with toil and care
The rich robes your tyrants wear?

"There's plenty more political verse: *The Masque of Anarchy, Prometheus Unbound, Queen Mab.* He was a famous infidel."

"Damn me, Jeremiah, I thought you didn't like poetry. You were so resistant to Mountstuart's."

"There were many things I liked about Xavier, just not his verse," said Blake. "He educated me. In the early years I was hungry for anything he passed my way: poetry, history, philosophy, geology. I thought if I could read the whole world, I'd understand everything." He took another swig from his flask, then shook his head and leaned back heavily on the gaslight, his face shiny with perspiration.

Anxiously, I cast about for a hansom cab, realizing I too was all in.

———————

*Blake would not let me* accompany him home, insisting rather that he would meet me at seven the next morning at the Crown and Anchor.

"You know," I said, "Heffernan reminds me of someone but I cannot think whom. You say you never forget a face. Who is it?"

He shook his head, clambered out of the cab and set off, half staggering up the street.

At the Oriental there were messages and invitations to dinner. But I longed for nothing but my bed and oblivion. I ordered supper and a bath in my rooms. I wrote letters to Louisa and Helen: a description of the day's events for my sister; a description of London without its darknesses, with promises to buy her something pretty, for my wife. Sleep descended upon me like a curtain, and once again I had the dream.

The men fly off the cliff one by one and I am unable to save them.

*I woke at six* as the carters and criers began plying their trade in the square and reached the Crown and Anchor well before seven. In the streets the hawkers were selling broadsides about "Woundy's Monstrous Murder" and the "Bookseller Butchered on His Own Press." I purchased one. There was a lurid description of the discovery of the body which owed a great deal more to the author's imagination than the actual circumstances, and no mention at all of Wedderburn and Blundell, nor thankfully of Blake and me.

I waited for Blake for nigh on an hour. When he did not appear I decided to go to his lodgings—concerned for his health, of course, but also secretly pleased to have a reason to see inside his living quarters.

The morning was bright and the city seemed less unfriendly. I retraced our route of the day before through Covent Garden, across St. Martin's Lane and Leicester Square, asking for directions when I could not remember, feeling with some satisfaction that I was starting to know my way about. The shops in Dean Street were opening as I approached his door, a great solid paneled thing at least a hundred years old, I would have said. I gave two smart raps with the great curlicue of a tarnished knocker and waited. Then I gave another two.

Presently a throaty voice protested, "Awl right, awl right, doan wake the house!" A large ill-tempered woman in a well-worn night bonnet and bed robe opened the door. She was wiping her hands on a dirty apron and was surrounded by an unpleasant, guttery smell.

"My apologies. I've come to make inquiries after Mr. Blake, madam. Is he in?"

"You an' everyone," she wheezed back grumpishly. "Dunno if he's here. Doan tell me nuffin. Doan usually entertain guests. What's your business?"

"My own," I said, pushing past her. "What floor?"

"Second," she said crossly. "And tell him to stop cooking those horrible furrin dishes. Stinks the place out."

I took the stairs as quickly and quietly as I could, the rough drugget covering them dampening my steps. The smell receded as I reached the second floor. Another old door, studded with woodworm, three panels, slightly ajar.

"Blake?" I said, pushing the door open in one swift movement. The room was cold.

He was on the floor, half on his side, his knees bent up to his stomach. One arm lay across his face, but I could see that he had taken a blow to the face. His nose and chin were smeared with blood and he had the beginnings of a black eye. Two men stood in the room: a very large one in a soft cap who stepped back in surprise when he saw me, and a shorter one in a gray worsted suit.

I threw myself at the taller man, catching him a blow full in the face. He staggered back, righted himself, brought up his fists and caught me in the stomach. I should have taken a fall but my blood was up and I threw myself onto him, driving my left fist, still holding my news sheet, into his face. He tumbled backward onto a chair. His hand shot up to his jaw, and he would have come back at me had not the smaller man told him to stay down, rather as one speaks to a dog.

"What the devil is the meaning of this!" I shouted.

"Avery," said Blake in a muffled voice, "my visitors are leaving."

"Mr. Avery," said the man in the gray worsted suit.

"*Captain* Avery, if you please. Good God! Sergeant Loin? Explain yourself!"

"I am sure Mr. Blake will do the honors," he said matter-of-factly. "No hard feelings, eh? After that blow you dealt my man here, Captain Avery, I think we might call it quits. Mr. Blake, remember what I said. I am deadly serious. Come along, you."

The large man followed dutifully, holding his jaw, glaring at me. Blake's eyebrow was cut; blood was dribbling into his eye and down his cheek. Perspiration streamed from his brow, he was shivering and his breath came fast and shallow.

"You have a fever," I said. "I must fetch a doctor."

"I just caught a bellowser to the stomach, that's all. It winded me. No doctor," he whispered. "A bit of *quing-hau* in the cupboard. And a knob of opium, that'll do me."

I helped him onto the settle and he winced with pain and clutched his ribs. There was a second room and I ran into it. On a bed, low and narrow like an Indian charpoy, were some blankets and a pillow; I took them and a shirt from a hook and a half-filled jug of water. I made him as comfortable as I could, then looked for his fever herb, *quing-hau*. It was in a small wall cupboard among rows of powders—the scents of India—in a tin box. It was the best cure for fever, sweet-scented and bitter-tasting. Next to it was a small pouch in which I knew the opium would be stowed. I started on remaking the fire to boil the water.

"Use the spirit stove," Blake ordered, his voice hoarse.

"No words from you, you should rest. Anyway what—"

"In front of you."

There was a painted Indian chest on top of which was a curious metal object: a round copper vessel with a trivet hinged over the top and a small brass bottle to one side, connected to it by a metal tube.

"The fuel's in the bottle. You need a match. Turn the lid, it lets the gas through. Light the trivet. Heat the water."

"Ingenious."

"Ha."

I turned the fuel bottle and placed my flaring match at the mouth of the tube; a small ring of flame danced under the trivet. I took a milk pan from a hook on the wall, poured in water from the jug and placed it upon the contraption. I dipped the shirt in the jug of water to wash away the blood, but he pulled it from me and simply pressed it against his head.

I poured hot water over the fever herbs and waited for them to infuse. To my relief Blake's breathing had deepened, though he was still too hot and the cut on his brow continued to bleed.

"That must be seen to. And your ribs. I shall get a boy to bring a doctor—is there someone you know hereabouts?"

"No doctor," he said, his eyes shut. "Give me a little of the opium ball. There's some gin in a bottle in the cupboard. It cleans fine."

I broke off a little of the opium ball, then propped him up and brought the mug to his lips. He swallowed a little, coughed and took the opium from me, then sipped the infusion once more.

"How is it that you think so much faster in these situations than you do the rest of the time?" he muttered.

"The truth is, I'm afraid, Jeremiah, that in these situations I do not think at all."

He gave a small smile and winced with pain. I tried again to clean the blood from his face. He pushed me away.

"You are a dreadful sight—not that it seems to deter the ladies."

He laughed this time and clutched his ribs.

"I am getting a doctor, Jeremiah. Not another word."

I ran downstairs. The old woman's door was shut and so I passed into the street where Miss Jenkins, her clothes as neat as the day before, was preparing to open her shop. She summoned a little maid-of-all-work from the back and told her to bring the doctor, taking a purse from her skirts. But I was ahead of her and gave the girl a penny, telling her there would be another when she returned, while Miss Jenkins collected a jug of warm water and a cloth and followed me up the stairs to Blake's.

Blake frowned mulishly when he saw us but said nothing. Miss Jenkins gaped.

"Oh, Mr. Blake, what's been done to you!"

Blake gave me a long-suffering look. "Just a few cuts and bruises," he said hoarsely.

"I always keep a supply of clean, boiled water, Mr. Blake. I have a bowl of it here. I must wash your cuts, and we will find something to put on your eye to reduce the bruising."

She sat on the edge of the settle and, with a hand that shook a little, began with infinite gentleness to clean the blood from his face.

The scene had an awkward intimacy. When she had finished, she handed him the cloth so he could stanch the blood from his brow himself, and stood up quickly as if she feared she might become too comfortable.

"The cut on your brow is deep, the nose is not broken, only bloodied, and you will have at least one black eye. I fear you have a few bruised or even broken ribs," said she. "I do quite understand that it is not my business, but I do worry sometimes at the state of you, Mr. Blake."

"You mean this has happened before?" I said.

She bowed her head.

"She means she has seen me after similar encounters," Blake rumbled. "I assure you, Miss Jenkins, I am fine."

She nodded her head obediently.

"And I thank you for your help, truly," he said.

She smiled at him: an adoring, hopeless smile. "I am always pleased to help after all the kindnesses you have shown me, Mr. Blake. But I must go and open up the shop. I shall, if I may, return later to see that you are not in need. I think I have a little sage which we might make into a compress for the bruising. Captain Avery, you should light the fire, and he should eat something. Do you have food?"

I'd seen nothing but a little bread and two bottles of small beer. She said she would send something hot and would make sure the doctor examined Blake's ribs and sewed up his forehead. I heard her descend the rackety wooden stairs carefully, one step at a time. Blake, conveniently, had drifted off to sleep.

I set about lighting the fire, then looked about the room. It was far from luxurious—worn boards, woodworm in the paneling, bare brick above—but it had some fine old features. The fireplace, though blackened and topped with a metal hoop over which a stewpot or kettle might be hung, was an elaborate one, far grander than the room deserved, with curling Greek motifs below the broad mantel. The paneling had once been very elegant, and the two windows overlooking the street were large and well proportioned, with handsome box frames. On the floor was a moth-eaten Indian rug, but of a complex and unusual design. There were Indian watercolors upon the wall: one of two tigers by a waterhole; another of a native man and a woman, playing chess. The settle had an aged, but again fine, Indian embroidery across the back. There was a round table by the window piled high with papers: his notes about Wedderburn, and the only hint of disorder in the room. And then there were books—on the deal shelves, piled upon the floor, on the tables—among them Montaigne's *Essays*, *The Philosophical Dictionary* by Voltaire, *Sketches and Essays* by William Hazlitt, Lyell's *Principles of Geography*, Thomas Paine's *Common Sense* and *The Age of Reason*, Percy Shelley's *Queen Mab*, a thick, battered copy of a book called *Chemical Manipulation* and another called *Chemical Philosophy*. I had read none of them, and not even heard of the last two.

In the back room along with a bed there was a small Indian rug, and a deep pot in which sat a set of bow and arrows and an Indian sword, a tulwar, in a fine leather sheath. Hung on hooks on the wall, among other pieces of linen, was a lavishly embroidered banyan robe. Outside the back window was a makeshift ledge with a few wrinkled apples and some cheese wrapped in muslin. Next to the bed was a low table with more books, among them something called *Extraordinary Popular Delusions and the Madness of Crowds*.

There was a gentle knock at the door. Miss Jenkins's girl had come with a pot of warm veal broth. Blake had woken. I tried to press a coin into her hand which she mutely refused, looking past me anxiously at Blake.

"Well?" I said at last, handing him a little broth in a cup with a few pieces of torn-up bread. He took a sip and regarded me gloomily.

"She is a spinster who was left a small annuity and bought a shop here, without any idea of what she was doing. The French tend to buy from their own, and the rest have barely the wherewithal for tea or trinkets, and so her stock declines year by year. I buy a little from her, share the cost of her maid, who brings me hot water in the morning and cleans my rooms from time to time, and I pay her to take my messages so I am not disturbed here. She is very efficient." He put a piece of bread in his mouth and began to chew laboriously.

"I did not mean Miss Jenkins."

I could have sworn Blake blushed, though it might have been the fever.

"Oh, Loin. He and his bone-breaker arrived when I was in the midst of the fever."

"The old biddy downstairs let them in?"

"I don't know how they got in. Loin said he'd come to deliver a message. He knew we'd been to see Heffernan, and the matter was bigger than I knew, and I must leave well alone and persuade Allington to do so too."

"He said that?" I said, my heart sinking. But I knew better than to disbelieve him: he had never lied to me. "Does he speak for the new police?"

"For someone in the police."

I took the cup from him and brought it up to his lips. He drank a little, then fell back, grumbling that he had had enough, and so we continued until the cup was finished.

"Can it be the new police who had us warned off Holywell Street?"

"They, or someone else."

"But the story is out now. It can't be silenced. Every patterer and broadside seller is crying Woundy's murder down the Strand."

"Do the broadsides mention the other murders?"

"No," I admitted. "Did he say more?"

"I asked him why the murders must be suppressed. He said it would be better if I didn't ask. I said, 'I'll find it out.' The bruiser hit me. Loin said, 'This will show you they're in earnest.' I said, 'Who are they?' The bruiser hit me again. I said I was sure he didn't like being kept in ignorance about Blundell and Wedderburn. He looked sour. I said, 'Things are being deliberately kept from you, Loin. How do you like it?' He said, 'There are things that you don't understand. The Chartists are the true danger. I know what they can do. I've seen it. There is a plan, a conspiracy for a rising in London. I shouldn't even tell you. Like Newport but far worse.'

"Perhaps you weren't back for Newport?" Blake's eyes closed, but he continued to talk. "After Parliament voted down the first charter in '39, some miners' organizers were arrested for illegal assembly in Wales. Five thousand Chartists marched on Newport to free them. They had pikes and a few guns and there was a pitched battle. Twenty, thirty Chartists were killed. It was said afterward that other risings across the North had been planned. But nothing came of them."

I had, of course, heard of Newport. It had shocked the country.

"The ringleaders were tried last year," Blake said. "They were sentenced to be hanged, drawn and quartered. But their sentences were commuted to transportation. There was a great wave of sympathy for them. There were petitions, editorials in every newspaper, votes against the government in Parliament. I had thought the lesson of Newport was that it had convinced the Chartists anew that the government can be swayed by the strength of public opinion. But it seems the coppers see it differently: that the Chartists are some great threat.

"I said to Loin, 'What do you know about the Chartists?' He said, with some force, that he knew plenty. He'd fought the Chartists in the Birmingham riots of '39. A unit of the new police from London was sent up there to deal with the unrest. Two of his mates were beaten so badly they never recovered from their injuries. He has no love for them. He said the printers' deaths were oil on fire. If there's noise about them, the Chartists will say that radicals are being murdered and the police are ignoring it. I said, 'But that is what you are doing.' He said I didn't know what they knew. I asked whether Blundell and Wedderburn were radicals, or tied up with the Chartists, or if it was just that some high-up was being protected. Loin said what he'd told me was the God's honest truth, and I should know how such things went. People were being watched and our inquiries would alarm them.

"Then he told me that if we didn't drop our researches, they'd pin Woundy's death on me. I was the first to find the body and I'd been heard threatening him, and you were seen fighting his bruisers, who have now vanished. It would be easy to make it stick."

"But that is absurd! Could they do this?"

"They could try."

"But you are a hero."

"There are parts of my time in the East India Company that could be made to look bad. I was demoted for insubordination, disciplined for disobeying orders." Blake had never spoken before about his demotion.

"And then?"

"I said that it must be a great satisfaction to him to be someone's messenger boy, which was not wise. So the bruiser hit me and kicked me in the ribs. Then you arrived."

"What can we do?" I said.

He tilted his head back. His voice was little more than a croak. "I do not like being threatened. I do not like leaving a case before it's cooked. I will not walk away from this. You understand. But you can."

"Ah, that old chorus!" I said. "Just now you could not make your way to the chamber pot without me. Besides, what is there to walk away from? We know nothing."

"I think we have happened on something. Why else would I be bleeding?"

"We must arm ourselves as best we can. We should visit Sir Theo Collinson or Lord Allington and explain all. They will stand by you."

"We cannot tell Allington. He will close down our work."

"But—"

"William, you cannot speak of it to him. You must promise me."

I bit my lip. "*You* do not give promises."

"I will not promise what I cannot be sure of delivering. But you must promise me this. You owe me a secret kept."

It was true, though it shamed me to recall it. "All right. Drink your tea," I said. "What of Sir Theo?"

"Oh, he'd believe us, but if the coppers asked him he'd hand over chapter and verse on my misdemeanors in a moment."

"But he made an agreement. He must protect you—if not, we will tell the truth about the Thugs."

"It's been four years, William. The moment has passed. All I have is some notes, and for all I know I still have enemies in the Indian Political Department."

"Is this Jeremiah Blake speaking? The most phlegmatic man I ever met?"

He shifted and pressed his ribs. "You don't need to stay," he said again.

"I swear if it were left to you, you would be dying in a ditch, protesting your good health," I said. "I shall stay as long as I need to. You may sleep."

He shut his eyes.

"But when I can, I will go to see Lord Allington, tell him about Matty and ask him if he will come to Coldbath Fields with us. His presence might help."

He opened one eye. "You will not mention Loin?"

"I said I would not. But let me ask you one thing: why did you refuse to come with us to see Matty's brother?"

He closed his eyes and brought the blanket up to his chin as if to fend off the question. "I know what a child in prison looks like," he said.

Down below, the door knocker cracked out a tattoo and the old harridan shouted out a litany of complaints. There were footsteps on the stairs, a knock on Blake's door and a voice announced itself as belonging to a Dr. McDouall, summoned by Miss Jenkins. There ensued a short argument during which Blake tried to insist he had no use for a doctor or stitches. I proposed the opposite and mentioned his fever, his breathing and his ribs, and the doctor—at first bemused by Blake's resistance—finally managed to take a look at his forehead and suggested politely but insistently that the cuts at least be sewn. He said that a little laudanum would help with the pain and encourage sleep, though it would also depress the breathing. I mentioned that Blake had already partaken. The doctor began to speak of a new "scientific" method for the relief of pain. At the word "scientific," Blake's interest was piqued. He was persuaded to sit up, and allowed the doctor to look at his ribs, the left side of which was blooming with a red bruise. The doctor wanted to bind them. I looked for something long enough and found a piece of embroidered Indian cotton, while the doctor poured a few extra drops of laudanum. We bandaged Blake's ribs as the doctor asked after Blake's fever herbs and in turn described the vapor called ether which could induce loss of consciousness and so permit painless surgery; though on an unfortunate number of occasions patients had failed ever to wake up. The doctor took out a needle to sew up Blake's brow.

"You may leave the patient with me," the doctor said. "I shall not leave until I am certain he is comfortable."

# chapter 12

Lady Agnes Bertram Vickers received me in the small cold drawing room at Charles Street. Mr. Threlfall stood in attendance, as ever a picture of simultaneous pomposity and obsequiousness. The lady was dressed, as usual, in black, though today the dress had sleeves fashionably puffed at the shoulder and was ornamented with tiny jet buttons and fine embroidery in raised black thread. At her waist was a chain of keys and a small notebook which dangled across her skirts.

Today the improving tract on the desk was *The Humble Spirit under Correction*, but the house was silent. There were no delegations or singing children, and Lady Agnes was distracted and impatient.

"Captain Avery, I was under the impression we should not see you until tomorrow. And no Mr. Blake, I see? What did he make of the tract I gave him?"

"I believe he gave it a good deal of consideration," I lied. "I fear he is indisposed. But I wished to ask His Lordship about a matter separate from our investigation. One I thought would be close to his heart, regarding a child in need. I had hoped he might spare me a few moments in what I believe to be a good cause."

"His Lordship is also indisposed," she said briskly. "You may deliver your request to me. I shall judge its merits and will pass it on should I consider it appropriate. I cannot, however, encourage too much hope. His Lordship is not well and when he recovers he will be extremely busy. I, too, have a great deal to do."

I had little confidence that she would present my request in any positive light. "More charitable works, Lady Agnes?"

She glanced at me as if she suspected I might be mocking her. "I may be but a poor weak woman, Captain Avery, but I strive always to be worthy of the role that the Lord has accorded me as my brother's helpmeet and lieutenant in charitable matters."

"I have no doubt," I said hastily.

"It just so happens, however, that I have another matter to raise with you. His Lordship received a letter this morning which casts a by no means attractive light on your investigations. It is from Mr. John Heffernan MP, who writes that you and Mr. Blake came to his house uninvited yesterday and gained access to him on false pretenses by invoking my brother's name. He goes on to say that Mr. Blake then extracted from him admissions which he felt in other circumstances he should never have made and which had no bearing on the matter of your investigation. In short, you harassed him. He says that he is considering commencing legal proceedings against you, and will certainly do so should you attempt to see him again."

"That is an outrageous misrepresentation!" I cried.

"Captain Avery!"

"Forgive me, My Lady," I said, lowering my voice, "but that is not how it went at all—"

"So you did see him?"

"We did visit Mr. Heffernan, Lady Agnes, but this description bears little resemblance to our encounter. We parted, I assure you, on good terms. I can only conclude that having made several very personal admissions—most relevant to our inquiries, I might add—Mr. Heffernan must afterward have regretted his candor. He seemed to me a most anxious man."

"Listen to yourself, Captain Avery, you hardly contradict Mr. Heffernan's account—he was in fear of you!"

I shook my head. "No—"

"But that is by no means all, Captain Avery. Another missive arrived this morning from the Office of Richard Mayne, the commissioner of the Metropolitan Police. This letter states that Mr. Blake's investigations are actively interfering with the police's own inquiries into the deaths of Mr. Wedderburn and the other man . . ."

"Blundell," I offered.

"Yes."

"But as His Lordship knows all too well, My Lady, the new police have made no inquiries into those deaths," I protested.

"Do not interrupt me, Captain Avery!" said she impatiently. "I will continue. In view of a number of matters the Viscount has asked me to suspend his employment of you both. Among these matters is the fact that Mr. Blake was found with the body of Eldred Woundy in circumstances that beg more questions than they answer and that it has been brought to the commissioner's attention that on several occasions during his time in India Mr. Blake's conduct was called into question."

"That is a flat-out lie!"

"Captain Avery!"

"I am sorry, but this is utterly unjust. Might I remind you that the very reason Lord Allington took up this matter was because of the dilatoriness of the new police, and that in our inquiries thus far we have found no evidence that they have taken any interest in either of the first two cases. I assure you, I would not behave in this manner did I not feel our honor had been unfairly calumnied. And though I do not in any respect wish to be impolite, madam—I mean My Lady—it seems to me that if these matters are to be raised at all, I should be discussing them with Lord Allington."

Lady Agnes passed her notebook from hand to hand. "Captain Avery, let me ask you this. Have you thus far made any headway in the cases?"

"We are unpicking many threads. Following them through takes time."

"I must tell you that if it were up to me I would withdraw my support from this inquiry altogether, and I intend to tell my brother this. And not merely because of Sir Richard's request. My brother should be bringing the gospel to the poor and needy, not associating himself with undeserving rogues and sinners."

"This you have already made plain. But it is not up to you, madam," I said, bringing myself under control. "And I humbly beg, may I please have just a few minutes with Lord Allington on a completely different matter?"

"You may not. And may I point out, Mr. Blake's absence hardly speaks well of him. Nor is your vagueness as to his whereabouts a recommendation."

"I presume you to be a just woman, Lady Agnes. Would you judge and condemn a man in his absence?"

She pursed her lips and beat her notebook against the palm of her hand.

"He is sick, madam," I said. "A fever from the old days in India. It comes upon him, it cannot be predicted."

"I see. If he is ill it is not unreasonable that you should both pause in your efforts until His Lordship is able to give this matter his full attention. In the meantime, Mr. Threlfall will calculate what we owe you for your labors."

"But, Lady Agnes—"

She had turned on her heel and was out of the room. Threlfall followed, daring me to try again.

Glumly, I pulled on my gloves and prepared myself for the street. Out in the gray hallway, however, Lady Agnes was mounting the staircase at speed, and from the upper reaches of the house there issued a series of desperate cries. Without a thought and before Threlfall had understood what I was at, I was already at the top of the first flight.

A footman and a maid were peering anxiously around a doorway. As Lady Agnes arrived, they parted for her.

"Frederick! If you please!" she said, her voice anxious. A footman followed her into the room. Through the doorway I saw Lord Allington. He was sitting on a dining chair wearing only a long white nightshirt, his eyes shut, his face pulled into a grimace of dreadful distress.

"He said that he could not bear having the door closed upon him, ma'am," the maid said fearfully. "He asked that it be left open. It did not seem so large a thing. But Frederick said—"

"When he has one of these days, the door is locked. It is for his own well-being," said Lady Agnes.

Lord Allington sagged in his chair. He opened his blue eyes, yet he seemed oblivious to the scene around him. He was a picture of inner pain and wretchedness. Lady Agnes stretched out her arms to embrace her brother, but he leaned away from her, and at this her face fell.

I walked through the door toward Lord Allington, past the maid and footman, ignoring Lady Agnes's sharp angry breath. I knelt by him.

"Captain Avery," he said. He spoke slowly, in a dull monotone. He looked me in the eye but he hardly seemed to see me. "Do you have more terrible things to tell me? I promise you, they cannot be worse than the abyss of darkness of my own imaginings."

"No, Your Lordship, I will not burden you. Will you tell me what ails you?"

A long silence.

"Captain Avery, I must ask you to leave," Lady Agnes said firmly. "It was your presence—you and Mr. Blake—which cast him down last time."

His Lordship roused himself. "He recedes from me and I am left in the dark. A small, small place, and the door is locked. I cry out but he will not come and let me out. I am so filled with fear I cannot move."

"There now, my dear, he is not here," said his sister. "He will never frighten us again. He cannot. We are safe now, you and I. You will never be alone now, I will always be with you. Captain Avery, please leave."

I cannot tell why, but I knew with absolute certainty that he spoke of his father. I understood those fears. "Your Lordship, look about you. The light comes in through the window. There are no dark corners here. The day is young. You need not despair. You do so much good, in yourself and by example."

Allington shook his head and gazed sadly into the distance. "I can see nothing to steer by. It all disintegrates. I see the world fall apart. I am found wanting and I fail. I despair. And despair is a mortal sin."

"*Captain Avery*," said Lady Agnes. She took hold of my shoulder. As politely as I could, which I admit was not very, I shrugged her off.

"Your Lordship, we do the most good with many small acts, not single grand gestures. You told me that. I come to ask your help with a small thing. Two children in desperate need, whose fate you can change. It is such a small thing for you, but for them there is no one else."

He took a long time to answer. Then he said, "I am used up, Captain Avery, I have not the strength nor the resolution to help anyone. Not even myself."

"Let me tell you of them," I said. I began to describe Matty as persuasively as I could—leaving out the matter of the thirty silver half crowns—and then Pen's situation and the sentence of transportation, observing that even were the boy guilty, the threatened punishment seemed to far outweigh the seriousness of the crime. I said that they needed a champion.

As I spoke, I fancied the dullness in his eyes cleared, just a little.

"They need you, Lord Allington," I said again. "There is no one else who can rival your knowledge and experience of these matters. You can bring attention to this injustice. I shall be at Coldbath Fields tomorrow at two. I would take it as a great honor if you would meet me there."

# chapter 13

I was eventually bundled out of the house by Threlfall, two foot-men and Lady Agnes, who charged me to swear on my life that I would mention nothing of what I had seen. I gave my oath freely, in my head exempting Blake from my assurances.

I returned to the Oriental, but realized I was in no mood to converse lightly on the races, court gossip and claret. So I excused myself from the dinner to which I had been invited by a wealthy former Company civilian, and—cold and damp, cursing the filthy London streets and wishing once again for my gaiters—returned to Blake's lodgings, the gorgon landlady complaining bitterly as she let me in and I mounted the stairs.

I knocked gently on Blake's door and when there was no answer tried the handle, which opened at once.

Blake lay prone on the settle, pale, eyes shut, and for a terrible moment I thought he was dead. I shook him and one swollen eye slowly opened. He pulled himself up, yawning and wincing, until he was almost upright.

"You didn't tell Allington?" he croaked.

"I could not had I even wanted to. You should not have left the door unlocked," I scolded. "I could have been anyone."

"Don't be such an old woman."

I locked the door. "How long have you slept?"

The other eye opened. His brow resembled a piece of needlework. He rubbed his ear. "What do you mean, you could not have told Allington?"

I described my visit.

"It seems the world is working very hard to get us off this case."

"I do not believe Lady Agnes would dare to dismiss us without consulting His Lordship. And he may yet come to Coldbath Fields tomorrow." But I did not sound confident, even to my own ears. "Do you think perhaps he is mad?"

He shrugged. "More likely melancholic. It seems these days are not unfamiliar to the household."

"He was in torment. I felt deeply sorry for him. And for all her haughtiness, she was no less anguished for him."

I made a cup of Blake's fever infusion on his clever little heated trivet, then warmed the last of the broth and fed it to him, as he protested. With considerable difficulty we got him into his bed, and he was unconscious within minutes. I dined on cheese and withered apples, not entirely able to put from my mind the dinner I would have had with my rich civilian. Then I lay down on Blake's settle.

It was dark and the fire had burned down when I was roused. It took me a moment to realize that someone was knocking quietly but insistently on the door. A voice called impatiently, "Mr. Blake! Mr. Blake! Open the door! Mr. Blake!"

I must have been half-asleep, but old habits are hard lost and I staggered up at once and went to the door, noticing my neck ached from the hard edge of the settle. Another sign of my creeping softness.

"Who is it?" I hissed.

"Where's Mr. Blake? I want Mr. Blake!" The voice was both pleading and importunate. I unlocked the door. A small huddling creature in a shapeless coat, swaddled in a large scarf, stood at the top of the stairs. It appeared to be carrying a cane. It pulled the scarf from its head and began to speak quickly.

"I must speak with Mr. Blake. I require sanctuary and he owes me. I told him I would need him, and now I do! You must let me in!" And he tried to push past me.

"Mr. O'Toole?" I said, confused. I stood back to admit him and he almost fell in through the door. "What time is it? How did you get in?"

"How the devil should I know?" he said. "Around one o'clock, I suppose. The old woman at the bottom did not bother to lock the door, I just came in. There is a very large bruiser of a man down in the street. Is he usually there?"

Renton O'Toole sidled over to the window and peeked out. There were few gaslights on the street, so little was to be seen. "I am being followed, I am sure of it. They are pursuing me," he said, and he threw off his shawl somewhat melodramatically. "I must take precautions."

"What's going on?" Blake shouted. I found him clutching his side, unable to maneuver himself up from his low bed. I set about getting him to his feet.

"Good God, man!" said O'Toole, who had sauntered in. "So they have got to you too!"

"They?" Blake shook off his befuddlement, edged himself awkwardly into his banyan and shuffled into the living room. His face, it had to be said, looked fairly bad.

"Why, the Chartists, of course!"

"The Chartists?" I said.

"I do not need an echo, Captain Avery, I require sanctuary," O'Toole snapped.

"In answer to your question, Mr. O'Toole," said Blake, "no, it was not the Chartists who got to me, but I should like to know why you think they might."

O'Toole looked as if he had been caught out. He covered his confusion by making a great dumb show of struggling out of his large coat, sinking down on one of the hard chairs by the window, drumming his cane against the side of the table and pointedly looking out onto the street.

"'Tis nothing. I exaggerate."

"We were told you had gone into hiding after Eldred Woundy's death. Feared for your life even," said Blake. He sat gingerly down on the settle, holding his side.

"Well, in a way," said O'Toole, looking over at the window. "'Tis some particularly determined pursuers, angry I exposed their vices. A group of gentlemen with an unholy appetite for strapping guardsmen. You can imagine the sort of thing. They plan to do me an injury. The usual, in others words. Just a little more insistent." He winked.

Blake rubbed the top of his ear skeptically.

"If I could just remain here for a few hours," O'Toole said, "perhaps you might then spirit me out of the city as quickly and quietly as possible."

"As you see, Mr. Blake is not well," I said testily. "He cannot 'spirit you out of the city' just now."

Blake said, "So you want to leave London on the quiet?"

O'Toole nodded.

"I don't have any truck with blackmailers. You will have to make your own way."

"Mr. Blake!" O'Toole said fretfully, but at the same time scarcely able to take his eyes from the window. "We made an arrangement!"

Blake shrugged.

O'Toole stood up, looked between Blake and me, took a great gulp of air and said, "Well, indeed, the matter is not blackmail exactly."

"Perhaps you want spiriting out because you murdered Woundy. Odd that you spent an evening blackening his name, he was found dead the next morning, and then you made such a thing of disappearing."

"Really, Mr. Blake, I'd never do something so stupidly obvious. In any case, I am entirely against physical violence and I enjoy very good relations with the new police."

"Let them protect you then."

"Mr. Blake!" wailed O'Toole. "I find myself in a quandary, that is to say, I am in an awkward position—"

"Get to the point, O'Toole. As Captain Avery says, I am not well and my patience is wearing very thin."

"Yes," said O'Toole, and he slumped miserably in his chair.

"Chartists," Blake prompted. O'Toole looked genuinely anguished.

"Damned if you do, O'Toole, damned if you don't."

"If I say what I know I could end up dead, Mr. Blake," said O'Toole. "I beg you, do not press me."

"I cannot help unless you tell me. And I am discreet. That is why you're here."

O'Toole scratched his chin with his cane. "The London Chartists," he began, "that is to say, a small group of Chartists . . . I have reason to believe that they are planning . . . that is to say, that something is being planned."

"Something?"

"There's a conspiracy, a plan, for a rising in London. Or rather a plan for a national rising, in which London rises first and stirs the rest of the country to arms."

"And how is it that you come to know this, Mr. O'Toole?"

"Oh, you know, Mr. Blake, I hear a lot of things," O'Toole said hurriedly, "keep my nose to the wind."

"Not good enough, O'Toole, I've no patience tonight," said Blake, and he stood up slowly and presented his back to the man. "Put him out, William."

"No, no, Mr. Blake! Look, I have always been a friend to the radicals—it is all there in my papers. I have done them good turns, sent a bit of useful intelligence their way, humiliated the powerful and privileged. And of course, there's the fact that many of us share the same homeland . . ." At my puzzled expression he added, with a hint of irritation, "Being Irish."

Blake did not turn around. O'Toole squeaked and ran after him.

"Wait, Mr. Blake! The truth is I have come to know some prominent Chartists. You could say I am not so much a court jester as a 'people's' jester." He laughed briefly but stopped when we failed to join in.

"Well, it so happens that I have become party to some confidential deliberations. I might have pretended to more enthusiasm for radical politics than I actually felt. I might have striven—for reasons of my own—a little harder than some might consider necessary to discover all the details. And now certain people have discovered what I know and are very displeased."

"Mr. O'Toole," I said, "you make no sense at all."

"He means," said Blake, sitting down again heavily and beginning to look quite ill, "that through a mixture of lies and guile he's got word of some Chartist plan, and now the men concerned have discovered what he's done, and are out to get him. What I'm asking myself is why, Mr. O'Toole, you should go to such trouble to find such things out. As you say, you are no Chartist yourself. And the answer that comes to me is that you're a nose for the blue bastards, which is why you enjoy such good relations with them, and they set you to finding out as much as you could about it."

"A nose?" I said.

"An informer."

"That is perfect nonsense!" said O'Toole, outraged.

"Is it? I had a visit early this morning from a pair of coppers, very much in earnest. These are souvenirs of their visit." He pointed to his face. "They went on about Chartist threats and Chartist plots. I think that on one of those occasions when you crossed the censor, or libeled some toff, or when some blackmail plan went bad, the coppers came to you and said they'd go easy if you would pass on any useful intelligence that came your way. That was how it started, wasn't it? I am familiar with the practice, Mr. O'Toole. It's no rare thing, believe me."

I had an intimation that O'Toole might bolt for the door. Sure enough, he picked this moment to hurl himself toward it, but not before I had stepped across and caught him. With a pathetic wail he fell back on the settle next to Blake.

"All right! But I must have help! I must leave London. They are looking for me. They are a bloodthirsty lot and they mean me no good."

"What about your friends among the coppers?"

O'Toole gave him a weary look.

"Tell me your story and I shall see what I can do." Blake propped his head up on his hands.

"Get a move on, O'Toole," I said, "Mr. Blake is sickening again and I have no patience for you."

O'Toole wriggled uneasily. He fiddled with his cane, put his head in his hands, then sat up. He said, "Some of them have set up what they call a 'Committee of War.' Very secret."

"Who is on it?"

"You would not know them."

"Names," said Blake.

"A Marylebone shoemaker called William Cardo, a physical-force Chartist delegate called Joseph Williams, a bookseller—a Northerner—called Charlie Neesom, a Scottish doctor, very cool customer, Peter McDouall, and a crazed Polish major called Beniofsky, a military man. He is to drill the men and plan the assaults. He loves to talk about blood and he is all for setting light to the city with bonfires. He talks of torches and little else. And knives. To my mind he is quite mad. There are a few other hangers-on."

"A doctor called McDouall?" I said, suddenly struck by this.

Blake closed his eyes. "I should have recognized him."

"You were hardly in a fit state," I said. "I certainly didn't."

"McDouall was here?" wailed O'Toole.

"Calm yourself," said Blake. "He is not here now."

"They are watching you too! Why are they watching you?" He stood up and sidled to the window again to look out.

"If you were seen coming here," Blake said, "there is little we can do now. Let us proceed one step at a time. We will think about McDouall later. We saw him and the Pole and met Neesom at a Chartist meeting."

O'Toole looked as if he might burst into tears. "You were at a Chartist meeting?"

"One thing at a time, sir. Who are the hangers-on?"

The little man gathered himself. "A writer called Harney, George Harney. Likes a swig. Likes to talk. Cannot decide if he is in or out—he wants to frighten the authorities with the threat of force, but is less eager to carry through. And there is a second tier of hothead young fools who have taken hard to revolution and fancy the notion of swinging a pike. I don't know all their names. They are all devoted to Neesom."

"Do you know Watkins? Small, lively man, a lay preacher," I said. "Is he part of it?"

O'Toole shook his head. "He is a moral-force man. Dead against such notions."

"How did you get in with them?"

"Through Harney. I've known him for years. Offered them my lodgings for meetings. I have a reputation among them of being a sympathizer, but not a signed-up Charter man. No one would suspect me, so they could meet in my rooms without fear of being suspected themselves."

"But it was the blue bastards put you up to it."

O'Toole hung his head and nodded.

"And now they've discovered you're a nose."

"They suspect me."

"How widely is this plan known?"

"It is a close secret. I think some other London organizers like Watkins may have an intimation and would not go along with it, being strong moral-force men, but equally would not give away their comrades. There are others who will hang back in order to see how it turns out."

"If they can no longer meet at your lodgings, where will they be based?"

"Neesom has a bookseller's shop in Brick Lane."

"What of the Chartist leader, Feargus O'Connor?"

"They do not trust him. Neesom's very much a temperance man and wants to make it part of the Charter. O'Connor disagrees and has attacked him for it. But the Committee believe that if their plans are successful, O'Connor will join them soon enough."

"And the plan?"

"They are convinced that the London poor are close to despair and sufficiently hungry and angry to rise. They have gathered a stockpile of pikes, guns and knives. I do not know where. They were to pick an organizer in each city division where there is a Chartist group. They may already have done this. Beniofsky, the Pole, was to train the orga-nizers, who in turn would select members they considered ready to fight. As I say, they may already have started. The plan is to organize meetings in taverns about London. At these, instead of talking of the Charter they will press home the terrible injustices perpetuated by the government, the tragic plight of the poor, hunger, unemployment and all that." O'Toole laughed cynically; Blake stared at him. O'Toole's levity quickly gave way to an embarrassed cough.

"These meetings are to gather support for a great outdoor assembly and march. I do not know the precise route or date—it is to be kept a tight secret from the new police and they are still arguing over it: whether to go to Clerkenwell Green, then to Lincoln's Inn and, from there, east to St. Paul's, the river and the Tower, or around the other way, toward Parliament. But the marchers are to assemble at Coldbath Fields prison. They call it 'the Steel,' you know, after the Bastille, where the French revolution began. There will be speeches to rouse the crowd. Weapons will be secreted among group leaders and hidden nearby.

"Even if the people do not rise, there are still plans to set fire to property and to the London docks, and the major wants to kidnap cer-tain prominent men who have opposed the Charter or spoken against attempts to help the poor, and even to assassinate them. Most of the others were wavering on this and considered it too extreme. I must say I find him frighteningly intemperate."

"You have no idea when this will take place?" said Blake faintly.

"In the next week I should say, but I cannot be sure. There was word that the price of wheat was to rise again. Food will be more expensive. People will be angry."

"Have you told all of this to the coppers?"

"Most of it. They have not afforded me the protection they promised me," O'Toole said sulkily.

"I think you knew they wouldn't. That is why you came to me at the Cyder Cellars."

O'Toole wagged his head in reluctant admission.

"I will help you," said Blake, "if you answer my next questions, understand?"

The little man stared at him, his eyes big with apparent sincerity; he nodded.

"What hand did you have in Eldred Woundy's death, and how are he and the other dead printers connected with this?"

"I had none!" O'Toole protested, stung. "And as far as I know, they are not connected in any way."

I could not remember ever having seen Blake more surprised.

"But you went into hiding the day Woundy was murdered!" I said. "Because of you, we had him down as our chief suspect for the Wedderburn murder."

"I cannot help that. It was the merest coincidence. I did dislike— all right, hated—the man. But this has nothing to do with him. After I left the Cyder Cellars that night, I returned to my lodgings and found Harney, Neesom and the surgeon, McDouall, waiting for me."

It must have been only hours after Blake and I had seen them at the Chartist meeting.

"McDouall is like stone, he gives nothing away. Neesom was angry but tried to hide it. Harney was hardly able to look me in the eye. He has never been a good liar—at least in the flesh—so I knew they had a notion. They wanted to know if anyone had come asking questions

about them. I assured them that no one had and that I myself had
been the soul of discretion. It was only afterward that I realized I had
made a mistake—they must have known the police had heard something, and by denying all I made myself suspect. I judged it sensible to
disappear."

"Instantly thereby confirming their suspicions of your guilt," I said.

"Why did you have your disappearance publicly announced at the
Cyder Cellars?" said Blake.

"I cannot help a small flourish here and there," O'Toole said. "It is
in my nature. Besides, I wished them to think I had left the city."

"Why did you not?" Blake asked stonily.

"Well, to be honest, I did not wish to leave town as old Cumberland
is back to visit the Queen. I have a little outstanding business with
members of his entourage. I immediately holed myself up in a room not
far from here, and then became concerned about going further. I cut
quite a figure in London, you know. I did not know who might recognize me and who might blab. But I must leave tonight. I must. Though,"
he added, looking faintly abashed, "I am also short of steven."

"I beg your pardon?" I said.

"He hasn't enough money," said Blake impatiently. "Did you have an
idea of where you might go, O'Toole? Do you have family in Ireland?"

"I'm not going back there!"

"Can you ride a horse?"

"I prefer not to."

"What precisely did you think I might be able to do for you?"

"Well, those who know say you are a man of great resource, Mr.
Blake, of elegant solutions."

Blake put his face in his hands, then lifted it up again as it had
plainly hurt.

"Mr. Blake," said O'Toole, his desperation reasserting itself, "I have weathered many threats and beatings. I have always confounded my pursuers. But I have not left London in twenty years, and I have no idea where to go. Still, I must go tonight."

"You say I owe you a debt. But the information you gave me brought me no closer to the murderer of Woundy, Wedderburn and Blundell. In some respects it actually made matters worse. The conspiracy you claim to have caught yourself up in has nothing to do with our case either. What you have done, however, is to draw us deep into a matter in which we have no business or interest. The coppers think I know something about this Chartist plot—they also appear to think Wedderburn and the other dead men had something to do with it—and now it seems the conspirators do too."

"But McDouall was here hours before I arrived," said O'Toole brightly. "I am not the cause, so."

"But if they are watching, your arrival will only have confirmed their suspicions," I said. "Can you not see, Mr. O'Toole, why Mr. Blake might not feel entirely obliged to help you? You might check the window again, by the way. I thought I saw a shadow pass across one of the gaslights."

O'Toole scurried to the window.

"McDouall does not seem to have done you any harm," I murmured to Blake. "He could have if he had wished to. Did he ask you any questions? Would you stoke the fire, Mr. O'Toole?"

"I cannot remember," Blake muttered back. "The fever and the beating loosened my wits and the laudanum slowed me down."

"What did he want, then?"

"He knows Neesom, Neesom knows the Wedderburn boy. Maybe that's why." He glanced at O'Toole, who was now piling the last of the firewood onto the grate and energetically poking it.

"Is anything missing?" I ventured.

"Will you look on the table?" he said.

I walked over. "Your notes are gone."

"All of them?"

I nodded.

"Well, they won't do him much good, unless he can read shorthand."

"Read what?"

"Never mind." He closed his eyes.

"Jeremiah, I am taking you back to bed."

"What about me?" said O'Toole, who was now stretching his feet out toward the crackling flames.

"Mr. O'Toole," said Blake, "I am sick. My mind is not at its sharpest. We are most likely watched. Give me time and I'll work out something elegant for you."

"By no means!" O'Toole cried. "I cannot stay here any longer, I cannot bear the thought. I must have a solution tonight."

Blake raised his palms in supplication. "I advise you to wait. But if you insist on leaving I can arrange something. I give you no guarantees that it will work, however. None at all."

"I shall take that chance. I have faith in you, Mr. Blake," said O'Toole fervently. "Now, I do not suppose you have something I could eat? I am quite famished. And perhaps a little something to quench a man's thirst?"

## chapter 14

At the rear of Blake's house there was a door that led out into an evil-smelling backyard. Upon reaching it, I let myself out, awkwardly picking my way through a veritable mountain of broken furniture, wooden shards and rotting rubbish, made all the harder as the moon was enveloped in cloud. Following Blake's instructions, I clambered through a hole in the old fencing into the yard of Miss Jenkins's building and then into the one farther along. There was an old gate in the back wall here, and I pushed it open and stepped into a quiet cobbled lane. On the other side were the back gates of a hostler's yard, described in detail to me by Blake. At my arrival the horses shifted uneasily in their stalls, and a man stepped out from a corner with a bull's-eye lamp.

I mentioned the name I had been given and told him whence I came. He called out. There was a rustling above me, and down a ladder, his hair interlaced with bits of straw, came a yawning boy of perhaps nine or ten. He listened to my instructions and nodded sleepily. He slid into one of the stalls, past an old dray nag who did not enjoy the disruption, and disappeared. The hostler went back to his corner, and I sat upon a straw bale and waited.

At last the boy returned and said all was in train and then disap-

peared again. More time passed. I struggled to stay awake, while un-
wanted thoughts thrust themselves into my head: Allington's terrible
dark misery; the monster who murdered and might do so again; my
confused thoughts about Matty Horner; my wife's expression when I
had told her I was going to London and the shame and relief I had felt
in going.

The boy reappeared and said that all was in order. I paid him well,
as instructed by Blake, retraced my steps and collected a nervous
O'Toole, who had bundled himself back into his coat and scarf until
he was barely identifiable as human. We descended the stairs, tackled
the backyard almost without injury and sidled through the gate into
the street, where there stood a very old and battered hackney carriage.
The plan—far from elegant but at least straightforward—was that the
driver, some familiar of Blake's, would take O'Toole to the Paddington
terminus, where he would catch the first train west, then a mail-coach
to Exeter, where he seemed to think he would find shelter. Should this
fail to transpire, I had reluctantly furnished him with a letter of introduction to my sister and had also written a letter to send in the morning to apprise her of the matter.

We crouched in the shadow of the backyard fence. The door of the
carriage stood open. The Irishman looked about nervously and took a
first step toward the carriage. From nowhere two men appeared. One
tried to push me aside and brandished a knife under my nose. The
other went for O'Toole, who, to my surprise, fought him off stoutly
with his cane, administering whacks with all the force in his small but
doughty arms.

I launched myself at my assailant. My fist reached across his body
and caught him in the face, then I seized his arm, jerked it back and
forced the knife out of his hand—I heard it skitter across the lane. I

kicked him in the stomach and threw all my weight at him, pushing him onto the cobbles, where he gasped, winded and unable to rise.

At this, the hackney-carriage driver took fright and took off. O'Toole howled, "No! No!" after it, the noise rupturing the night's silence.

O'Toole's man had managed to grasp one of his arms and was attempting to hoist him over his shoulder. Despite his proliferation of layers, O'Toole succeeded in eluding these efforts like a slippery eel, administering knocks to the man's head with his free hand and shrieking, "Unhand me, sir!"

I gave O'Toole's man a floorer, while O'Toole cracked him over the head. He threw his arms over his head to protect it and overbalanced. I seized O'Toole, kicked the other fellow—now on his knees—giving him a nose-ender (not a blow I was proud of), and ran to the hostler's yard. The moon had come out and the boy, alerted by O'Toole's shrieks, was standing in the shadow of the yard's open gates. When he saw us, he beckoned and ran into the stables, then into a stall, past a large old nag. I followed him, dragging O'Toole, who was terrified of the creature, behind me. In the corner of the stall the boy lifted up a piece of old canvas nailed into the wall to reveal a hole, before climbing inside.

Our pursuers had come into the yard. I propelled O'Toole and his cane into the hole after the boy and had just time to climb in myself before they reached the stables. The boy pulled at the Irishman's sleeve to follow him, but O'Toole would not, or could not, move. I did not press him, for I judged he might go off like an alarum if pushed too hard. The horses stumbled anxiously in their stalls. O'Toole took ragged breaths. The canvas covering the hole had folded back on itself a little and I saw their feet padding past our stall. One of them called for attention. The hostler had fled or was well hidden, for there was no answer. They debated what to do. One turned back into the stables; it became apparent that he was searching each stall one by one. I held my breath as he came nearer and nearer. In the stall before ours, however, he was almost trampled—the horses were growing more and more jittery—and so he gave up. The other man, meanwhile, had climbed into the hayloft, for we heard him stamping about above us.

At length they met again and decided we must have gone through the stables to the large inn on the other side. The boy began to tug at O'Toole's sleeve again. This time the Irishman was obedient. It was a tight place and he found it exceedingly difficult to turn, but he did so at last and we followed the boy on hands and knees until we came out into a larger space.

The boy lit a taper and I saw we were in a tack room: there were bridles, cart trappings, several sacks of feed into which the rats had made good inroads and an old cart with three wheels on which O'Toole made himself comfortable. It was almost warm. I mimed to the boy, asking if it was safe to speak. He nodded and said that Blake had told him always to have a safe place to hide, just in case. *Just in case of what?* I thought.

The boy, very pleased with himself and much enlivened by the night's activities, swore he could get O'Toole to Paddington for the first train. He said he was familiar with "the back ways" and that when they got as far as Hyde Park, he knew a cabbie who would take them the rest of the way. It did not seem a bad plan, but I worried at what might happen should they encounter any trouble, and O'Toole—previously so desperate to escape town—was now fearful of striking out at all. The alternative was somehow to regain Blake's rooms, a notion which would at least give us the benefit of Blake's judgment. The question was how to evade any observers. I wondered what Blake would have done. As almost in a dream, an answer floated in upon me like a memory from another world.

My pocket watch said it was near four in the morning. I asked the boy if he would be able to provide me with the necessary accoutrements, and gave him some money. He nodded, merry, disbelieving and very curious, but too deferential to ask for explanations. Having availed himself of the most comfortable spot, O'Toole was already nearly asleep, so I sat down in a pile of straw to take what rest I could find.

*I woke stiff* and, as I often did now, with a peculiar sense of apprehension. The boy was nudging me. I thought guiltily of Helen at home, without me, then I remembered where I was. I was very cold. I stretched and thought longingly of the bathtub at the Oriental Club. Light seeped in through the edges of a stable door. Under his arms, the boy carried a bundle larger than his head, with a paper parcel on top. He said it was nearly eight o'clock and we were expected. He untied the bundle and produced a dress of gray worsted, an apron and an old bonnet. We shook O'Toole awake—he was not in the best of moods—and presented him with the dress. I began to explain how in India many respectable British officers had escaped difficult incidents in women's dress. To my surprise he required very little persuasion. Indeed, he seized the clothes from me, unburdened himself of his own layers at once and almost leaped into the dress. It was immediately apparent that while his arms squeezed into the sleeves, the bodice would never button around his plump little figure. The ingenious boy, however, produced a moth-eaten cape to cover the great gaping hole at the back. O'Toole then arranged the apron so as, he said, "to make the dress sit plausibly," plunged his head into the bonnet and swathed his old scarf around his neck and chin to hide his emerging whiskers. When all was done, he gave me a low curtsey. The effect was most unsettling.

"Captain Avery, I am no stranger to women's *habillements*," he said gravely. "I take a keen interest in the stage. I have several times been called upon to give my 'dame.'"

The boy opened the paper parcel; inside were French pastries—I recognized them from having once or twice encountered them in India.

"Mr. Blake bought me one once," said the boy eagerly. "From the Frog bakery in Dean Street. Now they'll sometimes give me what's left at the end of the day. This one's a crescent. This one's a shohsun, like a jam turnover."

O'Toole had already seized two; the boy was sinking his teeth into another. I took up a fourth. It was ambrosial.

My notion was that the boy would lead O'Toole around to Miss Jenkins's (who had been kind enough to provide the clothes) while I would make my own way back to Blake's through the back door. Miss Jenkins would then escort her elderly female visitor up to meet Mr. Blake. That was as far as my ingenuity had taken me.

O'Toole then refused to give up his cane. "I have carried this thing through thick and through thin, Captain Avery," he said. "It has protected me against assailants in their dozens."

In vain we suggested that an old lady would be unlikely to be seen brandishing such an item. In the end I had to snatch it from him and promise that it should be returned to him once he attained Blake's rooms.

By the time I reached Blake's rooms Mr. O'Toole—still wearing his dress, his bonnet on his lap—had taken up residence upon the settle and was in full flood, in between helping himself to pieces of cheese. Blake was wrapped in his banyan, feet bare and gray-faced except for where he was shinily bruised. Miss Jenkins seemed admirably composed after her small adventure and had decided to ignore Blake's state of undress. The boy had returned to the stables.

Miss Jenkins leaped up and said she must return to the shop, but it had been a most exciting distraction, and O'Toole launched into a series of fulsome—and lengthy—tributes to each of us, during which I muttered apologies to Blake, and he grumbled that I should have sent O'Toole off with the hostler's boy. He asked if I had recognized any of our assailants and I said I had not, but added that I thought their intention had been to carry off O'Toole rather than to murder him.

"You cannot stay here," I said to O'Toole. I knew Blake would be oppressed by O'Toole's prolonged company, let alone the thought of him rooting around in his books and papers. "Blake must be allowed to rest quietly, and I have calls to make."

"But where then will I go?" said O'Toole, his face the picture of alarm.

Miss Jenkins immediately offered to take him in for the day, as I had hoped she might. Blake dismissed the idea. Miss Jenkins said that she would be happy to have Mr. O'Toole. Her aged house had a spare room and several small hidden spaces which she suspected had once been priest's holes. Should something go amiss, Mr. O'Toole might secrete himself in one of these. Unbidden, a picture of O'Toole's meaty little limbs bursting out of one of Miss Jenkins's small cupboards sprang into my mind.

Blake hesitated. It was clear that Miss Jenkins would have done anything for him. Clear, too—to me at least—that Blake knew this and wished it were not so. I foresaw an impasse.

"A capital and most courageous notion, Miss Jenkins," I said, before Blake could voice his opposition again. "Mr. O'Toole will of course pay for the time spent in your house and for his board and lodging. I think we have no alternative but to accept. Now I shall put Mr. Blake back to bed."

# chapter 15

T hey call it 'the Steel,' you know," said Henry Mayhew, gazing up at the forbidding gateway of Coldbath Fields house of correction in the afternoon gloom. "After the Bastille. Can't think why."

I had collected Mayhew from the Shakespeare's Head tavern in Wych Street, mere steps from Holywell Street. He claimed to be writing an editorial for his journal, though this seemed to be indistinguishable from enjoying numerous tankards of ale. We had agreed that we would not tell the warders precisely who he was, as he said that being too candid about his profession could produce unfortunate results. Matty was waiting in front of the gates when we arrived, clutching a parcel. She was so grateful to see us, and so slight and small against the prison's great walls, that I felt my anger and disappointment of the day before melt away. I introduced Mayhew and explained that we might be joined by someone of influence who could help us. I still had hopes that Lord Allington would come. I could not help but believe that if anyone could persuade the authorities to reconsider their judgment, it would be him. If he did not appear I would regretfully have to conclude that he remained in thrall to his demons.

The minutes passed. I grew less and less hopeful. To begin with,

Mayhew had asked Matty questions and scribbled in a small note-book. Now we simply stood. Coldbath Fields itself had a dejected, down-at-heel air; and the muddy green sward before the prison seemed principally arranged to attract chill gusts. The gateway, meanwhile, lent the prison an indubitably fortress-like aspect. On the great granite coping stones above the huge wooden doors were the words "The House of Correction for the County of Middlesex" and the date "1794." At the top of the two pillars supporting these stones dangled two pairs of giant black iron fetters. Within the great wooden doors was a smaller one, upon which was pinned the legend "No provisions, cloth-ing, or other articles for the use of prisoners can pass these gates."

Matty was carrying a bundle in which she had some food and cloth-ing for her brother.

"They let me bring him things cos he's being transported so soon," she said by way of explanation. Since we had met before the gateway we had both been very correct and polite. She shivered and pulled her shawl closely around her shoulders, though whether from cold or the dismal effect of the place one could not have said. Mayhew clutched a worn leather bag to him to protect his middle. The wind blew his hair up in tufts.

The turnkey thrust his nose out of the door again.

"If you doan come now, you won't be able to get in at all," he said.

I sighed. "Perhaps we had better go in."

Matty bowed her head. "I'm sorry that Mr. Blake isn't here."

We stepped through the small door, through the space between the outer and inner walls, then into a small, stuffy, dirty gatehouse.

"Back again?" said the turnkey to Matty. He was an unprepossess-ing man dressed in a too-tight dark blue uniform with a brass number pinned to his chest. It was plain she did not like him.

"I'm allowed to see him until he's transported."

"And who are these?"

"No one said I couldn't bring visitors."

"No one said you could, neither."

"The boy is lodging an appeal against his sentence," I said, in an attempt to sound official. "My colleague and I must see him in order to take testimony from him for his lawyers. Surely there is no problem, Warder?"

"I ain't heard nothing about it," said the turnkey. "You'll have to wait until I've asked me superiors."

I smiled pleasantly. "I have no wish to upset you," I said and, reaching into my pocket, I brought out five shillings and made to press it into his palm.

"None of that now," he said sourly, looking around as if someone might be spying upon him. "I could lose me job. Right, let's see what's in there."

Sullenly, Matty untied her bundle to reveal two small loaves, a chunk of cheese, two small withered apples, a bottle of small beer, a clean shirt, a small pot of ointment and a gray blanket of coarse wool. The turnkey picked up each item and examined it with exaggerated care. I suspected that had we not been there he would have taken something.

"You'll have to wait till I get a warder to take you in," he said, pointing at Matty. "You two—I dunno if you can even come in."

"I am sure the governor would not want us to be turned away. Perhaps you might ask one of the warders?" I said.

He bustled us into a bleak stone yard. There were more high walls all around, each with small, heavily barred windows. At the far end there was another stone archway, with a door armed with a row of spikes. Over the lintel was painted in black letters, "Consider your ways! For ye shall all stand before the judgment seat of Christ!"

"Wait there. And if you must talk, talk quiet, it gets the prisoners going. They ain't allowed."

"What, not at all?"

"Rules of the prison. Surprised you didn't know, you being in with lawyers and all." He disappeared back into his gatehouse.

I took out my pocket watch. It was fifteen minutes before three o'clock. A moment later the turnkey shot past, as if chased by a bullet, and disappeared into another doorway. He returned several moments later, followed by a troop of warders all tugging on their jackets and fastening their buttons.

"Captain Avery! You have waited for me." Lord Allington, graceful, firm of step, held a shining beaver hat and a plain but highly polished cane. He was followed by his footman, Mr. Threlfall, who ignored me, and a little behind them, Lady Agnes in a veiled black bonnet. She also chose not to acknowledge me. There was no hint in Allington of the distress of the day before—indeed it was almost impossible to imagine that broken creature in the man before me.

"Lord Allington, I cannot say how pleased I am that you came." I could not resist taking his hand and shaking it vigorously.

Mayhew and Matty stared at him, speechless. Matty blushed, dropped a clumsy curtsey, looked at the ground and mumbled something.

"May I introduce Matty Horner, Your Lordship, the sister of the prisoner."

He took her hand and gave her a kindly look.

"And Henry Mayhew, a writer and journalist—"

Allington's expression turned as if he had just caught an unpleasant odor.

"A highly respected inquirer into the conditions of the poorest and neediest," I went on.

Mayhew looked startled but simply nodded. It occurred to me with some pleasure that I was becoming quite an accomplished liar.

"He is hoping to be able to write an article regarding the conditions in prisons," I said. This appeared to pacify His Lordship.

From a doorway emerged a gray-haired man with abundant muttonchop whiskers, winged by two warders.

"Your Lordship!" he said, performing a deep bow. "I am Governor Chesterton. Had we known you planned to grace us with a visit—"

"I very particularly did not wish for any fuss, Governor Chesterton," said Lord Allington loftily. "I have come only to view the conditions for children here, and with Captain Avery and his friends to visit one child in particular. As I am sure you know, I am chairman of the Working and Visiting Society and am considering proposing a parliamentary committee to examine the welfare of children in prisons."

The governor begged Lord Allington to take tea in his house. Lord Allington declined. The governor, smiling far too much, said he was certain Lord Allington would find much to commend in Coldbath, which he had overhauled in the ten years since he had taken up the governorship. He glanced anxiously at Mayhew's notebook, and asked what the prisoner's number was.

"His number?" said Allington.

He explained that prisoners were given a number. It made for more efficient organization with upward of 1,300 inmates constantly coming and going.

"He is number 926, sir," said Matty, tremulously.

"You must address him as 'Your Lordship,' young lady," said Lady Agnes.

"Yes, ma'am," Matty whispered anxiously.

One of the warders disappeared and returned with a heavy blue register. "Number 926," he said. "One of the convict boys going to Australia. His cell is on the first floor of the boys' yard. He'll be picking oakum, I'll have him fetched."

"What is he convicted of?" asked Lord Allington.

"Larceny, sir. He stole five pounds and a tart. He was charged and found guilty. He is sentenced to transportation for seven years."

Matty stared at the ground.

"Twenty-five years ago," the governor observed, "the boy would have been hanged. We have come a long way. Transportation removes him from the temptations of the London streets, and the air in Australia is most healthy. After seven years he will be free to return to England, or to farm a small holding for himself."

"The boy and his sister protest that while he has indeed stolen small items before, and been punished for it, he is innocent of this particular crime," I said.

The governor and the wardens smiled thinly.

"May I ask why he is in Coldbath Fields?" said Mayhew. "It is not a convict prison, nor a boys' correctional house."

"The London convict prisons are crammed full of prisoners. There are the hulks on the Thames," said the governor, "but the magistrates do not like younger boys to be kept on them, and so they have seen fit to place convict boys with us until they are transported."

"And when will that be?"

"There is no precise date yet, but I imagine two weeks, if that."

"May we see the child?" Lord Allington said abruptly. He had not warmed to the governor.

"Of course. Perhaps I might walk you through the yards to the visiting room? I think you will find it most interesting. I shall be delighted to answer your questions, but may I entreat you to speak in quiet tones? As you may know, we have introduced at Coldbath a new and advanced regime. The inmates are kept, as far as is possible, in separate cells, and are forbidden to speak. Silence is the rule."

"No speaking at all?" said Lord Allington.

"No, Your Lordship. I found it an invaluable tool in the reintroduction of order in the prison. When I first arrived, ten years ago, the place was monstrously corrupt. The prisoners were entirely idle, those with money bought and sold prison positions, and the whole place was engaged in a vast illicit commerce of goods. I abolished all of that and, with it, all communication, in 1834. The silence helps in the maintenance of order: it prevents the relatively innocent from being further contaminated by the entirely unregenerate, and it forces the inmates to contemplate at length the seriousness of their crimes."

A warder took out a large ring of keys and began to unlock the door with the spikes. It opened onto a long stone hallway which led onto a large yard. The governor, Viscount Allington, Mayhew, Matty and I went ahead, and in a second group, slightly behind us, came His Lordship's entourage and two warders. I was relieved we were to be spared Threlfall and Lady Agnes.

The first thing that struck one—aside from a couple of Scripture texts printed on paper and attached to the walls—was how relentlessly gray it was. There was no ornament of any kind, just gray stone and black gratings. The second was that though the yard was filled with pale men—all dressed identically in voluminous gray trousers, a loose gray shirt with a canvas square upon the back on which each man's number had been inked, and a small gray cap—it was extraordinarily quiet and orderly.

"Behold," said the governor, stretching out his arm, "the treadwheel."

Two long sheds had been divided into thirty stalls. In each stall there was a prisoner. Each prisoner appeared to be continually climbing steps, but it was the wooden steps that moved—downward—not the prisoners. Those inmates not working the treadmill sat silently on the ground before it, resting from their labors.

"We have eight treadwheels at Coldbath. Prisoners are employed throughout working hours. Each must make twelve hundred steps a day. They work for twenty minutes at a time, are given a five-minute break, and then start again."

"What does the treadwheel produce?" Mayhew asked.

"Produce?"

"Does it grind corn or some such?"

"No. It makes nothing," said the governor. "It provides the prisoners with hard labor, as their sentences demand."

We passed through three more yards, all very much the same. In the first the governor informed us that these men had been imprisoned for larceny; in the next that these were in for more serious felonies such as assault; in the third that the men were serving sentences for vagrancy. At first I was impressed by the orderliness. I could see that the experienced criminals were prevented from recruiting the more innocent. But with each yard the sense of gloomy fruitlessness, the absence of voices, the feeling of the terrible isolation of each man, grew upon me. By the third yard I began to feel there was something dreadful in the way that the inmates, resting from their labors and surrounded by a hundred others, neither spoke nor even looked at their fellows. In the fourth yard, the Bible quotations set upon the walls seemed to mock the awful silence: "Behold, how good it is for brethren to dwell together in unity!" and "Swear not at all!"

It seemed to me that the faces of the silent prisoners had become strangely vacant and unnervingly disengaged from the deliberate lack of human contact.

In the last yard we passed a shed in which some twenty or thirty small boys were pulling apart bits of old tarred rope—"picking oakum," it is called—in silence.

"This is our boys' wing. We have another for women," said the governor. "The boy will be on the first floor." He bowed low and took his leave of Lord Allington.

At the end of the yard, the warder opened a thick wooden door which led to a staircase, and up we went.

This time we waited in a small, dark, ill-ventilated room. There was a table and two chairs. Lord Allington sat upon one, and Lady Agnes, who had not spoken a word, on the other. The rest of us remained standing. At length, the door opened slowly. There seemed nothing but darkness behind it.

"Pen, it's me," said Matty. "I've food and a clean shirt and something for your hands."

There was a shuffling sound. From the darkness behind the door emerged a small, gray, stumbling child, like a little patch of twilight. I was taken aback by how very small he seemed—the effect accentuated by the tall warder behind him, the oversized regulation gray trousers and shirt, and the white braces that trailed after him like a ghostly tail. He gave us a quick, suspicious glance filled with apprehension; I saw that his cheeks were streaked with old tears.

"'S'all right, lad," said the warder, "you can talk to your sister."

He looked at us fearfully, then threw himself into his sister's arms.

"Matty," he mumbled, hiding his head in the folds of her shawl while she stretched her arms about him and pulled him to her. On the back of his gray shirt, bisected by Matty's arms, was the canvas square with his number upon it, "926."

For a few minutes the only sound was of the boy's muffled sobs and Matty's half-audible words of comfort. We all looked away, even the warders, who seemed surprisingly affected by the scene.

At last the boy's warder prodded him gently and said, "Come now, boy, you don't want to use up all your time clinging to your sister's skirts."

Gently, Matty pushed him away from her, took hold of his wrists and turned up his palms. They were red raw and very blistered.

"Oh, Pen, they're bad this week."

"'S from the oakum," the boy said in a small voice, looking down.

"I brought a bit of ointment for them," she said.

"Won't do no good now, girl," said the warder, "his hands have gotta harden. That's the only thing what'll keep 'em from bleeding."

Matty smiled and ignored him. She laid her bundle on the table and took from it the small pot of emollient, quickly dabbing it on her brother's palms. The boy, meanwhile, leaned into his sister and muttered to her so quietly that we could not hear his words. He had the pinched look of the London streets, but his skin still had the peach-like softness of a child and his eyes were frightened.

She put her arms around him again and I knew she wished none of us were there. Then she pushed him away.

"Pen, you knowed I said something would turn up? Well, these three fine gentlemen—one of them's even a lord!—have come to see you today to find out if there's anything to be done. To try and help you." He looked up at us once again, this time more in astonishment than fear.

"Pen," I said, "my name is Captain Avery. This is Mr. Mayhew—he is a journalist and is interested in your case—and this is Lord Allington and his sister, Lady Agnes. They have been kind enough to come and hear your story."

The boy stared in wonderment at Allington, then glanced at Matty. Allington looked at him with great seriousness.

"Now, Pen, speak up. You must tell me the truth in all things. What is the prison like?"

The boy looked back at his warder, then at Allington. He seemed lost for words.

Matty nudged him. "His Lordship knows Mr. Dearlove, who runs the ragged school. No need to be afraid of him."

"I'm too small for the shinscraper, sir," the boy said, in a voice barely above a whisper, "so I pick oakum instead. Most every day. They give us gruel and hard bread." He was nervous and his breath came in gasps.

"The shinscraper?" said Lord Allington.

"The treadmill, sir—I mean, Your Lordship," murmured Matty.

Allington leaned forward, took Pen's hand and patted it. The gesture seemed to calm the child.

"Until I take the boat," the boy said, "they let Matty see me each week. The worst thing is the not talking. I got into trouble for talking and they docked my rations. And I'm alone in my cell all night and there's no light and it's so dark, and if you're frightened you're not to cry out, but even if you do, they carn hear you."

I fancied that the warders were touched by this. Even Lady Agnes seemed softened by the child's cruel situation.

"How old are you, Pen?"

"Twelve, I think, sir."

"Well, Pen, now I want you to tell me what happened on the day the police took you. But it must be the truth, for God will know if you lie and we shall not be able to help you."

The boy looked at Matty. "Mr. Taylor what's got a shop in Wych Street, he said I thieved from him but I never. Not that day. I never took the finny."

"He means five pounds, sir," said Matty.

"What did happen?" said Allington.

"I was standing outside his shop and he asked me in. Honest. He said did I want a tart, because he'd seen me in the street and knew I was hungry. I said yes. I was always hungry."

"So you already knew this man?"

Pen looked up suspiciously. "Yeah."

"Why was that? Had you stolen from him before?"

He hesitated. Then he nodded his head. "Only small things. There was never enough to eat. Matty, she tries really, really hard, but sometimes there's nothing. I get so hungry." He looked away as if he knew he had let his sister down.

"Stealing is a mortal sin, Pen."

"Yes, sir."

"So it is to be little wondered that you were not on the best terms with the shop owner, Mr. Taylor."

"No. But that day, he seemed kind. He's got a whole shop. I reckoned that with a whole shop you wouldn't miss a small thing."

"So you went in."

"I went in and he got it out. A penny tart with jam in it. He said, 'You'd like that, wouldn't you?' And I said I would, but I had no money. He said there was no charge, he could see I was really a good boy and if I'd promise not to thieve from him again I could have it. I said yes, I promised, and asked if there was anything he wanted me to do. He said, 'There,' just like that. I picked it up and said thanks, and that my sister would bless him, and I walked out of the shop. And I walked, like, a little way down the street, eating my tart, and he comes out of his shop shouting, 'Stop, thief!' And there's a copper with him, one what's chased me once or twice before, and they're pointing at me. And this man I never seed before, he takes hold of me. I didn't understand what was happening. And Mr. Taylor comes up to me with the copper and he says, 'See what this little thief has taken.' And he lifted up my jacket—it's a brown jacket that Matty got me and it's got big pockets— and the copper puts his hands in my pockets and he says, 'And look, five pounds.'

"I swear, I never seed that money before. I never took it. He says to the copper, 'Took it off the counter.' He said I'd come in begging for a bit of food and when his back was turned I took the tart and the finny, 'calm as you please, and strolled out of the shop.' And all these people gathered round and the copper said he'd have me up before the beak, and Mr. Taylor said who would come and bear witness? And the man that had stopped me said, 'I will, I caught him red-handed.' They took me to the beak's and they said all this had happened. And I swore it wasn't true and I hadn't never seen the money—I'd never stealed money." By now fat tears were sliding down his cheeks. "But no one would believe me. And they said it was larceny, and the copper said that given my previous—I'd been caught once or twice: food mostly, but once for some boxes—it'd be transportation this time." His voice faded away.

"Now, Pen, what are your circumstances? I mean, who do you live with?" said Lord Allington.

"When I was free, sir, you mean?" He wiped his nose with his sleeve. "With Matty, my sister. My ma died when I was a baby, and my pa when I was nine. My pa was ill and when he died we was on the street, but Matty looked after me. She learned me reading and sent me to Sunday school and kept us out of the pan."

"The pan?"

"The workhouse, Your Lordship."

"In the pan they separate you and they work you till you die, then they doan bury you prop'ly," volunteered the boy. "I doan never want to go there."

"All right," said the boy's warder. "Time's nearly up, I'm afraid, Your Lordship."

"May we see the boy's cell?" said Mayhew, looking up from his notes. The warder said no, but Lord Allington announced that he too would like to inspect the place, and so we set off, the boy clutching his sister's hand all the way and occasionally wiping his face on his sleeve, and the rest of us following after.

*We walked down* a long stone passage, lined on one side with small windows onto the yard below, and on the other with narrow wooden doors secured by bolts and bars. It was the last door and dark. The warder drove a key into the old lock. The door, barely wide enough for a man to walk through, slowly swung open with a wretched squeak. The boy thrust himself into his sister's arms again. Mayhew, meanwhile, ducked quickly into the cell. There was barely room for more than two and so I waited until he had emerged to take my look.

The room was entirely unlit save for the light that came in from the passage through a grating above the door, and so it took a moment for me to make it out. It was, I should say, six foot by nine foot, and very cold, its sole furnishings a hammock in which was folded a blanket; a three-legged stool—on which I judged the boy had to climb in order to get into the hammock—and an evil-smelling bucket. On the wall was pinned a piece of card on which one could make out the words "contemplate thy sins." On the cold stone floor there was a Bible, but it was too dark to read.

Lord Allington followed me in and out.

"Is there any light or heating in these cells?" Mayhew asked, notebook at the ready.

"No."

"What, not even in midwinter?"

"No."

Mayhew and His Lordship looked at each other. Their expressions hardened perceptibly.

*When the boy had been returned,* weeping, to the oakum sheds, we retraced our steps. Matty hid her face, mopping it with a rag. We averted our eyes.

At the prison entrance Lord Allington's coach awaited. Mayhew put away his notebook and pencil, bobbed a dutiful good-bye to the Viscount and his sister, and took my hand.

"I must thank you for asking me to come," he said. "I do not know if there is anything I can do for the poor child, but I can at least write about this dreadful system."

I said that Blake and I would attempt to verify the facts of the case, and that we would keep him apprised of our discoveries. Then he shook Matty's hand and strode off southwest in the direction of Ludgate Hill.

"Miss Horner?" His Lordship's voice was melodious, confident—such a contrast from the day before.

Inadvertently, I met Lady Agnes's eyes and felt sure she was thinking something not dissimilar. Matty, somewhat overcome, gave me an anxious look. I nodded reassuringly. She approached His Lordship and curtseyed.

"Miss Horner, I should like to know about your own circumstances. Captain Avery speaks well of you. I understand life has not been kind to you?"

"Well, Your Lordship, I do all right . . ."

"Miss Horner, I believe that in your hour of need you felt yourself alone. But the Lord never abandons us. My sister and I should like to do what we can to help you. We may be able to find you somewhere more suitable to live, and perhaps in time a position."

She gripped her shawl about her.

"I don't want nothing—I mean, anything—for myself, but if you could do something for Pen . . ."

"My dear child, the theft of five pounds is a serious matter—the law is very clear on this. And it was not his first time. Personally, I believe that the transportation of children for such offenses is excessive, just as I believe that the incarceration of children in prisons built to punish grown men is wrong. There are others who think as I do, but I fear our views will not change the system in a day."

She looked crushed but spoke up anyway.

"Sir, Your Lordship, I know that Pen didn't take that money. I know it. Mr. Taylor, he's a tartar, we all know that round our way. He's not to be trusted."

"But it comes down to a matter of your brother's word against that of the shopkeeper and his witnesses. And he was found with the items on his person. It will be very hard to disprove." He spoke gently. The disappointment on Matty's face was painful. Allington took her hand in his and brought his other hand upon it. It was clearly meant as a gesture of comfort, but I did not like it.

I said, "Blake and I will look into the matter, and perhaps we may come up with something."

"In the meantime, Miss Horner, I should like to do what I can to help you," said Allington. "I am on the boards of several homes and charity schools where orphans are given an education and found respectable positions. I think we may find you a place. I have been impressed by your perseverance and your loyalty."

"I had planned to escort Miss Horner home," I said.

"It is very cold," Allington said doubtfully, his hand still upon hers.

"I think perhaps it would be better if we drove Miss Horner in my carriage. Lady Agnes will act as a chaperone. My secretary Mr. Threlfall will take her particulars."

Matty gulped. She gave me a dazed look, as if seeking my permission.

"That is very generous, Your Lordship," I said, suppressing a surge of something—disappointment, unease, I could not tell.

"Yes, Your Lordship," Matty said, still staring at me. "Thank you, Your Lordship."

He put his other arm around her shoulder and walked her to the carriage, where the footman opened the door and Mr. Threlfall helped her in. Lady Agnes, who had volunteered not a single word, followed after.

"Captain Avery," Allington said, "we all owe you a debt of thanks. Myself, perhaps, most of all. Your kindly and charitable instincts do you credit. I know we have other business. I will give it my attention tomorrow and send you word on my decision."

The carriage rumbled away and I was left alone on the steps of the prison.

## chapter 16

The gates locked behind me, I contemplated the gloomy whistling emptiness of Coldbath Fields. It was now dark and there were no cabs to be seen and not a figure upon the road, so I set off in the direction in which I had seen Henry Mayhew go.

I believed it to be a southwesterly course, and reckoned, with my newfound confidence in my orientation around the capital, that I should eventually be certain to stumble upon some part of the city which I would recognize. But as I walked a fog got up, making it hard to deduce my position and muffling all sound. The chill gave a charge to my steps and I kept up a brisk pace for the best part of three-quarters of an hour, getting colder by the minute. I came to a large road which I was informed was High Holborn, but it was so jammed from one end to the other with unmoving carts and vehicles that I foolishly thought it better to continue on foot, though I was now damp through as well as cold. The fog deepened. I tramped across an expanse of mud and grass, and found a solitary wanderer who told me it was Lincoln's Inn and that the Strand was not far south and west. Joyfully I continued, taking a small lane due west that gradually became narrower and twistier and meaner, while the fog grew white and thicker, until I cursed myself for a fool and knew I had lost myself entirely, suspecting I had stumbled into a rookery—probably the very same that Blake had brought me into to meet Gentleman Joe.

A few sorry bundled-up figures had pressed themselves into the sides of the lane in quest of a little shelter. I stopped by a couple and asked for the way to Drury Lane. The answers were so muddled that after fifteen minutes I was more lost than I had been before and I seemed unable to shake off a couple of ugly-looking coves in ragged coats and became convinced they were following me. I accosted a couple more street dwellers, this time mentioning the Cock o' the Hoop tavern and palming them a sixpence. The answers were almost as bad as the previous ones, but I did what I could to follow them and at length was pleased to find myself before that very hostelry. There was already a crowd drinking and fighting outside, and I plunged in, hoping I might lose my attendants. I was at once assailed by the odor of old beer and herring and it was plain I was by far the most prosperous-looking person in the place and the rest of the customers had noted it. I looked about for Gentleman Joe—I remembered his warning that I might on this occasion not leave with my boots—but he was not to be seen. I made out the beefy, red-faced woman who had served us beer on our previous visit barging her way through the carousers, two large jugs in her powerful fists. I detained her, saying I had been in a few days before with Jeremiah Blake—I had no great hope that she would remember—and had spoken with Gentleman Joe, and had returned in the expectation that he had left a message for us. She shook her head witheringly, so I asked her to find someone to lead me to Drury Lane—a request I would have given a good deal not to make—saying there would be a reward at the other end. She landed her two jugs on a table and nodded for me to follow her to the counter, where she muttered to the man serving beer. No message, she said. Then she pulled from the counter a disreputable-looking creature in a bent hat who agreed to take me to Drury Lane, but demanded a small payment in advance, on which point the woman supported him. I had no great hopes that he would not either abandon me or try to rob me at the first opportunity, but I needed to get home and there seemed little to be done except hope that I might overcome whatever might be thrown at me.

We set off through the white murk, hardly able to see more than a few feet before us. Very quickly my guide turned what I judged must be north and I grabbed him by the collar, telling him that I was not a fool and if I thought he was taking me awry he would regret it. He cowered and promised to set me right and we went on for a while, twisting and turning, me holding firmly onto his sleeve, but with no notion where we were heading. At last I heard footsteps behind me, their sound subdued by the fog, and before I could do much but shift my weight to one side, I received a great crack on the shoulder—one that had clearly been meant for my head. I staggered and my guide slipped his sleeve from my fingers and ran off. Someone tried to grab my arms and another launched a blow at my head. I saw stars but managed to throw my weight backward upon one of my attackers and grind my heel down his shin and onto his foot. He stumbled and loosened his grip, and I broke from him and dashed into the gloom, I knew not where. I came up swiftly against a wooden strut—a door post—and pressed myself against it, working away from my assailants. They shouted to each other and cried out to me that I might as well give in, describing in bloodcurdling detail what they would do to me when they found me. Unsurprisingly, this made me ever more determined to elude them. I continued to move slowly along the wall until I came to an opening. With relief I blundered into it, losing my balance and letting out a gasp before I set off down it at a run. This was enough to alert my pursuers, who chased after me.

So we went on for some several hundred yards and several turns, their shouts sometimes receding, then suddenly near. My trousers were spattered with muck to my knees and with every step the mud sucked at me and threatened to make me slip. Thinking them entirely too close, I put my last breath into a final sprint forward but at the moment I did so there came a voice near me which cried, "Stop!"

Such was my surprise that I did stop and found myself on the edge of a pond of stinking water: a seething cesspool. Two more steps and I would have gone in headfirst.

"Who's there?" I gasped as I struggled for breath. A lean figure moved out of the gloaming, holding a lantern, with a thick comforter around its neck and its arms protruding too far from its sleeves. I peered again, not quite believing my eyes.

"Mr. Dearlove?" I whispered.

"Captain Avery?" he answered, no less amazed. "I heard someone running, I feared they—you—would fall in. It happens too frequently."

"I am being pursued, we must take care," I said. "Where can we go?"

He pulled me to one side into the shelter of some ruin or other and covered the lantern with his body. For some minutes we did not speak. We heard them pass some way away and then there was quiet. In a hushed voice I explained my situation.

"I have been visiting some families on the other side of this cesspool with food and succor," he said. "They are godly people but poor, and living so close to this sump of filth the children are often sickly. I know these courts and will take you to Drury Lane, of course. But, Captain, just before I heard you I made a terrible discovery of my own, one which must take precedence for the moment. I have found a body, in the water."

"A body! Good God!"

He winced at my language. I apologized and asked how I might be of assistance. Moving swiftly through the fog, Dearlove brought me to his ghastly find.

It lay facedown, entirely saturated with the stinking water. A big man, in good clothes, but without shoes.

"Did he drown?"

"I think he may have been stabbed but I did not get close enough to be sure. To be truthful, I could not bring myself to."

It was hard to make much out in the dark. I found a piece of broken wood and endeavored to turn the body a little, while Dearlove held the lantern up so we might see something of the face. I could not guess how long it had been in the water, but its features, while bloated and grayish white, had not been worn away. I had noticed before that dead men's faces were often hard to recognize, but something about it caught at my memory, and requesting that Dearlove hold up the lantern a little longer, I poked at the rough sodden cloth of its jacket and stared at the face, the most arresting feature of which was its large bulbous nose.

"What color would you say the cloth was?" I asked.

"I could not swear to anything but black."

"Blue, possibly?"

He nodded doubtfully.

I said, "I think this may be a man who was employed to guard the dead newspaperman, Eldred Woundy."

"You believe it may be connected to your case?" Dearlove's voice shook slightly.

"I cannot be sure, but it is possible."

We debated how to proceed, Dearlove explaining that, if we left it, the body might have disappeared by the time we returned, and that it might also prove difficult to find a single constable willing to make his way into the rookery by night. I offered to remain with the body while he went to the new police, but he refused, pointing out that I was now shaking and reminding me that my pursuers might return. I wondered aloud whether we might appeal to Gentleman Joe.

"You know him?" he said, taken aback.

I explained hurriedly that I had come across him once.

"You know he is the authority and thief master general in these streets," he whispered, "a murderous creature with no morals at all." We agreed in the end that there was nothing for it but to return to Drury Lane together and then proceed to the police station in Bow Street. I could not help wondering whether Sergeant Loin would take any more interest in this body than he had in the others we had brought to his attention.

# chapter 17

By the time we reached Drury Lane I had not stopped shaking and my head ached so badly it felt as if it were held in a vise. Dearlove urged me to go home, promising he would go to Bow Street police station, and would pass on my details should they wish to interview me. With a degree of shame but no little gratitude, I gave in and took a cab to Dean Street. Blake was definitely improved. He lay on the settle, wrapped in his banyan, and a decent fire crackled in the grate. O'Toole had gone to Miss Jenkins's, having been persuaded to pay for supper and lodging. He had initially sulked on being told that she did not allow spirits upon the premises, but had cheered up when I managed to convince her that half a bottle of port might be regarded as medicinal.

It took a little while for the shaking to stop, and the headache would not pass, so it was some time before I was ready to describe the rookery and my encounter with Dearlove. Blake listened with his eyes shut, and when I had finished said he would send to Gentleman Joe about the body and the two bruisers, for he was still owed a favor. I rattled slowly down the stairs to the back to call the hostler's boy, who came up and waited while Blake laboriously wrote a note, sealed it and handed it over with a blunt "You know where it goes."

The boy nodded, deadly serious and eager too, and took the stairs by twos.

Blake fell back on the settle. "Now, tell me about the prison." And I did.

". . . And so he took her off in the carriage. I should be pleased for her, but I cannot help it. I did not like it."

Blake did not smile, but listened intently.

"It is absurd, I know." I took up the poker and stirred the burning embers.

Blake said, "Why did you leave India, William?"

"Oh, a number of things. I was injured in Afghanistan. Helen wanted to return." Out of loyalty to my wife I knew I should say no more. And yet I wondered if the real reason I had come to London was to reveal my true thoughts to the only person to whom I felt such things might be said.

There was a brief silence. Then he said, "She never came round to it, then."

"No. I thought she might, but the place never held much charm for her. I think she imagined that it would all change once she was married, but of course the heat, the dust, the insects, the fevers, the strangeness remained the same. But she tried. She came to Afghanistan with me, you know. We were just married and many of the other army wives were going north, and so she decided to accompany me, though I told her she could stay and set up a household in Calcutta. We went first up to Simla. We missed the worst of the heat, but it was very hard for her—and, of course, it took months.

"We passed the monsoon months in Simla in the cool. Helen loved that. I was still the 'hero of Doora,' and she was part of Society and made a great fuss of."

"And what about you?"

"I am afraid I had tired a little of that, but I did not want to disappoint her since I was the reason she had come. I wanted to make her happy."

"And as a soldier?"

"Oh, I took to it. I am a born soldier, it turns out. They gave me an infantry unit to begin with, then an irregular cavalry unit. Then in Afghanistan they made me captain of an irregular unit of cavalry riflemen. I did well enough. Got my promotion, won my medals."

"In Afghanistan? Hard place. When did you go?"

"December '38. The Governor-General and that martinet Macnaghten—you remember him?"

Blake, his eyes closed, nodded.

"They said the ruler, Dost Mohammed, was in secret talks with the Russians. Threatening our borders, so we must depose him and reinstate the former king, Shah Shuja. Various senior army wives Helen admired were going, so she decided to come too. It was as if she had completely forgotten how much she had disliked the trip from Calcutta. I think she thought it would be like some adventure from the *Arabian Nights*.

"The initial campaign took about nine months. At first it seemed very straightforward. By August '39 we had taken the cities—there are only a few of them—reinstalled Shah Shuja and put Dost Mohammed to flight. But even then Helen was unhappy. She found the traveling hard and she hated seeing me go off to fight. She was sure that I was going to die and she would be abandoned. She was cheered a little when we took Kabul. Things were more settled. There were parties and banquets and plays. Then we found we were to be blessed with a child and so when many of the wives went home at the end of '39, she chose to stay on. I wanted her to return to Simla, but I could see she felt fragile and unwell."

"And what of you?"

"I felt the campaign had been too easy. But I liked my men, and my unit was very effective against the local tribes' ambushes."

"Go on."

"After most of the army left in December, there was a turn for the worse. It had become evident that Shah Shuja—an entirely unworthy creature, heartily despised by his own people—would never keep his throne without the backing of the Company, and there were not enough of us. The campaign began to decline into confusion. Obvious mistakes were made such as even I could see. We were sent out on sorties against tribes who were not, to begin with, our most significant enemies. I lost men pointlessly, but all the commanders would say was that we had to be 'kept on our toes.' Then the army moved to a new fort northeast of Kabul, far more exposed. Our supplies were left in Kabul. The perimeter was—is—too large to defend. If it comes to it, I do not see how the army will be able to defend itself. And," I said more sheepishly, "I came to feel we had no business to be there—in Afghanistan, I mean. It is an impossible place. I cannot see how the Russians could ever use it as a staging post to invade India. The terrain is impassable. The tribes are wild and lawless, their sole wish is to be left alone. They hate Shah Shuja, and increasingly they hate us. Of course, I could say none of this to anyone, and certainly not Helen. Even now—well, you are the only soul to whom I have spoken of it. Though I do not think I was the only one who felt things were going to the bad.

"In the new year Helen became ill. She lost the child in April. I did

not know what to do, how to make it better. I tried, but I could not
seem to bring her any comfort.

"A month or so later I was involved in a sortie against some tribes-
men outside Kabul. It was not my finest hour. I had a difference of opinion with a senior officer. Things did not go well. The matter was . . .
complicated. I was wounded, so my commanding officer decided to send
us back to Simla on the pretext that I was to deliver dispatches. My position had become difficult and I was injured. Helen was in a bad way,
and it made sense. I thought I should have felt humiliated at leaving, but
I did not. Save for leaving my men, I was happy to go. I could not abide
Macnaghten. He fell out with our local man, Alexander Burnes, who
knew more about the place than anyone else. Macnaghten will be the
death of them all. He is surrounded by men who bow and scrape and
agree with whatever he says. Well, perhaps I am wrong—I heard some
weeks ago that Dost Mohammed surrendered in November. But I also
heard that Macnaghten dismissed Willoughby Cotton and has put
General Elphinstone in charge."

"Elphinstone? The stupidest man I ever served under." Blake lay
with his eyes almost closed.

"Indeed."

"Go on," he said.

"The journey to Simla would have tried anyone. It was the last
straw for Helen. It was as if Afghanistan had drained all her reserves.
When we arrived she announced that she could not stay in India. I
could not blame her. So we returned."

"There was no alternative?"

I sighed. "I suggested we move back to Calcutta, or set up home in
Simla. I explained that in England I would not be able to keep her in
the manner to which she had become accustomed. I even proposed

that she return to England and I stay and send her funds. I thought she might prefer it. But she was anxious and the thought of being alone frightened her. As it was, the officials at Simla took a most sympathetic view. Offered me a pension. In fact I am perfectly well now—"

"Save for your limp," said Blake.

"Well, yes, you would notice. The wound healed very well. In India I had the native doctors clean my wounds with ghee, like you did. I swear by it now, but I still have the limp."

"And you are quicker to use your fists too."

"I know," I said, ashamed. *And I am sadder too and he knows that*, I thought.

"And you call out in your sleep."

"I do?"

"So you sold your commission," he said.

"There were plenty of takers—well, you would remember all that. We are reasonably well set up. I have leased a small estate. I train the local militia. Life is quiet. Seeing my sister Louisa again makes up for a good deal. But Helen . . ."

I stood up, went to the fire and rooted the poker around pointlessly in the embers.

"But Helen," he prompted.

I sighed again. "She would have done better to marry someone else. I do not think I will ever make her happy."

"She is not a child, William. She made her own decisions." The fire crackled.

"I have not forgotten, you know," I said in a low voice.

"What?"

"That you tried to tell me. Not to rush in, to take my time. I did not listen."

"Who listens to that kind of advice?"

"I hope the baby will make up for it a little." I stared at the fire. "Blake? Do you still think of your wife, of Anwesha?"

"I do, every day. But her face grows ever fainter in my memory."

*I dozed and woke* and dozed again. At last I woke and it was morning and Blake was shuffling about in his banyan. He had boiled water for coffee and was frying some eggs in a pan.

"Are you well enough to do that?"

He ignored me, then handed me a plate of eggs and a cup of coffee, which I did not refuse.

"Blake, perhaps we should surrender the Wedderburn murder to the new police," I said. I had been turning the matter over in my mind a great deal. "You would at least be safe. Who would be sorry?"

"I would be. The Wedderburns would be. His next victim would be. And you would be."

It was true. My blood was up and I was not ready to give up all and return home. "But if we continue, you may end up dead too," I said.

He did not respond but scooped up his eggs.

"I am with you, you know that," I said. "I wish, however, that you would tell His Lordship about Loin's threats."

Blake slurped his coffee.

"As you wish," I said. "Well, I should return to my rooms and change, and I will look in on Miss Jenkins and O'Toole. Can we not do something with him? Send him somewhere? She cannot be expected to put up with him for another day."

He stood up. "I'll come up with something. Now I'm getting up. I cannot spend another day here."

"Can you even walk? What of your ribs?"

Blake lifted up his shirt. He had removed his bandages and there was a dark bruise all along one side. When I remonstrated he brought out a little screw of paper. Inside was a small ball of opium.

I shook my head. "You are sure?"

He nodded, pulled a little off and ate it.

As he chewed it he said, "She's a nose, by the way."

"What?"

"Matty Horner. Is a nose."

"An informer? Oh, come now, Blake, enough of this! O'Toole I accept. We had it from his own mouth. But Matty? A spy? It is not British to do such things. It is, well, it is *French*."

"It may not be 'British' but it happens all the time. The authorities use spies and informers. Plenty of them. They just don't wish anyone to know it. I'd say they set Matty to keep an eye on us, and before that, to watch the Wedderburns, and maybe the whole of Holywell Street. It would explain why there's never a copper there. That way, they know what's going on, but they don't need to act on it."

A wave of disappointment washed over me. "What possible reason do you have to think that?"

"For one thing the coppers knew we had seen Heffernan."

"One might have followed us from Lord Allington's, and there was a policeman on Cheyne Walk."

He shook his head. "And when he came to see me Loin knew about my Judas notion too. Only you and I and Matty—"

"I recall it," I said curtly. The sympathy for Matty that had so sweetly revived in me drained away once more. "Was she spying on Daniel because of his Chartism?"

"Maybe. Maybe she was watching Nat."

"And all her professed affection for the Wedderburns was a lie.

And her words about improving herself. And when she offered to watch the street for us, all the while she was spying on us."

"She's on the right side of the law. I thought you would approve."

"Do not be facetious."

"You don't understand how such things happen," he said. "She's on her own. By running errands for the coppers she protects herself and Pen, she hopes. The coppers won't move her on like other street sellers. And for all we know, she was forced into it. Pen got himself into trouble, she did this in return. I reckon she cares for the Wedderburns and I'm sure she wishes to improve herself. She probably thought it better that she watched the Wedderburns rather than anyone else."

"If she hoped to protect her brother she has failed."

"I'd say she's got what she can out of the coppers. Theft is theft. Most felons in Coldbath get a visit every three months. She gets to see him once a week."

I laughed indignantly. "Damn me! I believe you *prefer* her as a liar, thief and spy."

Blake shrugged. "I know who she is now. She does what she must. She got herself off the street and out of the lodging houses. She's kept the blue bastards off her back. It takes nerve. I can't blame her for it."

"I swear," I said angrily, "she reminds you of yourself. That is it. You were a little spy too."

"Maybe she does."

*Matty's noxious cellar* was abandoned, the door swinging open upon its hinges. Not a trace of her presence remained; even the hiding place behind the bricks was empty. An old woman in the street told Blake she had not been seen the night before and that a cart had pulled up early that morning and removed everything.

"They have taken her off to some charity school," he said.

"Would she leave Pen so?" Despite my anger, I felt a creeping sense of unease.

"Time to visit Allington."

*At Charles Street* the daily tract on the little desk was entitled *Except Ye Repent, Ye Shall All Likewise Perish*. Lord Allington entered the chilly drawing room with his hands clasped around his back. Lady Agnes followed, taking up a position by the window.

His Lordship took in Blake's face and gasped. Lady Agnes, looking away from the window, saw it too. A small part of me enjoyed her surprise.

"I cannot think what you can be doing appearing here in such a state, Mr. Blake," she said in a lightly ironic tone. "Frankly, I find it discourteous. I can only conclude that you have been in a tavern brawl."

Once again, I had the strangest feeling that she was in some perverse way angling for his attention. I would have contradicted her but somehow Blake knew what I intended. He laid a hand on my arm.

"What leads you to that conclusion, Lady Agnes?" he said.

"Your face."

He half laughed.

"Mr. Blake and Captain Avery," said Lord Allington, looking at the ceiling, "as you know, a great deal of pressure has been brought to bear upon me to end the inquiry in which you have been engaged. After considerable thought, I feel I have no course but to bow to it. I have strayed beyond my calling. My work is to help and heal the laboring classes. The investigation must cease. I should like to thank you for your efforts. It is disappointing that they have come to naught. I will of course see that your work is rewarded and any expenses you have incurred are likewise met. I am sorry that our association should be brought to a close in this manner."

Blake bowed.

"I too am sorry, Your Lordship," I said. "We have also had a deal of pressure brought upon us to cease work on this case, though of a rather cruder sort than you. Two days ago Mr. Blake was visited at his lodgings by two men who told him to withdraw from Your Lordship's inquiry and threatened him with a dreadful fate should he not. I myself came upon them, by which time they had already inflicted considerable damage. That is why, Lady Agnes, he has been indisposed and his face is bruised. He asked me not to speak of it to you, like the stoic man he is. One might almost conclude that someone with considerable influence is actively working to keep the perpetrator of these awful crimes at large. And that thought dismays me. I should also like to add, Your Lordship, that when you requested our services, you said you sought men 'incorruptible and undeflectable.' Those were your very words and I beg you to reconsider."

"I am shamed by your words, Captain Avery. They are bravely said. But I must tell you, sir, I feel I cannot do otherwise."

"I suppose we must abide by your decision, Your Lordship," I said, "but before we go I should like to see Miss Horner. She did not return to her lodgings last night and all her belongings have disappeared."

"I am not sure Miss Horner's circumstances are really a fit subject for two men," Lady Agnes said.

"I beg your pardon?" I said. "We should like to see her now, please."

"That will not be possible," said Lady Agnes. "She is not here. One of our ladies took her to one of our clothing societies to find some suitable garments."

"I am glad you brought Miss Horner and her brother to my attention, Captain Avery," Lord Allington said, almost placatingly, "I truly am. And I should like to do what I can for them. The girl, in particular, appears to have conducted herself with courage and presence of mind. It seemed to us her current circumstances expose her to many dangerous and insalubrious influences and she would be best served by being removed from them. We decided to bring her here, where she was fed, washed and given a clean bed last night. Mr. Threlfall is inquiring whether there may be a place for her at the Union school at Norwood Hill, which takes children from poor and unfortunate backgrounds and gives them lodging and education. It may be that she is too old. If that is the case, we will endeavor to find her a position as a maid-of-all-work in a respectable household, since she seems to have had some education. For the time being she will remain here in the servants' quarters until a decision is reached."

"I see," I said.

"The brother's situation is less easily resolved," said Lord Allington, taking up a piece of paper from the desk. "He is known to our man at the local mission, Mr. Dearlove, who says that he is lively but prone to mischief and increasingly ungovernable. I suspect the only thing that may be done for him would be to try to have his sentence commuted from transportation. He would likely receive a prison sentence of two to four years, with a whipping at the end of it. It is not entirely clear to me that this would be a better outcome than transportation, which, though effecting the parting of brother and sister, might at least offer the prospect of a new start and a healthier life."

I thought of the small boy and his look of desperation as he had been pulled from his sister.

"She will see her brother before he leaves?" said Blake.

Allington hesitated.

"You must see that Coldbath Fields prison is hardly an appropriate place for a young girl," said Lady Agnes. "It may seem harsh, but she is embarking upon a new life—they both are—and they must prepare to be apart."

"But the girl must be able to make her farewell to her brother, and the boy's sole comfort is his sister's visit," I said, appalled. "Surely you can arrange for her to be chaperoned?"

"We will ensure he is visited by our people before he leaves. My brother mentioned he was short of warm clothes and bedding. He will receive them."

I looked at Blake, but his face was closed; it was as if he had already withdrawn from the room. I appealed to Allington.

"Your Lordship, would you reconsider this? Surely they should be able to take their leave of each other? In the meantime we are keen to follow Miss Horner's progress and to confirm she is happy with these arrangements. I should like to see her before I return to Devon. Will you allow me to do that?"

"I am sure that can be arranged," he said. "Perhaps tomorrow, Agnes?"

"I cannot promise, Allington. I shall be in Whitechapel visiting the lying-in hospital. One of the doctors believes he has discovered the means to relieve the pain of childbirth, a vapor. But we are uneasy about his work."

"Why is that?" said Blake, suddenly engaged again.

"If you must know, it is laid down in Genesis that women must bring forth children 'in sorrow,' and thus it might be said that such innovations go against Bible teaching. However, one of our Bible commentators says that 'sorrow' may be translated as 'toil.' We plan to discuss the matter more precisely."

Blake smiled woodenly. I could feel the irritation building in him. "It might be argued that God gave Adam just such relief from pain.

How does it go? 'God caused a deep sleep to fall upon Adam, and he slept; and he took one of his ribs, and closed up the flesh instead thereof.'"

"Unless your opinions have changed since last we met, Mr. Blake, you are an unbeliever," Lady Agnes said. "And therefore your citing of biblical authority can hardly be taken seriously."

"Agnes," said Lord Allington reproachfully. "Mr. Blake, may we return to this attack upon your person? Do you know who these men were?"

"I do."

"And . . . ?"

"As you yourself said, the investigation has ceased and our association has drawn to a close."

Lady Agnes snorted. It was an oddly unladylike sound for such a ladylike woman.

"I am sorry that you feel thus, though I *do* understand it," said Allington with such concern that even I found it slightly exasperating. Blake, I was sure, was starting to seethe. "Let me persist. Do you think your attackers may be protecting the murderer?"

"Perhaps. But they may have other reasons." Barely civil.

"Other reasons?" said Allington. "Do you believe you are any closer to finding the culprit?"

"Yes."

"And?"

"What's it to you, Lord Allington? You've just dispensed with my services."

"But you will continue with your pursuit?"

Blake gave a cursory nod.

Allington smiled. "Humor me, Mr. Blake. Tell me your theories."

Blake was silent for a moment. Then he said calmly, "I was working upon two suppositions. One is that the three dead men had a significant personal connection and that the key to the murders lay in their conjoined pasts. The other was that given the violence and strangeness of the murders, the murderer may be mad, and perhaps driven to kill, almost by a hunger for it. If this is the case, finding him may be more difficult, as such murderers may choose their victims on almost arbitrary grounds. However, since the murdered men had a common profession and are, I believe, linked in other significant ways, I persist in believing that by understanding their pasts we may arrive at the identity of the killer."

"A hunger to kill?" Lord Allington said warily. "My dear Agnes, I do not think this appropriate for your ears."

"I have spent my life facing down evil," Lady Agnes said. "I do not shy away from it now."

"We have discovered that Woundy and the others had a line in blackmail," Blake said. "They regarded it almost as a calling—an infidel calling, if you will. They regarded those wealthy men who bought their books, or visited Mr. Woundy's brothel, or who would pay to keep suppressed the stories of their less salubrious habits, as hypocrites of the worst order. Men who wished to present a respectable face to the world in order to justify their domination of it and their enjoyment of an unjust portion of its spoils. Men who rejoiced in condemning the poor and powerless for profane habits, minor vices and chaotic lives, while secretly indulging their own vices. They delighted in uncovering the secrets of these men and pursued them avidly, and believed they deserved what they got. Perhaps they blackmailed the wrong person, someone with an urge to kill, and thus they met their fate.

"You met Mr. Woundy some months ago, did you not, Your Lordship? Did he and Wedderburn try to blackmail you?"

It was such a very odd thing to say that I was for a moment unable to believe my ears. Lord Allington and Lady Agnes meanwhile stared at Blake, astonished.

Lady Agnes was the first to recover. "How *dare* you speak to His Lordship thus! You vile, discourteous little man! You *want* to drag his name into the mud! You are expressly forbidden to pursue the matter of the dead printers. We shall see that it is so!"

"*Agnes,*" said His Lordship, "enough! Mr. Blake, evidently I have offended you. I did not intend it, but I think it better that you leave." A footman rushed into the room. Blake raised his hands, walked out into the hall and was swiftly "helped" into the street. I gabbled an apology at Lord Allington and then Threlfall took my arm and drew me out into the hall. Lady Agnes was not far behind.

"Captain Avery," she said, "I want you to swear that you will never reveal what you saw here the last time you came. You must see, His Lordship's reputation cannot be sullied by such rumors. It would affect everything he does."

"I swear on my honor, My Lady."

"I thank you for it. I regret that we part on such terms." And at that moment I almost liked her.

I could not see Blake in Charles Street, so I strode, muttering angrily to myself, all the way to Hanover Square until at last I was outside the Oriental Club.

He was standing in the square, waiting for me. I could hardly bring myself to look at him.

"For God's sake, we could have persuaded him," I said. "He *wanted* us to continue. Could you not see it? And I spoke up for you. If you could have just kept a civil tongue in your head for a few minutes. Now we have nothing. No commission, no patron, no authority in this case. And we have lost sight of Matty. How are we to discover how she is, or if she is a spy? We are pursued by Chartists and the new police. Look at you, you can hobble a little, but how will you defend yourself if they come for you? The truth is that you prefer it that way. Jeremiah Blake, abjured by all, alone against the world! Well, you may have your wish. For I have had enough. You may take on the police and the Chartists and the toffs and the madmen all on your own. I shall return home tomorrow."

"I told you, William. There are times when I just cannot bear to dance for them another minute."

"Well, this time you chose your moment particularly ill."

He took something from his pocket and put it in his mouth.

"Is that opium?"

He nodded. I marched up the steps and into the Oriental.

# chapter 18

I had a vain hope that I would pass the evening quietly, but I was seized upon by one of the old Oriental Club hands. "Have you been at some secret heroics?" he said hopefully. "Perhaps you will dine with us?"

I gave my excuses and said I was retiring to my room.

"Ah, but afterward, sir? A man must eat."

So I agreed. An evening of familiar pleasures to put away the memory of the afternoon and to prepare myself for the return to Devon. I bathed and put on clean clothes, dined, and drank enough good claret to put myself into a good humor. The talk was of the cost of the repairs to the Tower of London, the wars in China and Afghanistan (of which there was little definite news), Mr. Carlyle's lectures on heroes, and Monsieur Lafontaine's marvelous demonstrations of animal magnetism.

Sometime near eleven o'clock there was a commotion in the hallway. I could hear a voice protesting loudly. We ignored it for some time, but at length a footman came to the table and with many apologies asked if I might accompany him to the entrance as there was a certain gentleman very insistently asking for me. With sinking heart I excused myself and followed.

"My dear Mr. Avery!" Looking somewhat the worse for wear, his hair teased into chaotic corkscrews, his coat flapping open, his arms revolving widely, Henry Mayhew was seeking to push his way between two liveried members of the club's staff. He was very excited.

"They will not let me in! I have news," he said, rather more loudly than was necessary.

"Mr. Mayhew!" I said. "Please, let the gentleman in."

The footmen fell disdainfully away. Mayhew, surging forward, seemed hardly to notice them.

"Call me Henry, please, Avery! I wanted to show you our editorial. I have written something very strong about the obscenity of children in prisons! I think you will approve! I must admit I am just a little ripped." His eyes were unfocused, but from his pocket he managed to bring forth a slim white journal. The title was *Punch, or the London Charivari*, and below it Mr. Punch was shown grinning evilly, his head in the stocks but his hands grasping tomatoes, as a gathering of little cherubs hovered above him on clouds, holding little scrolls and quills as if calling him to account.

"See, our new issue! It has just come from the presses. And inside on the first page, this."

The page read:

> In the puppet drama of Punch, our hero is cast into prison. He sings, it is true, but we hear the ring of the bars mingling with the song. We are advocates for the correction of offenders; but how many beings are there pining within the walls of

a prison, whose only crimes are poverty and misfortune? In certain prisons in our fair capital, moreover, the prisoners cannot sing and laugh, or talk at all, for while they climb the productless treadmill hour after gloomy hour, the rules forbid all speech and sound, and the heart can only hear the ring of the bars.

But worse than this, the incarceration of children in such places meant for grown men crushes and taints the child's spirit when their removal from the places of their fall should surely rather be an opportunity for instruction and renewal, not one of dull, unthinking punishment. We never looked upon a lark in a cage, and heard him trilling out his music as he sprang upward to the roof of his prison, but we felt sickened with the sight and sound, as contrasting, in our thought, with the free minstrel of the morning, bounding as it were into the blue caverns of the heavens. Such treatment is destructive of the child's spirit. It is nothing less than a crime against childhood!

I was touched by Mayhew's enthusiasm, if a little bemused by his determination to show me his handiwork so late at night, and had not the heart to tell him I would be returning home in the morning.

"This is most kind of you," I said.

"It's nothing. No really, it is. I have no idea if we will be able to get the thing off the presses. *Punch* is dreadfully in debt and on the very edge of bankruptcy, my dear fellow." He began to sag a little, then to topple in earnest.

"Might I invite you in for a nightcap?" I said, casting around for somewhere I could prop him up. The footmen kept their distance and pursed their lips. "We could take it in the library."

"Ver' kind of you, Avery," Mayhew said. "Ver' decent of you indeed. But no, I have more news to impart to you. I have taken more leaves out of your and Mr. Blake's books, so to speak." His mouth broke into a wide, sweet grin. "I have been looking into young Pen's accuser, Mr. Taylor, the shopkeeper. He is on Wych Street, you know, hard by the Shakespeare's Head where we write our modest publication. I have been speaking to anyone I could think of who might know of him, including the street people . . . in the streets. It has, I must say, been most exhilarating. Most exhilarating. I have learned much . . ." His voice, loud and excited, rang about the hall. "But I digress. I have news and have made a most interesting discovery, though I do not know if it can help the boy."

"Come, Mr. Mayhew—Henry—let us discuss this more quietly and privately, one never knows who might be listening," I said, realizing with some disappointment that I was now entirely sober.

"No, Avery," he said in a very loud and indiscreet whisper, holding on tightly to my sleeve. "I will not detain you long. But you should know that Mr. Taylor is not at all what he seems. The shop may seem entirely respectable, but he is well known as a receiver of stolen goods, and also as one who rents out rooms in his premises for, ahem, *assignations.*"

"Indeed?"

"A most unpleasant creature altogether. I have it on good authority—well, I have it on distinctly disreputable but probably truthful authority—that his enterprises are perfectly well known to the local new police. I was told that in return for turning a blind eye, they benefit from his industry to the tune of . . . well, to no small tune. I was also told that he recently went to some considerable effort to have a small thief transported. There it is, for what it is worth. I hope there may be something you can do with it." He let go of my sleeve and patted it a few times. "Now I must to my bed, Avery. I am exceedingly sleepy. Good night, a pleasure as always." And with that he turned tail and staggered out into the dark.

*I rose early* the next morning and sent a note to Lord Allington describing my regret and horror at Blake's rudeness, explaining I had not expected it, nor been party to it. I said it had been an honor to meet him and thanked him for his interest in me. I said I wished him only success in his philanthropic and reforming efforts. I requested that I might call briefly before I returned to Devon to see Matty Horner. I signed it, "Your affectionate (if I may) servant." I breakfasted. There was no answer. I set off for Charles Street. The doorman allowed me in, but I was informed that Matty Horner was not at home, and His Lordship and Lady Agnes were abroad too. The doorman thought the girl had been taken to the orphans' home in Norwood, but he could not swear to it. I waited half an hour in the hallway, then returned to the club, debating what I should do. There was a note from Blake requesting I meet him by the Crown and Anchor in the Strand.

It took me a moment to recognize Blake. He was bent over a stick like an old man and wore an eye patch over his more swollen eye. With his battered face, the effect was uncanny. He *was* an old man. He wore a corduroy jacket, torn at front and back, a greasy old cap and a pair of ragged gloves, which nevertheless were stuffed in the two fingers he was missing, so as to make his hand appear whole. He carried a large hessian bag over his shoulder.

"I have news," he said. No preamble. No apology.

"I, too."

"Thomas Dearlove was murdered last night."

It was as if the air was boxed out of my lungs all at once. "What? *No!*"

"At his school. Knife cuts and a long slash through the guts."

"Like the others?"

"Some resemblance, perhaps. That's as much as I know. Can't exactly ask the coppers. I had a message from Gentleman Joe this morning. An old man looking for shelter found him late last night."

"Thank God a child did not find him. Oh, I should have gone to the police station with him. I should have. Perhaps—"

"You might have ended up dead too. There's more. Joe says the body in the cesspool was Woundy's bruiser. The other skipped town: took passage on a boat to America a couple of days ago, said he'd come into money. Both were in the rookery the day after Woundy's death, avoiding the coppers, drinking mostly. He says one of them said Woundy had dismissed them the night he died. Said he was meeting someone privately. It happened from time to time."

"Does Gentleman Joe know who killed either of them?"

"He says someone had been inquiring after Woundy's men. Not a copper. A man. But I have no description."

"Dearlove . . . I cannot believe it. Where is he?"

"Police deadhouse in Bow Street."

"What shall we do?"

"I must see Dearlove's body. And I've been thinking about Wedderburn and the others. I am sure now that what bound them was not blackmail or lewd books but politics."

"Politics?"

"For one thing, Dearlove called Wedderburn an infidel, and Heffernan said he met Wedderburn twenty years ago at Spa Fields. In those days an infidel was not just a non-believer, but someone who heaped scorn on the Church and held republican opinions too. In the early twenties a community of radicals called the Congregation lived on Spa Fields. They held everything in common, shared earnings and labor and everything else, it was said—lots of stories about free love and revolutionary plots. I reckon Wedderburn and Connie lived there. And perhaps Heffernan and the others too."

"How do you know about Spa Fields?"

"I always know about such things." He smiled and shook his head. "No. I used to throw stones at them when I was a boy. Vicious little brutes we were, and my pa said they were mad, but that if they shared the women they couldn't be all wrong."

It was the first time I had ever heard him refer to his life before India.

"There must be a reason why the coppers are so concerned with Wedderburn and the others when they are also so preoccupied with Chartism. I was thinking about that copper outside Heffernan's: was he on the beat, was he following us or was he watching him?"

"But Wedderburn hated Chartism. He fell out with Daniel over it," I said. "That cannot be it. There could be so many other possibilities. What about Daniel's fury with his father? What about that unpleasant fellow Dugdale? A rivalry, perhaps, a falling-out among thieves? Or perhaps the police are protecting some fallen notable."

"You think evil old Cumberland has been creeping down to Holywell Street to murder publishers of lewd books? I never thought to hear you wonder aloud at corruption in high places, Avery."

"We have seen it before," I said glumly.

He shook his head. "I believe the key is in the past. I want to talk to Connie, try to get her to speak about Spa Fields."

"But even if Wedderburn was a radical, he gave it up long ago, and Woundy's main preoccupation was money. It is the Chartists that Loin minds—Daniel, not his father. In any case, we cannot go near Heffernan again."

"We may have to. So you're with me?"

I nodded. "What of the new police and Loin?"

"We'll have to do our best to keep out of their way."

He passed me his hessian sack. Inside there was a large greasy military coat long since out of commission, an appallingly garish dirty cotton waistcoat, a laborer's cloth cap, a pair of stiff canvas trousers and two square-toed boots such as the working poor wore. I sighed.

"You said you had news too," he said.

"I had a visit from Mayhew last night. It appears Pen Horner's accuser is far from honest himself. I want to try and do something for the boy. And I wish to make sure Matty is content."

He nodded.

"Have you eaten opium today?"

"Yes. It helps with my ribs."

"Have you heard anything from Theo Collinson? I cannot but believe that Allington will make a complaint against you."

"No."

"And what of O'Toole?"

"Miss Jenkins is nursemaiding him today in my rooms."

*There was a constable* in Holywell Street, the first either of us had seen there. For a moment he lingered outside Wedderburn's shop, then continued up the street. We wove between the stalls and shops, keeping as far from him as possible. The usual grim lines of handkerchiefs, neckties and coats were pinned outside Abraham Kravitz's shop, but the old man was nowhere to be seen. Inside, the musty smell of clothes assailed us and Kravitz appeared. For once he was divested of his many layers, revealed as a skinny, wiry creature, all hair and beard. Blake removed his cap and his patch and stood upright; I took off my cap.

"You two again!" He took in our togs and Blake's face and raised his eyebrows. "What you been up to? No good, I'll bet. I s'pose you heard about Woundy? And they're saying the schoolteacher copped it this morning. Where's Matty then? I've not set eyes on her since the day before yesterday. I've got something for her." He waved a dog-eared magazine at us. "Next bit of her story. What've you done with her?"

I explained that Lord Allington had taken up Matty and was looking into Pen's case. He looked skeptical.

"Lord Allington is famous for his charitable works and his religious observance," I said. "If anyone can get the child out of prison it is he, and he may well be able to find a good position for Matty. Either way, she would have received a hot meal and a warm bed."

"As to the boy, it'll take more than a miracle to get him off," the old man said, sniffing dismissively. "What d'you want then? Nice new coat? You could do with one."

"How long's that copper been there?" said Blake.

"Turned up yesterday. Seems we're back on the beat."

"We need to speak to Connie Wedderburn without drawing attention to ourselves."

"Thought you was on the law's side," said the old man beadily. "Yer face says not."

"If you'll go and ask her to come to the shop to see us, I'd be grateful and I'll pay you too. Tell her we've news. If you won't, we'll be off."

"Dunno as you've done much good to that family. Raising all that heartbreak again. Or to Matty."

"We'll leave then."

"Didn't say I wouldn't though," he grumbled. "I'll go. Ask her if she wants to see you."

Connie Wedderburn hurried across the street, head down, her shawl clasped over her head and around her shoulders. For the first time since I had met her she did not look like someone stupefied by grief. If anything, her movements had a pained precision to them, as of someone who had woken up to an unbearably bright sun.

As she came into the shop she caught sight of our garb and Blake's battered face and brought her hand to her mouth.

"Just a blinker. I've had worse," he said.

She took off her shawl, and under her eye was the unmistakable shadow of a bruise.

"I too," she said. She looked haunted and, truth to tell, the look became her. "You got something to tell me about Nat's death then?" she said to Blake quickly, before he could speak, but with no sense of anticipation. "You know who it is?"

"Connie, you're—"

"I don't want to speak of it." Her hand stole up to the bruise and she pressed it.

"I don't have an answer yet, but I figure we're close."

"Why'd you call me over then?"

"I've things to ask. There's more to say," he said, very gentle.

She sat then, and put her head in her hands. Abraham bustled over, patting her on the shoulder.

"You doan have to talk to them if you doan want to."

"Blue bastards gave me these, Connie," Blake said, pointing to his face. "They told me to leave Nat's death be. Three days ago. Then Avery had to use his fists against two men we think the Chartists sent."

The hand pressing the bruise withdrew.

"Mr. Kravitz," Blake said, "I wish to talk to Connie privately. If she will."

The old man tutted. Connie put her hand on his and he gave her an uncharacteristically soft look and took himself off to the front of the shop, grumbling quietly, then stepped outside and shut the door behind him.

"You must have heard about Woundy?" he said. She gave the briefest of nods.

"It was the same man that did for Nat," he continued. "I know it. There are things I need to know." He looked at her almost pleadingly.

She shook her head.

"Woundy paid for your food and the firewood?"

She nodded.

"What will you do now?"

"Shift for myself. Eldred always said he'd give the building to me. If it is mine, I can sell it, or take lodgers. If not, seamstressing—it's where I started. Or even teach school again." She gave a humorless laugh. "Take up my grammar. And if it comes to it, I have family out east, Lincoln way. We won't end up in the spike."

"It's a big thing, to leave you the building. He must have felt he owed you a good deal. There was a lot of history between you."

She gave him a sharp look. "Between the three of us."

"Will you tell me about Spa Fields?"

"I know what you're thinking and you are wrong. You don't understand. I'll not talk about it."

"All right," said Blake mildly. He paused, and I realized he had got the answer he wanted. "Do you know where Eldred lived? Did he have family?"

"No. There was some house he bought but he never went there. He kept a room in Charlotte Street."

"With the 'Governess of Love'?"

She gave him a cool look. "Yeah. Her. But he always kept a bed wherever he worked. Work, money, that was what he loved." She smiled sadly.

"Children?"

She shook her head.

"There's something I must tell you, Connie. The coppers who came to see me. There's word there's a Chartist plot. They have names. A man called Neesom." The color seeped out of her face. He spoke very quietly now. "Can you tell me why one of them is outside your door for the first time since before Nat died?"

"So you was never looking for Nat's murderer. It was always this?"

"You know that's not true, Connie. But I think they are connected and I am trying to understand how."

She closed her eyes and began to rock slowly back and forth. He took her hand.

"I am so afraid for him," she said. "So afraid. But what can I do? He won't listen to me. He looks at me as if he hates me. I can't lose him too, I can't."

"Why'd he hit you?"

"Doan ask."

"He's one of Neesom's young men, isn't he?"

She nodded. "I think so, but I know his head is full of pikes and knives and death to the toffs. He's so young. He won't listen." She thrust her hand to her mouth as if to push back a cry. "He's gone so far from me. He got hisself baptized. He won't eat sugar cos the government taxes it. He took the temperance oath cos drink is sin. I laughed when I heard. After all we went through. Nat went to prison for blasphemy and sedition over and over. I did time, we sold *The Rights of Man* and the *Republican*. We were reported to the beaks for sedition and infidelism by the Society for the Suppression of Vice. We reckoned we were fighting for the rights of freethinkers, for freedom, for land, the vote for men and women, to stop child labor, for the rights of infants not to be brought up hungry. See where it's brought me: I live in Holywell Street, my husband sold smut and my son is a temperance Christian."

"So Daniel has no idea that his father was a radical?"

"And his mother too. No, he doesn't know. After Nat got out of jail in '31, I told him enough. They'd tried to turn him informer. He could have come out and kept the appearance of a radical, all the time reporting back, plenty did. But he couldn't do that. And Daniel was growing and we had one more and another coming. We needed to feed them and keep them safe."

"So he hid his past?"

"*We* hid our pasts," she said. "We couldn't afford no more trouble. So we cut ourselves off from our old friends. But work was hard to find. I'd taught school before the babes came, but I couldn't with two and one on the way. Then six years ago Eldred offered Nat regular work, running the shop, selling his bawdy books. He said yes. It wasn't all I'd hoped for, but we'd've starved else, and Eldred kept us when Nat was arrested a couple of times for obscenity. The books were a joke on them—the swells and gentry who bought them, the only ones who could afford them. They guyed their hypocrisy, the way they come down on the poor for their immoral ways, while they do what they like where nobody sees. You'd be amazed at who bought the stuff. Never had much time for respectability. I've even less now. The old days felt more honest."

"Nat didn't join the Chartists then."

She looked away. "Our radical days were in the past. And the Chartists, there's no love lost between us and them. The National Union of the Working Classes expelled Matthew Blundell for bad morals. He was a drunk and a lecher, they said, and he ran his infidel chapel, made people laugh by preaching blasphemy and insurrection, but truly it was because he hated the Church with all his being. Chartists have no place for people like us. It's all churchgoing and respectability now. Nat and Woundy were even accused of trying to bring down certain Charter men. Nonsense! We fought for equality for all, for women too. For freethinking, fighting the lies of church and state, for what Nat called the Republic of Letters. That was what we believed in twenty years ago. But now, seems like all that has gone. It's church and Sunday best, and votes for men."

"What about Neesom?"

Her eyes welled. "We knew him from years back. He's Charter now, but I always thought him a good man. A kind man even. I thought he might make Daniel understand. But what he wants are soldiers and martyrs."

"Do you know anything of the plot?"

"If I did, do you think I would tell you, Jem Blake?" she snapped. "No, I know nothing. But I . . ." She took hold of Blake's sleeve, dragging his hand up to her face, and stared at him desperately. "I found two knives under Daniel's bed just before Nat died. Please, you both said you came to help us. Help me now. Please. Save my son from this. I can't lose him too!"

Gently, Blake pulled his hand back. "I can't promise when I can't be sure of succeeding, Connie. But I'll do what I can. Do you know where Daniel is?"

"He won't tell me, but Neesom lives out east, Brick Lane way."

"Have you tried to find him? Been down the rookery?"

"Why would I go there?" she said.

"Good place to get lost. Will you tell me how it ties up—this and Spa Fields?"

"Don't ask me about that." She stood up, suddenly angry. "It has nothing to do with it. I'm going back to the littl'uns. You said you'd help us. It's my son that wants helping." She swept her shawl back across her face and marched out of the shop without a backward glance.

Blake rubbed the top of his ragged ear uncomfortably. I thought it prudent to remain silent. Kravitz hobbled back inside. His eyes slid over us with distaste.

"Made a fine confusion of that, I'd say. Now she's unhappy and angry. Wish I'd never set eyes on you. Now 'op it. I've done my bit."

"Come on, Abraham," said Blake. "Who can I speak to about Nat's past? I reckon you know more about him than you said."

"Told you, gave you a name first time you was in here. Carn help it if you doan remember it."

Blake stood for a moment, his head bent so his eyes were entirely shadowed. "Dick Carlile," he said at last. "But you said he was dying and he'd moved long ago."

Abraham Kravitz sniffed. "There's someone in the street might know. But he won't talk to you."

Blake said, "Dugdale."

"He was an infidel like the rest, twenty years ago. Seems like old republicans make fine purveyors of dirty pictures."

Blake was already on his way out of the shop and shuffling over the road. I had to run to catch up with him as he pushed open the door of Dugdale's shop.

He was installed behind his counter. He looked at us twice—the first time to dismiss our poverty, the second to recognize us.

"Seems to me you've got a lot to be fearful about, Mr. Dugdale," said Blake, "with Woundy dead. If I were you, I'd be wondering if I was next."

"Thought I told you to keep clear of Holywell Street!" Dugdale said coldly. "You think I won't follow through? I tell you, you leave us alone or I will follow through!"

"So it was you that sent that blundering oaf to threaten us? Did the coppers tell you to get rid of me? You think they'll help you if he comes back for you?"

"Merrick!" Dugdale called out, throwing the word into the back of the shop.

"You think your bruiser will save you? Woundy's bruisers couldn't help him. And now one of them's dead."

"Get out of my shop! Merrick!"

A stout, slovenly creature lumbered out of the back. I stepped before him to block him, grinning.

Blake leaned across the counter and caught Dugdale's arm. "I reckon if anyone can save you it'll be me, Dugdale. If I catch him."

Dugdale squinted over at his nobbler, who had stepped away from me. "What do you want?"

"I want to know where to find Dick Carlile."

He laughed, incredulous. "Richard Carlile? You think he can help you? Well, you can try. He must be all but out of print, and if he's not he's not far off and living on his sons' charity. They've a print shop by Temple Bar. He might talk to you. If he's minded to. If he can still talk, that is."

———————

*We turned up Newcastle Street,* then left into Wych Street. "Where now?" I said.

"I need to see Dearlove's body."

"Yes, of course. But what about Daniel Wedderburn?"

"What about him?"

"Surely we must allow—though it pains me to say it—for the possibility . . ." I hesitated.

"The possibility of what?" he said.

"Why," I said, lowering my voice so that only he might hear, "that he killed his father and the others."

Blake limped under an awning to catch his breath. He held his ribs. At that moment my eyes alighted upon a shop sign.

"Herbert Taylor, marine stores and fine grocer's."

"An unusual combination," I said. The place looked cheap and un-prepossessing but relatively prosperous for the neighborhood.

"That must be the Taylor who had Pen Horner jailed and whom Mayhew says is a receiver of stolen goods."

My palm was already around the door handle. Blake said hurriedly, "Do not identify yourself. Take a brisk look. Pull down your cap so you will not be recognized. Ask him—"

But I was already away, hunching my shoulders and pulling my cap down in readiness as I entered.

The interior was cheaply paneled but recently painted, and was modestly furnished with a long brown counter on which there were scales with weights and one glass bell jar covering a bowl of boiled sweets. On the shelves behind the counter there were some boxes of tea, sugar, coffee and rice: the extent of the fine groceries. The rest of the shop was crammed with all manner of dusty, well-used junk and jumble: a couple of dining tables with leaves missing; odd chairs; several pairs of curling irons; a collection of assorted wineglasses; a number of muddy, unframed portraits; various tobacco boxes and watches in ugly, silver-plated cases; a moth-eaten fur mantle which bore the legend "worn by the second murderer in Kemble's Macbeth." Opposite the counter were piles of old chapbooks and "blood and thunders" and a stack of well-thumbed periodicals. I nosed among these, aware that I must not appear the most salubrious of customers. The man behind the counter cleared his throat expectantly, and I realized that if called upon to speak I would certainly not sound like a London working man and wondered how I might manage to engage him in an exchange.

"May I help you?" the man asked doubtfully. He was in late middle age, of medium height, and free of hair both around and on top of his head save for a few carefully teased tufts which he had endeavored to smooth over his bare pate. A bulge of flesh wobbled under his chin, and a paunchy stomach indicated a keen and presumably regularly appeased appetite.

I shook my head and muttered something unintelligible. Blake was standing in the middle of the street, looking impatient. I would have to risk a word or two.

"You Mr. Taylor?" I said, my words sounding appallingly strangled and wrong, even to my own ears.

He frowned slightly. "Might be. What d'you want?"

The only disguise I could think of was a thick West Country brogue.

"Errts a marssiff gray mixturr of thangs yoo 'arve 'ere."

He looked deeply puzzled. I might as well have been speaking Hindoostanee. I tried again.

"It is. A massive great mixture of things. You have here," I said slowly, retreating from deepest Devon.

"Oh! Yes," he said, his brow clearing with relief. "Not too many places you can get dry goods and such a wonder as the fur mantle over there. And we got all sorts at the back. Wych Street's best, if you know what I mean, which I'd be more than happy to help you with."

"Oh no," I ventured. "I'll just take two ounces of reg'lur tea. And a little shugur."

"Very well," he said ill-temperedly, weighing out the requisite amounts. I paid my tuppence and left, with little to show for my efforts, and gave my modest report to Blake.

"It'll do," he said. "Little more we can discover today."

"Funny thing," I said. "He has piles of copies of *Master Humphrey's Clock* in there, the one which has *The Old Curiosity Shop* in it. Matty was reading them. It made me recall the part where the boy, Kit Nubbles, has five pounds planted upon him and is sentenced to transportation. It made me think of Pen."

"Say that again," said Blake.

I repeated it. He rubbed his ear.

"Gracious, Blake, you do not think . . . ?"

"There you are," he said. "A lesson. No reading is ever wasted. Give me the bag."

I handed the old hessian bag to him. He retreated under an awning and with an air of utter confidence, together with great speed, dispatched the eye patch and cap into its depths while simultaneously retrieving a clerk's coat and slipping his arms into it. From its pocket he brought out a pair of round spectacles. In his new garb he had the air of a meek man who found the world a worrying place.

In he went, and I, loitering, followed a moment later, making a show of admiring a large stuffed carp. Taylor gave me a suspicious look but turned his attention to Blake.

"May I help you, sir? Anything ail you?"

"I must confess I am taking shelter in your shop. I have come into town to meet my nephew who wishes to take me to the theater later. I am not altogether comfortable in these streets. I have recently had a most unpleasant experience with some footpads. I was lucky I escaped with just these bruises." He gestured at his face. "Forgive me for saying so, but I have always found this area somewhat rough, with pickpockets and such, and the locals quite brusque in their manners." He rubbed his hands together. "But for all that, I am not averse to spending a few pennies should I find something I like."

"I understand your concern, sir," the man said, smoothing his few strands of hair over his head, "but I can assure you we shopkeepers, who are a respectable bunch, have the matter in hand. Wych Street is now regularly patrolled by a constable of the new police, and we are determined to raise the street's tone. I myself was engaged in the capture of the ringleader of all the local pickpockets just under a month ago. Now he is to be transported and his cohorts are blown to the winds."

"The ringleader, you say?" Blake said distractedly.

"Why, yes, sir. Caught red-handed."

"Good gracious!" said Blake. "My congratulations, good riddance! Mr. er . . ."

"Taylor, sir."

Blake ran his hands over the pile of *Master Humphrey's Clock*. "I cannot resist Mr. Dickens."

"The death of little Nell, sir," Taylor said, with a dramatic sigh. "A masterpiece."

"Heartrending. I had it from a circulating library. It would be a pleasure to glance over some chapters again. How many issues do you have here?"

"I could give you a good price on those."

"Mmm," said Blake wistfully. "What a world he draws us. Such lessons."

Taylor laughed suddenly, gleefully. "Funny you should mention that, sir. I've certainly found there's a deal more to be learned from Dickens than you would expect."

Blake looked up innocently. "Whatever do you mean?"

"I'd best not go into it too deep," Taylor said, clearly very pleased with himself, "but I found that Mr. Dickens was of great help when I least expected it."

Blake came up to the counter and placed the pile of magazines upon it. "You've captivated me utterly now! You cannot leave me in suspense!"

Taylor leaned forward. "Let us just say that I fixed that evil trouble-making pickpocket who had blighted our streets with the help of *The Old Curiosity Shop!*"

Blake gasped. "How marvelous! Literature coming to the rescue of life. Might I ask . . . ?"

Taylor smiled, his eyes shining. "A boy has five pounds planted upon him—"

"You mean you planted five pounds?"

"Well," said Taylor, aware that he might have said too much, "I'm not saying—"

"But that is what you did?"

Taylor couldn't resist a satisfied nod.

"How did you manage it?"

"I cannot really give out the details, sir, but believe me, we've bound him up good and proper."

"That is interesting, Mr. Taylor." He gave an odd emphasis to the word, and the man looked up sharply. "And I've a witness too." Blake pointed at me. "Captain Avery?" I straightened up and took off my cap.

"What? Who are you?" Taylor looked at Blake and then at me.

"Jem Blake, Mr. Taylor. I'm an inquiry agent. Perjury is a serious matter."

"I don't know what you mean. I want you to leave my shop."

"I'll be doing that presently, but I want you to retract your accusation against that child."

"You cannot make me."

"You just admitted to fitting him up."

"I'll deny everything. You cannot pin it on me."

"Think carefully before you say more, Mr. Taylor. You don't want to cross me."

"Get out! You've no proof."

"We'll see about that."

"Well, he admitted it to us but he will deny it to anyone else. What can we do?"

"He does not need to deny it. He needs to drop his accusation."

"And how, pray, is he to be persuaded to do that?"

"It's in hand, William, I promise you."


*The Bow Street police station* was five stories high and had a very grand façade of elegant classical stone. The effect was somewhat mitigated, however, by the unedifying collection of rogues and drunkards that hovered around the entrance. Blake had retrieved his nasty eye patch and odorous corduroy jacket and wished to slip in on his own, undetected. I asked why we could not simply and openly pay our respects to a good man.

"A police deadhouse is not a place to pay one's respects," said Blake grimly. "And the last thing we need is to draw the coppers' attention to us. This is Sergeant Loin's station, and as far as he is concerned you are on your way home and I am recovering from a beating. But if I were to be taken—which I won't be—I'd need you to be free to make your politest representations to Collinson and Allington."

"But I was the last to see him," I protested. The more I thought of poor Dearlove, the more certain I was that I had made a terrible mistake in allowing him to report the body on his own. We argued for some minutes and then Blake limped off toward the station, leaving me loitering outside for all the world like one of the idle loafers I had scorned the first day I had walked down Holywell Street. And thus quite as well disguised as he. Why should I not follow him?

The interior of the station was a good deal less impressive than the grand façade: a series of plain whitewashed rooms leading onto a bare courtyard, on the other side of which there were gray-looking cells from where a constant ruckus of calls and drunken shouting emanated.

I could see Blake hobbling through the courtyard after a constable. I had hoped simply to follow him, but there was a skeptical-looking policeman sitting at a desk in the front office through whom it was clear I would have to go. Thankfully there was no sign of Loin. I asked—employing a light Devon burr of which I was quite pleased—if I might pay my respects to Mr. Dearlove, who I'd been told was dead and who had been a rare kindly face in the courts and brought food and succor to my family.

The policeman looked up from a book in which he was making notes with pen and ink. "What do you know about the murder?" he said sharply.

"Nothing."

"What's this about?" he said. "There's another just asked the same. It's not a sight I'd choose to see."

"Just wanted to pay my respects. Didn't know where he might be taken after this, not having no family of his own, so far as I knew." This was no more than the truth.

He continued to eye me suspiciously and insisted on taking my name—one I invented—and my address—I gave Matty's—then bade me follow the old man and the constable with the keys through the courtyard. Blake gave me a sour look and the constable, selecting his keys, ignored me. At the farthest, coldest end of the courtyard we descended some stone steps to a large wooden door. The constable opened it. It gave with a long painful squeak into a still dark cellar. The constable took a candle from his pocket and lit it. The room was cold as a tomb, the air damp and heavy, and there was a sharp, heady, metallic smell—I was grateful for it as it masked the smell of death. The body lay shrouded in a sheet on a long table that might have been an old door on trestles. Blake gestured and the constable, carrying his candle, went to the head and pulled back the sheet so we might see the face. Relaxed into the stone-gray repose of death, Dearlove seemed thinner and gaunter even than I remembered. I was glad his features had not been marred by wounds and knife cuts, but that was the barest consolation. There was no need to pretend to distress.

"Might I say a prayer over the body?" I said. Blake, I could tell, was impatient to examine Dearlove more closely.

The constable did not relish the idea, but could hardly refuse. I shut my eyes ostentatiously; Blake folded his hands and also assumed an observant pose. Through half-closed eyes I saw the constable had closed his too.

"Receive into thy hands, oh Lord, thy servant Thomas Dearlove," I intoned as loudly as I could manage. "He was a good man, a devout man, who devoted himself to the poor and the needy and brought succor to those without . . . those without." There was an awkward silence while I searched for something more to say. "He was a good man . . . he visited the sick and lost in the rookeries. He met with resistance and violence, but he persevered and he was respected. He taught the little children . . ." I rambled on for as long as I could and, when inspiration declined, began on the Lord's Prayer, so as to warn Blake I was coming to an end.

As the words "Thy will be done" issued forth, however, the constable protested, "What are you up to?" He had Blake by both arms and the sheet had slipped from the body, revealing Dearlove's bare torso and a number of ghastly slashes.

"What is it, Constable?" I said, my horror unfeigned.

"He was poking round the body! He was sniffing it! What's your game, you old monster?"

"He should be reported to your senior officer at once!" I said, and seized Blake's other arm, dragging him up the stairs. While the constable locked the deadhouse door, I offered to hold Blake. I began to walk him through the courtyard. As luck would have it, prisoners from the cells were being brought out at that very moment to a waiting covered van, to be conducted to various prisons. The process was far from orderly and so we ducked through the queue and made off as fast as we could. Two constables tried to pursue us, but Blake slipped into one narrow alley, then another, and pressed us deep into the shadow of an old doorway where we both gasped for breath.

"Was it worth it? What did you see?"

"Slashes to the stomach like the others, but not so elaborate. And something else I need to think about. Either way, it won't take long for Loin to work out it was us," he said. "We will have to make the best of what time we have left."

———————

*On the river side* of Temple Bar was a row of ancient doorways, some prosperous, some less so. On one unfeasibly narrow shopfront, cobwebbed with age, its windows darkened, was a discreet but smartly painted sign, "Alfred and Thomas Carlile, printers and booksellers." On either side of the names was an old white pattern of thorns and leaves. It looked oddly familiar but I could not recall why.

The interior was dimly lit with oil lamps and hung with mildly suggestive prints—ladies with large amounts of exposed bosom beaming invitingly at fat, overeager gentlemen in white court wigs. The man at the counter, a florid-looking fellow with pockmarked skin, looked up.

"What d'you want?" he said brusquely. "Nothing here you can afford."

Blake took off his hat, then his eye patch, then his gloves, pushed his hair back from his face, placed both hands on the counter as if ostentatiously to display his missing fingers, leaned forward and stared into the man's eyes. The transformation was impressive and accompanied by an air of menace. The man's eyes flickered uncertainly and he took a step back.

"My name is Jem Blake and I need to talk to your father."

"He is sick."

"All the more need then."

The man frowned. "He has done nothing wrong. Paid his dues. Leave him alone."

"I'm no bluebottle."

"Does he know you?"

It seemed to me that Blake hesitated. "No. But I need to ask him about something that happened a long time ago. Seems everyone else has short memories. Want to ask him about Spa Fields and the *Republican*."

The man considered Blake's words. "I'll ask him if he wants to see you. If he won't, that's it."

"Can't say fairer than that."

He disappeared into the back. When he returned he said, "He'll see you. But don't upset him. Don't tire him. He has had enough pain in his life. Who's your friend?"

"He comes with me."

He gave me a hard look. "All right. Take off your hat. You'll be in the presence of a great man."

At the end of a corridor we came to a dim, stuffy room. In an old chair bolstered by cushions sat an old, tired-looking man, a thin blanket across his bony knees and a stick across his lap. He stared into the embers of a small fire burning in the grate. His hair was cut close to his skull; his eyes were sunken, blinking out of dark gray shadows; his cheeks were hollow and his skin had a dried-out, whiskered look. Slowly he shifted his gaze to us, and I saw that he was not as old as I had thought. I imagined him robust as his son now was; hardship had wasted him.

"So, you want to talk about the old days, do you?" he said. It was a West Country voice, hoarse and strained but unmistakable. No one, it seemed, was truly from London. "Well, you are the only one."

"Come to ask you about Spa Fields. The bookseller Dugdale says you're the one that remembers."

"Bookseller, eh? Is that what he calls himself?" He turned back to the fire.

"Tell me, Mr. Carlile, what is the significance of the white thorn and laurel on the shop sign?"

"Oh, you saw that, did you? Smart fellow. Twenty, thirty years ago it was the infidels' sign, the symbol of republicanism and freethinking. A sop from my sons."

I recalled now that I had seen the same embellishment on Wedderburn's, Dugdale's and Woundy's premises.

"I need your help, Mr. Carlile," Blake went on. "Five men have been murdered, three of them printers whom I think you knew twenty years ago—Eldred Woundy, Nat Wedderburn and Matthew Blundell—and I suspect it was Spa Fields that tied them."

"Did Dugdale also tell you that I was in Dorchester jail for most of that time? What makes you think that I can tell you what you wish to know?"

"There'll be more dead if you don't."

"So you are a bluebottle. Why trouble me? Think I did it?" He laughed, a cracked, mirthless sound. "In all the years when the law came after me I was never accused of murder. And now chance would be a fine thing. Look at me. I've not been out of this house since before the winter. Like as not I never will again."

"I'm not a copper, Mr. Carlile, and I've not come after you. Coppers want to put a lid on it. They think it's powder for Chartists' guns."

"You think to tease out my words by abusing them. You'll have to do better than that. Come here, let me see you. Tell me your name again."

"Jeremiah Blake."

"Some pretty bruises. You related to—"

"No."

He shrugged. "As you like. You have the look of him. Do you know who I am?"

"Richard Carlile."

There was a silence. Carlile's eyes slid back to the fire. "So you do not."

I could not forbear to speak. "We've been many years in India, sir. He cannot be blamed for that."

Carlile looked at me briefly, dismissively.

"India," he said, and he frowned with distaste. "'Small islands, not capable of protecting themselves, are the proper objects for kingdoms to take under their care—'"

Blake interrupted: "'But there is something absurd, in supposing a continent to be perpetually governed by an island.'"

I had no idea from what they quoted but I had seen Blake perform this trick before.

Carlile said, "'Common sense will tell us, that the power which hath endeavored—'"

"'To subdue us, is of all others, the most improper to defend us.'"

The older man added, "'Such is the irresistible nature of truth—'"

"'That all it asks, and all it wants, is the liberty of appearing.'"

"'My own mind—'"

Blake did not hesitate: "'Is my own church.'"

"So you know your Tom Paine, Jeremiah Blake. I went to prison for selling *The Age of Reason* and I named my son Thomas Paine Carlile for him. I raised my boy downstairs and his brother with his ideals of freedom and liberty, his notion of the tyranny of church and state. I gave them the weapons of rational argument and clear thought, the education I struggled and sweated for. I taught them to use a printing press, the greatest gift of man to man, the greatest disseminator of truth and knowledge. And how do they use their education? As Nat Wedderburn did, by printing filth and selling it to those who can afford it. Tom Paine said, 'What we obtain too cheap, we esteem too

lightly; it is dearness only that gives every thing its value.' He was talking about freedom. I have learned its truth in other bitter ways. For all
I know, your father schooled you in those words and they mean nothing to you either."

Blake said, "I had no father. I need to know about Spa Fields. I
mean to catch the monster who has done these things. I'll do it with or
without your help."

"Why do you not ask Connie Wedderburn?"

"She is blinded by grief and she will not talk of the past."

Carlile sat back in his chair and closed his eyes. "I heard of Woundy's death. And Nat's. I was sorry. I did not know about Blundell. I
have not heard his name in many years. I wondered if anyone would
remember or come." He brought his hands together. The sensation
seemed to cause him pain.

"I'll tell you what I remember, Jem Blake, for all the good it will do
you. Twenty years, is it, since Spa Fields? Doesn't feel it. I was in jail
most of the time, as I said. They put me away in 1819. Charged me with
blasphemy, blasphemous libel and seditious libel. I wrote things about
the government it did not want the people to read. The first two charges
were dismissed, but they had me on seditious libel. Three years I got.

"I had been at the Peterloo massacre, you see. One hundred thousand men and women gathered peacefully to demand the vote. People
were going hungry. The government had suspended habeas corpus,
said the country was on the edge of revolt. It was tyranny by any other
name. The local magistrates issued warrants for the arrest of the
speakers, and the army went in and used their swords on the crowd.
Men and women went down before them. I saw a woman hacked to
death by a soldier."

I had, of course, heard of "Peterloo." But the account I had been
given had been very different. A tale of a rioting criminal mob.

"I escaped, got to London and published an account of it. The government confiscated the copies and closed us down. I got hold of a new press, wrote another version. That was the first edition of the *Republican*, my newspaper. We denounced the corruption and iniquity of the government. We demanded true representation. The government branded us traitors, and put a duty of four pennies on the press, so the poor couldn't afford it. We ignored the stamp and we sold more copies than *The Times* itself. More than *The Times!*" He cackled. "They got me in the end, gave me three years, then let me out and gave me another two because I couldn't pay the fifteen-hundred-pound fine. In all I did over nine years in jail. All those years in the damp cells ruined my lungs. Now I'm dying.

"The *Republican* never paid the stamp, and the government kept arresting us. But it never closed us down. When I was jailed, Jane, my wife, kept it going. When she was jailed, my sister Mary took over, until she was arrested. But there were always people to fight on. One hundred and fifty men and women went to jail for selling the *Republican*. Among them were Matthew Blundell, Eldred Woundy, and Nat and Connie Wedderburn.

"They were members of the Spa Fields congregation. It had been started in 1821. There must have been about two hundred odd: freethinkers, infidels, republicans, radicals of all different hues. It was to be a community of like-minded souls, living together, holding everything in common. They took some houses round Spa Fields and in Guildford Road, pooled their labor and undertook to govern themselves democratically through debate and democratic vote, the women with the same rights in the community as the men—at least at first. They farmed some of the common land, advertised their trades. They had a communal kitchen, a laundry, and all the children were minded and schooled together. Connie Wedderburn—Connie Sharp, as she was—taught the younger ones. The notion was that the community would support the individual. If a man went sick, his family would still eat. If he needed medicine, the community would pay. When I was first in prison, the Spa Fields congregation helped my wife. When I came out after three years they gave us shelter. I was grateful for that.

"Nat Wedderburn was an apprentice shoemaker with a fancy to be a literary man. Woundy came from Wales—his father was down the mines, I think. Blundell was a compositor and a former lay preacher who had lost his faith. The three of them ran the Spa Fields press. Printers were always keen on learning and education—which was how I knew them. They wrote to me when I was in jail. Lord! How young they seemed then, and I was only ten years their senior. They wanted to sell the *Republican* and they asked me for advice on politics. I told them we must have a democratic republic and open debate, education for all, the rights of men and women, and we must fight the corruption of organized religion.

"Nat was the leader: direct, clear-headed—people were drawn to him. Woundy was a good organizer and good with money, but he was domineering and impatient with debate. He listened to Nat though. Blundell was an infidel, a performer, a clown—blasphemous, lecherous, but people would laugh as they heard his message."

"Do you remember a man called Heffernan?"

He looked mystified.

"Irishman, landowner with radical sympathies."

Carlile's dull eyes lit up. "The Irishman? I've not thought of him for years. He didn't live in Spa Fields. He took a house nearby. Never took him seriously. He seemed to me a callow creature, but he idolized Nat. And Connie too. Nat wanted to learn the law, and Heffernan had studied it in a casual way, so he helped him. I always thought he was playing at politics, and at the first sign of trouble he would rush back to his comfortable life, and so it proved."

"How long did Spa Fields last?"

"It worked well enough for a while, but it could not sustain itself, and there were always factions and disagreements. There were many different breeds of radical. Most of us were Spenceans, but there were Owenites, blaspheming infidels, those who believed in free love and those who did not. Those who advocated rebellion and revolution, those who thought we should farm in common. Those who championed equality and the rights of the female, and those who thought women should keep their mouths shut. Those who had a taste for power and wished to dominate just for the sake of it. And these divisions were sharpened because Spa Fields never produced quite enough to get by. Heffernan's money, I believe, met some of the shortfalls."

"Where did Wedderburn and his friends stand?"

"Does it matter? Never came to much."

"I think so."

"They wanted the abolition of the stamp on the newspapers, universal suffrage, education, the rights of women and infants, they denounced the corruption in government, and scorned the Church that justified it. They wanted the wholesale reform of Parliament, land reform and redistribution. Nat went to prison for the right of free speech, he sold books banned by the government. He attended political gatherings."

"I thought Spenceans believed in revolution," said Blake.

"They did, and you can see how well they succeeded."

"How did Spa Fields end?"

"It fell away around '24. It was too hard to keep it going and feed everyone. Some blamed its demise on Connie and Nat."

"Why?"

Carlile closed his eyes slowly. A spasm of pain passed across his face. Then he opened his eyes again.

"Connie held that marriage vows were the bonds of women's servitude, legalized prostitution. She said she would belong to no man and her body was hers to do with as she wished. You should have seen her at twenty. She was a fine-looking woman, capable and bold—some said too bold—afraid of no man's censure. She had arrived on her own, took over the teaching of the little children, and took up with Nat. He was entranced by her. The others, Woundy and Blundell, were no less enthralled, and for a while she seemed to bind them all closer. It was about the time I was released from jail. Then she took Heffernan as a lover. He was puppyishly adoring, and handsome in his milk-sop way." Carlile's mouth puckered with disapproval.

"And he had money," I said.

Carlile glanced at me. "I should have said that money was not of great importance to Connie. Having taken them both as lovers, she announced that she would live with them both."

"How did Nat take that?" said Blake.

"He said he shared her belief in free love. To tell the truth, I think it hurt him but he accepted it, and perhaps it was eased by the fact that Heffernan's passion for Connie did not diminish his idolization of Nat."

"And Woundy?"

"There were those who said she went with Woundy too. Maybe she did. She had the measure of him and he took her at her own estimation. He was an argumentative soul, ready for a spat, ambitious, and from what I heard, age never mellowed him, but I believe he cared more for her and Nat than for anyone else.

"Well, some denounced Connie's connubial arrangements. Many of the men argued that women were the weaker sex and should not have an equal voice. They held her up as an example of the dangers of letting a woman have her head. Some of the women worried their men would take other women. There were yet others who coveted Nat's position in the community and wished to undermine him. Some called for them to be expelled, others supported them. They divided the community.

"Eventually Connie fell pregnant. She would not say who the father was. Nat and she chose to leave.

"I heard Woundy left the cause sometime in the late twenties and set about making himself a fortune. Much good it did him. Blundell I heard little of after Spa Fields. He went on making his speeches for a while, but he spent more time in his cups than out of them. As for Heffernan, he disappeared back to his lands and privilege. Perhaps his father threatened to disown him. Never heard of him again, until a few years back, there he was, a Whig Member of Parliament. The party which perpetrated the workhouse, and imprisoned Chartists and radicals alike.

"I kept up with Connie and Nat for some years. We were all scratching a living. He was in and out of prison for selling banned books, seditious libel—much the same as I. They brought the boy—what was his name?—up as Nat's, though most thought he was Heffernan's son.

"I took over the Blackfriars rotunda in 1830 and renamed it the Temple of Reason. We held political debates and lectures. Nat spoke once or twice, Blundell did too, I recall. But Nat never quite became the leader I hoped he would. Then he wrote to me in the early thirties saying he was giving up the cause. He simply walked away from it. He was worn down, I suppose, it was too hard on Connie and the children, and he did not like the new breed of radicals. They judged us and spurned our republicanism. They had no interest in public education or women's rights. It seems to me they are no closer to getting what they want than we were.

"I heard Nat was in Holywell Street selling lewd books. I suppose he was driven to it. Plenty of radical printers from the old days took to it—Dugdale and Woundy among them. I am told," he said disdainfully, "that it provides a decent living. I did not see Nat again. I lost the little I had and went to live in Enfield. London was too hard, and I could not bear what my sons had become. Now I live on their charity and must be grateful for it."

"You beat stamp duty," said Blake. "We have a free press."

"Yes. They brought it down to one penny in '36. Then the steam presses came and the paper got cheaper. Now the poor can buy and read what they will. And what do they choose? *Woundy's* fucking *Weekly*. I hope Eldred enjoyed the joke while he could." He began to cough, and the sound brought the son, Thomas, to the room.

"That's enough now," he said, fussing over the old man's blanket. "You must conserve your strength, Father."

Carlile moved only his eyes. "For what?"

"Why, to get better, Father."

The old man gave him a look and the son retreated behind the chair. "Let me finish, Thomas," Carlile said. "I get few enough visitors."

"You believe you failed," Blake said.

The old man scowled. "The people would not rise. They did not care enough. We were too divided. And we were riddled with informers. Authorities knew our every move. I know that now. Didn't then. They tried to turn me a few times in prison. I always refused, but others were tempted."

Blake said, "Do you know a man called Charles Neesom?"

The old man lay back on his bolster. "He was a bookseller. Good enough type. Tight with the Chartists now."

"Did Wedderburn know him?"

"Dunno. But we are a small tribe, the radical booksellers and printers. We congregate at the same places—the Harlequin in Drury Lane, the Mulberry Bush up near Islington."

"Where would I find Neesom now?"

"He had a bookshop in Brick Lane. Perhaps he still does."

"Do you know Renton O'Toole?"

"The fool O'Toole? Dirty, grubbing little fellow. Believes in nothing. I came across him."

"He had quite an animus against Eldred Woundy."

Carlile gently rubbed the skin around his mouth with a finger. The flesh seemed tender and he winced a little. "I would not know about that."

"Do you have any thought as to who might have killed these men?"

"No." The old man gave a rattling cough. "Honestly, I do not. I always hoped that man could be ruled by rational thought and reason, but I have come to think that almost anyone, under the right circumstances, is capable of inflicting great cruelty and violence on their fellow men. How else do you explain how the well-fed, rich men of Parliament can so basely and brazenly deny the needs of those who suffer so visibly before them on the streets of London?"

"Father," said Thomas anxiously.

"No, never enough!" said Carlile, suddenly riled. "Never enough! I have seen such injustice, such poverty, such mistreatment of the poor, such unjust bondage. I have seen so many men spent and used up in the struggle against it. And yet it seems to me worse now than it ever was. The city is on the edge of the abyss, the poor packed into ever smaller rookeries, living in their own shit.

"I never had much time for poetry, satires and allegories and such. They seemed to me to be a way of hiding what ought to be said straight out. But there's a poem by old Billy Blake—William as he liked to call himself, the man from whom, Mr. Blake, you are so keen to disclaim any association—which cuts to the heart of things." In a sudden movement Carlile rolled back his blankets and levered himself onto his feet, using the arms of his chair. He swayed for a moment, then pulled himself erect, fixed his eyes on a point above our heads and began to declaim. As he did so he rapped out a rhythm with his stick on the floor, and though his voice was now hoarse and much diminished, one could tell that in its prime, it had been a powerful instrument.

> "I wander through each chartered street,
> Near where the chartered Thames does flow,
> And mark in every face I meet
> Marks of weakness, marks of woe.
> In every cry of every man,
> In every infant's cry of fear,
> In every voice, in every ban,
> The mind-forged manacles I hear.
> How the chimney-sweeper's cry
> Every blackening church appalls,
> And the hapless soldier's sigh
> Runs in blood down palace-walls.
> But most through midnight streets I hear
> How the youthful harlot's curse
> Blasts the new-born infant's tear,
> And blights with plagues the marriage-hearse."

As he finished speaking, Carlile sagged. Blake caught him and helped him back into his chair.

"No one remembers old William Blake," Carlile said, his breath coming in wheezes, "except old men like me. He was mad much of the time, and he abandoned the true struggle for his visions. But what he wrote is as true now as it was then. The rich own the city, the poor are exploited and suffer, and in the end all are blighted by inequality and cruelty."

He closed his eyes and he seemed to diminish and become once more a sick old man.

"I have said all I can, Mr. Blake," he said. "I am used up. You will have to fathom the rest out for yourself."

# chapter 19

B lake, his eye patch on, his shuffling gait adopted once more, had passed through Temple Bar into Fleet Street toward the east.

"Jeremiah!" I shouted after him—the noise was, as ever, too great almost to think. "Surely we must go back?"

He continued on his way and I was forced to run after him. "We must relieve Miss Jenkins of O'Toole and you must rest."

"It won't be long before Loin comes looking for me. There's always a chance he may find me. So I must do one more thing today. And Miss Jenkins will manage, though she's likely to be eaten out of hearth and home and talked to death by O'Toole."

"Where do you wish to go?"

"To see Neesom, the Chartist, in Brick Lane."

"The Chartists? Who set a watch on your rooms, sent a spy to steal your papers and attacked me?"

"I must have my notes, and I said to Connie I would do what I could for Daniel. I am sure Neesom knows where he is. Besides, I need to warn them."

"*Warn them?*" I said. "Jeremiah, please tell me you are joking. These men are dangerous revolutionaries."

"Your natural order is not necessarily my natural order, William."

"I see," I said between gritted teeth. "Yesterday you casually in-sulted Lord Allington. Today you plan to warn a band of dangerous conspirators their plot is known. Men who plan the downfall of the country and regard you as an adversary. It is stupidity."

"The conspiracy is doomed," he said. "London will not rise. It never does. There are informers everywhere. You and I uncovered two in a day. The coppers already know everything they need to."

"They are desperate men who will find some other violent way."

"Neesom is not foolish, he is desperate in support of a cause he believes doomed to failure. You heard what Carlile said. They see their fellow men starving and in distress. They have spent years working peacefully for their cause to no avail. They are driven to conspiracy, but they are doomed to failure."

"Good men. Even the Pole who wishes to set light to everything?"

"The Pole, I grant you, is mad."

We seethed at each other. "I do not understand this."

"I should not expect you to," he said. "You are a perfect example of your class."

I turned on my heel and walked away.

"Avery!" he called. I kept walking.

He caught my arm. "It may be the only way to save Daniel Wedder-burn from arrest and transportation, if not hanging."

"But what if he did kill his father and the others? He is intemperate and violent. He has a part in a revolutionary plot. He hated his father and Woundy. He has beaten his mother. He keeps knives in his bed. What she fears is that he killed his father. Perhaps she knows it."

"Then he should pay for that crime and not for one he has yet to commit."

"For God's sake, Jeremiah, why do you choose to do what you do?

You work for Collinson's grandees yet you profess to hate them. Your role in the world is to bring order after crime has disrupted it. And yet you do not believe in the very order you reimpose. I do not understand you."

Blake rubbed his face with the palm of his hand. "Look, the killer of Blundell and Wedderburn and Woundy, whatever you make of them, he is a monster. We must catch him. I believe Neesom knows something. Even if he does not, I must speak to him."

"I think this is utterly wrong, dangerously wrong," I said. "But it is a familiar refrain, is it not? You do as you wish with no recourse to me, and if I do not like it my only alternative is to leave. Just as in India. As if I had no investment myself in the resolution of our endeavor. As if nothing I think or say is of any consequence."

"William," he said.

"I have been a fool," I said. "I have made a mistake. I have come too far from my own beliefs and my own world. I am not made for this. You have said it many times—I am of no use to you. I will return to my lodgings and pack for Devon. I have real obligations there. I find this uneasy twilight world, these half-explained exchanges, exhausting. I am a country squire and this city is more than I can take."

"Self-pity does not become you, William," Blake said.

I shook my head. Blake blew slowly out of his mouth. The air steamed. He shifted his weight from one foot to the other and back.

"Do not go."

"Why not?"

"I trust you."

I sighed. We eyed one another. I sighed again. "Our beliefs, our understanding of the world are too different."

"We both know what is right and what is wrong."

"Do we?"

"And there is Matty. You cannot leave without seeing her. Come with me, Avery. If nothing else, I'll likely have need of your fists."

I thought for a moment. "I want something from you in exchange. My company for some truth. About when you were a child. How you know the rookeries. The lock-picking. You must tell me."

He gave a brief smile. "I was born round here. Up in the St. Giles Rookery. You must have guessed as much."

"Not enough."

"My pa was a thief. The man I called my pa. Started out as a pick-pocket in his younger days, went on to become a cracksman—a house-breaker. You can't do the street stuff forever, you lose your dexterity. I was the oldest and I was trained up for a buzzer—a street thief—from my first steps. He apprenticed me to a pickpocket for a while. I was good enough. I stole everything: laundry off lines, money off kinchins—other kids. And I had a line in diving—trying doors and windows to see what was open. If I was caught I could always talk my way out and then run fast. I must have been seven or eight then. Later my pa took me on for house-breaking. I was a scrawny thing and I could climb anything, get in through anything.

"I learned a bit about good silk, good china, good glass, good jew-elry. Stole my pa's tools and taught myself to pick locks—he gave me a walloping for it. I was shaping up for a fine career in crime. My pa was satisfied, when he wasn't beating me."

"Were you only caught the one time?"

"I had a few turns in Tothill Fields and in Newgate."

"You must have been very young."

"Eight or nine the first time."

"Did you know you did wrong?"

"There were many of us. If we hadn't thieved we'd have starved. It seemed to us that outside the rookery the world cared nothing for us.

We reckoned it could do with being relieved of some of what it had. And it was what I'd been raised to do."

"Did you have any schooling?"

"No."

"Church?"

"Never. My pa had no time for it and it had no time for us."

"So you only stole from the rich?"

"Anyone was fair game. I'm not claiming we were right."

"And your father was caught?"

"Both my parents. And me. We robbed a house and were caught as we were carrying the stuff out. They got my ma for possessing stolen goods from another job. They still passed hard sentences in those days. My pa got hanging, commuted to transportation along with my ma. Someone thought to send me to India. A cheap mascot for a Company regiment."

"And what became of your parents?"

"Don't know. Don't care. They took what they wanted from me: I paid my way from the age of four or five. I owed them nothing."

"Did you have brothers and sisters?"

"Four or five. Another three or four died."

"What became of them?"

He shrugged. "I was left to shift for myself. I did."

"They could be here! Living still!" I said.

"That part of my life is over."

"Is it? You are still picking locks. Does Gentleman Joe know?"

"I've never spoken of it."

"Is your name not recognized?"

"Blake was my ma's name. I took it when I went to India."

"That poet, William Blake. You did know him."

"I never knew him. My ma said he was a great-uncle or some such. I don't know. She'd come down in the world. I never knew her family. I remember she talked of old Billy Blake. He wrote verses and made prints but he was a bit crazed in the head and if you knocked on his door he'd like as not open it naked. Wanted to be ready for Jesus when he came for him." He rubbed his ear and cleared his throat. "And that's as much as I've said about myself in as long as I can remember."

*The cabbie carped* about our rags all the way out east, but he took our money happily enough. It was dusk when we discharged ourselves from the carriage, and the streets were as quiet as any London streets I had stood in. Unnervingly quiet. And the old red-brick houses had a forlorn, abandoned air.

"Spitalfields," said Blake. "These were some of the finest streets in London. The French silk weavers lived here. Princes among artisans. Their silk was like spun gold. The northern steam looms killed their trade, and the whole place is starving before the city's eyes."

To the left of us was silhouetted a large hill like some strange, brutal, gray volcano.

"The Nichol refuse pile," Blake said. "It grows like a poisonous weed." He took off his patch and straightened up. "If Loin has followed me here, he deserves to catch me." He touched his ribs gingerly, then stopped when he caught me watching.

"No more lectures," I said. "Let us get to our destination."

He took us down a side street of silent shuttered houses. Behind us a gang of fellows, swaddled in caps and scarves, muttered and whispered. We turned left into another street, just as quiet and dark. They followed us. We took a right, at the end of which I could see a wider,

better-lit road, and there they were again. Before we achieved the end
of the road, another group of shadowy figures, one of whom carried a
lantern, stepped out in front of us.

"Don't want any trouble," Blake called out. "We're looking for
Charles Neesom. Want to talk to him."

"What makes you think he wants to talk to you?" said one of the
men. The lamplight showed a makeshift club studded with nails
stuffed into his belt. His neighbor appeared to be carrying something
heavy and round, a bludgeon wrapped in cloth.

"I say vee finishing zem now," said another man with an unfamiliar
foreign accent and elaborate whiskers. He opened his jacket to expose
a long knife on one side and a metal bar on the other.

"I think Neesom will want to hear what I have to say," said Blake,
"Major Beniofsky."

The first man commented that it was late to be making a social call,
and the Polish major, for it was he, ignoring Blake, asked his companions if we had been followed. Our pursuers said we had not.

"Ought to take more care," the first man said, turning back to
Blake. "They's rookeries and whatnot near here. Some of they'd kill
you soon as look at you."

"I'll mind it for the future," said Blake calmly. "Take me to Neesom."

There was some debate as to whether they should simply knock us
out and leave us in the street, or take us to Neesom. At first it seemed
they all preferred to murder us, but at length the first man suggested
that Neesom should decide our fate. He demanded, however, that we
submit to being searched. Blake agreed, laying a restraining arm on
mine. They went through our pockets, undid our belts and made us
remove our shoes, jeering and laughing all the while.

The Pole and the first man muttered together. "Neesom's is round the corner, on the left," said the first man. "The white thorn and the laurel. We'll take you."

In Neesom's window a guttering candle put out a little light; above it was the sign with the familiar white pattern. A small bell tinkled as we entered; the Pole and his men piled in behind us.

The room reminded me a little of a library, though the titles were such as would have confounded most keen novel-readers. Shelves of books by Thomas Paine, Percy Shelley, Lord Byron, all read many times before. *An Address to Men of Science* by Richard Carlile. Piles of thin pamphlets with names like *The Principles of Nature* and *Wat Tyler*. In a corner, sitting up at a tall clerk's desk, was Charles Neesom in his thin-rimmed spectacles.

"Mr. Neesom," Blake said.

"Jem Blake," he said, looking coolly at us over his spectacles. "And Captain Avery, isn't it? Peter, would you come through, please." There was the sound of a chair scraping the floor and McDouall the doctor appeared. He started very slightly. The room felt very crowded.

"Peter said you were somewhat the worse for your injuries," said Neesom, standing.

"He did a good job," Blake said. "I do not believe I thanked you, Doctor."

The doctor nodded cautiously. "The swelling still has some way to go," he said.

"May I ask what brings you here?" said Neesom.

"I have some information and some questions," said Blake. "You may know that we seek a murderer. We think he must kill again. Our goal is to stop him. Nothing more, nothing less."

"Then you should take yourself off to the blue bastards. They know more than they say."

One of the men behind us laughed.

"They are not saying it to me, whatever it may be," said Blake. "We mean your cause no harm, Neesom. We merely want to stop this man. Call off your boys."

"Anything else?" said Neesom. Blake shook his head.

"Come, Blake," I said, taking his arm, "let us depart. They are rabble after all."

The men behind us muttered and stirred threateningly.

"Take care, Captain Avery," said Neesom, "our friends are touchy. Major Beniofsky, perhaps you might take your men outside?"

The foreigner looked me up and down, said something obviously coarse in his own language, pulled his knife from his belt and ushered the others through the shop door. They stood ostentatiously outside, occasionally peering through the window. I had no doubt that if Neesom summoned them, they would instantly burst in and murder us.

"I can see that the coppers might want to keep me from something they wish hidden," said Blake. "But I cannot see what you have to gain from watching me, stealing my papers and threatening us. Is it truly more important than letting a monster go on killing? If that is the case, you are not the men I thought you were."

"Do not talk of principle to me. I know the kind of work you do, the men you work for. You're the toffs' creature. Your patron, Lord Allington, hates us. He would be delighted to have us guilty. All those talks at which I saw you. You were a nose all the time. Your Tory friend simply confirms it."

"Don't give me that. McDouall had a good look at my rooms, and you've seen my papers. My politics are my own. Do you think that if I were a nose, I would present myself here in such odd company as Avery? We are what we seem."

"The broadcloth gentry answers to the old lag?"

Blake smiled. "Just so."

McDouall said dourly, "Why do you use a secret code if you have nothing to hide? Your notes are unreadable."

Blake almost laughed. "No code, Doctor, just shorthand, a means of writing quickly. It is used to take down parliamentary speeches." He pulled off his gloves, stretched his hands and rubbed the stumps of his fingers. Neesom stared at them, fascinated.

"They say you lost them fighting next to Xavier Mountstuart as he died," Neesom said.

"I can vouch for it," I said.

"You say you have information for us," said Neesom.

"Your plot's discovered. The coppers have your names: yours, Cardo, Williams, Beniofsky and McDouall. They know about your weapons. They know about Coldbath Fields, the training, the plans to rise, to set alight buildings and the docks, the kidnappings. They are preparing to make examples of you."

McDouall started. Neesom removed his spectacles and began slowly to polish them with the bottom of his shirt.

"Why should we believe you? For all we know you're just a cat's paw for the bluebottles yourself."

"I could be, but I'm not. Your membership is riddled with informers, Neesom. The coppers who knocked me about could talk about little else but your plot—wanted to steer me off Wedderburn and his friends, keep it quiet lest it rouse anger among the poor and they rise with you."

"That is what you have for me, the whisperings of a few blue bastards?"

"And a long story from a police nose in fear of his life."

Neesom bent forward.

"They are coming for you, Neesom. This time it may go harder with you."

"Harder?"

"I read the papers. January 1840, the *Morning Herald*. You, Williams and Beniofsky. Arrested for conspiracy."

"You'll know then that the charges were all dropped."

"And this time?"

"Who's the nose?" Neesom said. "Harney?"

"No."

"Who then? O'Toole?"

Blake said nothing.

"And they are determined to get us?"

"As far as I know they've just informers' confessions and they don't want to admit to how many informers they have. I reckon you can get out of this. But if there is evidence, you'll have to give them a sop: a few pikes in the back room of the Mulberry Bush tavern and someone willing to go down for a few months. As for noses, I daresay there's more than one."

"Why'd you tell us? You are not, as you said, a joiner."

"I believe in the suffrage. But the city'll never rise for you, and it seems to me you are playing into the hands of the authorities. If the winter is as hard as it promises to be, you'll have a good few more members by the end of it and next spring you'll have a bigger petition for Parliament."

"There'll be a few more blameless creatures dead of cold and starvation too. As for petitions, in May we collected over one million three hundred thousand signatures to petition Parliament to pardon the Newport rebels. One million three hundred thousand! More signatures than for our first petition in 1839. More than anyone has ever collected for anything! It took eight masons to carry it from the Old Bailey to Westminster. There was a debate in the Commons, and you know the outcome: the vote was equal, fifty-eight to fifty-eight. The Speaker, damn him, voted against. No reprieve. We have abided by the rules. We have shown what the people in this country want," Neesom said drily. "Those in power do their best to frustrate us. A few of the Tories toyed with us, but they have since concluded we are the great danger of the age. And all around we see great need and great hunger. Only force can now bring what we want." He replaced his spectacles, pushing them up the bridge of his nose.

"What reason do you have to watch me?" said Blake.

"Wanted to know why the bluebottles were so keen to keep an eye on you," said Neesom.

Blake shook his head. "Dr. McDouall?"

The man remained silent.

"Why are they so certain Wedderburn and the others were connected to your conspiracy?" Blake said impatiently.

"I don't know," Neesom answered. "I swear it. Maybe they do believe that if there's a fuss about their deaths it will start riots."

"Perhaps you don't want the murderer found because you can use their deaths to do just that. You are looking to raise the city. What could be more certain to make people angry than the discovery that the authorities care so little for them, they allow murderers to roam free, and innocent men's deaths to go unavenged? If you chose, you could have the story echoing in every tavern in London, and yet you've chosen to keep a lid on it. Until it suits you, perhaps?"

"No. I'll tell you what I know—though it's just rumors and whispers. People say that the blue bastards want the murders forgot. They have been doing their best to quieten talk and hush those with notions. Among the notions are ones you'll have heard: that Woundy and Wedderburn blackmailed someone who took his revenge sharp and nasty, like. And that there was an old quarrel between them and us and we killed them. I deny that."

"You knew Wedderburn and the others. Ten years ago you were on the same side. I have it from good sources."

"I'll not deny I knew them. But not well."

"Then they were men who'd deserted the cause. Judases. For all I know you could have set some of your men on them. Not short of angry men, are you."

Neesom laughed. "To what end? I may be worldly but I am no cynic, Mr. Blake. I would never sacrifice lives so callously. If you truly thought I had, I don't think you would be here. I didn't delight in the road Wedderburn and the others took, but we were hardly enemies. They said they'd paid enough and they didn't like the religion and re-spectability of Chartism. I didn't see how their dirty trade was a proper alternative, but they were not the only ones who withdrew from the struggle. I found succor, faith and a new vigor with the Chartists. They did not. But I will say that if we were to trumpet the injustice of their deaths, no one could blame us."

"What about Daniel Wedderburn?" I said.

"What about him?"

"He is a very angry man," I said, "and he was not with his family the night his father was killed."

"It is true he was in a great rage with his father—"

"A rage," I interjected, "his mother says you fostered and exploited, and could have calmed had you so chosen."

"Nat and Connie could have told him about the past. They chose not to. How is she?"

"How would you expect?" I said scornfully.

"I don't believe Daniel killed his father and the others," said Neesom. "He is a believer, he has a fire in his belly, but his passion is for politics. I see no sign of mania."

"But as you say, he is in a great rage."

"The cause needs young men of passion, believers—soldiers, if you like—to carry it on."

"Young soldiers who will fall at the first charge," I said, sarcastic. "Oh, martyrs, you mean."

"Do not mock me, Captain Avery," said Neesom mildly. "I have spent my life fighting for things you take for granted: for rights and laws and justice, to vote, to eat, to work fair hours for a fair day's wage in conditions that will not take years off a man's life. Things which all men—and women—deserve and few enjoy. I've given my life to the cause, lost everything three times over, had years taken from me. And still, the government ignores us and guards its privileges in all its unjust forms. We may fight for decades more, or, God forbid, for longer than that. One must have conviction, and anger, and new blood, to carry it on, as the old lose strength and fade. To keep the cause going we must pass the fight and the fire from generation to generation. The costs are high to those who choose to lead, so yes, I need my angry young soldiers, men willing to risk all. If I did not have them, nothing would ever change."

"I'd like my notes returned," said Blake suddenly, "and the watch taken off my rooms—your men are wretched at tailing me. I want to be left alone to catch this man. If you have a reason for obstructing me, tell me to my face."

"Dr. McDouall, will you bring Mr. Blake his notes?" said Neesom. McDouall disappeared upstairs.

"That was a fine speech," said Blake quietly. "It would be finer if you were not playing both sides, Neesom."

"I don't follow."

"If you were not a nose for the coppers yourself."

Neesom took his spectacles off. He spoke even more quietly.

"Take care. You are not necessarily among friends."

"I have no interest in your horse trading, Neesom. I've no doubt you have your reasons. Five, six arrests. Years in prison. Possessions confiscated. Threats to your family. A whisper in your ear, and a calculation. The movement is filled with informers, but the cause continues. I think you know all too well that it will not be force that changes things but time and belief. And if you feed a little to the coppers you can continue your work under their noses—converting, educating, 'passing the fight and the fire from generation to generation.' There are problems now, however, with other informers who have exposed what you have not told the coppers, and if your fellow conspirators knew what you were doing they would not be kind. Especially those angry young soldiers so willing to risk all."

Neesom smiled. "That is preposterous."

"I know how such things work. In India I ran men such as you. Men with dreams very different from my masters', but who would feed me a little information to survive."

Neesom shook his head as if he could not believe what he was hearing.

"What if I were to call them all in from outside and accuse you," Blake said, "what would happen? You might order them to kill us, but Avery would take at least one with him, if not two or three, and I'd do my part. Most would not believe my words, but a few would wonder: would he have said anything so rash if there had not been something in it? How quick Neesom was to have him killed. Could it be? There would be a rot among your believers, a stealthy loss of faith in you. And then we would be missed. The companions of Mountstuart. And eventually they would come to you. What a coup for the coppers. But all of this could be avoided. All I want is my murderer. For that I need a favor and some intelligence."

Neesom laughed wryly. "This is all nonsense," he said. He licked his lips. "What favor?"

"I hear there's to be a Chartist meeting tomorrow at the Orange Tree tavern in Holborn. There's something there I need. You'll help me to acquire it. I'll send you instructions. You'll need do nothing awkward or incriminating, I assure you."

"And what is it that you want to know?"

"Where is Daniel Wedderburn?"

"I swear I don't know. He hasn't been seen in a day or two," Neesom said.

"Was he here on the nights that the men were murdered?"

"He stays here often, but he isn't here every night. If you tell me the dates I will try to remember if he was. But as I say, I do not believe he is your killer, however intemperate he may seem."

"Do you expect him tonight?"

"No," said Neesom.

"Are you worried for him?"

"I am certain he will appear when he is ready. Will you let me have O'Toole?"

"He is not your man and I do not have him," said Blake. "Mr. Neesom, how do you pay for these 'arrangements'—the pikes, the books, those men out there?"

Neesom pursed his lips. "Membership is by subscription, Mr. Blake. All comes out of that. There's little left, believe me. As I said, I myself have been beggared three times."

"I'll send you my requirements. I'll be discreet. If I may say so," he went on more loudly, "your men out there are armed with weapons more naturally seen in a rampsman's armory. They don't look like Chartists so much as footpads."

"Desperate times, Mr. Blake," said Neesom, and for the first time he looked discomfited. "Our plans require men with a greater experience of physical measures."

"When you tangle with those types, things become complicated," Blake said. "And you do not need me to tell you that Beniofsky's an unpredictable man."

"Well, it appears we shall be reconsidering our plans, so they may not be our men for much longer," said Neesom.

McDouall reappeared in the doorway. "Your notes, Mr. Blake. They are all there."

Blake took them. "See, just shorthand, no code. I will teach you sometime if you are interested, Dr. McDouall."

"Would you be so good as to call Major Beniofsky in on your way out?" said Neesom. "We have matters to discuss."

Blake had his hand on the door handle. "Dr. McDouall, do you recall when you stitched my head that you mentioned the use of the vapor ether? I wondered if you had encountered it yourself. Can you describe the smell?"

"Why, yes, just once," said McDouall, puzzled. "A very strong, pungent odor, sharp like distilled alcohol, but stronger, such that it made my eyes water."

*The streetlights in Brick Lane* were gloomier and smokier than those in Mayfair. Within a few hundred yards the night became muddily black and we moved beyond sight of Beniofsky's men.

"I have never seen a more murderous-looking crowd," I said. I still did not understand why Blake had disclosed the discovery of the plot to Neesom, and it had not escaped me that the man had given very little in return, and nothing about Daniel Wedderburn's whereabouts.

"Intelligence is currency," Blake said. "I gave Neesom a warning because I'll likely betray him in the end."

It seemed obvious to me that one way or another we must give the details of the plot to the police and betrayal had nothing to do with it, but I let that pass.

"It seems to me now that Daniel Wedderburn is our most likely suspect," I said, "though it grieves me. He has gone into hiding and Neesom clearly protects him. I think we must consider giving some kind of lead to the police about him. It might shift their attention from you."

Blake bowed his head. "I cannot do that."

"By God, why not?"

"I could not hand him to the coppers unless I was certain. Now that Woundy's dead, and the subject is such a sore one, it would be easy to bang him up and have him on the gibbet in days. A young angry Chartist would fit the bill just right. That is how it would work. Believe me."

"And if he is the killer and then kills another, that would be on your conscience."

Blake rubbed his ear. "The chance of another victim against the hanging of a man who may be innocent," he said. "A nice conundrum." He closed his mouth, set his chin and picked up his pace. I knew I should get no more from him on that score.

"How do you know Neesom is an informer?"

"I've a nose for it."

"You can do better than that."

"He did not deny it when I put it to him. I expect the coppers came to him when he was in prison. That's how they do it. Threatened transportation or worse."

"So he is a Judas in his own way too."

"As I said, I knew men like him in India. He is a believer, he thinks that one way or another they will win in the end, either through force, or simply through time. He calculates that to continue his work he must feed the police a few tidbits, but it will make no difference in the end. In the end it is an idea he fights for, and ideas are hard to suppress."

We walked on toward Spitalfields. Blake began to hold his side.

"Why did you not bring up O'Toole's ambush with Neesom? We must get rid of him, by the way, move him somewhere," I said.

"No. We must keep him close."

I felt the cogs of my mind move painfully slowly. "Keep him close?"

"I could not let him get away. He needed to be convinced to stay."

I felt my palms tingle and the rage begin to rise. "You knowingly left him with Miss Jenkins. And the ambush, it was you! Ah, Jeremiah! If you were in better health I should . . ." I set off at a run, for if I had stayed near him I should have punched him.

"I do not suspect him," Blake said raggedly, when he finally caught me up. "But I thought he might know more than he said. Even if I did suspect him, we know his preferred victims are not single ladies of a certain age. I'm sure Miss Jenkins is safe. Unless he has talked her to death."

"Not amusing," I said.


*There were still* a few people on Dean Street when we returned. At least two might plausibly have been watching us. Blake insisted we enter through the backyard, so we doubled back and went round by the hostler's yard. In his rooms a fire was dying in the grate. O'Toole snored on the settle, still in his dress. Miss Jenkins slumbered on the elderly armchair. The table between them was covered in empty, crumb-covered plates and half-filled teacups of fine porcelain. Miss Jenkins jerked her head up and opened her eyes, confused by the sight of us. I was gusty with relief.

She sat up and went pink, protesting that she would not have had us find her thus for anything, and apologizing for dropping off.

"Mr. O'Toole is a most animated talker. Really, I heard things I thought I never should—"

"Half of them untrue, I'm sure, Miss Jenkins," I said.

"Most probably," she admitted, "but he does not stop, charming as he is. I gave him some port. I must admit I was quite glad when he fell asleep at last."

"I assume he has eaten all your supplies," said Blake. "I shall make that good for you."

She protested that if she could be of assistance she was happy, and blushed again.

Someone began to rap on the door.

"Mr. Blake!" came a voice from the other side. "I know you are there. You would do well to let us in!"

O'Toole sprang from sleep, looking blearily but anxiously about.

"Mr. Blake is not here," I called out. "Who is it?"

"Is that Captain Avery? You'd better open the door. This is Sergeant Loin of the Metropolitan Police."

"You must hide me," O'Toole squealed.

"Be a man, O'Toole," I hissed back.

"I'll write you something to give Loin, then I shall take Mr. O'Toole next door," Blake said quietly. "Perhaps he can climb out the window. There is a ledge he could balance upon."

O'Toole's face was such a picture I almost laughed.

The door received two hard blows that caused it to shake on its hinges.

"Sergeant Loin, I told you, Mr. Blake is not here, but there is a lady present. I will not open the door if you persist in your violent manner."

The blows ceased.

"I must compose myself," Miss Jenkins called out, smoothing down her dress, while Blake scribbled on a scrap of paper.

"Sergeant Loin! Give the lady a moment, she is most upset." When we unlocked the door it was to discover Loin framed by two uniformed constables. Miss Jenkins managed to look dreadfully pained and anxious.

"I am sorry to have alarmed you, madam," Loin said awkwardly, and made a small bow.

"You startled us dreadfully," I said. "What could possibly bring you here, Sergeant Loin? As I said, Mr. Blake is not here. Miss Jenkins is his neighbor and is most concerned for him. Neither of us have any idea where he is."

"You know why I am here. He is wanted for questioning with regard to the murder of Eldred Woundy."

"I can vouch for the fact that Mr. Blake is no longer working on that case. Lord Allington has discontinued the investigation."

"That's as may be. It did not stop him making his visit to the Bow Street deadhouse—a foolish move. We will have to search for him."

"You cannot simply walk in here," I cried as Loin pushed past me into Blake's bedchamber. As he did so, there came a shout.

"Hi! There!" O'Toole was pointing out the open window.

"O'Toole?" said Loin, incredulously.

"The very same, Sergeant Loin," he said, turning and making an extravagant bow.

"What are you doing here? And why are you wearing a dress?"

"Well, Captain Avery was kind enough to allow me forty winks. As you may have heard, I am somewhat unpopular in certain circles. I was woken by your voices. As for my costume, well, that can wait for another occasion. I could not help hearing that you were looking for Mr. Blake. I just saw the very man about to climb in through the backyard. Something made him reconsider his plan, for he suddenly withdrew and rushed down the lane in the direction of Oxford Street. That was when I shouted. He should not be hard to find: long gray coat, much patched, old gray moleskin cap, black gloves, slight limp."

"Mr. O'Toole!" I said.

Loin looked between us, unable to decide whether he was being gulled or losing crucial moments of pursuit.

"And do you mean to take me in too?" I said recklessly. "After all, we both found Woundy's body and it was I who engaged Woundy's bruisers in fisticuffs."

"My orders do not include you," said Loin.

"This is absurd!" I said.

"It is in truth very simple, Captain Avery," said O'Toole. "You are a gentleman and a war hero. And Mr. Blake is not."

"We shall return soon enough if we do not find him. I shall leave a constable here."

"Not upon the premises, Sergeant Loin," said O'Toole, silkily. "That of course is not permitted."

"He will wait outside," said Loin ill-temperedly, preparing to run down the stairs.

"Sergeant Loin, Mr. Blake asked me to give you this." I drew out Blake's note and thrust it into his hands. "And could you not take Mr. O'Toole with you?"

Loin put it into his pocket, ignoring my words, and pulled the door shut after him.

"Where is he?" I rasped as loud as I dared.

"Clinging onto the wall outside like a veritable human spider," said O'Toole, "an indomitable snail, a resolute vine! Never in all my born days have I seen the like!"

The rest of O'Toole's peroration was lost to me as I was already leaning out the window. In the moonlight Blake looked exceedingly strange, ghostly white and adhering to the wall though there seemed nothing for him to hold on to. I put out my hands to him and had O'Toole hold my middle to ballast me, and thus we pulled him in. He lay on the floor, holding his ribs, his eyes closed in pain and exhaustion. Miss Jenkins called gently from the parlor, offering smelling salts, and I blessed her once again.

"So," O'Toole said when Blake was somewhat recovered. "The new police search for you and I ask myself why."

"The Chartists search for you and I know why," Blake gasped irritably. "And it would be very easy to let them know where you are."

"I understand," said O'Toole, far too genially for my liking.

Miss Jenkins returned to her rooms, bidding a loud good night to the constable outside. We put Blake to bed on his charpoy. O'Toole lay on the settle, his snores breaking through the night's quiet almost as soon as he lay down, while I stretched out upon the carpet, tossing and turning. Eventually sleep ambushed me.

## chapter 20

The Orange Tree tavern near Holborn had a large hall in which about three hundred persons were gathered. The chill of the day was mitigated by the crush of bodies, and the effect, though thankfully warmer, was not altogether pleasant. I had expected a roomful of ragged-trousered revolutionaries. Many of them, however, were respectable-looking men in their Sunday clothes; others looked to be honest working men in corduroys and moleskin.

On a platform at the front of the hall, Neesom smiled benevolently and Dr. McDouall wore his forbidding face. Another man from the previous meeting, Harney, sat next to them. And Watkins, who had led the previous meeting, stood, smiling beatifically and raising his hands for quiet. Over their heads was a banner embroidered with the words "Metropolitan Charter Association." Gradually the buzz ebbed and stilled until there was near silence. I had looked over the crowd repeatedly, but could not see Daniel Wedderburn anywhere.

"Welcome, friends, brothers and guests!" Watkins shouted, and called the meeting to order, offering himself as chairman.

Someone shouted out, "Seconded!" There was a deal of surprisingly orderly voting and "aye"-ing, then Neesom stood up. He introduced two pale, haunted-looking men, a cabinetmaker and a silk weaver, who he said would speak eloquently of the suffering of their communities. He told the audience that two years before, the Chartists had tried to bring their situation to the attention of Parliament but had failed. Now they were more numerous and organized than ever before, especially in London.

"Join us, and London will not lag behind this time! Parliament will be at last rescued from its own corruption! The terrible need of the country will not be denied, nor the rights of the needy!"

There were noisy cheers.

The cabinetmaker began to speak. His tale was a terrible one of desperation and loss, of prosperity giving way to distress and hunger, of children starving, of mothers dying. He spoke simply, without rhetorical skill, but I had never heard want described so painfully, so immediately. On it went, the terrible, unignorable litany of pain and deprivation. When he finished, the weaver spoke of the calamities visited upon his fellow silk workers in Spitalfields, who he said had formerly been "the aristocracy of labor" but were now, in the face of the mechanical looms from the North, starved of work and reduced to burning for fuel the very looms on which they had plied their trade.

I did not trust what I had seen of Neesom. I was more than wary of the Chartists. I had seen famine and want in India. I had read of the complaints of the northern operatives, and in *The Times* read stories of poverty in London. But I had never heard it given tongue like this. My heart was wrung. I could not deny these people had cause to complain. About me, the faces of the audience were somber, there were murmurs of agreement and sympathy, and when the two men sat down it was to sustained, respectful applause.

Neesom stood and spoke of how in London something different was happening than in the North: apprenticeships had been broken and skilled men who had once worked for themselves were driven to seek employment in larger factories owned by a few masters who paid a lower wage, while women and children were sweated in slop shops, and fine old skilled trades died out.

"We make more," he said, "yet wages decrease."

Now Harney leaped up, waving to the assembly with his red cap and calling excitedly upon his "brothers" to sign up to the Charter.

"We shall gather in such numbers that we shall force Parliament to understand that we will not go away, we will not cease from the struggle until every honest working man in the country has a vote, until life improves for the toilers."

He announced there would be a new petition and they would gather millions upon millions of signatures demanding the vote, and present it to Parliament.

"We shall collect so many names that one hundred men will be needed to carry the petition into the Houses of Parliament. The procession will stretch all through London. People will come out to greet us. It will be more splendid and more representative than anything yet seen. A great celebration, and when Parliament sees how we represent the people, they will have to listen to our demands. They will not be able to dismiss us."

I found Harney's brittle rhetoric less to my taste, but my mind was still overthrown by the descriptions I had heard.

Neesom asked the assembly to join the movement while a young man recited a dirge-like poem about "the heroes of Newport."

The assembly formed itself into a slow column and approached the platform, where each signed a paper and brought out a few coins. The young man continued with more poems in a similar vein, all of which had a great many verses.

Not far from me was a man, a Northerner, who had muttered to himself throughout the speeches, despite drawing angry glances from his peers. He had a rough beard and a coarse, swarthy look. As the last poem ended and the column of signatories abated, he began to shout in earnest.

"Our families starve and you tell us to sign a paper?"

Those about him endeavored to shush him, but he ignored them.

"Who am I to speak? I'll tell you. I am every man and woman who starves on a flagstone floor when the work is gone and there's no kindling for a fire. I am every man that walks the streets with bairns keening at home for food. And you say to me, 'Wait'? 'Sign a paper'?"

The assembly stirred uneasily. Those about him told him to hold his tongue. But others called out, "Aye!" And one shouted, "We signed before and we got nothing!" Another said, "Why should we listen to you?"

"I've heard Mr. Harney speak for force," said the Northerner. "Why does Mr. Harney not speak for force now?"

Harney looked highly discomfited but said nothing.

Watkins the cleric held up his hands again for order.

The swarthy Northerner shouted out, "This is a fool's paradise! Nothing can bring us what we deserve save cold iron and force of numbers. Why do you not tell them that? You are just O'Connor's mouthpiece, the blarney merchant. He made his peace with the government. He's in its hands now, while we are crushed and oppressed."

Suddenly Daniel Wedderburn stepped onto the platform. Despite his size he looked very young. A few in the crowd called out, encouraging him to speak. He drew a deep breath.

"I, too, have come to believe that acts of oppression must be met with resistance. In '39 we did not support our brothers in the North. Are we once again to have the rest of the country cry 'Shame!' on the men of the capital? I say no. I say, in London we will plant the tree of Liberty and if necessary bleed the veins of government to succor it."

At this there were furious shouts from some in the audience and cheers from others. I tried to push my way to the front, but fighting had broken out in one part of the crowd. Watkins again waved his arms and called for quiet. It seemed chaos was about to descend.

Then there was a piercing whistle and a loud crack on the doors.

"Police!" came the cry from outside.

"We are raided!" someone shouted, and as one the crowd began to shout and struggle, all looking for some means of escape. Watkins and Neesom called for quiet, but the crowd did not heed them. Wedderburn stepped off the stage into the melee and I lost sight of him. I pushed toward a wall to avoid the surge and press about me. The police began to force doors. Neesom, McDouall and Harney disappeared from the stage; Watkins remained, still calling for calm. A group of men on the left side of the hall charged a small side door and eventually broke it and began to rush out. In the middle of the room people began to scream and push each other. The police were now in. One fellow climbed upon his friend's shoulders, took off his shoe, broke a high window and climbed out through it, mindless of the shards of glass. I followed a small group who made their way toward the back of the platform, the way the speakers had gone. There was a door and then a honeycomb of small rooms, one of which had a low window through which people were climbing out.

I ran past this, through two doors to my right into a room with a desk on which there was a large black ledger. I took it into my arms.

*Blake's sour-faced landlady* opened the door to me.

"There's a regular crowd up there," she muttered crossly. "Too much noise." I caught a gust of the drains and another of her sour breath as she coughed in my face. The constable from the night before had at last taken himself off, and in Blake's rooms O'Toole was tucking into bread and butter and a crusted pie of considerable girth, while Miss Jenkins poured him a cup of tea. O'Toole was speaking between mouthfuls.

". . . and, Miss Jenkins, you would not believe what a certain duke paid me to keep quiet about his string of mistresses all kept at great expense in one street in St. John's Wood, and his lady wife at the county seat all the while."

"I think you might have described this one to me before," Miss Jenkins said faintly.

"I'd not say no to something a little stronger, madam. You know I have some talent as an actor. If we have time later, I might, if you are very good, give you my Lear . . . Ah, Captain Avery, what have you there?"

I ignored him.

"Mr. Blake is here," he continued regardless. "He arrived in a remarkable manner. Covered in grime he was. Bearded, like some railway navvy. Strutting and fretting his hour, I should think. That is *Hamlet*, by the way, Miss Jenkins."

Blake appeared in the doorway of his bedchamber, wiping off the face of the angry Northerner from the meeting.

"Miss Jenkins is leaving," said he.

"Oh no, Mr. Blake, I truly do not mind," she said.

"Any more of O'Toole's gabble will mash your brains, Miss Jenkins. I insist. Anyway, O'Toole, there is really nothing to keep you here any longer."

Blake beckoned me into his room and closed the door, leaving O'Toole gazing beadily after us. "If I must spend another hour in that man's company I think I will be driven to murder myself." He spied the ledger. "Is that it?"

"It was all as Neesom described to you, and was in the room you directed me to."

He took it from me and began to leaf through the pages.

"Will it do?"

"Admirably. I must make use of what time I have." He pulled on something like a seaman's jacket and a comforter, grasping the ledger to himself. "We must visit Heffernan."

"Is that wise?"

"It must be risked. And this"—he pointed at the book—"is our lever. Now I must tell you about Matty." He swung open the door. O'Toole, clearly eavesdropping, was backing away, nursing a cup of hot rum and water in his hands.

"Anything that might interest yours truly?" he said brightly.

"I'm sure it would," said Blake. "We're going out. The hostler's boy will watch you. I know where everything belongs." He lowered threateningly at the little man for a moment, and I truly thought he might do him harm. O'Toole sat down and buried his snout in his cup.

*The maid at number 23 Cheyne Walk* was even more reluctant to let us in than she had been on the earlier occasion.

"Master's not here," she said loudly, attempting to shut the door in our faces.

"We will wait then," said Blake, slipping his foot between door and frame. He tipped his elbow to me and I set off for the back of the house.

"This is not lawful." I could hear her crying as she tried to push him out. "I'll call the peelers!"

"You do that," he said.

I was outside the garden door when Heffernan emerged wearing a perfectly pressed coat with an elaborate fur collar and clutching his hat and cane, his face a picture of furtive anxiety. I realized then why he had seemed familiar to me. Seeing me, he began to stutter.

I took his arm, and he struggled lamely and protested in confused half-sentences.

"We mean you no harm, Mr. Heffernan, but there are things to be said," I said firmly. "We will return inside, I think."

He slumped against my shoulder and nodded forlornly. When the maid saw me with her master, she shrieked.

"Calm yourself, Martha," said Heffernan, attempting to reassume some dignity. "We shall go to the green study. Bear with me, gentlemen." With exaggerated care he removed his expensive coat and handed her his cane and hat. "Some tea, Martha, and a glass of brandy. I shall need it."

Blake sat himself down on one of Heffernan's perfect walnut chairs. He carried the black ledger in his arms. Heffernan fell into another. I remained standing by the door.

"You will not remove your coat, Mr., er, Blake?"

"No."

"Will you have some tea?"

"No."

Blake gave Heffernan the look that few were able to endure for long without feeling obliged to speak.

"Tea, Captain Avery?"

"Kind of you, but no thank you, sir."

The silent scrutiny continued. Heffernan tried to sit still but he could not. He rubbed his hands back and forth over his knees. He sat back and tapped his fingers upon his thighs. He chewed his lip. His eyes darted about anxiously. Blake moved not a whit. At last, when even I felt that the silence had gone on long enough, Heffernan jumped up from his chair, pressed his fist against his mouth and blurted out, "I am sorry I wrote to Lord Allington. I had my reasons. What do you want of me?"

"You knew all of them, Blundell, Wedderburn and Woundy, twenty years ago at Spa Fields."

Heffernan shook his head vigorously.

"I had it from Richard Carlile himself, and in the end from Connie too," said Blake, stretching the truth just a little.

"No. No!"

I said, "Daniel Wedderburn is the picture of you."

The words seemed to startle him. He looked at us both, his eyes brimming with tears, and turned away.

"I was young," he said in a low voice. "Carried away by the wish to do good."

"Why do you go to such lengths to deny it?"

"Why, man, I was arrested for selling seditious literature! Only my father's connections got me released. Do you think I would be where I am now if this were widely known? Now the Chartists are so feared, a past dalliance with political radicalism is regarded as more danger-ous for one's reputation than one with a notorious courtesan!"

"Mr. Disraeli is happy to talk to the Chartists, even to defend them in Parliament. He spoke for the Chartist petition in 1839."

"The Tories' relations with the Chartists are quite different. Mr. Disraeli is a young man with no history."

"Explain it to me." Blake's voice was curious, gentle even. Heffernan leaned toward him as if Blake's words were a lifeline.

"It was a youthful indiscretion," he said pleadingly. "We were dis-tributing Thomas Paine's writings when they were banned. We were nearly transported. My intentions were of the very best. I wished only to give the poor the voice they deserved. But it went too far. Plenty of men in public life have committed far worse derelictions. Why, Melbourne and Palmerston had strings of mistresses."

"And Connie Wedderburn was yours."

"Do not speak of her so!" Heffernan cried. "Have you come merely to rub my face in my own shortcomings or do you have something of substance to say?"

"These three men you knew have been murdered. Do you not have anything to say about it?"

"It was years ago! I was a different man! What would you have me say? It pains me. I am sorry. I had nothing to do with it."

"Does it not make you even a little concerned for your own safety?"

"Should I fear for my own safety, Mr. Blake?" His voice caught and he fiddled with his necktie as if to loosen it.

"Some might speculate that it would suit you well if they disappeared. I am told you are a coming man among the liberals."

Agitation was supplanted by horror.

"I could not do such a thing! I would not know how! I swear to you. What kind of man do you think I am?"

Blake did not answer. "So you no longer have any association with political radicalism?"

Heffernan looked startled. "No!"

Blake nodded. He opened the black ledger and studied it. Heffernan chewed upon his lip. "Mr. Heffernan, when we visited you last time, you quoted a poem, do you recall it?

> "Who fought for freedom more than life? Who gave up all,
>     to die in strife?
> The young, the brave, no more a slave, Immortal Shell! That
>     died so well,
> He fell, and sleeps in honor's grave."

"I cannot say I do."

"Do you recall Mr. Heffernan quoting those lines, Captain Avery?"

"I do."

"Well, it is a well-enough-known poem," Heffernan said. "Must be twenty years old. It is about Shelley. As I say, it dates from a time when I was a firebrand."

"It does not. It was written just two years ago by a young Chartist poet, after the siege of Newport."

"What can I say? I have always had a quick memory. Things I have heard only once I can recall."

"And yet you did not recall saying the lines. Where do you think you would have come upon such a poem?"

"I do not know. In one of the radical papers, perhaps. I see them from time to time. One needs to know what these people are thinking."

"It has never been printed in any newspaper, Mr. Heffernan. It has been recited at a couple of Chartist meetings and there are copies of it in Charles Neesom's bookshop. I think you thought to twit us."

"No, I swear—"

"Mr. Heffernan, we know you kept up your association with Wedderburn and the others. That is partly no doubt because of Daniel, but also because you are still engaged in radical politics. Do you recognize this ledger?"

"I do not."

"You should. It belongs to Charlie Neesom's Chartist group. It has in it, set down, the money you and Woundy have given to his physical-force Chartists. Not a very sensible thing to do, it must be said, but it's all written down here. Captain Avery took it from the offices of the Orange Tree tavern in Holborn not three hours since. Your name is here. In pen and ink."

Heffernan ran his hands through his handsomely coiffed hair. "I did not kill them, Mr. Blake. I did not. I would not know how." He fell back into his chair and put his hands over his face. There was a small whimper.

"Come now, Mr. Heffernan," I said as warmly as I could, drawing close to him. "Would it not be a relief now to speak of it?"

Heffernan did not move.

"Eldred, Nat and Matthew are all dead," said Blake, "and two more now, a teacher and a guard. You must be starting to fear for your own safety."

Silence.

"Mr. Heffernan," I said, "our task is to find out who killed your friends and to prevent more deaths. Perhaps to save your own life. We wish to help you, but we cannot if you do not tell us what you know."

Heffernan lifted his hands from his face. He took a handkerchief from his pocket and dabbed at himself. "You do not understand," he said. "It is all falling about me. Everything."

"What happened after Daniel was born?" said Blake.

Heffernan wrapped his arms about himself. He did not look at either of us. "I did not see Connie and Nat for some years. She did not wish to see me, and would not say for certain that the child was mine, though I was sure he was. I wanted to set her up, but she would not come away with me, you see. She knew I could not marry her, and she would not be a kept woman. Perhaps she loved Nat more than me. I was angry. I returned to Ireland, took my law exams, placated my father. But I did not forget them. I sent money to Spa Fields for the child. I believe it helped them through some difficult times. Nat was in jail on several occasions, as was she. But eventually they left Spa Fields and I lost all knowledge of them.

"Some nine or ten years ago I returned to England and entered Parliament. It was just before the so-called Great Reform Act in '32. Two things came to pass. I worked to get the reform bill through: deals were brokered, promises made and broken, points urged and withdrawn. When finally the bill was put through, the Whigs congratulated themselves on how they had reformed the system and had selflessly given up their privileges. But to me it was a deal of air and effort expended over nothing. The vote was only minimally extended, corruption remains. Parliament disappointed me."

"And the second thing?"

"A year or so after the act passed I was given a place on a committee to look into stamp duty on newspapers and the matter of censorship. The post amused me—although I was known as a radical, no one in Parliament knew about my history. Then Nat came in with a group of petitioners appealing for the reduction of the stamp. Time had dealt harshly with him, but we knew each other at once. He waited for me afterward and asked me if I would meet him. I agreed. I wished to see Daniel, who was then ten or eleven years old. There was no question but that he was my son. Connie was still a fine-looking woman. I offered to take the boy and bring him up as my own. They refused but it was done with no anger—at least on Nat's part. Connie and I, well, she made her choice. Nat and I fell to talking of the past. We found we were of a mind in our disappointment with the Reform Act. Nat said he was done with campaigning. Prison had worn away at him, the old radical groups had been overrun with informers, and now the movement was changing in a direction he could not follow."

"You still believed in the principles of Spa Fields," Blake prompted.

"Yes. It was clear Nat was in some financial difficulty. I tried to press money upon him. He refused it but asked that I see what I might be able to do for the cause—our cause. Connie took the money I offered, though she could hardly bring herself to thank me for it. Through Nat I met Woundy and Blundell again. Woundy had had several busi-

nesses. Blundell had lost his old exuberance but was still devoted to
Nat and, like Nat, was struggling to make ends meet."

"What next?"

"We agreed to take up the torch again when we could, but to do so
privately."

"Secretly, you mean," I said.

"It was you who lent Woundy the capital to set up his businesses,
was it not?" said Blake. "You are his backer."

Heffernan looked shocked.

"I have some friends at Westminster Hall," Blake said. "I've been
told you were lucky to escape prosecution and keep your seat in 1834
over an accusation of fraud."

"It was a mistake, the matter was dropped."

"I found the papers for the case. The other man accused was Eldred
Woundy. You seemed quite tied up in each other's pockets."

Heffernan gulped and fell silent.

"Woundy had a real talent for making money. From his brothel and
his lodging houses, and his mechanism for blackmail. He made you a
pretty fortune too. You helped him."

Heffernan bridled. "He made Nat and Matthew secure. Raised
them out of poverty."

"To sell lewd books and blackmail on his behalf, and take the
heat of the magistrates, while he appeared respectable," I said. "Very
principled."

"You do not understand, young man," Heffernan said. "It was a living, and in the spirit of our beliefs. The books skewered and satirized
the rich hypocrites who bought them. They were the butt of the joke.
And Nat, it transpired, had quite a way with such material. As for
those who handed over money for the protection of their reputations,
they had only themselves to blame. Nat and Eldred disdained them."

"Would not some call you a hypocrite, with your secret son and your secret beliefs, funding a man who made his money through black-mail and brothels and stuffing the poor into lodging houses?" I said, repelled.

"Eldred was always torn between money and principle, but he was true to our principles at the last."

"And have you been true to them?"

"I think so—it is the best part of me. What I have done—what we did—was for a higher cause."

"Giving money to Charles Neesom and the physical-force Chartists, whom I thought you and the others hated," said Blake.

"Chartism is currently the only hope for democracy and freedom. It may have been ambushed by the Christians and temperance men, but there are true spirits within it."

"Charlie Neesom."

"Neesom worked with Nat against the stamp. They never lost touch. He decided to cleave to Chartism, but he works from within to reclaim the old truths and keep the faith."

"But he's Christian and temperance," I said. "And he's planning an armed rebellion."

"Perhaps that is what it will take. But even if it fails, do you have any idea how much money those northern manufacturers pour into the Anti-Corn-Law League's coffers each year?" Heffernan said. "Thousands upon thousands. They can pay for anything: offices of writers and speakers, whole newspapers, bills, halls to speak in. We proceed upon the passion and the faith of poor men already fatigued by sixteen hours' labor before they can turn their thoughts to a better day. These men need help. Support. Money. And believe me, I am not the only man of higher station who has contributed."

"Who else?"

"You have the ledger."

"I do. You made introductions. Brought respectable men to Woundy, who found ways to extract money from them. Blackmailed them."

"You cannot have any proof of that."

"Connie thinks Neesom will send your son to his death," said Blake, changing the subject. "She asked us to save Daniel from him."

Heffernan looked pained. "I will see that he is protected."

"And how will you do that?" said Blake impatiently. "The police already know of the plot, in almost every detail."

"You told them!"

"Not I. The movement is stuffed to bursting with informers. Every inch of it."

Heffernan crumpled. "I cannot believe that."

"And yet it is true."

"Does Daniel know you are his father?" I said, thinking to distract him.

"Connie did not want him to know, and I came to think that it was, perhaps, better that way. Connie said he was asking questions, and it seemed politic not to become too familiar. Sometimes I travel to the Strand and watch him in the street. A tall, strong, handsome young man, don't you think? Do the new police," he spoke tremulously, "do they know about me?"

"Your name is in the book, but we have that. What becomes of it depends upon you. Who knew about you? Perhaps you would kill to ensure you were not found out."

"No! No, I swear it, I did not kill them." He began to weep. I looked away.

"When did you hear about Nat and Blundell?" said Blake.

"Woundy sent me a message the day after Blundell died. He came to tell me of Nat's death. He said the police had turned a blind eye, a cause both for relief and fear, and said he was taking precautions to guard against attack. You cannot imagine the terror I have lived with since Eldred's murder."

"What is it that you fear?" said Blake quietly.

"At first it was exposure and disgrace," Heffernan whispered. "Then that he would come for me and kill me as he had the others. So I keep at home, waiting for I know not what. I have dismissed most of the servants. I have had every door and window locked. Every knock at the door, every rattle at the window, leaves me terrified. I keep a pistol here"—he gestured to his desk—"and another under my pillow. I fear I shall go mad. I have no idea whom to fear."

"I can protect you," said Blake, "and keep your name from the press, I promise you—and I never promise what I cannot deliver. But you must tell me the truth. Otherwise . . ." He held the ledger by his forefinger and thumb, letting it dangle perilously.

"Yes," said Heffernan, "I admit it. I made introductions for Eldred to men of prominence and wealth. He would work them. On their weaknesses and their sympathies, whichever was more effective, then threaten to expose them. They paid handsomely. And it has not been altogether unhelpful to my political career to have such information in reserve."

"So you have used blackmail to extract advantages for yourself. You have good reason to fear Eldred's victims."

"I only used it once or twice, and that was some years ago. Never since. I have always taken great care to ensure that my connection appeared as tenuous and innocent as possible."

"And yet your name is in this ledger and you are shaking in your boots."

"I . . . I . . ."

I looked out the window toward the gray slick of the Thames.

"There is a policeman standing outside the house. I think he has been there for some time," I said.

Heffernan slid from his chair and cowered on the floor.

"Mr. Blake, you could protect me," he said suddenly. "I would pay you handsomely. Save me from this monster! Do not tell the police of my involvement with Neesom, I beg you. I beg you!"

"Who do you fear, Mr. Heffernan?"

"I do not know, I cannot be certain. But when you came to see me, then I felt most fearful."

"Why?" I said.

"Because Mr. Heffernan was the one who introduced Viscount Allington to Eldred Woundy," said Blake.


*"Allington?" I said.* We left through Heffernan's backyard, and turned the corner to walk back round to the river where the cabs went.

"Sweet heaven—Matty! Do you think he—"

"I am not sure what to think, but we must see him. And I must tell you—"

"He will not admit you."

"We will see."

My mind teemed. I could hardly take it in. "I cannot believe Heffernan's name was inscribed in that book," I said. "How could they have been so foolish?"

"They were not."

"I beg your pardon?"

"They were not. There were no names in the ledger. See for yourself."

He handed it to me. The pages were inscribed with minutes of dull meetings in a tight, tidy hand. No names.

"What did I risk? What time have we wasted, for this?" I said incredulously.

"I needed to provoke a reaction both from Neesom and Heffernan,
and I did not know how long I would have before the coppers got wind
of me. The day we went to Westminster Hall to find Heffernan, the
clerks hinted there was talk about him. They have long memories. I
sent the hostler's boy with a few shillings and got wind of the old fraud
case but no mention of Woundy. I finessed that out of Heffernan.
When we saw Neesom, it suddenly seemed obvious that the rising
needed money. Who else but Woundy could supply it?"

"And you chose not to tell me."

"You believed in the ledger. You convinced Heffernan. Now, about
Matty—"

We turned the corner into Cheyne Walk and ran straight into a
party of new police led by Sergeant Loin. Tucked into the left of Heffernan's house was a covered police van drawn by two horses. I would
have run, but Blake let them take him like a lamb. Two constables
rushed forward and roughly grabbed his arms, pressing his hands together. Loin produced a pair of iron cuffs and enclosed his wrists. I
demanded what the charge was. Loin ignored me.

"How did you find us?" I said.

"Your friend Mr. O'Toole tipped us off," said Loin.

"No friend of ours," I said bitterly.

"So you acted on my note about the Mulberry Bush tavern then,
Sergeant Loin," said Blake. "Did you find a good cache of pikes?"

Loin wrenched his wrists together.

"Listen to me," Blake said. "It's true I have not left off looking into
these murders. But who else will search for the culprit? And do you
think he will stop? You know he will not. And I am so nearly there."

"It is not up to me."

"You don't like being told to look the other way, and given no good reason for it. You know I had nothing to do with these murders."

Loin pushed Blake forward. He stumbled.

"You do not like to be given orders you cannot see the reason for, or to place blame where you know it does not belong. But how far would you go in this? Would you see me hanged for something you know I did not do?"

"Be quiet!" said Loin, attempting to put his hand across Blake's mouth. Blake broke away.

"I can pull together all the pieces of the Chartist plot for you—perpetrators, plans, all of it. I just need more time."

"If the Chartists rise, all the better," said Loin. "We shall prevent them and have ourselves a good haul. And they shall be punished as they deserve."

"I do not believe you think that. People are hungry and angry. If the rising starts, who knows where it will go: there will certainly be riots. It will be your men upon whom the anger and resentment will be visited, your men who will have to remake things afterward, not the commissioners and superintendents. You know I am right, Loin, and you know what is right."

Loin gave Blake another push. "Put him in the van, boys. We'll take him to the cells. Tomorrow he'll go before the magistrate."

"You've not arrested me yet," said Blake. "Are you going to arrest me?"

Loin ignored him.

"You'd better charge me or I won't come quietly," he said grimly, beginning to struggle in the constables' grasp.

Loin grunted. "Jeremiah Blake, I am arresting you for the murder of Eldred Woundy."

"You cannot do this," I said, placing my hand on Loin's shoulder.

"This is not lawful. You have no evidence. I can swear he was with me all night, standing guard over Connie Wedderburn and her children. Others saw him. I am not without influence."

"Take your hand off me, Captain Avery," said Loin.

"What shall I do, Blake?" I appealed. "Tell me! And what about Taylor and Matty and Pen? We barely have a day!"

They began to bundle him into the van. "Avery," he shouted over his shoulder, "I received word from the Norwood orphanage this morning. Matty is not there." They pushed him down and he spoke no more.

"This will not stop, Sergeant Loin," I said. "The printers were one thing, but what of the deaths of Dearlove and Woundy's bruiser? I have witnesses to swear that Blake was far too weak after your beating to leave his rooms when they were killed."

"What do you mean, Woundy's bruiser?"

"The body that Dearlove and I found in the Drury Lane courts three nights ago. It was one of Woundy's bruisers. Dearlove reported it at Bow Street police station the day before he died."

"As far as I know, Mr. Dearlove did no such thing," he said.

# chapter 21

I tried in vain to think as Blake would have, but I could only think as myself. There seemed nothing for it but to go to Charles Street, though I had little idea of what I would say and little hope that it would do any good.

Even as I stood on the doorstep, I wondered whether I should be collecting witnesses for Blake, but then the footman appeared, and I presented my card and the note I had prepared. It said that I was returning to Devon, and wished to say good-bye to Matty Horner. Also that I should like to pay my respects to His Lordship before I left, and that I wished to apologize once again for Jeremiah Blake's impoliteness.

I was told I might wait. I was shown into the usual bare drawing room. Today's pamphlet was entitled *And the Lord shall deliver me from every evil work, and will preserve me unto his heavenly kingdom: to whom be glory for ever and ever. Timothy, chapter 2, verse 4.*

Outside the door I could hear voices. I could not make out the words, but it seemed to me that one was remonstrating with another. At length, Lord Allington appeared, followed by the ubiquitous Threlfall, who closed the door behind him and remained mulishly in the corner. His Lordship took his seat behind his desk, carefully placed his wrists upon it and interlaced his long, slender fingers.

"You are well, Your Lordship?" I said, my head full of questions.

I fancied he winced a little. "Thank you, Captain Avery, I am. So, you are to leave London?"

"My wife is with child, sir. I must be getting home. I wish to say good-bye to Miss Horner, and also to express my shock regarding the ragged-school teacher, Mr. Dearlove. He was the reason, after all, that the matter of the printers came to light. I was most upset by his death. I hope the new police are able to find his murderer."

"I, too, am deeply troubled by it. Deeply. And he is a great loss. A great loss. I prayed for his soul when I heard. I assume this dreadful matter has once again spurred Mr. Blake to action?" Allington's absurdly long lashes swept down. He twisted the one plain gold signet ring he wore on his left hand.

"If you mean does he still think about the murders," I said, "I know he does. He is convinced Dearlove's death is connected to those of the printers."

"I commend his persistence. As St. Paul says in Corinthians, 'Stand fast in the faith, quit you like men, be strong.' Has he made any progress?"

"I think he would say he has," I said carefully, "though he has come up against an obstruction." I could not help but wonder whether Allington knew, or had even had a hand in, Blake's arrest.

"I am sorry I abandoned the investigation," said Allington. "I am forced to admit the police have made little progress. I should like to hear Mr. Blake's conclusions now, though no doubt he would be reluctant to give them to me."

"I am surprised to hear you say that, Your Lordship," I said, "and I will happily answer that question once I have seen Matty Horner."

"I'm sorry?"

"This is the third attempt I have made to see her since she came here, Your Lordship. Each time I have failed. I was responsible for bringing Matty into your orbit. It is not unreasonable to ask to see her and be sure she is content with the great change in her circumstances."

"Captain Avery, I am sorry, I must confess to some confusion. Miss Horner is not here and has not been for some days," said His Lordship.

"Then I am mystified, Your Lordship," I said, "for I have been informed that as of this morning, Matty had not arrived at the Union school in Norwood."

Lord Allington turned his pale blue gaze upon me. "Perhaps you have made inquiries at the wrong establishment."

"I am sure that is not the case, Your Lordship."

"If I may, Your Lordship," said Threlfall, and I started, for in all our dealings with Lord Allington, Threlfall had barely ventured a single comment in the company of his master. "It transpires that Norwood did not have a place for a girl of her advanced age. Lady Agnes has, I believe, made arrangements to place Miss Horner in a respectable household as a maid."

"May I have the address?" I said. "I should like to visit today, before I leave town."

Lord Allington looked at Threlfall expectantly.

"I do not know where it is," he said awkwardly, smoothing the sides of his mustache.

"Well then, Threlfall, will you go and find Lady Agnes," Allington said, with a hint of impatience.

Threlfall hesitated, as if he should have liked to say something more, but instead he backed obediently out the door.

I now felt exceedingly uneasy.

"As I was saying," His Lordship continued, "I should be very glad if you would enlighten me regarding Mr. Blake's discoveries."

There seemed nothing for it but to comply. "Well, at first Mr. Blake assumed the printers' deaths must have come about as a result of the victims' illegal dealings, but we could find no evidence of this, and so he became convinced that they must have died for some other reason. We have since discovered that they met twenty years ago, brought together by their radical political convictions. And that the Right Honorable John Heffernan MP was also part of their circle."

"Heffernan?" said Allington faintly. He ran one elegant hand through his hair. He seemed genuinely surprised.

"Yes, sir. They were all republicans and infidels, and Heffernan toyed with political radicalism. They all eventually publicly renounced their pasts, but continued to work in secret for their cause. Recently they had been giving money from the sales of their illicit publications to the physical-force branch of the Chartists, and Heffernan has been helping them."

"*The Chartists*. So they were part of it."

"Yes. Lord Allington, you said you met Eldred Woundy some months ago. I must ask you, was it John Heffernan who introduced you?"

Allington was already pale. His skin seemed to take on an almost blue whiteness. He did not speak for some time.

"Why, yes, it was."

"But you did not mention it when you told us you had met Mr. Woundy," I said, aware that I was about to trespass over the bounds of courtesy.

Lady Agnes chose this moment to sweep into the room, her thick brown hair pinned simply but perfectly to give an impression of unassuming modesty. Threlfall trotted after her like an obedient little dog.

"Captain Avery wishes to see Miss Horner before he leaves London, Agnes."

"I would be most grateful if you could give me the address of her new employers," I added.

"I am not sure she should be disturbed so soon after taking up her position," said Lady Agnes.

"Agnes?" Allington frowned at her.

"Madam, I believe I have a good claim upon her attention and I have important news for her regarding her brother," I said.

There was a short silence. "That is to say," she said awkwardly, "she is to be placed in a respectable household. I have selected it."

"Then where is she?" I said.

Lady Agnes struggled with herself for a moment. "She is here, but she has not been well. Exhaustion and a malady of the stomach."

"My apologies, Captain Avery. I had no idea," said Allington.

"Her health was perfectly good when last I saw her," I said. "I should like to see her now."

"Do not trespass too much upon our good faith, sir," said Lady Agnes.

"I wish you had kept me abreast of this," said Allington. "Is she well enough to receive visitors? What did the doctor say?"

Lady Agnes hesitated. "I think she would likely be ill at ease if visited in her current state."

"I wish to see her now," I said.

Lady Agnes made a silent appeal to her brother.

"My dear," he said firmly, "you will arrange it."

There was a hint of mutiny in the look she gave him, but then she cast her eyes down and left the room, Threlfall in her wake.

"Where were we?" Allington stood and began to pace. "You asked about Mr. Heffernan. It is true that he introduced me to Mr. Woundy. No doubt I should have mentioned it but I am introduced to such men all the time, and through many different avenues. It was just as he was launching his eponymous newspaper. Heffernan described him as a respectable man of modest background with energy and ambition in the philanthropic line, and I had no reason to doubt him. Heffernan has a reputation as a rather 'sociable' gentleman, but is also much engaged in social reform and philanthropy."

"Your Lordship, Mr. Heffernan admitted to us that he made introductions between Eldred Woundy and a number of men of wealth and high station, and that Woundy found ways of playing upon either their vices or their political sympathies, and then blackmailed them."

There was another silence, then, "I see."

"It seems that some of this money was passed to the physical-force Chartists, who have used it to fund a conspiracy to try to raise London."

If it were possible, Allington seemed to grow yet paler. "I can think of no worse destination for it," he said.

"I am sure you will be relieved to know then," I hurried on, "that Mr. Blake has helped in the discovery and apprehension of the plot and the perpetrators."

"That is some comfort."

And so I asked the question I had been dreading. "Your Lordship, were you one of those whom Eldred Woundy blackmailed?"

"I was not."

I did not believe him. "I am sorry, Your Lordship, I had to ask."

"Did you?" he said, considerably less amiably. "May I ask where Mr. Blake is?"

"He has been arrested for the murder of Eldred Woundy. It is a travesty of course. I spent the night of Woundy's murder in his company." This was not strictly true.

"Then it should be a small matter to get him released."

"The police seem determined to have him. I fear corruption in high places. Your Lordship, if there is anything you can remember, anything you can say to aid his release, I implore you to do it."

"I cannot think what you mean."

Threlfall appeared. "If Captain Avery will come upstairs?"

"Do, Captain Avery," said Lord Allington, "then take your leave. We have no more to say."

I followed Threlfall up the elegant staircase past the first and second floors, and then continued up into the servants' attic realm. We walked the length of the house along a dingy, low-ceilinged corridor. At the last door Threlfall stopped. Matty was lying on a small pallet bed. She wore a gray nightdress and her feet were bare. She was scrubbed and clean, and her hair shone, but her face was gray and there were beads of perspiration on her forehead though the room was chilly. She was struggling to keep her eyes open. I bent over the pillow. Her breathing seemed very labored.

"I thought you would never come," she mumbled. "I thought you had forgotten me."

"Never," I said, "I would never forget you."

She tried to rouse herself. "I knew him," she whispered. "I knew him when I saw him at Coldbath Fields. I'd seen him before. At Nat's." Her eyelids fluttered. She tried to speak again but she could not.

"What have they done to you?"

There was a crack on my head and something slapped me in the face. My eyes burned, I could not breathe. Someone took hold of my arms. I could not break free and I felt myself fall into the dark.

*All things were blurred.* My eyes stung, my throat burned and I could not breathe through my nose. I felt slow and stone-headed. I could not move my hands. Gradually my eyes settled.

I was in the same attic room. Threlfall was slumped on a chair by the door, snoring quietly. Matty lay on the bed, utterly still. There was a candle on the chest of drawers. My hands were tied behind my back. For some time I shifted and tried to stand, but my legs were quite useless. Then Threlfall opened his eyes and saw I was awake. He stood, stretched, and left the room without meeting my gaze. I would have shouted but my throat was so raw I could hardly speak.

Again I tried to call out to Matty, but all that emerged was a dry croak, and my attempts to move myself across the floor were hopeless. I prayed that we might be left alone until I was more recovered.

But now Threlfall returned with Lady Agnes. He was anxious, she matter-of-fact. She glanced at me, then directed him to the far side of Matty's bed. Neither spoke a word.

Threlfall took hold of the girl's hands as she tried feebly to resist. Lady Agnes picked up a small glass bottle and forced open Matty's mouth. Again Matty tried to resist. As Lady Agnes attempted to pour the contents down her throat, she choked and coughed and thrashed from side to side, and the liquid splashed across the sheets. Lady Agnes slapped her.

I, able neither to move nor to speak, could only sit and watch.

Then there were footsteps on the creaking boards outside, the door handle turned, and there was Allington, or the back of him. He came slowly into the room, his hands raised. And behind him, a pistol in one hand and a knife in the other, came Blake.

Seeing me, he grinned.

Threlfall uttered a small scream. Lady Agnes cried, "What have you done!" The bottle she had been feeding to Matty was nowhere to be seen. The scene was so unlikely I wondered for a moment if I were dreaming. Realizing it was real, I could not decide if I was glad of Blake's entrance or should be fearful for what it meant.

"Please, Agnes, be calm," said Allington. He looked oddly ungainly with his hands raised, his elegance suddenly gawky. "Mr. Blake will do us no harm, we must simply be calm."

"I may not do you any harm," said Blake, "but then again I am a desperate man and therefore capable of anything. Moreover, while I'm not a bad shot at this range, I am excellent with a knife. So you'll oblige me by moving into the corner." They did.

"I'd hand you the gun, Avery," he said, apparently unsurprised to find me tied and dazed, "but I suspect you're not yet fit to hold it." He put his knife in a pocket, came up to Lady Agnes and in one fluid movement wrested the bottle from her sleeve and smelled it. "Laudanum," he said.

He bent over Matty and inhaled her breath.

"Agnes? Threlfall? What is this?" said His Lordship.

Blake brought his face up close to Matty. "What she has given you, it is like poison. We must bring it up. Do you understand?"

Matty's eyes were open but it was by no means clear that she had understood.

"Matty, we think we have a way to help Pen. But you must harken to me."

There was a bowl and jug on the chest of drawers. Blake grabbed the bowl and put it on the bed, then hauled Matty up, leaning her against his right side, his right hand still aiming the pistol at Allington. His left hand he thrust down her throat. She gagged and doubled up and a thin gray watery liquid spewed out of her mouth into the bowl. She coughed and retched again and more came up. And then again.

"That's it," he said, and patted her gently. When Matty had ceased coughing and retching, he laid her down and pressed his head to her heart, the pistol all the time trained on Allington. "Her heartbeat is slow. Can you stand yet, William?" he said to me.

I nodded, though I was not sure I could. He took hold of my shoulder, pulled me up and cut the cords holding my hands. He brought his head near mine, sniffed, and lifted an eyebrow.

"Stay away from the candle," he said, "or we will all burn, guilty and innocent."

I felt light-headed and as if my legs might at any moment give way. He dragged me over to sit next to Matty.

"You must keep her upright and awake," he said. Then he turned to Allington. "What your sister poured down the girl's throat was enough to kill her."

"That is nonsense," said Lady Agnes, "it was just to quieten her, that is all."

"Enough to damage her heart and brain, enough to stop her breathing. Enough to kill her," Blake said.

Matty's eyes were open and she stared at me. I dabbed at her mouth, tipped a little water down her throat and smoothed stray wisps of hair from her face. "You must stay awake," I murmured.

"Agnes, I am sure you can explain to Mr. Blake and Captain Avery why Miss Horner is here."

"I shall do no such thing. The man is a desperate criminal."

"Sister!"

"I should think it has something to do with the fact that before Mr. Threlfall knocked me out Matty told me that she recognized His Lordship from Nat Wedderburn's shop in Holywell Street," I said hoarsely.

"We had no sinister intention. It was simply to protect your reputation," Lady Agnes said, as if it had all been entirely reasonable.

"We planned to keep her here until Tuesday, then place her upon the same ship that was to transport her brother to Australia. Brother and sister were to be reunited after all."

"So Woundy got his claws into you and you went to Holywell Street to pay up," said Blake.

"Yes," said Allington, sadly, "I did pay him."

"I think it is time you told your part," said Blake.

"Allington!" Lady Agnes said. "Do not—"

"Enough, sister!" He shuddered and clasped his hands together tightly. "I must speak of it, though it shames me more than I can say. It was Heffernan who introduced me to the man Eldred Woundy. I found him more persuasive than I expected. He said he wished to contribute to our school for orphans. He spoke of his disgust for the Anti-Corn-Law Leaguers and the factory owners, and he understood how much effort and expenditure it took to make any true impression on the causes of want, and how slowly that was forthcoming. It was obvious that his opinions were closer to the Chartists' than mine, but I reasoned that Mr. Disraeli had found things to praise in them, and perhaps I might too.

"I wonder, Mr. Blake, if you can imagine how frustrating it is, watching the legislation one has worked on for year after year endlessly eroded by one's colleagues, for their own interests? I was tempted, and I fell. I met with Woundy and his cohorts, that coarse little creature Blundell, and Wedderburn, who seemed meant for better things. We spoke on several occasions about how to counter the Anti-Corn-Law Leaguers and feed the starving. I was drawn into the discussions. Then they began to talk about turning the world upside down, the death of the aristocracy, their hatred of religion, the so-called temptations of revolution. They turned on me, divulging how they raised their funds. I saw I had been tricked and I took my leave amid their sneers. The drunkard Blundell arrived here a week later, demanding payment. He threatened me. He said that it would be most damaging if it was discovered that I had had dealings with former revolutionaries and sellers of lewd books. I refused to pay, of course. But he returned with Wedderburn, and they showed me the articles they proposed to print if I turned them down again. Accusing me of having dealings with physical-force Chartists, infidels and Holywell Street printers, of hypocrisy and betraying my party. It would have destroyed my work and my position. And so, in answer to your earlier questions, Captain Avery, yes, they did blackmail me, and I did pay. Twice. To my shame."

All was silent.

"It was not your fault," said Lady Agnes. "You were too good. Too trusting."

"May I ask then, Lord Allington," I ventured, my voice still little more than a wheeze, "with the new police having buried the matter, why on earth you employed us to rake it all up again?"

Allington drew a deep breath.

"It was only a few weeks after I had made the second payment that I heard about Wedderburn's death. And then about Blundell's. I admit that in the moment of hearing of their terrible fates I felt relief, though I knew it was wrong of me. Then the ragged-school teacher persisted in reporting how nothing had been done. A few more questions and I learned that the investigations into their deaths had been all but abandoned by the police. It was then that I knew God was testing me. He was telling me it was my task to ensure their murderer was found."

"And then there were more deaths," said Blake. "Woundy, and Thomas Dearlove, felled on the table in his school, and Woundy's personal guard, discovered by Captain Avery and Mr. Dearlove in a rookery cesspool, the night before Dearlove died. All those people dead. Woundy had a second guard, you know, who took passage to

America two days after his death. Second-class ticket, paid in full in advance. Convenient, don't you think? Keep her up, Avery. Shake her if necessary."

I shook Matty a little and her eyes opened but she still could not speak and her breathing was labored. I think Allington would have tried to help, had not Blake waved the gun at him. For myself, my throat burned and waves of nausea washed over me.

"Blake," I wheezed, "she needs a doctor."

"She needs to be kept awake and given water. A doctor would do no other," he countered.

"I am deeply sorry for Dearlove," Allington said. "I know nothing of the guard. I had nothing to do with their deaths. I swear on my life that I did not. I have harmed no one. If I had, why would I have employed you?"

"In my experience the apparently most rational men may commit the most irrational and destructive acts. Perhaps you wish to be caught. Ask yourself how this appears. A girl drugged almost unto death hidden in your attic. My colleague attacked and bound. Why would I not suspect you?"

"Godless man," said Lady Agnes. "Of course he is guiltless."

"Why did Threlfall attack me and tie me up?" I whispered.

"To protect His Lordship," said Blake. "You murdered those men, didn't you, Allington? You thought them Judases, betrayers, and you dispatched them as someone for whom the Bible is the fount of all counsel and inspiration would. You strangled them first, painted Blundell's hair red and left the twigs by Woundy, then slashed their stomachs because Judas's mouth was purified by the kiss he gave Jesus when he betrayed him, and therefore his damned soul had to depart his body through a hole in his stomach. Then you cut them and painted them with ink to show the stain of their dirty profession and their ungodly beliefs."

"I did none of this. You must believe me," Allington said, almost pleading.

"No, no, Allington, my dearest, of course it is not true," said Lady Agnes. She stretched out her arms to him but he ignored her. "Do not press him!"

"I believe that you wished to be discovered and you want to confess," said Blake. "That is why you chose us for this: two men 'incorruptible and undeflectable.' That was what you wanted. Two men who would persist when the police and the authorities turned a blind eye. You knew who I was, a non-believer with a certain reputation. The part of you that yearns for light wants to admit to it, and the part of you that is dark longs for punishment. You wanted me to catch you. You want to confess."

Allington hid his face in his hands.

"You are a man with dark desires, Lord Allington. You told us you are drawn to hangings. You cannot keep away from them. What is it that draws you? A guilty excitement at seeing the bodies swing? A twisted longing for punishment, or for the moment when the rope presses the air from your throat, and you are agonizingly suspended between life and death? Is that why you killed them, or was it because it was so heady an experience, and gave you such a terrible satisfaction, that you could not resist repeating it?"

"Stop it!" cried Lady Agnes.

Blake's words had a horrible mesmeric power about them. I wished he would stop. Equally, there was something dreadfully crushed about Allington's response, as if all his defenses had collapsed. He lifted one arm over his head like a child defending himself from a rain of blows.

"Captain Avery told me that you spoke to him of the abyss of your dark imaginings. About how you feel that God recedes from you, and you are left in the dark and in despair. There is a good reason for it, isn't there? Because you are filled with dark, transgressive thoughts. And because you murdered these men."

"No, I could never do such things, I could never do such things," said Allington, and his voice broke.

"You killed Matthew Blundell, Nat Wedderburn and Eldred Woundy. You overcame them, strangled them, undressed them, hauled them onto their presses and then stabbed them in the stomach."

Allington cradled his head in his hands and began to rock backwards and forward. He uttered a long low cry as if in dreadful pain.

"What is that but an admission?" said Blake.

"This is not about your pitiful accusations," Lady Agnes answered, pushing past Blake and taking Allington's head in her arms. She kissed his hair and he caught her hands and pressed them to his forehead. "No, no, my love," she said tenderly. "You are safe. You are safe. No one will hurt you. They cannot destroy you. I shall protect you. He is pure as the lilies," she said to Blake contemptuously. "He is the sinned against, not the sinner. And besides, where is your proof? It is you, Mr. Blake, who will be punished. Charged with murder, escaped from the police, forcing entry and threatening your superiors with such weapons. It is you who will hang. Make no mistake, I shall bring the full weight of this family's influence to ensure that you suffer for it. And then you will go to hell. 'The unbelieving, and the abominable, and murderers, and whoremongers, and sorcerers, and idolaters, and all liars, shall have their part in the lake which burneth with fire and brimstone: which is the second death.' Revelation 21, verse 8. That will be you."

"I have nothing to lose then," said Blake. "If I must hang for something I did not do, then first I will make sure that the real perpetrator is punished for it."

Blake turned the pistol again upon Allington.

"Blake! Please!" I said.

"Ah, William," he said wearily. "If there's one thing I've learned it's that the rich and powerful usually get what they want. And I am sick to death of it. But this time it will be different. Stand up."

Wordlessly, Allington stood.

"Please, Blake," I begged. "There must be some other way . . ."

"I'm sorry, my friend," he said. He cocked the pistol and took aim at Allington's head.

Lady Agnes flung herself at him. Deftly, almost gracefully, he stepped aside, caught her by the arm and twisted her round so that he had her trapped against his waist. Again he took aim.

"Stop!" she cried. "He did not do this. *I* killed them!"

"You would say anything to save him."

"You do not believe me!" She was almost exultant. "Just like the others. You underestimate me. I killed them. I confess it freely! And they deserved it. Blackmailers, infidels, evil all."

Though I had seen her pour the laudanum down Matty's throat, a thousand objections rose in my breast. It was not possible.

"You are right, I do not believe you," said Blake, but he let her go.

"They did not suspect me, just as you did not. They depreciated me. They welcomed me into their grubby premises, rubbing their hands, but I had the advantage. Drunken, disgusting Blundell, pathetic Wedderburn, coarse, greedy Woundy. Damned, all of them. Woundy was only too happy to dismiss his guards when I said I had something private to ask of him. So easy to manage. A simple creature of base appetites."

Allington collapsed back onto his chair. "Agnes?" he said, hesitantly.

"And how did you overcome these men who were twice as large as you? Woundy, for example: he was a big man."

"Why, I used the vapor."

"The vapor?"

"The ether. From the hospital. On a sponge or a cloth. It renders them unconscious," she said. "Blundell was half-drunk, it was simply a matter of holding him by the arms while I pressed it onto his face. We were new to it then and spilled some. I almost passed out myself. When the body was found, a candle was brought in and everything caught alight. My arrangements were not appreciated. But I suppose it meant there was less fuss. Wedderburn needed a blow to the head while I gave him the vapor. Woundy too. He struggled. He required a blow to the head—two—then we had to put the cord round his neck while we administered the ether. Threlfall helped, of course. He always came with me. He does what he is told."

Threlfall brought his hand up to his mouth. "No!" he said. "It is not true."

"As for the little schoolteacher, he weighed nothing. Barely two breaths and he was unconscious."

"Why did you do it, Lady Agnes?" said Blake.

"Allington is a bright shining star," she said, as if surprised. "Nothing can be allowed to compromise him. They betrayed him, they tried to tarnish him, they threatened his reputation. They thought they had him. I could not allow it. And they were nothing. Who will miss them? Creatures of the gutter who had already damned themselves."

"And why bother with all your 'arrangements,' as you call them?"

"Why *bother*?" She looked puzzled. "They were Judases. It was how it had to be."

A short silence while Blake contemplated this.

"And how, madam, may I ask, did you ensure the deaths would not be investigated?"

"Why, we are related to the highest in the land. Allington is too good to understand such things, but I knew that I could make sure that the police turned a blind eye to the matter without revealing who was being protected or who had asked for it."

"You forgive me if I seem unconvinced."

"I took tea some weeks ago with Sir James Graham, the Home Secretary. He is a cousin several times removed. I took an aunt, quite deaf, with me as a chaperone. I told him confidentially, and with a maidenly blush, that I must impart something that had been discovered in the course of our charitable works. A printer from Seven Dials had recently died in mysterious circumstances and he, along with several other insalubrious booksellers, had been supplying shocking and lewd material to certain high-ranking members of the Cabinet, including one very prominent member whose intimate relations with these men were so disreputable that they would instantly cast a terrible slur on the government. This, of course, was not true. All Blundell's papers had burned in the fire and the police had shown very little inclination to look into his death. But Sir James had no reason to disbelieve me. I am a very honest person, and he has come to regard my brother and I as experts on the matters of factory hours, child education and the condition of the poorest. He immediately ordered that the police give a wide berth to those particular booksellers. And when Wedderburn perished—"

"When you killed him."

"I wrote to the Home Secretary again, letting him know that he had almost certainly met his end as a result of some low rookery feud, but that investigation into his death might bring to light his association with those members of the Cabinet. And so once again he let it be known that the police should not devote too much attention to their deaths." She smiled, as if well satisfied with her work.

"And when Woundy died," Blake said, "the seed was so well established you did not need to say anything. It did not occur to you that the order to abandon the investigation of the murders might have come about because Graham assumed that you were trying to protect your brother, rather than nameless 'members of the Cabinet'? That you have inadvertently raised suspicions at the top of the government about your brother?"

"Why, no," she said, frowning.

"It certainly made it a harder task for us," Blake said almost conversationally. "The police suspected Woundy and the others were tied in with the Chartists and their plot. They assumed that the order to look the other way was about the plot. It left us most confused."

The idea seemed to give her some satisfaction.

"I assume you searched Woundy's office after you killed him," said Blake. "Did you find what you were looking for?"

"Woundy's ledger with all the names in it? Yes. I found it, and I had Threlfall burn it."

"And Woundy's bruisers?"

"Woundy's guards? I was not sure how much they might have seen. I sent Threlfall to arrange for them to take passage to America. One went, the other did not. He was warned, he did not listen. Threlfall found a fellow to perform the act and dispose of the body."

Threlfall bridled. "This is not true!" he whined.

"Then the schoolteacher came to me after he found the guard's body. He had the temerity to ask me to pray with him! He did not know everything but he had begun to guess, for we had asked him how to go about finding someone in the rookery. He was thoroughly too close to the whole matter. No one would have seen that Blundell and Wedderburn were tied together if he had not said so."

"But he was a good, devout man."

"I may be the weaker vessel, but I am a very capable woman," she said, "and I do not shrink from what must be done to protect my darling." She laid her hand on Allington's arm.

He pulled away from her. "Agnes, what have you done?" he said.

Matty sagged in my arms. I shook her, but her eyes had closed and I could not get her to open them.

There came the thud of feet up the stairs.

"We are saved! The police have come for you, Mr. Blake," said Lady Agnes.

"But you confessed!" I said.

"Oh, Captain Avery, I was merely marking time. Who do you think they will believe?"

Sergeant Loin and a band of constables burst through the door. Blake tossed the pistol on the floor, but they fell upon him anyway, beating him with their truncheons.

"Stop!" I cried, my voice still weak and hoarse.

"Thank the Lord you are here, Officer," Lady Agnes said, her hand fluttering around her neck, her eyes wide. "You have saved us!"

"Are you hurt, madam? Is His Lordship quite well?" said Loin.

"We are quite unharmed, Officer," Lady Agnes said, "but my brother is deeply shocked. That man stood not a foot away from him and held a pistol to his head. He would have shot him if you had not arrived."

The constables dragged Blake up roughly by his arms. There was a ripe red smear on his cheek and his nose was bloody.

"Leave him be!" I said. "She confessed, Loin, Lady Agnes, she confessed to killing them all, with the servant, Threlfall. It was her. They knocked me unconscious. See where my wrists were bound."

Loin looked at me and Matty. We made a strange picture.

"I am sorry, Officer," Lady Agnes said. "Captain Avery is quite under the spell of Mr. Blake. He would say anything to save him. Is it not true, Threlfall?"

Threlfall nodded, a little sullenly. "He is not to be trusted."

"What is wrong with the girl?" Loin said.

"They poured half a bottle of laudanum down her throat," I croaked. "I have it here. She saw Lord Allington at Nat Wedderburn's when he came to pay them off. Lady Agnes intended to silence her. She must see a doctor."

"The child is an opium eater," said Lady Agnes calmly. "She cannot control her appetites. We were trying to help her. I fear it may be too late."

"That is a lie!" I said.

Loin looked between Lady Agnes, sister of a viscount, daughter of an earl, and me, and made up his mind.

"On your feet, Blake," he said. "I am sorry you have had to suffer this ordeal, Your Lordship, My Lady." He bowed.

Blake could hardly stand. He struggled for breath. "You are a monster, Lady Agnes Bertram Vickers," he said with great calm, his voice hardly above a whisper.

I think Loin would have struck him, but saw that he would probably never have risen again.

"But I was right about Judas, wasn't I?"

Lady Agnes smiled gently. "Mr. Blake appears to have an obsession with the story of Judas's betrayal and the superstitions that surround it, Officer." She sounded almost sorrowful. "You will find, I think, that he employed details from these stories when he committed his terrible crimes: red paint signifying Judas's red hair, elder twigs to signify the tree on which Judas hanged himself. And of course, the thirty half crowns."

I was shocked at her audacity. "Allington, please!" I implored. But His Lordship would not meet my eyes.

Blake did an extraordinary thing. He laughed aloud.

"I never said anything about thirty half crowns, Lady Agnes. Only Matty Horner, Avery, Loin, whom I told not three hours ago, and I knew about them. And the killer. And I never mentioned the twigs were elder."

"Everyone knows that Judas sold our Lord for thirty pieces of silver," she said.

"Avery stinks of ether, Loin," Blake said. "Keep the candle away from him."

Loin did an odder thing. He came to the bed, leaned toward me and sniffed. He paused, then waved his hand and two of his constables took hold of Lady Agnes.

"And the servant too," he said.

Threlfall began to shake. "I did nothing wrong!" he shouted. "She forced me to do it!"

## chapter 22

Matty was still unconscious when I got her to Dean Street. I had no idea what to do with her save to get her somewhere safe and sheltered. The admirable Miss Jenkins saw us and immediately insisted she be put to bed in her own lodgings.

The doctor who attended advised that Matty be closely observed to see whether the drug had affected her heart or her mind, and whether she had developed a craving for it. He recommended a nurse whom I engaged, and left a small bottle of laudanum lest she became dangerously agitated or worsened.

O'Toole, unsurprisingly, had disappeared.

Blake limped into Dean Street not long afterward. His face was a grim patchwork of old and new bruises, and when he coughed he held his ribs. He told me that Loin had been rank led by his orders to look the other way, and knew perfectly well that he was innocent. He gave Blake three minutes to make his case. Blake had told him about the thirty half crowns and his suspicion that Lady Agnes Vickers had used ether to render her victims unconscious before she killed them—and indeed it was what Threlfall had used upon me.

Unsurprisingly, Loin had been skeptical. As far as Blake knew, no doctor in the country had actually used ether thus, but Dearlove was still in the deadhouse and Loin agreed to visit the body and smell it, and Blake reminded him that Woundy too had had a strange odor. He told Loin that Lady Agnes was one of a handful of people who knew about the power of ether because of her position at the Whitechapel hospital, where a doctor had wanted to experiment with it. It was, he had discovered, not hard to purchase from certain druggists, for small quantities went into many tonics. And it was dangerously flammable, which explained why Blundell's house had burned after the murder.

Loin had struck a bargain. In return for the details of the Chartist plot—Beniofsky and his men were arrested not long after—Blake could have an hour of freedom to pursue his case. After three hours he had still not returned, and so Loin had come after him.

I asked Blake when he had realized that Agnes Vickers was his quarry. He said that it had come to him gradually: the smell of the ether on Woundy and Dearlove, her mention of the Whitechapel doctor's desire to introduce the vapor to help with the pain of childbirth, then Matty's disappearance, and finally Heffernan's admission that he had introduced Allington to Woundy.

I told him I had thought he was truly about to shoot Allington. He gave me his inscrutable look.

"She had to admit it willingly," he said. "I could not have her say I had forced a confession from her. It would never have stuck."

"How far would you have gone if she had not?"

"I do not know," he said.

That night Blake wrote to Charlie Neesom, informing him of Lady Agnes's confession and asking that Daniel Wedderburn might now go and see his mother. Neesom had evaded arrest but was being watched by the new police. We agreed to visit Connie Wedderburn in the morning, and then Taylor to see if we could persuade him to sanction Pen's release.

"You will not tell me why you are so optimistic he will agree?"

"Let it be a surprise," he said. I could not summon the effort to argue.

*We found Connie Wedderburn* with Daniel and the children. They had already heard the news and she was wreathed in smiles. Blake gave a careful account of what we had discovered, and gave great credit to Matty.

"Beniofsky and a good number of his men have been arrested," he added. "But Daniel is safe, for the time being."

She thanked him extravagantly, telling him he had saved the family. She looked as handsome as I had ever seen her. "Can I ask you one more favor?" she said. "A considerable one. Tell Daniel what you know about Nat."

Blake cleared his throat and looked exceedingly awkward. She asked him again, and it seemed to me she tossed her hair in such a way that made it hard for a man to refuse. He agreed. I went to play with the children, who, regarding me owlishly as always, patiently taught me their dice game and relieved me of half a crown.

Before Blake ended, Daniel had begun to wipe his eyes.

"Why did you keep it from me?" he said to his mother.

"I made Nat promise to give it all up. I had seen so much lost in pursuit of our cause, and children suffering because of it. He wanted to tell you, but I would not have it. I wish with all my heart I had let him." The boy fell into his mother's embrace and the other children surged about them, holding on to whatever piece of skirt or trouser they could reach.

Connie Wedderburn took Blake's hand and held it, smiling steadily into his face. Daniel fidgeted. Blake detached himself gently and she followed him to the door.

"How will you live?" he said.

"Woundy left us some money. I don't know what we shall do. We might return to Lincoln or Daniel may take over the press. I may set up a small school to teach reading and writing, now the teacher is gone. Come and see us, Jem."

He looked down, again awkward. "John Heffernan wishes to do something for Daniel. He may write to you."

Her face clouded. "It is too soon," she said.

*The old man was* in his familiar position, sitting amid his pipe smoke, wrapped in his many layers of musty cloth. He affected not to notice us until we were standing before him, and only then did he slowly raise his eyes to acknowledge us.

"You," said Abraham Kravitz, his voice thick with irritation. "I knew you was trouble. What have you done with her? I've not seen her for days."

"She is sleeping in the rooms of Mr. Blake's neighbor Miss Jenkins." Briefly I explained what had happened.

"So you delivered her to the evangelicals and they nearly did for her," he said. "And her brother's to be transported Tuesday. I knew you'd be no good for her."

"Yes. It'd take a miracle to get Pen Horner released," said Blake. The old man conceded this with a suck upon his pipe.

"But you could make it happen."

Kravitz laughed incredulously. "Don't take your meaning."

"Come now, Abraham, you know which shop Pen was accused of stealing from."

"I heard the tale. Never been in there. No reason to go." Another suck.

"Really?"

"Why should I?"

Blake pulled his shoulders up to his ears as if he were stretching. He yawned. He said softly, "You said you had a brother who'd converted. I saw the resemblance the moment I laid eyes on him. Kravitz means tailor in Yiddish, doesn't it, Abraham?"

He started to sputter, waving his pipe around. I was not sure who was more surprised, Kravitz or I. Blake smiled at him.

"You can shout all you like, you can't deny it. Now, shall we go inside, Mr. Kravitz? I think there are matters arising."

Reluctantly the old man shuffled into his shop, leaving the door to slam into our faces. "When did you see this?" I muttered to Blake.

"Did a little work for some Jew clothes dealers in the Houndsditch, picked up a few words then of Yiddish. When I saw Taylor I recalled the translation."

The old man stood among his musty damp mounds, bullish and mutinous. Now that Blake had named it, I could see that he was a taller, finer-featured version of his smaller, paunchier sibling.

"So?" said Blake.

"Chaim, his name was. I don't like him, he don't like me," he said gruffly.

"Didn't stop you from doing a little trade together though, eh? Those old copies of *Master Humphrey's Clock* that you gave Matty are from your brother's shop. No one else round here has them. So some exchange is going on. Get those nice silk neckties from him too?"

"Not against the law."

"It is if he's a fence." This said with an air of weariness. "It wouldn't take long for me to put it together. And my currency's high with the police just now. But the fact is I don't want to."

"What do you want then?" said Kravitz sullenly.

"You claim to care for Matty. What would you do for her?"

"Look, the boy may not be a pickpocket yet, but mark me, he's bound for no good. The girl, she's special. One way or another she'll make something of herself. But the boy—he's a millstone. Transportation's the best thing for him."

"Maybe you're right, maybe you aren't. You've not answered my question though, and he isn't guilty, or not of what your brother set him up for. She'll take it very bitter too, if he goes. Worse if she knows that you knew."

"You'd tell her?"

"I would."

He made a sour face. "And I must do what?"

"Tell your brother he must retract his accusation against Pen Horner. If he won't, then you'll take what you know to the police."

"So I'll land myself in it."

"So he'll know you are in earnest."

"Or what?"

"I shouldn't need to threaten. But I can."

He lifted his eyes to Blake and met his gaze at last without ire.

"The boy'll just be back in there in time. A few months, a year."

"Perhaps," said Blake. "Or perhaps if she has a steady place and clean lodgings he won't."

"If," said Kravitz.

"Come on, old man. Let's finish this."


*Herbert Taylor,* formerly Chaim Kravitz, was putting a taper to his gaslights, for the morning was dark. The peculiar assortment of objects looked most macabre; the dust on the merchandise seemed to catch the light in such a way as to give the curling irons a sinister gleam so they resembled nothing so much as a pair of torture instruments, while the murderer's cloak from *Macbeth* was lent an eerie volume, as if it might get up and leave of its own accord. When Taylor saw Blake, he rested his taper and folded his arms.

"I told you I'd call the police on you," he said. "Be off."

"We brought Mr. Kravitz with us," said Blake. "You don't mind, do you, Mr. Taylor?"

The sight of his brother brought the shopkeeper up short.

"What do you want?" he said, looking away from his sibling.

"It's all up, Chaim," said Abraham quietly.

"Don't call me that!" said Herbert Taylor angrily. He peered out the shop window, then pushed us aside, locked the door and pulled the shutter across the window. "What nonsense is this!"

"You must withdraw the accusation against the boy," said Abraham. "You went too far."

"And what have you to do with this, Abraham? What's brought you across my threshold for the first time in decades?"

"I told you, you went too far."

"You didn't protest when he was taken. They got something on you, have they?"

Kravitz took a breath. "No, they got something on you. You withdraw it or I'll go to the authorities and tell them about your dodges, my brother."

"You'd not escape, you're up to your ears in it."

Abraham rolled his shoulders back and stretched his hands out before him. "It's a wrong that should be righted, brother. I told you, it's all up."

"You're mad! That girl turned your brain. Fancy you'll get under her skirts, dontcha? Dream on, old man."

Abraham stared balefully at Taylor. "Always with the filthy mouth, brother. Shall we be along then, or shall I accompany these gentlemen to the station alone?"

Glowering, Herbert Taylor considered the alternatives.

"You need do no more than withdraw the accusation," said Blake. "Say it was a misunderstanding. Say that the boy's youth and his sister's goodness have softened your heart."

"What of the constable?"

"The one you bribed? I daresay you can come up with something on that front."


*Pen Horner* was released the following day. Mayhew and I met him at the gates of Coldbath Fields, dressed in the clothes in which he had entered prison—a grimy assortment of items both too small and too large. At first he was almost dazed by the great muddy green space outside the prison walls and extremely wary of us. He looked anxiously around for some sign of his sister as we tried to make him understand what had come to pass—needless to say, the authorities had told him nothing of why he had been released. Once he realized Matty was sick and abed, he began to cry, and it was all I could do to persuade him that she was somewhere safe and warm. He cheered up a little at the prospect of traveling to Dean Street in a hackney carriage. Then we presented him with pastries from the French bakery. He inspected them initially with great distrust, then fell upon them with great enthusiasm.

As for Matty, I took my turn watching her over the days, cursing myself for my misplaced desire to help her, wishing that I had never introduced her to Allington. The drug's progress was cruel. At one time she was dreadfully feverish, at another she was racked with coughing, then gripped with cramps. It appeared that Agnes Vickers had begun to dose her with laudanum the morning after she arrived at Charles Street, when Matty had let slip that she had seen Lord Allington in Holywell Street.

We took Pen to see his sister at once. We had hoped she would make steady progress but it was still not clear if she would fully recover. We left them to their reconciliation, but it was hard to ignore the sound of tears through the walls of Miss Jenkins's small apartment.

The singularity of Lady Agnes Vickers's crimes, let alone the horror of them, meant that it was on every newspaper's front page. She was variously denounced as a she-wolf and as monstrously unnatural. Among atheists and freethinkers her case was chewed over and brandished as evidence of the hypocrisy of the evangelicals and religion. The evangelical community denounced and disowned her at once. As he had promised, Blake gave a complete version of our investigation to Mayhew and Jerrold, who wrote an admirable account of it, leaving our names as far as possible out of the story. Thus it was that Sergeant Loin got a good deal of credit for Blake's discoveries.

After a week, however, the stories began to diminish. There were few new details, and Lady Agnes was soon removed from prison and placed under the care of a doctor well known for his treatment of rich lunatics, until the trial. Allington's parents publicly disowned her, but other members of the family endeavored to have her declared insane. Jerrold believed that she would thus avoid the noose, Mayhew that she would hang. There was no doubt, however, that Threlfall would swing.

The public turned in preference to other stories: news of the Queen's baby son, the story of the foiled Chartist plot and the failed attempt of that other notorious murderer of the day, Brealey, to plead madness just before his execution, which was followed by his wife's suicide. It occurred to me that people simply did not want to dwell upon the fact that a woman could perform such terrible acts.

Allington immediately gave up all his charitable and political work, retired from Parliament and ceased to go into Society. He was said to be distraught. For myself, I feared that he would never recover. His retirement was seen as a terrible loss to the philanthropists and social reformers.

O'Toole was rumored to be visiting relatives in Ireland. Neesom was questioned for several days, but the authorities released him without charge. The Polish major was charged with various crimes. The police seemed convinced that he had taken some part in the Tower of London fire but could not produce any proof. He was given seven days to leave the country. Blake told me that Neesom had written to inform him that the Chartists were planning to collect another vast petition of names to present to Parliament to ask for the vote. "Perhaps," the message went, "this time we may persuade you to sign it."

I received a letter from Sir Theo Collinson, Blake's patron, commending me for my work and assuring me that all my expenses and more would be taken care of, but voicing the wish that it had all been done a little more discreetly. The same day I received a letter from my sister urging me to return home. My wife, she said, was nearing her confinement and starting to complain bitterly of my absence.

Matty was improving daily by then and the question of what she would do became pressing. Blake suggested she might work for Alexis Soyer, the chef we had met at the French dining room. Apparently he liked to employ women, for he said they listened better than men, and posts were opening up at his vast new kitchens at the Reform, the political club set up to draw the Whigs, liberals and radicals together.

There might also be something in the portering line for the boy. I remembered Soyer, the exotic grinning dandy, and I did not like the notion at all, though I knew my reasons were selfish ones. I told Blake it was a capital idea.

Soyer took Matty on, gave Pen a post as a messenger boy and porter and arranged accommodation in the club's new servants' quarters. Everyone, especially Miss Jenkins, was extremely pleased. After several days out of prison and off the streets, Pen Horner had entirely lost his shyness and become an exhausting houseguest.

When I came to take my leave of her, Matty was tucked in a blanket, sitting in one of Miss Jenkins's neat, threadbare chairs. She wore a fitted gray cotton dress with a clean white apron and Miss Jenkins had done her hair very prettily. She looked like a young woman.

She was delighted to see me.

"You said you'd save Pen and you did!" She grasped my hand in both of hers and brought it to her cheek. "And me. I thought they'd lock me up in that room forever. And you came. I can never thank you enough. And now Mr. Blake's found me a position. I used to dream of having a chance, and you and Mr. Blake . . ." She was most uncharacteristically overcome and had to stop, turning her face from me.

"Matty."

"I can never do enough to deserve it," she said, her eyes blinking.

I almost said that I had come to think that life had very little to do with what one deserved. But I did not.

She wiped her eyes. "You know what I did," she said. "I spied for the coppers on the ones I cared about. I lied to them and to you. I stole the money on Nat's body. Blood money."

"To protect yourself and Pen," I said.

She shook her head. "I sinned. I should be in jail."

"You kept your head above water when the world left you to drown,"

I said. They were the words Blake would have said. Now I believed them.

"You know I lost the money. I went back to get it and it had gone. It wasn't meant for me."

I held her hand for a while, then I said, "I have come to say good-bye. I must return to my home in Devon. My wife is soon to have her confinement."

Her face fell. "Your wife? A baby? That is good news. You won't be in London then. I thought you might stay till Pen and I started with Monsieur Soyer."

"I cannot. But next time I am in London I shall come and dine at the Reform Club, and send my compliments to M'sieur Soyer, and there you will be, congratulated on the port jelly, or the cabinet pudding, or the lemon posset."

She gave a small laugh, unconvinced. For my part, I knew that as a Tory I could not dine at the Reform.

"And so, my dear, I must bid you adieu and wish you good fortune." I leaned forward, aware of the softness of her skin even before I touched it. I kissed her forehead, held her hands for an instant too long and then dropped them.

"Good-bye, Captain Avery," she said.

"William, please," I said.


*My thoughts turned* to the winter fields of home, my unborn child and my marriage, such as it was. I resolved to do my best to try to mend it. There was no one at the Oriental Club whom I wished particularly to see again, though I knew my family would be glad I had expanded my acquaintance. So I dutifully exchanged cards, and when asked gave an expurgated version of our—or rather Blake's—apprehension of Agnes

Vickers. Events, I was mildly amused to discover, appeared only to have enhanced Blake's reputation in that quarter. I was repeatedly asked if I would try to persuade him to allow the club to honor him.

Of all my new acquaintances it was Henry Mayhew and Douglas Jerrold whom I hoped to see again. I knew my family would most certainly regard them as alarmingly disreputable and liberal. Mayhew was somewhat low the night Blake gave them his account of our investigations, as *Punch* was at death's door and he deep in debt.

*Woundy's Weekly* closed but was almost immediately succeeded by a host of new Sunday newspapers, each vying for the circulation that the *Weekly* had forfeited by its untimely demise. There were also a few heated calls for the publishers of Holywell Street to be shut down, but nothing came of them.

*Mayhew and Jerrold came*, with Blake, to see me onto the train to Swindon. There was some time before the engine departed, and so they ushered me off for a glass of ale at a noisy hostelry nearby. We spoke of Mayhew's plans to save *Punch* with a Christmas almanac of the best drawings thus far published, while Jerrold shook his head and made various jokes about Mayhew's intentions toward his daughter and Mayhew looked somewhat pained. Blake was almost entirely silent. I said I hoped to visit again within the year, and Mayhew said he would write. Jerrold was a member of the Reform and announced his intention to keep an eye on Matty. I shook hands vigorously, and strode into the station with my baggage. I turned, and there was Blake behind me, like a genie.

"Have you names for the child?" he said.

"Frederick Henry if he is a boy, Constance Mary if a girl." I remembered with a sudden awkwardness his own child, stillborn. "I hope it shall not be three years until I see you again. And for God's sake get yourself better, take some rest, let those ribs set."

He shook his head as if in disbelief and put his hand on my shoulder. "Good-bye, William. Good luck."

The train's piercing whistle sounded. A sudden spume of dirty white smoke enveloped us and for a moment I could see nothing. I felt my way anxiously onto the train. When I turned around, he had gone.

# *historical afterword*

Holywell Street was well known in the first three-quarters of the nineteenth century for its pornographic—a word which, frustratingly for my purposes, didn't come into use until the second half of the nineteenth century—bookshops, as well as secondhand clothes. Along with its disreputable neighbor, Wych Street, it was demolished in 1902–1903 to make way for the area now known as the Aldwych.

By the early 1840s central London was on its way to becoming the modern city we know. Nelson's Column, Trafalgar Square and the Houses of Parliament were in the course of being built. The two houses of government met at Westminster Hall while the building works were going on. Other parts of the capital, however, were very different from today. The River Thames was much closer to the streets (the Embankment, which runs down the north side of the Thames with its network of sewage pipes underneath, would not be built until the late 1850s). You could walk a few steps down from the Strand to Hungerford pier and catch a boat across the river; Cheyne Walk in Chelsea was only separated from the water by a grassy verge and a fence.

What would now be unrecognizable were the old "rookeries" sprinkled around the city, the spiderwebs of broken-down alleys and cul-de-sacs that had degenerated into overcrowded slums for the poorest. Labyrinthine, famous as criminal heartlands, they were often avoided by the police. The best known was St. Giles, at the east end of Oxford Street. These areas would be systematically cleared and demolished during the 1840s and '50s by property and railway developers. One of the initial effects of this was to create more overcrowding and worse conditions, as the newly homeless crammed themselves in with those already occupying what was left.

Coldbath Fields prison closed in 1877; the area, famed for its swampiness, was optimistically renamed Mount Pleasant. There is nothing left of the fields or the prison, which became the site of Mount Pleasant Sorting Office in Clerkenwell, the biggest post office in Britain. It now borders Farringdon Road and Rosebery Avenue. Spa Fields park, a 350-yard walk east from Mount Pleasant, the site of a radical community between 1821 and 1824 (and a political riot in 1816), is still there.

*The early 1840s* saw an explosion in publishing and communications. Steam presses revolutionized the speed of printing, paper had become cheaper, and the government repealed the stamp duty which for decades had made newspapers too expensive for any but the rich. Alongside respectable and expensive publications like *The Times*, Britain had long had an energetically scurrilous press industry which included broadsides—a single sheet purporting to report on the latest gruesome murder—as well as publications like the *Satirist*, a journal that covered goings-on about town, including reviews of brothels and courtesans, and was notorious for running stories about scandals. The editor, Barney Gregory, would send the draft of an article to its subject and demand a bribe to keep the story out of the paper. Although the *Satirist* would struggle on through the 1840s, most of its fellow publications had foundered by the late 1830s.

*Punch*, first published in 1841, was set up in deliberate contrast to the scurrility and explicitness of papers like the *Satirist*. It was radical, critical of the government's social policy, and comic but not dirty. Its founders, who included Henry Mayhew, later to write groundbreaking books about the London poor, recognized that there had been a shift in public attitudes to morality: "the age is more delicate in words than any former one," he wrote. However, the paper struggled in its first two years to find a market and almost went under more than once. Journalism was a precarious and by no means respectable living.

Much more successful was Edward Lloyd, who pretty much invented the Sunday newspaper with *Lloyd's Illustrated London Newspaper* in 1842. A small-time publisher of penny dreadfuls—cheap sensational serial stories illustrated by woodcuts—atlases and "penny miscellanies," Lloyd recognized that there was a potentially huge market for a cheap newspaper with a mix of sensational but not rude news, "educational material" and social comment, and that the new technology could allow him to produce it. His paper was swiftly followed by the *Illustrated London News* and the *News of the World*. By coincidence, Douglas Jerrold became editor of *Lloyd's Weekly Newspaper* in 1852, and made a huge success of it.

*The Chartists* were the first British working-class political mass movement. Between 1838 and 1848 they campaigned, through a mixture of mass gatherings, vast petitions which they collected and presented to Parliament, and occasional riots and unrest, for universal suffrage—

namely that everyone (all men, that is) should have the vote, irrespective of income or position. Their name came from the six-point People's Charter their founders drew up in 1838.

The Charter demanded the vote for all adult men who weren't insane or in prison; a secret ballot so no one could be intimidated into voting a certain way; the abolition of property qualifications for MPs, and the introduction of a salary—at the time only men with a certain income could stand for Parliament, and they weren't paid; the redrawing of all political constituencies so they were of equal size—it was still the case that there were parliamentary seats that were based on a voting population of a few dozen people, while others in cities represented hundreds of thousands; and annual parliaments. This last idea was impractical but was an attempt to address the problem of voters being bribed. No one, they reckoned, would be able to afford to bribe voters every year.

The Chartists were concerned by other issues such as working hours and conditions in factories and mines, low wages and the price of food—bread in particular was kept expensive by the Corn Laws, which prevented cheap foreign wheat from entering the country while allowing the British agricultural interest (i.e., the landowners, who mainly supported the Tory party) to sell their own wheat at elevated prices. The Chartists believed that political representation was the best way to get these other issues addressed.

The grassroots support they received was extraordinary. The three petitions in 1839, 1842 and 1848 were so huge and long, they had to be brought to Parliament in carts and carriages, and it took dozens of men to carry them into the House of Commons. The 1842 petition was signed by 3.3 million men—an amazing number when you consider that England had a population of about 16 million people, half of whom were women and 45 percent of whom were under twenty (the voting age was twenty-one).

The majority of members regarded themselves as "moral-force" Chartists: they wanted to campaign within the law and they hoped to persuade Parliament to give them the vote by showing the extent of the desire for it in the country. Perhaps because of their civilized behavior, Parliament felt quite able to dismiss their demands entirely. However, others in the movement, "physical-force" Chartists, thought the only way to achieve their aims would be to frighten—or even to go further and threaten force against—the Establishment to make it give them what they wanted. Aside from several much-reported small risings and demonstrations in Wales and the North, however, they never dominated the movement. Chartism disintegrated in 1848 after a vast mass meeting in Kennington in south London and the delivery of the petition to Parliament. Why it did so has been much argued over. Its leadership in particular was criticized, but the fact that the government felt quite safe in repeatedly rejecting the Chartists' politely presented petitions must have contributed to the movement's eventual loss of steam.

The Chartists never made common cause with the other great political movement of the period, the Anti-Corn-Law League, which campaigned for the repeal of the Corn Laws. The Chartists felt that the League, set up by rich northern manufacturers, with a middle-class membership, was a distraction from the real story—political power for the working man. They also accused the League of being a political weapon to attack Tory landowners wielded by Liberal-voting northern manufacturers, who wanted to get rid of the Corn Laws so that they could pay lower wages to their workers.

The Chartists were not the first generation of politicized working-class radicals. The French revolution, fifty years before, had inspired decades of working-class agitators and campaigners, who had also demanded democracy, press freedom and better pay.

Richard Carlile (1790–1843), a forgotten hero of the fight for a British free press, belonged to this earlier generation. The son of a Cornish shoemaker who died when he was four, Carlile was a self-educated atheist and self-described "infidel," who spent most of his career as a printer and publisher being hounded for his support for radical causes. The British government that came after the end of the Napoleonic Wars in 1815 was unpleasantly authoritarian and obsessed with the threat of "sedition." It suspended habeas corpus, passed a series of repressive laws called the Six Acts, which banned all public meetings and the works of writers like Thomas Paine, and put a seven-pence stamp duty on journals and newspapers in order to crush the radical press and discourage newspaper reading by the poor. Carlile campaigned for universal suffrage, universal education, the rights of women, the regulation of child labor and the rights of agricultural workers, but most of all he fought for a free press. He was repeatedly arrested for "seditious libel"—for publishing material which might encourage people to hate the government, and for refusing to pay stamp duty on his publications.

Like many of his generation, Carlile didn't join the new Chartist movement when it began to gather steam in the mid- to late 1830s. The radical firebrands of his generation had held more extreme views than the Chartists: they were atheists, fiercely anti-church and anti-government (with good reason), with dreams of overthrowing the established order. They tended to belong to a more eighteenth-century world of looser moral conventions. They had little interest in what would become respectable middle-class values, and some of them had convictions as pimps, for drunkenness, blasphemy and extortion. By the late 1830s and '40s, however, many of this previous generation had given up on political agitation. The historian Iain McCalman has researched what became of them, and discovered that not a few of the best known went on to earn a living as muckraking, blackmailing journalists and pornographers, many of them operating out of Holywell Street off the Strand. Carlile himself died in poverty in 1843, having been taken in by his two sons—who to his dismay had themselves become successful pornographers. Incidentally, almost everything we know about this earlier generation of radicals comes from reports from informers recruited by the Home Office and the London police.

The Metropolitan Police had been created in 1829 under the auspices of Sir Robert Peel, then Home Secretary and by 1841 Prime Minister. For several decades afterward they were known popularly as the "new police," and also as "coppers," "bobbies" and "peelers." The London poor and street people, whom they had instructions to move on, had less enthusiastic names for them: "bluebottles," "bludgeon men," "raw lobsters" and "blue bastards" among them.


*The character* of Lord Allington was inspired by the 7th Earl of Shaftesbury, Anthony Ashley Cooper. Shaftesbury was a remarkable social reformer and philanthropist—but while given to occasional melancholia there's no evidence at all that he was bipolar. A patrician and Tory to his fingertips, and, unusually for his class, a devout and evangelical Christian (unloved by his famously unpleasant, chilly parents, he was brought up by a servant who was herself devoutly evangelical), he campaigned against child labor, and for better working hours and conditions for

workers, and statutory free education for all children (he was president
of the Ragged School Union). He was also instrumental in the reform
of the treatment of the insane, and in the campaign to ban child chimney sweeps.

His motivations were complicated. Though he felt real empathy for
the poor—and for children in particular—he was obsessed with the
idea that their conditions must be improved so they would have time
to attend to their own salvation and go to church. Shaftesbury was
also absolutely committed to aristocratic government and hated the
thought of political change, but was convinced that the ruling classes
must show that they cared for the welfare of the poor, or they would be
in danger of losing them to what he regarded as the evils of socialism
and Chartism. Even so, he spent his whole life as a tireless campaigner
for and spearhead of social reform and the betterment of conditions
for the poor and their children, and he helped to set the agenda for
social reform from the 1850s. In 1893, after his death, a winged statue
was set up in Piccadilly Circus to honor his extraordinary achieve-
ments. It's widely known as Eros, but in fact it represents Anteros, the
symbol of selfless, nurturing love.

*Ether (diethyl ether)* was the first widely used anesthetic in the West. It is
a liquid at room temperature but easily turns into a vapor and can be administered on a towel or sponge. Its first published use took place in New
York State in 1842, when a dental patient was given ether for a tooth ex-
traction. Several months later a doctor from Georgia used it when removing a cyst. It seems, however, that English doctors were aware of its
anesthetic properties as early as 1840: it had been used as a tonic for decades, and the scientist Michael Faraday had noted its potential as an in-
ducer of unconsciousness as early as 1818. So I've allowed myself a little

poetic leeway in suggesting that it may have been discussed or even used informally by doctors in London in 1841. Less dangerous when applied in large doses than its successor, chloroform, ether had a very strong smell like nail varnish remover, gave the user a very sore throat and streaming eyes and was also highly flammable.

# acknowledgments

I first stumbled on the historian Iain McCalman's book *Radical Underworld* (1988) in the London Library in 2012. The story of a generation of poor aspirational political campaigners and would-be writers turning into pornographers and extorters just as the Chartists were becoming a mass movement seemed to me completely fascinating, and I owe him a great debt—as well as having stolen some of the more lurid details and names from his books and articles. I've read a great deal about London, but I was particularly inspired by (and shamelessly plundered) Judith Flanders's *The Victorian City*, published in 2012 (as well as her other excellent books on nineteenth-century social history, especially *Consuming Passions* [2006]), and Jerry White's *London in the 19th Century* (2007). On Chartism I found Malcolm Chase's *Chartism: A New History* (2007) and David Goodway's *London Chartism* (2002) particularly useful. One of my other secret weapons has been Kellow Chesney's terrific *The Victorian Underworld*, first published in 1970.

I owe huge thanks to my agent of over twenty years, Bill Hamilton, a constant source of encouragement, support and good sense. And to Juliet Annan, my UK publisher, who kept sending back the manuscript until it was the best I could do, and whose editorial nose I utterly trust. Thanks also to my U.S. publisher, Sara Minnich, whose comments were exceptionally useful. Caroline Pretty, my copyeditor, was once again a pleasure to work with. Finally, I owe an undischargeable debt to John Lanchester, who, as always, told me to take out the boring bits.

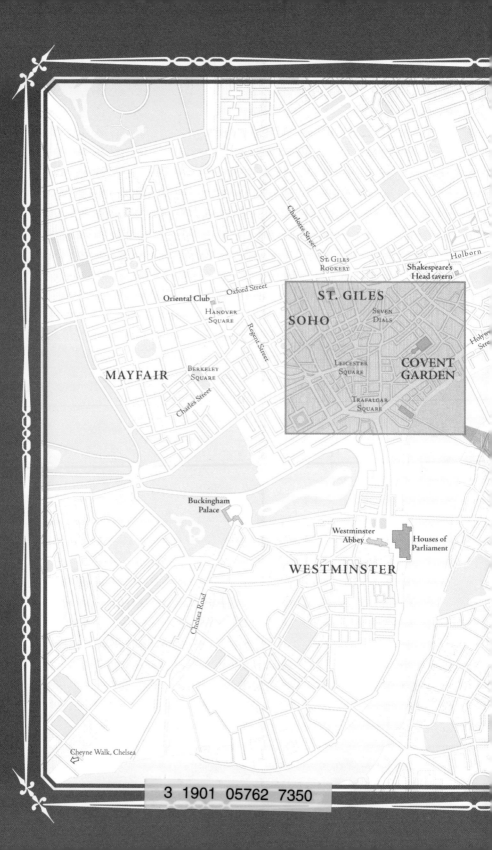

ST. GILES
ROOKERY

Shakespeare's
Head tavern

Charlotte Street

Holborn

Oriental Club

Oxford Street

ST. GILES

HANOVER
SQUARE

SOHO

SEVEN
DIALS

Regent Street

MAYFAIR

BERKELEY
SQUARE

LEICESTER
SQUARE

COVENT
GARDEN

Holyw
Stre

Charles Street

TRAFALGAR
SQUARE

Buckingham
Palace

Westminster
Abbey

Houses of
Parliament

WESTMINSTER

Chelsea Road

Cheyne Walk, Chelsea